midnight on the marne

midnight
on the
marne

SARAH ADLAKHA

A Tom Doherty Associates Book
New York

This is a work of fiction. All of the characters, organizations, and events portrayed in this novel are either products of the author's imagination or are used fictitiously.

A Forge Book
Published by Tom Doherty Associates
120 Broadway
New York, NY 10271

www.tor-forge.com

Forge® is a registered trademark of Macmillan Publishing Group, LLC.

Library of Congress Cataloging-in-Publication Data

Names: Adlakha, Sarah, author.
Title: Midnight on the Marne / Sarah Adlakha.
Description: First edition. | New York : Forge, a Tom Doherty
Associates Book, 2022. |
Identifiers: LCCN 2022008299 (print) | LCCN 2022008300 (ebook) |
ISBN 9781250774590 (hardcover) | ISBN 9781250774606 (ebook)
Classification: LCC PS3601.D5485 M54 2022 (print) |
LCC PS3601.D5485 (ebook) | DDC 813/.6—dc23
LC record available at https://lccn.loc.gov/2022008299
LC ebook record available at https://lccn.loc.gov/2022008300

Our books may be purchased in bulk for promotional, educational, or business use. Please contact your local bookseller or the Macmillan Corporate and Premium Sales Department at 1-800-221-7945, extension 5442, or by email at MacmillanSpecialMarkets@macmillan.com.

First Edition: 2022

Printed in the United States of America

0   9   8   7   6   5   4   3   2   1

To Philip and Annelise Festoso.
This one's for you, Mom and Dad.

Goodbyes are only for those who love with their eyes. Because for those who love with heart and soul there is no such thing as separation.

—**Rumi**

part I

part 1

prologue

MARCELLE

Soissons, France
May 1991

The diary arrived on a Monday. It was old, the pages worn, and the words faded. Even with her strongest reading glasses, Marcelle couldn't pick out more than a phrase or two. English was a language she rarely read, though it was one of many she spoke.

The package had come from America, bound in a roll of tape that had barely managed to hold it together as it had traveled across the ocean to reach her. The author, a man Marcelle hadn't seen in over seventy years, was dead, and while she had often thought they would meet again one day, life had other plans for them both.

There were other treasures in the box: newspaper clippings, photos, letters. If she'd been ten years younger, Marcelle would have already pored over them, but ninety-four years had taken a toll on her eyes, and, like everything else in her life, reading was something she couldn't do for herself. Instead, she waited patiently for five days, for Friday, for the day her daughter would arrive from Paris.

Liliane had offered to read the diary to her, but this was not something Marcelle wanted to share with her caregiver. Not an hour of Marcelle's day passed without company. Daytime caregivers. Nighttime nurses. Doctors. Therapists. Dietitians. Gabriel had secured only the best for his mother, the guilt he felt over his absence in her life softened only by the level of care he could provide for her.

Juliette, on the other hand, didn't have the financial means to help with caregivers and specialists. When she had finally given up trying to move Marcelle in with her, she had insisted they at least spend the weekends together. Marcelle's only daughter divided her time between a Paris apartment during the week, where her days were spent with her daughter and her grandchildren, and Soissons during the weekends with her mother. It wasn't an easy commute, especially for a woman nearing seventy, the ninety-minute drive taking her over roads that were starting to resemble the speedways they had heard about in Germany. But Marcelle had refused to abandon her home in Soissons. She wouldn't do that until it was time to join her husband and her sister and her parents in the cemetery behind the cathedral square.

"Bonjour, Maman." Juliette leaned in and planted a kiss on Marcelle's cheek before she sank down onto the sofa beside her. She was right on time, as usual. "What are you doing inside? It is such a lovely day; I expected to find you in the garden."

Marcelle nodded toward the box on the table before them. "I got a package on Monday. I thought you could help me with it. My eyes, you know."

"A package?" Juliette pulled the box on the table closer, her eyes scanning over the shipping label. "America? Who do you know in America?"

"An old friend," Marcelle replied, not sure how to explain to her daughter who George had been to her, not even sure how to explain it to herself. She had met him on only two occasions, but what he had done for her, and what she had felt for him, was nothing she could put into words.

"A man friend?" Juliette pulled an aged photograph from inside the box before turning it over to read the inscription on the back. "George Mountcastle," she said. "He was a very handsome soldier. I did not know you had an American boyfriend before Papa."

The tremor in Marcelle's hands worsened as she took the photo from her daughter and squinted at the image. It was no use. The face staring back at her was as blurred as the one that had lived inside her memory for over seven decades. "He was not a boyfriend."

Juliette rifled through the box, past the newspaper clippings, and the letters, and the keepsakes. "This one looks like a movie star," she said, pulling out another photograph and reading from the back of it. "Philip Foster. Was he a boyfriend, too?"

"My goodness, Juliette." Marcelle shook her head and sighed. "There were no boyfriends. And I do not remember any Philip."

Juliette laughed as she tucked the photo back into the box before pulling out a yellowed newspaper clipping. "How about this one?" she asked, scanning over the article. "Max Neumann. He was a German. Do you remember him?"

"No . . . I do not think so . . . but maybe . . ." Marcelle shook her head again, frustrated. Her memory had started failing her years ago. Names she couldn't put with faces. Places that seemed both familiar and foreign at once. The term "Alzheimer's" had been tossed around lately, but Marcelle refused to listen. She would not allow her mind to be taken by a disease that had been named after a German. She was simply old; her mind was tired.

"It was a long time ago, Maman." Juliette refolded the article and placed it back into the box before closing the top. She was a perceptive woman, always in tune with the people around her and sensitive to their emotions. Nothing like her brother. "How about a cup of tea in the garden?"

Marcelle's rose garden was almost as famous as her mother's had once been. Her mother had lost interest in gardening after the first war with the Germans, upon returning home to Soissons from Paris and finding nothing but rubble and weeds. Marcelle had planted a new garden to go with the home they had rebuilt when the Germans had surrendered, a place where her mother could spend the rest of her days surrounded by a symphony of colors and the budding of new life. It was a mercy that her mother had passed before the Second World War, before the color had been drained from their lives once more. It would have destroyed her.

Marcelle's teacup rattled against the saucer as she tried to place it onto the table beside her wheelchair. The garden was in full bloom, and as she watched a plump bumblebee bounce from bud to bud, she found herself defenseless against the memories that washed over her.

"It was the summer of 1918," she said, as Juliette took the cup from her hands. "That was when I met him."

"Maman, you don't have to do this." Juliette waved away her mother's words. "There is no reason for you to go back there."

Marcelle's daughter was no stranger to war, or to German occupation. They rarely spoke of the war they had lived through together, and Marcelle had never shared her experiences of the first war with her daughter. The Forgotten War. It was hard to believe a war that had toppled four imperial dynasties could be forgotten.

"You should know what happened," Marcelle replied. "Once I am gone, there will be no one left to tell it."

Juliette pulled the diary from beneath her chair and held it up in front of her mother. "It is all in here," she said. "I took a glance through this while I was preparing the tea, and it looks like this man, George, has already told your story."

"What could he know about my story?" Marcelle huffed. "He barely knew me."

"Shall we find out?" Juliette opened the journal and held it up so Marcelle could see that one lone sentence was scrawled across the middle of the front page. She squinted out of habit, but the ink ran together. "It reads, *the real story of The Great War.*"

Juliette turned the page, and Marcelle listened as her daughter brought life to the words and awakened memories that had long ago been put to sleep. The night the Germans had bombed Soissons at the start of the war in 1914. The cellar beneath her father's store where they'd taken shelter. The train station in Montmirail where she and her sister had volunteered as nurses.

"How is this possible?" Marcelle whispered, interrupting her daughter's reading. "How could this man know all these things about me? I never told him any of this."

"Do you want me to stop, Maman?"

Marcelle didn't have an answer for her. There were moments in the story of her life that she had fought to erase from her mind, but there were also moments of joy that had escaped her memory unknowingly, gifts that were being given back to her through her daughter's words.

"Maman!" Juliette gasped as her eyes bounced over the pages before her. "Were you a spy?"

It was a secret she had kept for seventy years, her husband guarding it well for her. He'd understood why they couldn't share it with her sister or her parents after the war. She smiled at her daughter and nodded in response.

"Did Papa know?" Juliette asked, and again, Marcelle nodded. "Why wouldn't you tell us this, Maman? This is remarkable."

"It was a long time ago, Juliette. And it was not as glamorous as it sounds."

As her daughter flipped through the diary, the fog began to lift from Marcelle's clouded memories. She could see George, the man who'd written the words on those pages; she could feel the sun warming her skin on the day they'd first met; she could hear his voice as he'd delivered the message that would save her life. Perhaps it was a mistake giving that journal to her daughter. Perhaps those memories should have been buried with the people who'd made them.

"Maman." Tears glistened in Juliette's eyes when she looked up at Marcelle after skimming through a few more pages, an equal amount of sorrow and disbelief battling through her features. "How could you keep all of this from us?"

"All of what?"

"That you were a prisoner in a German war camp."

"I was never . . ." Marcelle tripped over her thoughts, trying to find a sliver of truth in her daughter's words. "That is not right," she finally managed. "I was never a prisoner in a war camp."

"But it says right here." Juliette pointed at the page, at a cluster of indecipherable words. "You were captured and taken to a prison in Jaulgonne."

"No, that did not . . . it almost happened . . . but . . ." Marcelle had imagined that scenario so many times in her life, what might have happened if George hadn't stopped her, that it often felt like a real memory. But it wasn't real. Was it?

"It says right here," Juliette continued. "After the Germans won the battle at the Marne River . . . in July 1918 . . ." Juliette skimmed through the pages, reciting disjointed pieces of a story that felt strangely familiar, but one that Marcelle knew was false. ". . . they marched into Paris . . ."

"No. That is not true, Juliette. I was there. It was July of 1918. We had been at war for four years, and the Americans had just joined the fight. We held the Germans back at the Marne River. They never got to Paris. Our troops pushed them back until they surrendered a few months later. I was there." Marcelle pointed to the journal in her daughter's hands, remembering the celebrations in the streets when the Germans had surrendered. The music. The laughter. The dancing. The day George had come back. "It did not happen this way," she whispered, unable to still the worsening tremor in her hands. "The Germans did not take Paris."

"I'm sorry, Maman." Juliette closed the book and returned it to the spot beneath her chair before reaching out to her mother. "Maybe this was not a good idea," she said, pressing her hand into Marcelle's. "I did not realize it was a made-up story."

Was it a made-up story? Was it fabricated by a man who had known things about Marcelle that were impossible for him to know? It didn't happen that way, did it? But if it was made up, why did it feel so true?

"Could you start from the beginning again?" Marcelle asked, before clearing her throat and forcing a calm into her voice. "I would like to hear the entire story."

chapter 1

MARCELLE

Soissons, France
September 1914

The winds shifted outside the window as the light faded, the burdens of the world clawing at Marcelle's beautiful life and trying to rip it to shreds. She was dutiful in her indifference to it, ignoring the empty house around her with a steadfast determination.

She dreamed, instead, of Pierre. She occupied her thoughts with stolen kisses, secret engagements, and romantic wars. Not the kind of war that took place on battlefields and in trenches, not the kind that men wrote of. She dreamed of the war she had envisioned when the Germans had first announced their intentions to invade France: the soldiers in their crisp uniforms; the troops in their perfect formations; the lovers in their final embraces. She would be a soldier's wife soon, and what could be more romantic than that?

Pierre had left for the front just two days earlier, along with Marcelle's brothers, and, while the proposal hadn't yet been announced, she was certain that when they all returned for Christmas in a few short months, it would become official. She would be eighteen next year, old enough to be a bride.

Madame Fournier.

The name tasted sweet on her tongue, like the candies her father had brought home from the store last year after Madame Martin's nephew had visited with an armful of goodies from America. He had bartered them for an expensive bottle of Bordeaux from her father's cellar, and Marcelle had never tasted anything sweeter.

But that was before her father changed, before everything changed. Her brothers had tried to explain the dynamics of the war to them at supper the night before they'd left, but it was a convoluted tale, and Marcelle wasn't certain they'd understood it themselves. From what she had gathered, the archduke of Austria had been assassinated by Serbians three months earlier, leading to a war that pitted one faction of European countries against another. Austria-Hungary, Germany, and Turkey were the aggressors, while France had allied itself with Russia and Great Britain to defend Serbia.

Marcelle's father had said it was a bit like a chess match, but Marcelle thought it sounded more like a schoolyard brawl, just a bunch of bullies taking sides and fighting. What it boiled down to for her was that two days earlier, her fiancé and her brothers had been marched out of town to defend their north-eastern border with Belgium, not one hundred kilometers away, because Germany was poised to strike.

Marcelle felt certain that the Germans were in for a devastating defeat. How could they fight a war on two fronts? Russia to their east; France and Great Britain to their west. The boys would be home before Christmas. She was sure of it.

The sun continued to sink outside the window, but Marcelle waited until the sky had almost succumbed to darkness before she wrapped a shawl around her shoulders and walked the short distance from their home to her father's store down the street. The shop was empty when she arrived, so she followed the soft light filtering in from above as it guided her down the stairs to the cellar. The jewelry box was the first thing she noticed. It sat on the wooden table against the far wall of the room, looking out of place by the sacks of food that had been tossed down beside it: potatoes, flour, sugar, beans.

"Que fais-tu?" Marcelle asked. *What are you doing?*

From a darkened corner just beyond the light's reach, her mother stepped forward.

"Nothing, dear," she said. "Just tidying up. Doing some rearranging."

"Stop lying to her, Eva." The wine bottles clinked as her father stacked them beneath the wooden table, his temper in full bloom. "She is practically a woman. We need everyone's help here. Stop trying to shelter her from this."

"Shelter me from what?" Marcelle stepped forward, eyeing her sister, who was handing the bottles to their father. Rosalie was an obedient girl. Despite sharing their mother's womb and every minute of their lives thereafter, they had so little in common.

Marcelle was five when she had first realized they were special. She had seen her reflection in her mother's mirror at home, so she knew it was the same as her sister's, but it was not until her mother had taken them to the river for a picnic on their fifth birthday, and she'd seen their reflections side by side in the pool of water, that she had really understood what they were: two different versions of the same person.

Marcelle was the achiever. Nothing was beyond her reach. She was one of the few girls in Soissons to complete her second-level examinations, and she excelled in her studies, eager to learn every nuance of history and language and mathematics. Her plans had once included making the one-hundred-kilometer trek southwest to Paris upon her eighteenth birthday to find work as a teacher. She had never shared that dream with anyone. Her parents would have discouraged it, and by the time her second-level examinations had rolled around, she had already fallen for Pierre.

Rosalie, by contrast, was the pleaser. She was a quiet and serious girl, sullen, to a certain extent, especially since talk of war had arrived at their doorstep. Life was a chore for Rosalie, a tedious undertaking that required following all the rules in all the right order. She would never have dreamed of running off to Paris without their father's permission. She did what was expected of her.

"Come, dear," her mother said, smoothing her hair back and pinning the strays into place before gripping Marcelle's elbow. "Let's get you back home. The air down here is not good for you."

"No." Marcelle pulled her shoulders back and straightened her spine, pressing her heels firmly into the soft earthen floor and standing almost as tall as her mother. "I demand to know what is going on here."

"You demand to know?" Her father almost banged his head on one of the low-hanging beams of the ceiling when he spun around. "You are a little girl with her head in the clouds. Open your eyes if you want to see what is happening here. The Germans are coming. If they have not already killed your brothers or taken them hostage, they will do so tomorrow. And then they will be here. They will destroy our town and take what they want, and we will be at their mercy."

Marcelle stepped back at the assault of his words.

"You want to know what we are doing here?" he continued. "We are trying to survive. We are trying to save our family. And your sister is the only child I have left who is strong enough to help me do that."

"Mon Dieu, Gabriel!" Her mother stepped between them, wrapping an arm around Marcelle and forcing her up the stairs. The light from outside was muted when they crested the final step and entered the store, and it wasn't until Marcelle looked around that she spotted the crisscrossed mesh that had been taped to the windows. She hadn't noticed it when she had entered just moments earlier, or the bare shelves, or the silence.

The streets were empty. The men who spent their afternoons smoking and arguing and laughing outside of the store were missing, the women who shuffled arm in arm from shop to shop were gone, and the children who chased the dogs from one side of the cobblestone street to the other were nowhere to be seen. When had this happened?

"What is that?" Marcelle pointed to the mesh that was taped to the windows.

"It is to prevent glass from shattering and spraying into the store." Her mother hesitated before she continued. "If the Germans shell us, we need to be prepared."

Marcelle simply nodded and followed her mother home in silence. She sat on the mattress she shared with her sister, the one her brothers had once shared, and tried not to imagine where they might be now. She tried not to think about Pierre and the letters she had already written to him. She tried not to hear their voices or see their faces. She tried, but her father's words would not leave her: *If they have not already killed your brothers . . .*

She didn't come out for supper that night. Her mother tried to take her some bread, but Marcelle refused to eat. She refused to speak or change her clothes or acknowledge her sister when she came to bed. Her father was right. She was a naïve little girl with her head in the clouds. She had refused to see the signs all around her. She had sent the men in her life off to war believing they would return safely to her.

But hadn't they deserved that?

For all she knew, her father was mistaken. He was not the Almighty; he could not possibly know their fates. He was a man like any other man, and Marcelle would keep her head bowed in prayer to the heavenly Father, who *did* know the fates of all men, the Father who could perform miracles and was the only One who could deliver her brothers and her fiancé from evil.

～～～

The thunder started shortly before dawn. Marcelle didn't realize she'd fallen asleep until the booming in the distance woke her. The storm was far enough away that the rains would not reach them for at least another hour, so she pulled the quilt her grandmother had made and gifted to her parents on their wedding day up under her chin and curled into a tight ball. She would sleep until daylight stole the darkness.

The rains never came that day, because the thunder was not born from the heavens. To the west, the sky remained a cerulean blue, but to the east, a haze of smoke floated above the horizon where men were killing men and families were fleeing for their survival.

Rosalie was the one to drag her out of bed and hand her a bag so she could pack two days' worth of clothing. Marcelle followed her back to their father's store and down the cellar stairs to where their family would wait out the long days ahead. She didn't argue with her sister. She didn't argue with anyone. She stepped in line and did as she was told, clutching her grandmother's quilt to her chest as she watched some of the men from town help move mattresses to the cellar.

Monsieur Fournier was one of the men. Pierre's father was forty-six, just like Marcelle's, and they had both avoided being sent to the front by the grace of age. Soissons seemed to be shrinking by the day. The absence of the young men was made more obvious by the disappearance of families who had fled toward Paris as the Germans neared. Marcelle had overheard her father discussing similar plans with Pierre's father, but Monsieur Fournier wasn't ready for it yet; he was worried his daughters would not be strong enough. As she sank down onto the mattress beside her mother, who was cutting an apple and portioning the pieces onto plates for the men, Marcelle wondered if her own father felt the same way about her.

"Do you think I am weak?" Marcelle reached over and slipped one of the apple slices into her mouth before her mother could swat her hand away.

"I think this world does not suit you," her mother replied, replacing the apple slice before moving the plate out of Marcelle's reach.

"Is that why you tried to shelter me from it? Because I am not strong enough?"

"Not at all. You are stronger than you give yourself credit for." She took a bite of the last apple slice before handing the rest to Marcelle. "Your father does not think you are weak, either. He is simply trying to protect you, and he is worried that you are not as careful as your sister. You speak up when the world expects you to be quiet. This could get you into trouble one day. You do not have your brothers to protect you anymore."

"But I heard some of the men talking earlier, and they said there is still a chance that the boys are alive out there."

Her mother nodded. "I hope they are right," she said. "There is no greater sorrow than losing a child." She squeezed Marcelle's hand before she continued. "You will be such a beautiful mother one day."

It was not until late in the night that Marcelle really thought about her mother's words. The thunder grew louder as the shells rained down around them, and, while silence filled the space between blasts, Marcelle knew that no one slept.

She couldn't stop hearing her mother's words: *You will be such a beautiful mother one day.* Did she really believe that? Or did she think that cellar would be their tomb?

The night stretched on indefinitely. Pierre's parents had taken refuge with them, along with their two young daughters, Lina and Marie, who whispered to each other in English until the lanterns were extinguished. Marcelle wondered what they were saying. Were they comforting each other? Were they scared? They were shy children, always giggling when Marcelle came around. Pierre's grandmother was British and had insisted that her grandchildren be raised to speak English, but Marcelle had never heard either girl speak French, and she often wondered if they even knew how.

The cellar was only large enough for four mattresses since Marcelle's father had refused to move the wine bottles or the wooden table against the far wall. Sleeping conditions were tight, to say the least, and though no one made a sound all night, Marcelle felt certain it wasn't because anyone slept. It wasn't until her father pulled the cellar hatch open, and a current of fresh air swept in around them awakening all the stagnant fears and anxieties that had festered throughout the night, that anyone stirred.

Marcelle clambered up the cellar stairs after her father, so desperate for air that she didn't even bother with shoes. A glint of sunlight reflected off a fractured window that had not survived the night, and before she could blink away the glare, she knew she had made a grave mistake by following him.

German.

The man standing beside her was speaking German. She recognized his voice and understood his words, but she couldn't force a breath into her lungs, and the tunneling of her vision was threatening to land her on the ground at his feet.

"Hier spricht niemand Deutsch." *No one speaks German here.*

Monsieur Bauer. It was her German teacher from school, lying to the German soldier by his side about one of his most accomplished students. He had written that on her final evaluation not even two months earlier: *Mlle. Marchand is gifted in conversational German. She is one of the most accomplished students I have had the pleasure of instructing.* He was the one who had told Marcelle about the all-girl schools in the bigger cities and the boardinghouses for unmarried women who dedicated their lives to the education of children, the one who had placed those dreams of independence in her head all those years ago. He had not been happy when Marcelle's attentions had shifted from school to Pierre.

"Monsieur Marchand," he said, addressing Marcelle's father in French and gesturing to the German soldier accompanying him. "Hauptmann Krause here has asked that all citizens of Soissons be present outside the cathedral at midday today for an important announcement. He has also commanded anyone who speaks German to come forward and assist as a translator for his troops who will be billeting in the homes along this street. I have already informed him that no one in your family speaks German and that your house is available for his troops."

Marcelle's father nodded along to Monsieur Bauer's words, skillfully avoiding the gaze of the German soldier, who, judging from the medals weighing down his coat, must have been someone very important.

Marcelle could feel the man's eyes on her. She hadn't thought to pin her hair up before leaving the cellar, and she wasn't even sure she had buttoned her blouse up around her neck. She felt exposed and vulnerable, and despite the chilled morning air, beads of sweat formed on her upper lip. She stood frozen in place, her senses heightened like a doe caught in the sights of a wolf, wondering if the predator beside her was waiting for her to bolt, if he delighted in the chase.

"Oui, Monsieur Bauer." Marcelle's father nudged her back toward the cellar. "Our house is open for the troops. We will gladly take comfort in the cellar, and I will be certain to spread the word about the meeting at the cathedral today. Merci."

Marcelle didn't notice the musty stench of the cellar when she descended the stairs, or the darkness that enveloped them when her father closed the hatch. The cold of the tomb-like stone walls and the dampness that endlessly clung to them was a welcome relief. It wasn't until her father lit the oil lamp that she had to face her consequences.

"You will be more careful from now on." His voice never rose above a whisper, but venom laced his words. Marcelle did not fault him for it. She had been reckless. She had not been paying attention, but she would not make that mistake again.

"Oui, Papa," she mumbled, ducking into the shadows and feeling her way to the mattress she shared with her sister.

The glow of the oil lamp reached only as far as the adults who gathered around it, her parents and Pierre's. From the periphery,

Marcelle and Rosalie watched its shadows dance across their faces, unmasking the fear they tried so desperately to hide. The cellar wasn't big enough for privacy.

Plans were being made. Besides the meeting at the cathedral square, there were supplies to gather and families to visit and meals to be made. As expected, Marcelle's chores—childcare and meals—would never bring her out of the cellar, but she was wholly unprepared for the task her sister would soon inherit.

Rosalie jumped at her father's words, always eager to please him. She was, without question, his favorite daughter. Maybe even more revered than their brothers. Through the anemic glow of the oil lamp, her sister's eyes shined with pride.

"You will come with us to the meeting at the cathedral square today," her father said. "And from there, you will accompany Monsieur Fournier to fetch a wagon and some food supplies from his storage shed."

"No." Marcelle's words were cutting through the thickness of the cellar air before she'd realized she was even speaking. "You cannot mean to send her out there with the Germans. I will not let her go."

"This does not concern you, Marcelle." Her father's eyes flashed to the darkened corner, but Marcelle was already at her sister's side.

"Of course it concerns me. I will not let you send her out there. You saw how that German looked at me. It will be the same for Rosalie."

"Rosalie can handle herself. We have no other choice."

"Why can't *you* do it? Or Maman? Or Madame Fournier?"

"Enough, Marcelle." If not for the company of the Fourniers, her father would not have been so charitable with his patience. His voice trembled with contempt. "There are other tasks that need to be done, and Madame Fournier's children need her here. This is not open for discussion."

"Then I will go with her."

"You will not!" When his hand slammed onto the wooden

table between them, Marcelle was silenced into submission. "You are a reckless child. You think nothing through, and one of these days your carelessness will get people killed. You will not leave this cellar until I tell you it is safe. Do you understand?"

Marcelle slunk to the mattress in the corner without answering him, but she could feel him pressing into the darkness, hovering above her, and refusing to relent without her promise.

"Do you understand me, Marcelle?"

"Oui," she mumbled, but turned her body away from him. She would say whatever words he needed to hear, but she would not abandon her sister. She would never send Rosalie out to the wolves on her own.

chapter 2

She watched from the shadows.

Marcelle had bolted from the cellar when her mother had gone out to gather supplies and Madame Fournier had dozed off with her daughters, and then she had slipped into a crowd of people who were making their way to the cathedral square.

Monsieur Bauer was doing the translating again for the German commander, but Marcelle didn't need it. She understood perfectly well what "Wir werden deine Stadt niederbrennen" meant without having to be told.

We will burn your city down.

Insubordination would not be tolerated. Monsieur Bauer's voice struggled to be heard over the roar of the commander's words that echoed in German through the town square. Everything about the man was severe: the lines and angles of his face; the boom of his voice; the penalties for breaking his rules.

Loitering, missing curfew, and not saluting German officers were not fatal transgressions, but most of his orders ended with the words "wird mit der Todesstrafe bestraft."

. . . the penalty is death.

"All weapons are to be turned over at once. If you are found with firearms in your possession, the penalty is death."

"All collaborators will be treated as enemies of the state. If you are found to be a traitor to Germany, the penalty is death."

"All food stores and farm produce are now the property of the

German Empire and will be rationed as seen fit. If you are found stealing from the Reich, the penalty is death."

When he finished, he had the gall to ask the crowd if there were any questions, but, of course, no one dared raise his hand. There was not so much as a cough or a sniffle from the people of Soissons as they waited to be dismissed.

When they were finally ordered to return to their homes, no one lingered. Not even Rosalie and Monsieur Fournier. Even with this new threat of death, they slipped through one of the side streets north of the cathedral and disappeared into the shadows as they headed toward Pierre's home.

Marcelle had to quicken her pace to keep sight of them, weaving through the back streets of Soissons past the shuttered butcher's shop and the bombed-out bakery. The alleys were filled with people racing to get home and off the streets where the German soldiers stood like sentry men. Marcelle was just coming up on the alley behind Pierre's home when she was stopped in her tracks.

"Halt! Stehen bleiben!" *Halt! Stop right there!*

The words jumped out at her, their bite like an unsuspected strike from a snake, and the gunshot that went with them echoed through the now empty cobblestone streets of the city.

She heard Monsieur Fournier's body hit the ground just a moment before she turned the corner and found herself face-to-face with the German soldier who had shot him. The man glanced back and forth from Marcelle to her sister, trying to reconcile the double image, before pointing the gun at Rosalie.

"Du stiehlst." *You are stealing.*

Rosalie didn't respond. She didn't understand his words, and her eyes darted back and forth from the gun in the German's hand to the body of Monsieur Fournier at her feet, the blood from his head pooling around her shoes.

"That food no longer belongs to you." The German soldier

pointed with his gun to the sacks of food that had already been loaded onto the cart. "Do you know the penalty for stealing?"

"Bitte." *Please*. Marcelle stepped forward with her hands raised to her chest, stopping only when the German took aim at her head. "My sister does not speak German. Please, let me explain."

"There is no explanation necessary. She was taking what belongs to Germany. The punishment for that is death."

"There must be another way," Marcelle pleaded, and when his eyes ran over Rosalie's body, she wondered if she had just doomed her sister to a fate that was, perhaps, worse than death.

"There might be another way," he agreed, and while Rosalie could not follow their conversation, when the wolfish grin surfaced on his face, she understood his intentions.

"I will do it," Marcelle said, stepping forward as if to shield Rosalie from the man's hunger. "My sister is ill. She has the fever that took our mother, and I fear she will not survive. If we could just take the cart to move our mother's body to the cemetery, I will come back and pay for the crime. Please."

The German stepped back as Marcelle moved even closer to her sister. He pointed the pistol toward Monsieur Fournier's lifeless body.

"Is that your father?"

"He is a neighbor who has been staying with us. He offered us the cart but insisted on retrieving supplies from his home on the way."

"Did he have the fever too?"

"I do not know," Marcelle replied. "But it is spreading fast."

Marcelle's story was woven from thin and tattered lies, but when the German muttered something about *dirty French swine*, she was certain his hands would never touch them. He pulled the sacks of food from the cart, each one hitting the ground with the same thud Monsieur Fournier's body had made, and when the cart was empty, he aimed the gun at Rosalie's head once more. "I should do this as a favor to you," he said. "Before you end up like your mother."

The earth shifted ever so slightly beneath Marcelle's feet as she stepped in front of her sister. There was no rational thought involved; it was an instinct as natural as self-preservation. Her sister's life was worth her own.

"Bitte," she whispered. "Please do not kill us."

They watched each other through a thick and heavy silence, the German's eyes locked on hers, and in that brief moment, Marcelle was suddenly aware of the freckles sprinkled across his nose and the thin scar running down his chin and the crooked tooth jutting from beneath his lips. Things that made him human. Things that made him look like a boy. Like Pierre. Did he have a girl waiting for him at home? Was she excited to be a soldier's wife, too?

When he lowered the gun and nodded toward Monsieur Fournier's body, Marcelle was quick to shake the thoughts away. She and Rosalie worked in a rushed silence as they dragged Pierre's father to the cobbled road, heaved his flaccid body onto the edge of the cart, and then rolled him toward the center to balance his weight. They didn't dare look back as they lugged the cart toward the cellar and prayed that a bullet would not find them before they made it to the door.

Marcelle descended the stairs first. Her father was almost too angry to spit out his words, but when he found his voice, it thundered through the cellar.

"What have you done, Marcelle?" His rant was short-lived when he noticed the blood smeared across his daughter's blouse and caked onto her skin. When Rosalie climbed down the stairs, Marcelle got a glimpse of what her own reflection might have revealed if she'd had a mirror.

The red streaks across her sister's face were a stark contrast to the icy blue of her feral eyes, which danced feverishly across the room. The gold of her hair was matted and clumped with the blackened and dried blood from Monsieur Fournier's head, and the blouse she had been so careful to button and tuck before heading out that day sat draped open at the neck and askew on her limbs.

"Where is Monsieur Fournier?" her father asked, glancing up the stairway behind Rosalie. "What happened?"

"They shot him." Marcelle searched the darkened corners of the cellar for Madame Fournier, who sat with her arms wrapped around her daughters as if to shelter them from the news. "I am so sorry. We brought his body back."

"I told you to stay here, Marcelle! Why did you do this?" Her father gripped her arms so tightly that Marcelle's feet were almost off the ground. "You got a man killed!"

"She did not get him killed." Rosalie's words pierced them like an arrow and commanded an immediate audience. "Monsieur Fournier was shot before Marcelle showed up. I would have been shot too, and worse, if she had not been there to save me."

When her father loosened his grip around Marcelle's arms, she stumbled back away from him, searching for the dampness of the cold stone wall.

"They killed him because he was trying to take his food with him," Marcelle said, as her legs quivered beneath her body. When she slid her back down the rough-hewn stones of the cellar wall and onto the dirt floor, she knew she would lack the strength to pull herself back up. "They will come for ours too," she continued, unable to ignore the sobs from the far corner of the cellar where the few survivors of the Fournier family were huddled together. "And they will take our mattresses and blankets and whatever else they want. We will not survive long by hiding out down here."

"What other choice do we have?" Her father sank down onto one of the mattresses, dropping his head into his hands. He had inherited a widow with two young daughters, and, while he had his own broken family to worry about, he was not the kind of man to skirt his responsibilities. "We cannot run. We cannot fight. All we can do is keep our heads down and hide."

He was right. There were no good options. There was no amount of prayer that could have warded off the evil that had descended upon them, and there was no amount of preparation that could have changed the outcome.

Marcelle refused to pray that night. She refused to ask God for forgiveness or hope or mercy. She had seen death for the first time in the face of Pierre's father, the man who would have been her father-in-law, and she hadn't the stomach to call on a God who had acted so unjustly.

If she had known the cruelty to come, if she had been warned that what she had witnessed that day would pale in comparison to what her future held, Marcelle might not have fought so hard to survive that winter. She might have offered herself mercy.

chapter 3

GEORGE

Châteauvillain, France
June 1918

"Easy, girl."

George held his palm out as he approached the mare, but she bucked and snorted in response, narrowly missing his head before he dove under the fence to safety. Her nostrils flared as she pawed at the dirt ground and pranced around in circles, daring George to give it another go. If she hadn't been starved to the point of near exhaustion, and if her black coat hadn't been caked with a layer of dried mud and dust, she would have reminded him of Calypso.

He missed that horse. The only one in his herd who couldn't be rehomed when he'd left for army training in North Carolina the previous year. Her reputation was unparalleled in their small Alabama town. The daughter of the devil, his neighbor had called her, and no one had been willing to step up and risk his life for her. George's father had begrudgingly offered to keep her fed, but without any handling, she'd be as wild as this mare if he ever made it back home.

He'd been in France for less than a month with the rest of the Third Infantry Division, and, while the weeks had blended together, the days were terminally long. Lessons in trench warfare took up most of their time, but when word had gotten out that George was a bit of a horseman, he'd been commanded to get the newly arrived herd into working shape. Every spare moment of the past week had been devoted to this lost cause. Even if he'd had a year and unlimited supplies of grazing pastures, trainers, and fencing material—of which he had none—he'd be hard-pressed to complete the task. Over two hundred horses had arrived in the last shipment, emaciated and stressed and packed together like cattle. They weren't warhorses. They were family pets that had been starving along with their owners, and they'd been sold for barely enough francs to buy a loaf of bread.

The sun was still rising in the sky when George glanced over the fields to the east, toward the town of Châteauvillain, where they'd been staying while learning to do battle with the Germans. He was working alone again. Of the twelve other men who'd been assigned to the horses with him, only one ever showed up with some regularity, but even Philip had grown tired of watching horses starve to death.

The little girl was back. George's most reliable companion at the horse corrals couldn't have been much older than seven or eight, her fiery red curls glowing beneath the rising sun. She never spoke, but there was an easiness to their company that he didn't find with many people. She was typically a serious girl, but George had caught her giggling once when the black mare had run him out of the corral. He'd tried to tease her about it, but she'd darted off through the woods and hadn't returned for two days. He liked her company too much to try that again, and since none of the locals spoke English, he figured she wouldn't have understood him anyway.

She spent most of her time watching him from a distance, sitting in the tall grass and tying daisy chains like the girls back home used to do, waiting for George to grab his buckets so she could trail him to the well. She was always on the lookout for danger. She reminded him of a sparrow, flitting around in one moment and then vanishing in the next, no trace of her left behind.

She was gone when he returned from the well that day, the threat that had driven her away sitting on the highest rung of the broken gate.

"Do these horses ever sleep?" Philip hopped off the gate and followed George to the water trough. "I never see them lying down."

"Horses sleep standing up. It's a survival mechanism for fight-or-flight animals. They always have to be ready to bolt."

"Do they die standing up too?"

"What are you talking about?" George sloshed half the water over his pants and boots as he lugged the bucket toward the trough. "Why don't you help me with this and stop asking stupid questions."

"Because I'm pretty sure that one over there is dead but just doesn't know it yet." Philip's laughter unsettled the corralled horses, who were already fussing and snorting. Of all the men they'd picked to help him, Philip was the least qualified to be tending to horses. He was a Pennsylvania native who was hard not to like, and he was as strong as an ox, but his high energy made the horses uneasy. He and George had formed a quick bond. They were as different on the outside as two men could be, but the rhythm of their friendship had developed seamlessly from the moment they'd met.

"It's time to head out, Mountcastle." Philip took the bucket from George's hands and dumped the water into the trough. "Hand grenade practice today. The French have more to teach us about killing Boches. We best not remind them of what a shitty job they're doing in this fight and hope they're better teachers than soldiers."

George looked once more for the little girl before he followed Philip through the overgrown pastures that would have made ideal grazing land if they'd had enough fences to build more corrals. If their victory against the Germans was dependent upon their horses, they were destined for a monumental failure.

The training grounds were little more than a maze of hastily built trenches they'd dug out the previous week under the direction of their French and British allies. They'd been instructed to make the trenches their home, to find comfort eating and sleeping belowground in preparation for battle, but George and the rest of his regiment had so far not heeded that advice. The way they saw it, they hadn't trained stateside for a year and traveled thousands of miles just to live like moles.

France had been at war for three years before the Americans had joined the fight. After losing too many American civilians at the hands of German submarine captains, President Wilson had finally declared war. The troops hadn't seen much combat yet, especially on the front lines, but it was coming. The Russians were in the midst of their own revolution and had recently signed a treaty with Germany, ending their participation in the war. This had allowed the Boche to move most of their troops from their eastern front with Russia to their western front with France, and there were rumors they were planning a push to Paris soon.

Of all the units, the one George found himself in was the least disciplined. The Thirty-Eighth had been without proper leadership for weeks, and when they'd finally been assigned a colonel, he'd shown up with his own discipline problems. Colonel McAlexander was a West Point graduate who'd already proven himself on the battlefields of the Spanish-American War, but he didn't take instruction well. He'd been relieved of duty from another unit earlier in the month for the way he'd expressed his disapproval of the French commanders who'd been trying to teach him about trench warfare, and when he'd strode into Châteauvillain barking orders at troops and officers alike, no one questioned the rumors they'd heard about him.

Colonel Mac was a bulldog. He pushed his men night and day to hone their battlefield skills, and, since he didn't think the war would be won in the trenches, most of their training was done aboveground. Bayonet drills started first thing after breakfast, followed by grenade launching and artillery training, and then, after a break for lunch, the men perfected their marksmanship and compass skills.

George learned a lot about himself after Colonel Mac showed up: He was not designed for hand-to-hand combat, he had no inherent navigational abilities, and his analytical nature made his reaction times sluggish, at best. But he was a natural marksman. His hands were not only steady with the Springfield rifles the Americans had sent over with the troops, but he could handle the kick of the French Chauchat machine gun better than anyone. When it wasn't jamming. Philip, who was almost half a foot taller than him, bayonetted burlap dummies with a savagery that couldn't be matched, but behind the barrel of a rifle, no one was George's equal.

Grenade practice had already begun by the time they'd arrived from the stables, blasts rumbling in the distance as men hunkered behind trench walls and lobbed explosives into an empty field. It was one of the few training drills they did from within the trenches, and always one of the most dangerous. There was never enough room. In addition to the soldiers who were packed in on top of each other, there were ammunition caches, grenade boxes, and radio sets, even gas masks that ended up underfoot and underground. They'd been issued to the soldiers a week earlier and were supposed to have been strapped to their faces at all times, but few of the men could tolerate them. George rarely wore his, certain that suffocation would end him well before poisonous gases ever could.

By the time he and Philip settled in with the rest of their regiment, tremors from the explosions a quarter of a mile away were spilling loose soil and rocks over their heads, and Philip was already rambling on about something. He never shut up. He even talked in his sleep.

"Have you guys heard the one about the English fighter pilot who was shot down over Germany?" He glanced down the trench line to make sure he had time to finish his joke. "So, this poor chap wakes up as a prisoner in a German hospital, badly injured, and the German doctor tells him, 'Ve haf bad news. Ve haf to amputate your arm.' So, the English pilot says, 'Well, that's bloody unfortunate. But can you do me a favor? Can you have one of your pilots drop it off over England, so I know it will rest on home soil?' The German doctor thinks it over and says, 'Ya, ya. We do zis for you.' Well, a few days later, the German doctor returns and says, 'Ve haf more bad news. Now ve haf to amputate your leg.' The Englishman is distraught and says, 'Bloody hell! Please. It would mean so much to me if your pilots would drop it over England again.' This time the German doctor hesitates, but finally agrees. The following week, the German doctor again visits the patient and says, 'Now ve haf to amputate ze ozzer arm.' Despondent, the Englishman asks for the same favor, to which the German doctor suddenly shouts, 'Nein! Ve do zis no more! Ve sink you're trying to escape!'"

Philip was the only one laughing when the blast threw them into the muddy trench water at their feet. George could see the men around him scrambling and yelling for help, but a high-pitched ringing had replaced their screams. The explosion had buried what was left of the man who'd been holding the grenade and the others who'd been crouched down beside him. They'd been at least twenty-five yards down the line from George, but the walls had collapsed and entombed everyone and everything between them.

Philip was already at work clawing through the mud and plucking grown men from the trenches like he was plucking potatoes from the ground, and in that moment, George could see so clearly the divide between them.

Philip had stepped into this role like he'd been groomed for it his entire life, but George couldn't do anything but watch from the sideline, frozen with fear. It was someone else's battle. Someone stronger and braver and tougher. Someone like Philip.

By the time George had dragged himself from the trench, his hearing was slowly returning, and all the men had been pulled from the ground. Three fatalities and a host of injuries were enough to keep the medics busy, and Colonel Mac had given the men three hours to recuperate, eat lunch, and return for afternoon training.

George walked home alone. The farmhouse he and a dozen other men shared was a good mile down the road and he didn't have it in him to listen to Philip rehash the events of the last hour. He couldn't shake away the thought that kept spinning through his head, circling back around and around:

He wasn't suited for war.

He'd been foolish to think that a man with no propensity toward violence could navigate this kind of world. He was a farmer. He'd only joined the army to prevent being drafted and to escape the tedium of farm life in the tiny Alabama town that had been smothering him since birth. He hadn't considered that he might not even live to see his first German.

"You okay?"

Philip stood in the doorway. He looked like a warrior with streaks of dried mud smeared across his face and uniform. He was larger than all the men in their unit, and though he was barely twenty, a full three years younger than George, he was the natural leader of their crew.

George nodded.

"It gets easier." Philip dropped his helmet and field pack onto the ground by his bedroll and hung his jacket over a chair before unlacing his boots. "I don't know if that's a good thing or a bad thing, but we had a few training accidents stateside, and somehow it seems that death gets easier the more you see it."

George nodded again, though he didn't agree. He'd seen plenty of death, and it never got easier for him. He'd never forget the night his mother's screams had echoed through the house as the doctor had called for more linens and towels. It had turned out there weren't enough towels in the world to stop that bleeding. The doctor had finally left when the screaming had stopped, and though George had been just six, he'd known that meant his mother was dead. The baby she'd been carrying didn't fare any better, and George had never been able to shrug off the resentment he'd felt toward his father for suggesting it was a blessing in disguise, that an infant wouldn't have survived without its mother.

Two years later, George's twelve-year-old brother—the only person he'd ever loved besides his mother—had been killed in a farming accident. That was the summer he'd found refuge with the horses; the summer his father had told him he'd need to step up and do his share to keep the farm running.

"The rest of the boys are at the river getting cleaned up before lunch," Philip said. "You want to head out there with us?"

"You go ahead. I'll meet you out there in just a bit."

The river was nothing more than an anemic stream, a dead-end branch of the Aujon River that ran through Château-villain. They'd been bathing in it for weeks, but there was a restlessness running through the men that day, like getting a glimpse of their own mortality had energized them, reminded them they were living on borrowed time.

The water churned with mud and blood and whatever else came off their bodies, and George watched from atop a lonely boulder twenty yards away as each man became more reckless than the next, their voices thundering up into the air and through the windows of the chateau on the water's edge. It was rumored to have been abandoned and then turned into a hospital for wounded French soldiers, but, until that moment, George had never seen anyone coming or going.

The woman who descended the hill was obviously a nurse. Her white cap bobbed up and down, her brown curls bouncing beneath it, as she stormed across the stretch of field to where the men were still frolicking like otters in the stream. George could only hear a word or two as she pointed up toward the open windows of the chateau.

. . . Soldiers suffering
. . . Men dying
. . . Americans gallivanting

The gallivanting came to an abrupt end as the men dropped their heads in shame and retrieved their clothes before scurrying up the hill toward the road. The nurse followed them to the base of the hill.

"Louise!" Her voice drifted over the field until it got trapped in the trees on the far side of the road. "Louise! Allez, mon enfant."

The little girl with the flaming curls who'd watched George at the horse corrals darted from the forest edge and into the waiting arms of the nurse. He watched them for a moment before dropping from the boulder and starting his own climb up the hill.

"Excuse me." The nurse's accent was British, and when George turned to face her, he noticed the red cross on the front of her white apron, the same one the Voluntary Aid Detachment nurses from England wore. She was holding the little girl's hand as she approached. "May I speak to you for a moment?"

"Of course," he replied.

"I'm Anna," she said, "and this here is Louise. I know she follows you out to the old stables sometimes."

"Yes," George replied. "She's been out there a few times. Is she your daughter?"

Anna laughed as if the idea was preposterous, but there was no shortage of affection in her gaze as she looked down at the little girl who was still clutching her hand.

"No. She's not my daughter. I took care of her father in this hospital when he came back from the war, and I got to know Louise when she would come for visits."

"You're English?" George gestured to the cross on her apron.

Anna nodded and glanced back to the chateau behind her. "I work with the Red Cross and spend most of my time in there. But Louise lost her mother to influenza last year and then her father this year, so I've been taking care of her. She's not a particularly trusting child, so I assume you are a decent man since she seems to like you."

"Oh," George laughed. "Well, I enjoy her company, too."

Louise's brown eyes were turned up at such an angle that the sun's reflection off her pupils could almost trick George into believing the light was coming from within her. He'd never spent much time around children, but there was something so different about Louise, some kind of depth or sorrow in her eyes that drew him to her.

"The chateau has a barn," Anna said, pulling George's attention back from the little girl. "There are no horses there anymore and everything is just gathering dust these days. Perhaps it could be of use to you?"

"That's very kind of you. We could certainly use whatever you can spare."

"Consider it yours, then." When a lock of curls escaped from beneath her cap, she tucked it behind her ear as a blush crept into her cheeks. She didn't seem like the type of woman to blush, and that in itself made George smile. "Take care of yourself out there," she said. "I hear the Americans will be leaving for the front soon."

George nodded and tipped his cap to her.

"Yes, ma'am," he said. "I certainly will."

It wasn't true. The next stop for the Americans would be a town called Toul for more combat training, but that didn't sound as dangerous and exciting as heading to the front, and George wanted to be both of those things. He wanted to impress the pretty nurse standing in front of him. He wanted to be the soldier he knew he wasn't.

George never did gather any of the supplies from the chateau's barn. He could never convince the other men to help him, and there wasn't enough time. The train took them away a few days later; soldiers were needed at the front.

He never got to see Anna again, either. It was just one of the many regrets he left in Châteauvillain, along with the horses. The day the train rolled out, he spotted little Louise in the crowd of people who'd gathered to see them off, standing alone on the platform with her bare feet. He watched her for a moment, wanting to wish her a final farewell, but by the time he called out her name, the train was already picking up speed and his voice was swallowed down by the roar of the engine.

chapter 4

July 1918

The train drummed a rhythm into his bones, the cold metal of the floor beating into his body an ominous and worrisome tune. The men beside him were subdued, each lost in his own thoughts and expectations of what was to come. Even Philip had offered them peace after one or two jokes about German submarines.

No one knew what was coming. They weren't battle-tested soldiers, and, when their orders sent them to Château-Thierry to face off against the Germans instead of to Toul, anticipation and excitement had turned into trepidation and fear.

"Mountcastle, what do you think we'll see out there?"

George turned to the man beside him, a twenty-two-year-old dock worker from New York who'd landed at Ellis Island not two years earlier from Italy. He was one of many immigrants in their unit, but his English was far better than the others'.

"I don't know, Ricci," George replied. "I guess we'll find out."

"I'll tell you what we're going to see out there," Philip said, weaving his way over from the far side of the train car and wedging himself into the small space between them. "A bunch of dead Germans."

"You gonna kill them with your jokes or your good looks, Foster?" Matthews was another New Yorker, a jovial guy they'd nicknamed Ace on account of his burning desire to be a fighter pilot. He'd gotten through flying cadet training school at Cornell, but during his physical exam it was determined he had partial blindness in his right eye from an old childhood injury. It wasn't bad enough to keep him out of the army, but his flying days were over before he'd even gotten a chance to get off the ground.

"I can't help what the good Lord gave me, Ace."

The laughter and chatter that was beginning to spread through the troops fizzled out as the train slowed and came to a jarring stop, throwing a few of the men on top of each other. Profanities rang through the air as helmets and gas masks, which were supposed to have been secured, went flying through the train car.

A mechanical issue was plaguing one of the Cadillacs that had been carrying the division commanders, the men who were too important to be riding in cargo trains along with their troops. They weren't too pleased that they'd already waited three hours for the mechanics on the train, and since the mechanics had little to no experience with Cadillac engines, they were all in for a long delay.

The temperature was steadily climbing, the July sun conducting its heat into the metal train cars and cooking the men inside. The only shade was from a tree-lined ravine that the men were ordered to march to on the far side of a meadow across from the tracks. If not for the clusters of vine-encased tomb markers scattered throughout the field, George wouldn't have known they were marching over a recent battleground. With a rifle slung over his shoulder and his helmet strapped to his head, he trudged through the overgrown meadow of wildflowers that had been cultivated from death, unable to read the French-inscribed grave markers.

"Those your horses, Mountcastle?" Milo was the one to point the herd out to George. He was an Alaskan whose family had emigrated to the United States from Serbia a generation before he and his seven brothers were born, and, though he insisted he was twenty-three years old, his skin was coursed with the crevasses of a man twice his age. No one could pronounce his last name—Milosavljevic—so they called him Milo, which didn't seem to bother him. He was a man of few words, and those he used were reserved for matters that, for whatever reason, he deemed important. His name was not one of them.

By the time George spotted the horses on the horizon, Milo was already stretched out beneath the canopy of trees with his eyes shut, his legs crossed, and an unlit cigarette dangling from the corner of his mouth. He looked like a man without a care in the world.

The horses were suffering. Even from a distance, their low-hanging heads and staggering gaits were burdensome to watch. The black mare from the corrals was among them, tethered to a draft horse and moving at a glacier's pace. Whatever fire had once burned inside of her had long been extinguished. George crossed the field and stepped onto the dust-covered path that followed the train tracks to the front, stopping in front of the two horses.

"Step aside, son."

He didn't pay any mind to the man beside him. If not for the grip on his shoulder, George would have shrugged him away, but the man pulled him back a step or two just as the whip cracked over the back of the black mare, sending her stumbling forward.

"There's nothing you can do for her at this point." When George turned around, he was surprised to find Colonel Mac by his side. "I'm afraid we're about to find out just how useful a healthy herd of horses would have been."

The colonel didn't stick around to discuss the matter, and George had a sudden wave of nausea as he watched him walk back to join the other officers in the Cadillac that was finally sputtering to life. A throbbing pain was hammering at the base of his skull, and by the time he turned back toward the horses, they were already fading into the distance.

Over the horizon, a black cloud of smoke from an approaching train billowed into the air to announce its presence. The train had slowed to a crawl by the time it reached them, and the men from George's unit were zipping around the cattle cars and hurling insults through the barred windows. The cargo was German prisoners. Hundreds of corpse-like men packed together so tightly there couldn't even have been room for the dead to fall. They were being taken from the front, but where they were going was anyone's guess. Most of them were just boys. Not the monsters George had been led to believe they'd face on the battlefield.

It was one of the men from George's train car who decided to hop up onto the side of one of the compartments, his fingers clinging to imaginary ledges. He might have held on longer if he hadn't insisted on being a fool. But then he probably wouldn't have been swinging through the air on the side of a moving train if foolishness wasn't in his nature. It happened so fast that when George was later asked for an official incident report, he could only say that one minute the man was waving his arm and pumping his fist through the air, and the next minute he was on the ground and that same arm was missing. George didn't see the moment it was ripped off by the metal disks of the one-hundred-ton train.

By the time they pulled him from the tracks, the train was gone and the arm unsalvageable. The man was mumbling in a language that George couldn't understand while the medics wrapped the wound with gauze and towels and whatever else they could find to stanch the bleeding. Everything was soon saturated, and no one, least of all the medics, had any expectation that he would survive the rest of the trip.

George sat by his side in the back of the train car, more out of duty than want. He watched the countryside roll by, the caravans of refugees hobbling away from the front with everything they could carry on their backs. Old men, women, children, babies. He tried not to listen, but he couldn't stop hearing the bleeding man beside him with his endless questions.

Is this the train to Barstow?

Yes.

Am I going home?

Yes.

Will my mother be there?

Yes.

What else could he say? It wasn't until the questions stopped that George realized the man had lost consciousness, and within moments of the silence, he spotted the black mare on the side of the tracks. She'd had enough decency to step off the path before collapsing, before being untethered and left behind for dead.

Nothing good came from the front. It was like a tornado, a vortex that sucked everything nearby into its dark and foreboding center. Whatever made it out, which wasn't much, had been battered or ripped to shreds, no resemblance to what it had once been.

The man with the missing arm was somehow still alive when they rolled into the station at Montmirail. George lost sight of him when the medics collected him from the train car and hauled him to the surgical tents, and it wasn't until he looked down that he realized he'd forgotten to hand over the man's belongings.

If the road to Montmirail had been tumultuous, then the station itself was pandemonium. It had been converted into a hospital of sorts, platforms made into surgical suites and lawns turned into wards. Bodies were everywhere, some alive and some dead. George wandered through the mass of people coming and going, everyone seeming to know what direction they were headed but him. A British orderly was the one to finally point him toward the surgical tents, physically turning his body and nudging him forward until he walked straight into them.

It was a nurse he noticed when he first poked his head into the tent. He couldn't see her face, but her voice was as beautiful and melancholic as the song of an Alabama whippoorwill on a cool spring night. Her accent was French and her words soothing as she sat beside the American soldier who'd lost his arm on the train, stroking his face and assuring him that he would soon be home, that he'd fought bravely and sacrificed himself for a noble cause. For the briefest moment, a pang of jealousy ripped through George's body as he watched that man die beneath her touch.

He stepped into the tent just as the nurse pulled the sheet up to cover the man's face, and when their eyes met, his feet stilled. It wasn't just the beauty of her face that stopped him. It was the intimacy of her features. They were so familiar that he was certain he could close his eyes and draw them from memory.

"Did he suffer?" George pulled his hat from his head as he stepped further into the tent, nervously squeezing its brim between his fingers and glancing from the nurse to the man on the bed behind her.

When she opened her mouth to speak, he could almost hear the rich cadence of her voice before her words even emerged. He was surprised when they came out in French.

"Je ne parle pas anglais."

"I'm sorry," he said, shaking his head. "I don't speak French."

She hesitated before responding, weighing her words as if they might not come out the way she intended. "No English," she finally said, and George was certain he could hear the moment his heart fractured inside his chest.

"Of course." He dropped his gaze to the blood-soaked sheet covering the man whose name he'd never bothered to learn, the man who'd been sung to sleep *in English* by the beautiful nurse standing before him. "There's one thing you got wrong about him, though." George gestured toward the bed with his hat. "He never fought bravely. He never got the chance."

Her eyes dropped, and the slight bow of her head gave George a new perspective of her face. The even lines of her cheekbones, the flutter of her eyelashes, the slope of her nose. He could stand there forever discovering her from every angle and it wouldn't be long enough. The laugh that escaped her lips was almost decadent. She wiped something from the front of her apron before she looked back up at him.

"I am sorry about your friend," she said, in English. "But you should know that he did not suffer."

"So, you do speak English." George pulled out a smile that a girl from his hometown had once said made him look like a young Teddy Roosevelt. "Is it just the Americans, or do you try to avoid the British soldiers as well?"

"Both," she replied, and this time her laughter was infused with a girlish lilt that could almost convince George she was flirting with him.

"Are we really that bad?"

Her eyes flickered beneath her lashes, revealing the most magnificent shade of blue he'd ever seen. She shrugged before she glanced up at him one last time. "Not all of you," she said.

When she started for the door, George almost tripped over one of the empty stretchers on the ground, his mind frantically searching for something witty to make her stay. "Wait," he said, catching himself mid-fall. "Please. I have to know your name."

Her smile never faded, but a sorrow passed over her features with the subtlety of a thin cloud barely eclipsing the sun on a breezy summer day. The light came back before George even had a chance to miss it, and as she pushed the tent flap back, she sighed into the space between them.

"Marcelle," she finally said. "My name is Marcelle."

chapter 5

MARCELLE

Montmirail, France
July 1918

"Où as-tu eu ça?" *Where did you get that?*

Marcelle took a long, slow drag of the tightly rolled cigarette before holding it out between her fingers and studying the craftsmanship that went into making it.

"Un Américain," she said, blowing the smoke up toward the ceiling and then offering it to Pierre.

"What did you do for this cigarette?" He took it from her before pulling the sheet up to hide his body as Marcelle rose from the mattress and gathered her clothes from the floor. She was not ashamed of her nakedness. She was so rarely alone these days that she relished the few nights a month she shared Pierre's bed and could freely examine her ever-wasting body.

At seventeen, it had been soft and full, more like a woman's than it was now at twenty-one. She was no longer made of smooth curves, but of sharp angles, and, as she ran her hands over the jutting edges of her ribs, she wondered if she might shrink away to nothing. Was that possible? When the food ran out for good, would her body wither down to nothing and be swept away by the wind?

The morning light was spilling through the curtains that covered the sliver of window, giving Pierre's basement room a voyeuristic view of ankles and legs and anything else that was not properly covered by the unsuspecting pedestrians who ventured too close to it.

"Why do these American men give you so many gifts?" he asked.

Marcelle huffed in response as she pulled on her under-garments and shook out her skirt and blouse. She had never known Pierre to be a jealous man, but war had taken a toll on them both, turning them into a different version of the couple they had once been. Her eyes flickered to the stub that remained of his right arm, the rest having been left to the battlefield that took it. Everyone from Pierre's past, his mother and his sisters and his friends, was certain he was dead. Pierre would not discuss the details of the battle in eastern France that had taken the rest of the young men from Soissons four years earlier, but he made it clear there would be no reunions after the war.

"Jealousy does not suit you, darling." Marcelle winked at him as she buttoned up her blouse and tucked it deep into her skirt. "And there is not a man in all of America who could steal me from you."

The Americans had been trickling in to join the fray over the past few weeks, and, because they didn't understand hunger and had yet to learn the importance of rationing, the nurses were gifted with their excesses. Marcelle never turned their generosity down, but she rarely engaged with the men. Her knowledge of the English language was a well-guarded secret that spared her from both diplomacy and civility. One conversation with an injured private from New Jersey was enough to teach her that Americans were sociable to the point of being intrusive and courteous to the point of being intolerable.

"Is that right?" Pierre scooted to the edge of the mattress, the sheet still covering the bottom half of his body, and reached for Marcelle's hand. "And is this Marcelle talking, or is this Josephine?"

Josephine. She had become Josephine LeBlanc two years earlier when Pierre had walked back into her life, returning from a fate he never should have escaped. Together, he and Marcelle worked within a network of people whose masked identities were critical to their survival. They were supposed to know nothing of each other's pasts, and, as far as their superiors knew, they didn't.

Marcelle had been working as a nurse beside her sister in Château-Thierry when a British intelligence agent had overheard her lying in flawless German to an injured prisoner who had been captured the previous evening. Gangrene had already eaten through his legs and seeped into his blood, and while Marcelle did not understand the intricacies of the infection, she knew he was due for an agonizing death, and she could do no less than offer him grace at the end. Unbeknownst to her, the British agent who had been eavesdropping on her conversation heard all about the soldier's mother who would be getting a room ready for his return, and the girlfriend who would be waiting to greet him as he stepped off the train, and the friends who would welcome him home with drinks and laughter and celebrations that would last for months.

Shortly after the man's death, the British agent introduced himself as Charles and made her an offer she couldn't refuse. He was extremely moved by her words and was convinced that if a pretty French nurse could coax a man so seamlessly into death, she could also coax information—like enemy positions and battle plans—from beleaguered and battle-weary soldiers who hadn't seen their wives and girlfriends in years.

Until her work with Charles, Marcelle and Rosalie had been lodging with the other nurses, mostly British and properly educated, in a tent outside of the Montmirail train station. But her service with British intelligence had bought them access to a shared room in a local house with one mattress and three tenants. Crowded as it was, shift work made it possible for all three women to coexist and occasionally have a night to themselves on the scratchy, bug-infested mattress that was an unquestionable step up from their tent lodgings.

Marcelle's sister never questioned their accommodations. Rosalie knew nothing of Marcelle's espionage, and she would not have approved. If she'd had any inclination of what Marcelle had been up to, or that Pierre had returned from the front alive, she would have dragged them both kicking and screaming to their families. The Marchands and the Fourniers, what was left of them, had slipped out of Soissons during a skirmish between the French and German troops, shortly after the German occupation four years earlier, and had found accommodations with a widow in the outskirts of Paris. Marcelle's parents insisted the old woman had extended her offer to house them as a courtesy, in return asking only that they kept her gardens blooming and her chickens fed, but she had seen her mother's sterling silver necklace around the woman's neck shortly after they'd arrived, and she knew better.

The tasks were menial, but the provisions were not enough to sustain them all, so Marcelle and Rosalie, on a whim of patriotic duty and sheer boredom, had joined the Croix-Rouge française as voluntary nurses. With no formal medical training, calling themselves nurses was a bit of a stretch, but on-the-job training more than made up for their lack of education, and within months of registering, they were sent to Château-Thierry, where the French and their allies were barely holding the line along the Marne River. When the shelling got too close to the camp hospital, they were moved to the train station in Montmirail about thirty kilometers from the front, but the Germans would soon be upon them again, crashing over the defensive line of Allied soldiers like the bludgeoning waves of a high tide. It would not be long before the Parisiennes were speaking German.

As it turned out, Charles's rendezvous with Marcelle had not been by chance. Pierre had orchestrated it. He had watched her for months, waiting for the perfect moment to approach her, to step back into the life they had surrendered years earlier. Young lovers, bold and reckless and naïve. But that would have involved giving up his cover and forfeiting his work with

British intelligence, which, at the time, he was reluctant to do. When he finally accepted the impossibility of the situation, he did the only thing he could think of that might draw them back into orbit together. He planted a seed in Charles's head about a young French nurse who could reportedly speak flawless German and might have some use to the network.

Marcelle didn't learn that truth until months after her first meeting with Charles. She had turned out to be a much more valuable asset than anyone had expected, securing vital information from German prisoners, especially the higher-ranking ones, and was both feared and revered by the Kaiserreich. There was even a rumor they had given her a nickname: die Hexe des Flusses. Or in French: la sorcière de la rivière.

The witch of the river.

For the sake of the empire, German soldiers, especially officers with classified information, were encouraged to take their own lives upon capture rather than being seduced and manipulated by the witch. In fact, she had garnered so much attention that Charles was beginning to fear for her safety. It was shortly after she became the witch of the river that he'd started introducing Marcelle to a few select operatives, some for safety and others for collaboration. Adrien Rousseau would be one of them. He was a French soldier as proficient in English as Marcelle was in German and would act as her interpreter to the British intelligence agents who were unable to speak French. The information she had been given about him was that he'd been at the front lines near Soissons early in the fight, losing an arm along the way, and that he spoke English with a Cockney accent he had learned from his grandmother, who was from Surrey.

Marcelle's heart had raced at the description of him, but she had not allowed herself to hope, to believe that Pierre might have come back to her. On the day she was to meet Adrien Rousseau, she'd stepped hurriedly through the streets to the dimly lit basement apartment where she was routinely given her orders, to find that he had already arrived. His face was gaunt and hollow, his youthfulness stolen years too soon, but there was no doubt it was him. Her fiancé, Pierre. Back from the grave. The subtle shake of his head was all that had stopped her from spilling her emotions onto the half-rotted wooden floorboards between them. Charles had been none the wiser. He'd made the introductions and left them on their own.

Two years had passed since that meeting. Two years for Marcelle to perfect her English and to no longer have need for an interpreter. These days, their rendezvous were more like covert missions, surveillance having become second nature to them both.

"I have to go," Marcelle said, smoothing out her blouse as best she could before pinning her hair into place and gesturing for Pierre to check outside the door so she could make a discreet departure. Charles wasn't the only person on their radar. War had eased social expectations to an extent, especially near the front, where liberties with wine and profanity and promiscuity were accepted, but nurses—particularly French ones— were to be godly in all pursuits. Nurses from the Croix-Rouge française had been sent home from the front for far less than sneaking out of a man's room shortly after dawn, and Marcelle had no intention of returning to Paris in shame.

Pierre pulled his trousers off a three-legged chair that sat in the corner and slipped them on beneath the covers. "The Germans will cross the Marne River soon," he said. "And more men are going to be needed at the front."

Pierre was done hiding. Four years had turned out to be his limit. His behind-the-scenes service was more valuable to his country than any time he might have spent on the battlefield, but it was not the kind of service that would ever make headlines, and the guilt was starting to consume him. It was accumulating on his skin, layer by layer, like thick coats of paint that would soon dry and stiffen until he could no longer breathe. He wanted his dignity back. He wanted to make Marcelle his wife, see his mother and sisters one last time, and fight with his countrymen. Even if it meant dying.

"I am still capable of fighting," he said, buttoning up his trousers. "And I would feel better if you were in Paris with your father."

"I am not ready to return to Paris," Marcelle replied. "I enjoy my work here."

Pierre wrapped his arm around her waist and pulled her onto his lap, the pungent scent of tobacco lingering on his breath and twisting Marcelle's stomach. "Marcelle Marchand," he said. "Why won't you marry me? I want to know you as Marcelle Fournier just once before I die."

"Stop that." Marcelle pulled herself from his lap, straightened her skirt, and stormed to the door before turning around to face him one last time. "Stop talking about dying, Pierre. You will not die. And you will not go out there and fight with one arm. Do you hear me? I will not allow you to go."

"Marcelle, wait . . ."

She breathed out a hefty sigh before she yanked the door open and marched out of Pierre's room with no shame or worry about what the neighbors might see or say. When she reflected on that moment years later, it wasn't the anger she would remember. She wouldn't think about the scorn that had carried her across town and back to her boardinghouse or the way she had scolded Pierre for his careless words. The only thing she would recall from that day was the way her name had sounded on his lips when he had asked her to marry him and she had been too proud to say yes.

chapter 6

The sky was blanketed in a thick fog by the time Marcelle made it to the train station. The sun was fighting a losing battle of burning through the smoke and haze from the cannons and hand grenades and gas cannisters that were endlessly being launched from one trench line to another less than thirty kilometers to the north. The ambulance trucks were already making their rounds, buzzing around crater holes and downed trees like scurrying beetles evading the light. They stopped only long enough to drop off the dead and injured at the railway platform and pick up the walking wounded, who were then carried back to the front.

Marcelle spotted her sister walking between the rows of corpses that had been lined along the road, collecting identification tags from around their necks. She hesitated before calling out Rosalie's name, a moment of uncertainty that the nurse she was watching was her sister and not a woman twice their age.

War had done that to her. Malnutrition had stripped the sheen from her hair and the blush from her cheeks, and Marcelle couldn't help but wonder if the stoop in her shoulders would ever be righted.

Rosalie sensed her sister's presence, turning to face her before Marcelle could even call out her name. A gift from God, their mother had said of them. Two souls so entwined that they could feel the other's presence, and absence. Neither sister had argued with their mother, but they had both understood, even if they hadn't voiced it aloud, that it was as much a curse as a gift.

To have your soul tied to another person from birth was like holding your heart in your own hands and watching it beat beside you, knowing you cannot live without it or leave it behind, but desperate to unburden yourself from it. Desperate for freedom.

Marcelle followed the path between the dead that led to her sister, the breathy words of Rosalie's Hail Marys spiraling into the fog above them as she yanked off identification tags, one by one, and slipped them into a bag. They would be sorted later and dropped in with the letters that would travel around the world to countless families who would shoulder their grief mostly in silence.

"You should get some rest," Marcelle said. "You are going to wear yourself out." She tried to block out the clinking of the identification tags as they landed in the bag, each one pounding into her head like a hammer coming down on a nail, like a coffin being sealed for eternity.

"I am almost done," Rosalie sighed, nodding toward the end of the row. "Just a couple dozen left. Elise was worried about you this morning. She said you were not in bed when she got back to the room last night. That you never came home."

Elise was their third roommate, and as far as Marcelle knew, she was supposed to have been working the previous night. She and Marcelle had worked alternating shifts for so long, she hadn't thought to double-check Elise's work schedule. She was getting sloppy.

"I was . . ." Marcelle's gaze was caught on the bag of identification tags in her sister's hand. Lying to Rosalie was infinitely harder than pulling information from German prisoners of war. It was only when the clinking stopped and Rosalie turned to face her, waiting for an answer, that Marcelle could feel the drumming of her heart beneath her sternum.

"I know where you were." Rosalie sighed again, before turning back to the soldiers and finishing the Hail Mary she had left undone. "You were with the English nurses in their tent."

"Yes." Marcelle breathed out the word with more force than she had intended. "I didn't realize Elise would be home last night. I thought she was working, and I was so tired of being alone. I certainly didn't mean to worry her. I will make sure to apologize."

"You need to be careful, Marcelle. The British nurses are not like us. Do not forget that. They serve men and we serve God."

When had piety taken over her sister's life? And why had war had the opposite effect on Marcelle? God had forsaken them so many years ago that Marcelle couldn't even remember what faith felt like. She had given up being manipulated by her convictions, and she had vowed to never allow man or God that luxury again.

"Of course," she replied to her sister. "I will be more careful."

The screeching of iron on iron drew their focus from the field of corpses to the railway platform. It was a familiar sound, one that would frequent Marcelle's dreams for years to come. The inbound trains carried soldiers. Some alive. Some dead. Most incapacitated in some way. They both watched the train come to a stop before they spoke.

"Looks like there is some work for you," Rosalie said. "I know you are lonely, Marcelle. Maybe tonight when your shift is over you can join me for mass."

Marcelle nodded as she leaned in to kiss her sister's cheek. They never spoke of her refusal to attend mass, but it weighed heavily between them. It was an anchor that Marcelle would have freely tossed overboard if not for the fact that it had been tethered to her sister. Rosalie would have drowned from the weight of Marcelle's faithlessness, her infidelity to God. The words of her sister's Hail Mary danced around in the mist of the morning air as if shadowing her as Marcelle made her way back to the station platform.

———～——

English was the language pouring from the train as the compartments opened. American English. And the men who descended upon the platform were fresh-faced, well fed, and mostly garrulous. There must have been hundreds of them, but Marcelle weaved her way between them, her head bowed and her eyes to the floor until she found her way to the hospital tents. It was an eerily quiet morning inside the surgical tent.

The ambulance drivers had brought mostly corpses back from the front that morning, and the train carrying the American soldiers held only one injured man, who was very near death. His arm was missing, and from the pallor of his skin, Marcelle was certain that most of his blood was missing, as well. He was alone, and not quite dead but gone from the world. She kneeled beside him and took his hand between hers. It was already cold.

"Good night, my love," she whispered to him in English. "You have fought bravely, and now you are going home. Rest well."

The man was dead by the time she finished speaking. How many times had she repeated those words? To how many men? In how many languages? She covered his face with a bloody sheet that had been lying by his side, suddenly aware that she was not alone. The man watching her from the other side of the tent was also an American. He wore their uniform and carried their gear, but he didn't look like the other men who had come off that train. He was more refined, less like a warrior. His dark eyes danced back and forth between Marcelle and the man beneath the sheet, and she couldn't seem to pull her gaze away from them.

"Did he suffer?" The man removed his hat from his head

and kneaded the brim between his fingers before stepping closer to the bed. There was something so intimate and familiar in the way his eyes landed on her skin that Marcelle was almost compelled to break her own rule and answer him in English. She shook the thought away before it could take root and blossom into something she couldn't undo.

"Je ne parle pas anglais."

"I'm sorry," the man responded, shaking his head. "I don't speak French."

Marcelle watched him for a moment, certain that if she gave her memory enough time it would pull up his name for her, reveal the date they had last spoken, remind her of the place they had once stood. But it was impossible. She had never met this man. Had she?

"No English," she finally replied, but the man standing before her knew better.

— — — —

Marcelle's cheeks were still aflame when she stepped out of the tent and into the blinding sunlight. Pierre would have been disappointed in her. After assuring him just that morning that no American could ever steal her heart, she had shamelessly allowed herself to be swept up in another man's attention. George was his name. She couldn't remember the last time she had giggled and blushed under a man's gaze. Even Pierre's.

The ambulances were making another round through the station, but this time the corpses had been left on the battlefield. The hospital was overwhelmed with wounded soldiers long before darkness clipped the final strands of light, and it wasn't until Charles showed up that Marcelle took a moment to stretch out the cramps that had leached their way into her back.

Charles stood to the side, a handkerchief over his mouth and nose as Marcelle disinfected a gangrenous foot. She could feel his eyes running over her bloodstained apron and the crusty layers of sweat and salt that had dried on her skin throughout the day.

"I have a favor to ask of you," he said. "I hate to do this, but I have no one else."

Marcelle nodded and finished wrapping the soldier's foot, before she tried to brush away the grime from the white blouse beneath her apron. It was splattered with blood that would likely never wash out.

"I have a message that needs to be run," he said as he glanced down at his watch, "and all my girls have left town for good, I think."

Charles's messages were typically run by local girls, young women who were either from the area or passing through with their families on the way to Paris. He had already learned from experience that a rendezvous between a man and a woman might draw the attention of nosy neighbors, but it rarely roused suspicions of espionage. Lately, though, rumors had been swirling that the German front, sitting on the other side of the Marne River, was about to make its move, and people were fleeing even faster to Paris, leaving him shorthanded and resorting to other means. Marcelle had already run a handful of messages for him. There was nothing to it, really.

"Of course," she said. "But I don't have a change of clothes, and my sister will be at home by now. I do not believe she will let me leave again after dark. Especially alone."

When Charles ran a hand through his hair, she could see that it was thinning on top, its color an almost perfect match to the ruddiness of his complexion.

"I have some dresses in my boarding room that I keep for reasons like this," he replied. "Something in there should fit you."

The night was eerily quiet as they walked the short distance to Charles's boardinghouse. Marcelle thought the shelling sounded more muted and sporadic than the last few nights, but maybe it was just the comfort of having Charles by her side that made it seem so. He was a difficult man to read most of the time, except when he was angry, and she was endlessly trying to discover something about him. Anything. If they had met before the war, she would have guessed he was in his fifties, but since war seemed to age people at a much faster rate, she had to assume he was quite a bit younger. He wore no ring, but she imagined he had a wife back home, maybe even a few redheaded children.

His lodgings were a bit of a letdown. The room he rented in an all-male boardinghouse was no bigger than the one she had snuck out of just that morning, and it didn't even have a three-legged chair. He pulled a satchel from beneath the bed that looked more like a doctor's kit than a traveling bag, and Marcelle was eager to see what was inside of it. A wooden cigar box sat on top, and, despite his careful hands, the top fell off when he placed it on the bed, spilling out a few letters. He shoved them back into the box and under the pillow before Marcelle could read any of the words, but the precision of the penmanship was so beautiful, she was certain she had never seen its equal.

"We keep this for emergencies," he said, pulling the satchel wide and rifling through the garments before realizing he was holding up a slip between them. The color in his cheeks swelled with a rose-colored blush a few shades darker than the one he typically wore as he dropped it back into the bag and coughed into his fist. "I'll step out for a bit. Let you find something that suits you. I'll be just outside the door when you're ready."

It was the red dress that Marcelle noticed first. She held it up to her body and twirled around in place, watching the skirt flare out around her like a parasol. The waist was cinched, and the plunging neckline gave way to long and elegant sleeves that were hemmed with lace at the wrists. Marcelle had never worn a dress like it before. She had never even seen one, and as she thought about the drabness of her life and the probability that she would never reach her twenty-second birthday, she couldn't resist.

Charles seemed a bit off balance when she finally opened the door, and Marcelle was suddenly aware of how the fabric clung to her skin and outlined the shape of her body. She couldn't stop running her hands over it.

"I . . . um . . ." Charles cleared his throat before he gestured to the dress with his hand. "You look quite lovely. But I'm not sure if this is the best choice for this particular occasion."

Marcelle glanced down at the black belt that was cinched around her waist and ran her hands over the buckle, feeling once again like the little girl with her head in the clouds that she thought she had left in Soissons four years earlier. But here she was again, playing dress-up in the middle of war.

"Of course," she said. "I am sorry. I just . . . well, I had never seen such a beautiful dress, and I thought maybe just this once . . . I am sorry. I will get changed." She stepped back into the room and was closing the door behind herself when Charles reached out and grabbed the handle.

"You are dazzling, Marcelle," he said. "Someday, when this war is over, you are going to step out in a dress even more beautiful than this one, and men will swoon over you."

Marcelle shut the door before the tears could fall. Did he believe that? Did he think they would survive this war? Did he find her dazzling? None of it mattered. She had a job to do, so she pulled out a gray smock of a dress that was as colorless as the life she was living and dropped the red dress into the case. As she bent down to slide it back under the bed, wondering whose skin that red dress would touch next, she remembered the wooden cigar box under the pillow.

It was wrong. She had no business rummaging through Charles's things, but the yearning to know whose beautiful penmanship had crafted that letter was almost physical. The clock was ticking; if she spent any more time thinking about it, she would lose her chance.

My Dear Joseph,

Our daughter made her entrance into the world last night. Evelyn Rose Granger is as beautiful as she is feisty. She is perfect, my love, with your fiery red hair and my insufferable insomnia. We needn't have worried about her all this time. She is plump and healthy and already attended her first air raid drill. Edward was quite disappointed he didn't get the brother he was hoping for, but his sorrows were assuaged by the jam tarts Fannie brought him this morning. She will stay with us until your return, so please don't worry yourself, darling. We are in loving and capable hands, and . . .

The letter went on, but Marcelle could hear Charles pacing outside the door, so she folded it back into the envelope and dropped it into the cigar box as she struggled under the weight of her guilt.

Joseph Granger.

She chided herself for her selfishness. This was exactly the kind of thing Charles had warned her about. She couldn't even blame naivety or ignorance, because she had known full well what she was doing. She slid the box back under the pillow and when she opened the door to the hallway, Charles gave her outfit a nod of approval before glancing once more at the watch on his wrist.

"We have to run," he said, closing the door behind her and rushing them out to the street. He folded the message into the front page of a book that Marcelle had never read and showed her how to carry it, and then he quickly rehashed the details of her upcoming encounter:

"Oncle Henri" would be waiting at the bottom of the stairs outside the boardinghouse for elderly men displaced by the war, just blocks from the Montmirail train station. He would wear a black beret and have a pipe hanging from his mouth, although the pipe would not be lit. Marcelle would address him first, offer the book to him, and the man would then accompany her back to the hospital at the train station, where Charles would be waiting with her uniform so she could return to her boardinghouse and her sister without suspicion.

Charles walked her as far as the train station, and from there, Marcelle continued to the boardinghouse alone. She had just rounded the corner when she caught sight of a red glow beneath a cherry tree at the base of the stairs, and the scent of burning tobacco hit her with such a force that she was reminded of summers when her grandfather would visit them in Soissons.

The man with the black beret did indeed have a pipe hanging from his mouth, but it was a lit pipe, and he did not wait to be approached as Marcelle had been told. When he spotted her, he snatched the pipe from his mouth and pasted a broad smile across his face.

"Josephine!" His voice boomed across the vacant road and the pipe in his hand glowed through the darkness as he waved her over. It zigzagged through the air with a dizzying effect as Marcelle's thoughts jumped from one inconsistency to the next. The pipe was not supposed to be lit, and she was supposed to address him first.

A tingling sensation spread through her limbs and the leaves spinning at her feet knocked her off balance as she stepped forward. She hesitated just briefly, but for the rest of her life, there would never come a day that Marcelle would not relive that moment, that split-second decision to approach the man with the black beret, that lapse in judgment that had cost too many lives.

"Oncle Henri," she replied, leaning in for a kiss on the cheek before handing him the book from her hands. His eyes were the last thing she saw. They were dark, not just in color, but in temperament, as if they were so consumed with sorrow and regret that they could no longer hold light. Marcelle would spend years wanting to believe the sorrow in that man's eyes was because of the guilt he felt for his betrayal. Whatever his reasons, she would never know. She would never see him again, and eventually his eyes would lose meaning to her, and she would forget about them altogether.

The burlap bag scratched against her cheek as it was thrust over her head, but the terror that coursed through her did not linger. A sharp pain splintered through her head, and, as she felt her body listing from the blow, she slipped away into the darkness.

chapter 7

GEORGE

Château-Thierry, France
July 1918

The nights were darker than any George had ever seen, the light of the moon and stars unable to pierce the impenetrable smoke and fog that endlessly blanketed them. It was the kind of dark that tricked you into thinking your eyes were shut when they were, in fact, wide open.

But it was the day that terrorized them. The light. Without the cover of darkness, there was nothing but trenches to shield them from the low-flying German pilots who not only gathered intelligence for the Reich, but also liked to pick off American soldiers in a fatal game of cat and mouse. The German front sat less than fifty yards away from them, just across the Marne River, so they labored through the nights, when the darkness could shield them.

George's unit had been assigned to protect the Surmelin Valley, a low-lying expanse of open wheat fields and farmhouses that extended for miles from the south bank of the Marne River. According to Colonel Mac, the thin strip of land they were defending, at the base of two hills that rose up on either side of them like amphitheater seating, would be the location of the next German assault. It made no sense to George. Why would the Germans want to sit on this stage, exposed and vulnerable, nowhere to hide?

It was a precarious position. An American unit was digging in on the hill to their left, but the hill to their right was being defended by a French unit that was already beleaguered from years of battle. As far as George could tell, they hadn't even begun to dig in. If either unit retreated, the Thirty-Eighth would be an easy target from high above.

Colonel McAlexander, who seemed to live his life in a constant rage, was, of course, livid when he'd learned the French would be covering one of those hills. He was so certain they'd flee the minute the fighting started, leaving their entire right flank open, that he'd requested permission to take partial control of the hill. George had a sneaking suspicion that it was the tone of Colonel Mac's voice, rather than the content of his request, that had gotten it denied, but, whatever the reason, the hill was off-limits to them.

Sleep was a luxury that eluded George in the valley, adrenaline surges keeping him awake for the first seventy-two hours. Philip slept soundly beside him, while George lay with his eyes wide open, unable to acclimate to the planes and bombs that dropped in from overhead. He spent most of his time trying to remember the exact shade of Marcelle's eyes. The French nurse from the train depot lived in his mind. Her eyes, her laughter, her smile.

On the fourth day, his body so fatigued from the long nights of labor that neither bombs nor airplanes could reach him, he slept. He dreamed of trenches, of hardened earth that wouldn't yield to his shovel, and of the blisters that never had time to heal.

Colonel Mac walked the perimeter of their territory at dusk each day, always returning with the same orders to his field commanders: more trenches. For a man who thought the war would be won on an open battlefield, George thought he had his men spending far too much time tunneling through the terrain like ants. But he couldn't fault him for it. The flat and open valley provided no protection, so the men of the Thirty-Eighth begrudgingly split the land with their trench tools, carving lines through the earth.

For weeks, they went on like that: sleeping during the day,

digging at night. When they were done, they had five trench lines running parallel to the river, each about a mile apart, starting at the hill to their east and ending miles away at the hill to their west where their neighboring American unit was setting up a similar pattern of defense.

An elastic defense.

That's what the field officers called it. When the Germans attacked, landing on the south shore of the river, the men defending the first trench line would put up a brief small-arms fight before falling back to the second trench line a mile south. The Germans, thinking they'd scored an easy victory, would ferry their troops and heavy weaponry across the river to take control of the valley. Only then would they be met by the main force of the machine gunners from the second trench line and the heavy artillery of the third and fourth lines.

Because he was tasked with defending the trench line closest to the river, the one the Germans would hit first, George didn't think it was a sound strategy, but Philip wouldn't have been happy anywhere else. He believed in his leaders and his unit, and he was ready for the Germans to make their move.

"Do you think horses remember people?" Philip was patting one of the draft horses that George had just untethered from an artillery gun that they hadn't been able to move into position. He was a Percheron, a workhorse, his gray coat matted with dried mud and blood, and he would have labored until his last breath if George hadn't stopped him.

"Of course," George said, watching Philip run his hands over the muscles of the wasted animal. For all his bravado, Philip was a reflective man; it was likely the reason they enjoyed each other's company.

"I had a dog once," Philip said, brushing the Percheron's mane out of his eyes. "His name was Otis. He used to follow me to school every morning and bark at the door until the schoolmaster would run him off. I loved that dog." The smile slipped from his eyes as Philip's memory took him back to the moment all young boys remembered: the death of their first pet. George knew better than to ask him about it. Some memories were sacred, meant to live only in one man's thoughts.

"What should we do with this thing?" George nodded toward the artillery gun. The horses had given out like he'd known they would, and they would need to find another way to get the guns into place. He could already hear Colonel Mac barking orders at his lieutenants, who would then come down on the troops. There were never enough trenches, never enough guns, never enough artillery. George agreed. He would have preferred more guns, too, but without the horses, what could they do?

Reconnaissance missions, if they could be called that, started a few weeks after they'd dug in at the front. Capturing German soldiers with information about enemy positions and targets was the goal, but more often than not, the Americans came back from their excursions empty-handed.

George hated those missions. They would wait until well past midnight to set out in tattered and plugged-up rowboats that floated so low in the water, it was just a matter of time before they sank. Figuring out which direction to swim was George's biggest concern, aside from what they'd do if they actually captured a German soldier. Philip and Ace would have swum beside the boat if they could have sacked a Boche, but, so far, luck was on George's side.

It was about halfway into July when George felt certain his luck had finally run out. Ace was the pilot, as usual, the one to row them across the river as George and Philip scanned the north bank of the Marne for any signs of movement. A rustle in some low-lying bushes caught their attention, and when Ace dipped his paddles into the river, slowing the boat so they could get a better look, the form that took shape in front of their eyes was undeniably a man. Even under the moonless sky, George could see that he wore an officer's uniform and that he was unarmed.

A dull throb began to beat at the base of his skull, and the same nausea that had gripped his gut as he'd watched the black mare march to her death along the road to Montmirail was taking its hold. He was too dizzy to stand, certain he would lose his balance and fall into the river below if he tried, and when he pointed to the shore, to the man standing on the bank, he couldn't tame the tremor in his hand.

"Look," he whispered, before noticing the letter in the man's hand. "He's just standing there. Like he's waiting for us."

Philip's eyes scanned frantically over the horizon of the shoreline, passing over the man as if he wasn't even there, and by the time George turned his attention back to the bank, the man was gone.

But it wasn't possible. No one could move that fast. He'd just vanished, disappeared into the night without a trace.

"What are you talking about, Mountcastle?" Philip asked, his rifle aimed at the shore and his finger resting on the trigger as Ace rowed them backward with quiet strokes away from the bank. "Did you see someone?"

George could still see the man's face, the letter in his hand, the pins on his uniform. The hammering at the base of his skull began to fade as they drifted further from the shore, and by the time they'd made it halfway back to the south shore, and Philip had lowered his rifle, the nausea had subsided as well.

"I guess it was nothing," George mumbled. Was it stress? Insanity? He leaned back, untensing the muscles in his shoulders before shaking away the image in his mind. "Why don't we head back to shore?" he said. "Back to our unit. I think I just need to get some rest."

chapter 8

George couldn't sleep.

The French were having a raucous celebration in honor of Bastille Day. Wine flowed like water as they toasted and cheered and sang songs to commemorate the men who'd fought and died for their freedom over one hundred years earlier.

The Thirty-Eighth had been given the night off as well, but unlike Philip, who was snoring beside him, George couldn't turn off the chatter in his mind. He stared into the blackness of the moonless night, trying to remember the exact position of the stars in the Alabama sky he'd left behind. When the first of the mortar shells came blazing through overhead, he wondered if he might have imagined it, painted a shooting star into the scenery of his mind. It wasn't until it hit, and the ground shook, that he realized they'd spent the night in an unfamiliar silence.

Something wasn't right.

It was a fleeting thought, like the moment of anticipation between grabbing a hot iron and feeling the sting of its burn. Within seconds, mortar shells were exploding all around them, and bursts of blinding light were swallowing up the stars that had floated through his mind just moments earlier.

The pungent scent of mustard and garlic filled the air as George fumbled with the straps of his gas mask. His hands trembled from the combination of fear and adrenaline, and he couldn't get it secured to his face. Philip had to do it for him.

He tightened the straps and straightened George's goggles before he moved down the line to help the next man.

The earth shook as bombs rained down, burying whole companies of men beside them, and George couldn't tame the panic surging through his chest. It burned like an inferno, starting in his gut and reaching its tendrilled fingers up into his chest until it squeezed the breath from his lungs. The walls were closing in on him. They would bury him alive.

He clutched his rifle and clawed his way to solid ground, thrusting the bayonet tip blindly into the air as he inched forward. The sky was lit up like the Fourth of July, mortars and grenades streaking through the yellow and green smoke that hung over their heads.

His vision was blurred, but he couldn't blink away the fog that danced just in front of his goggles. He was so disoriented, he didn't know if he was heading toward friend or foe, or if he was even moving at all.

Bodies were everywhere. Some alive, some not.

The men around him were panicking, scattering through the night in a frenzy like a flock of chickens who'd just realized a fox had entered the yard. What were they supposed to do? They'd spent months learning how to shoot a rifle and launch a grenade and man a cannon, but this was something different. No one had prepared them for this moment.

George hadn't made it very far when a hand reached out and grabbed his leg, yanking him back into the trench.

"Where the hell are you going, Mountcastle? You're going to get yourself killed!" Philip ducked his head just moments before a bullet whizzed through the air above them. "They're shelling us from the far side of the river. Their troops haven't crossed over yet. Our best bet is to hunker down here until we can make a run for it."

"How do you know they're not out there right now?" George asked. "Where are the field commanders?"

"I don't know who's running this show, but I can tell you

the Boche aren't dumb enough to send their troops in and then bomb the hell out of them. We stay put until it's safe to move."

The tree line to the south was engulfed in a blaze that was spreading to the woods behind it, and all along the horizon, scattered fires burned. The shrieks of the mortar shells that whistled through the sky swallowed down the screams of men, and, through the fog of smoke and poisonous gases, hundreds of bodies could be seen strewn across the valley floor.

George couldn't breathe.

He wanted to rip his gas mask off and go running across the valley, past the miles of trenches and fortifications that were never going to hold, past the train station where he'd met the beautiful French nurse, past the ocean that had carried him to this ghastly place. He wanted to go home.

Ricci was on top of them before either Philip or George could react. If he'd been a German, they both would have been dead. His gas mask muffled his screaming voice, and George wasn't sure if he was speaking English or Italian until he ripped it off and threw it to the ground.

"Damnit, Ricci! Put your gas mask on!" Philip picked it up and was trying to force it over Ricci's head as he coughed and gagged from the poisonous gases that were seeping into his lungs.

"Ricci, please," George said, but his voice was muffled by his own mask and the explosions that were still slamming into the ground all around them.

"Dobbiamo uscire di qui!" Ricci yelled, clutching his rifle as his hands shook and the vein running down the middle of his forehead bulged. He paused just briefly before throwing his rifle over the edge of the trench wall, pulling himself out of the hole, and darting off into the night.

Philip threw Ricci's gas mask against the wall and sank down onto the ground, as George tried to hear the orders that were trickling in from the commanders. They were to stay put, hunker down in the trenches until the shelling eased up, and await further orders.

Minutes ticked away, maybe even hours. Time had no meaning but to carry them to morning and break the darkness. Would the dawn bring an end to this? Would the light drive the Germans back into hiding like it did every other morning?

It wasn't until the shelling slowed down that the other men around them started to move. Bodies that George had thought were corpses were suddenly popping up like prairie dogs in a field, peeking out over the trench walls and peering into the horizon. Orders from their field commanders soon followed.

It was time to fall back.

The Germans were crossing the Marne faster than expected, constructing floating bridges and bringing with them tanks and artillery guns and Sturmtruppen. The elite stormtrooper units were something of legend to the Americans, an admirable foe that many of the men from the Thirty-Eighth had vowed to best in battle.

Not George, of course. He'd had too much sense and not enough bravado for such foolishness. Philip had been one of the most outspoken, but whatever words he'd said about the Sturmtruppen were long forgotten, left on the training grounds in Châteauvillain. He and George were two of the first men over the trench wall, retreating through the wheat fields of the Surmelin Valley as fast as their legs could carry them. The rest of their company wasn't far behind, but the chaos of the night drove a wedge between them, and, instead of moving as a cohesive unit, each man was in his own fight for survival.

Retreat to the second line of defense.

Those were the orders, but the wheat fields were disorienting, and George felt certain they were carving a tortuous path that would take them straight back into the German front. The further they ran, the more the shelling intensified, lighting up the sky to reveal a scene so riotous that George would spend years trying to forget it.

Soldiers scurried beneath felled trees like roaches when the exploding incendiaries stole the cover of darkness and turned them into easy targets. They hid under railroad embankments and behind stone walls, struggling to quell the panic that was stifling their ability to do the most basic of things. Breathing was the most difficult.

Some men couldn't take it. They ripped their gas masks from their faces, gulping the poisonous air deep down into their lungs, convinced it was the masks suffocating them and not their own fear. They suffered for it. George couldn't watch as they clawed at their burning eyes and vomited into the masks that they struggled to pull back over their heads.

George's legs burned as he fought to keep up with Philip, not allowing himself to rest for fear he would lose him. Before long, four or five other men had joined them, latching on behind George. They moved in a line, one long living and breathing unit, a serpent sliding through the tall grass and over bodies that, unlike the hardened earth, gave beneath their feet. It wasn't until they came upon a stream that they finally stopped.

"Shit!" When Philip spun around, he seemed startled to find ten sets of eyes upon him, each man waiting for the private from Pennsylvania to tell him what to do. No one knew where they were. No one remembered the stream. It was narrow and shallow, more like a creek, and as some of the men started arguing about whether or not they should cross it, George was suddenly aware of the silence that was stretching around them. He could hear the wind blowing through the tree above his head and the dried wheat cracking beneath the boots of the soldier beside him.

It was too quiet.

The blasts of the mortar shells were off in the distance now, as if the land they were standing on was sacred, spared from the carnage. Philip's words rang through his head:

The Boche aren't dumb enough to send their troops in and then bomb the hell out of them.

"Get down!" The voice was a whisper, but it hissed up at them from the edge of the wheat field not fifteen feet away. The man's uniform was stark against the amber of the sun-dried wheat, and his finger was jabbing at the air, pointing to the woods on the hill behind them, across the creek.

They dropped where they stood, each man scuttling into the wheat like crabs burrowing into the sand at low tide. Before their bodies had even stilled, German words were floating across the stream. George swallowed his breath, fearful that the terror gripping his body with its viselike claws would break free and reveal itself to the enemy. Would it come out as a scream? Would he get them all killed?

Wir überqueren den Fluss nicht . . .

Besser auf dem Hügel . . .

Waffen hier . . .

The voices were so close that every enunciated syllable was crisp in his ears, and the fact that George couldn't understand their words was meaningless. Someone would flinch. Someone would break. Someone would give them up. George hoped it wouldn't be him.

Whispers were spreading through the group of men beside him on the ground. On Major Rowe's command, they were to stand and shoot, and they weren't to stop until all the Germans on the other side of the creek were dead.

The command came sooner than George expected, before he could convince himself that this was a job for other men, real soldiers who knew how to fight. When the signal came, he didn't hesitate. He sprang from the wheat field, his rifle at the ready, and fired into the group of Germans on the other side of the creek. They dropped like bowling pins, three or four going down together, then one or two picked off alone. It was like a game at a carnival, but, instead of a teddy bear or a chalk doll, the winner got to walk out alive. By the time the bullets stopped flying, there were at least a dozen dead German soldiers littering the forest floor.

They were on the move before the last body had even fallen, sticking to the stream, and weaving in and out of the wheat fields while keeping a steady pace. Major Rowe was the commander, but his company had taken enormous losses, so he'd been collecting men along the way to fill in the holes. He knew the terrain well, cutting across patches of forest and ducking under bridges before bringing the men to rest at an abandoned farmhouse. He sent five men from his own company to clear the house while the rest of them huddled behind a stone wall on the far side of the property.

They were close to the second trench line, but they'd somehow taken a southeasterly course instead of heading due south, landing them at the base of the hill the French were defending to their east, the hill that had already been overrun by the Germans. This was the scenario George had feared all along: the Germans positioned high above the valley and taking aim at the Americans below.

There were no more than thirty men with them, some with wounds that, at any other time, would likely have proven fatal. But the horror of that night had somehow diminished the urgency of the gaping chest wounds and the nearly severed limbs. Those things could wait. They *had* to wait.

One of those men was Milo. Two fingers on his left hand were missing and the bandage that was holding the third and fourth in place was soaked through with blood. George wouldn't have known it was him, but Milo recognized Philip, and, by default, Philip's sidekick.

"This man can ride" was how Milo greeted them, still a man of few words. He was standing over them with Major Rowe by his side and pointing down at George.

"I need a runner," the major said, pulling a map from his pocket and squatting down beside them. "I have to get a message to Colonel McAlexander. Communication lines are out, but there's a horse corral about half a mile from here."

When he shined his pocket light over the map, the first

thing George noticed was the worn-out, crisscrossed edges that were starting to rip from where it had been folded and refolded too many times.

"The corrals are here, and Colonel Mac's dugout is here." He ran a finger to the far side of the map. "It's a good three or so miles from us, and if we send a runner on foot, it'll be too late."

"Too late for what?" Philip asked. "What's the message?"

"The French have retreated. The Germans have taken Hill 231. Our right flank is not protected."

The major wrote the message down on a piece of paper that George tucked deep into his coat pocket. Milo and Philip had volunteered to escort him to the horse corrals, and, while there were no two men he'd rather have by his side, George feared the major had picked the wrong man to deliver the message.

The shelling intensified the closer they got to the stables, and George's reluctance to go any further, to enter back into the nightmare of explosions and mangled bodies and scream-ing men, was so visceral and overpowering that Philip had to physically prod him on. The flames were still blazing, the mortar shells ripping the trees from the ground around them and tossing them into giant heaps as effortlessly as twigs being tossed into a campfire.

Milo turned out to be an excellent guide, leading them di-rectly to the smoldering boards and ashes of the corral from the map. If not for the dead horses littering the ground around them, they wouldn't have known they'd reached their destina-tion. Nothing was left. If any of the horses had survived, which seemed unlikely, they were long gone by now.

"We have to get to the second line," Milo shouted, and, as if his body had a built-in compass, he set off in a direction they would soon learn was due south.

As they neared the second trench, the turmoil heightened, and, soon enough, they were caught in a crossfire. German ar-tillery shells pitted the ground in front of them, and American bullets from the machine gunners of the second line were zipping by their heads. With their bodies flattened to the ground, they slid through the field, from one crater hole to the next, sheltering themselves with the dead when they were caught out in the open.

By the time George rolled his body into the second trench line, fatigue was setting in. The scene around them was mayhem. Bodies were everywhere. The dead were being tossed over the trench walls to make room for the living, but many of the living were grievously wounded, begging for their mothers and wives and girlfriends, pleading for death. The medics sprinted back and forth, some intrinsic need forcing them to keep the dead alive, to refuse them their peace.

Communication lines were out everywhere. Field commanders, men who'd been tested in battle, were panicking alongside the men they were supposed to be leading, and the news that the French had fled, leaving their right flank open, was of no importance to any of them.

Like George, they had only one goal: to survive the night.

Milo and Philip were on the move again, George trailing behind them. They stopped only long enough to take a map and a pocket light off a dead field officer before diving into a crater hole.

Milo's left hand was useless, the two remaining fingers barely attached, and the blood-soaked bandage mostly unraveled. He shook out the map with his right hand and pointed with his chin while Philip shined the light over it.

"Colonel Mac's dugout," he said, and, after a quick scan over the rest of the map, he handed it to Philip to fold, and they were on their way again.

The wheat fields had turned into forests and, in the inky shadows of the night, avoiding downed trees that had been ripped from their roots became more troublesome than dodging the mortar shells that had chased them through the open fields. The obstacles were as ubiquitous as the dead, and a journey that should have taken them no more than thirty minutes was well into its second hour by the time they arrived.

"What do you mean the French are gone?" Colonel Mac's words thundered through the air as he stabbed at the map Milo handed to him, at the spot where the French troops were supposed to have formed a connection with the Thirty-Eighth. "This is where they should be! This is what we agreed upon!"

"Sir," Philip said, stepping up and saluting the colonel. "Major Rowe sent us. We got here as soon as we could, but the stables were destroyed, and we had to come on foot. The French were completely overrun. They retreated hours ago."

Colonel Mac leaned forward over the makeshift table that held his own map and ran his finger along the stream where George and Philip and the rest of the men in their ragged troop had shot down the German soldiers earlier in the night. He placed his palm over Hill 231, the hill that was now crawling with German troops, and slammed it down with such force that all the men around him jumped back.

"Dammit! Those sons of bitches! I knew they'd flee! And this Goddamn elastic defense. I told them it wouldn't work."

When a nearby explosion rocked the ground around them, George flinched. Everyone flinched, except the colonel. They followed him from the dugout and into the night, where incendiaries split the sky open like bolts of lightning. They marched along a trench wall, stopping only long enough for Colonel Mac to gather troops from nearby units.

"Listen closely," he said, his eyes landing briefly on the face of each man he was about to send on a mission from which there would likely be no return. "If we don't stop the Germans on that hill, we're done. They'll sweep in over our right flank and surround us, and we won't even have a chance to retreat. This Surmelin Valley is the gateway to Paris, and you men have been tasked to defend it with your lives. We must not fail. We must take back that hill."

The plan was to take out the artillery guns that were now pockmarking Hill 231 and prevent the Germans from advancing through the forest to the east. It would be a stealth mission, since they were lacking in numbers, but the Germans would be unsuspecting, and the element of surprise would be on their side.

George thought it sounded more like a suicide mission, and, as he looked at the men around him, beleaguered and weary, he wondered how many of them would live to see the morning. They listened in silence as Colonel Mac finished laying out a battle plan that, on the best of days, would have been met with failure.

This was not the best of days, and when they set off together, a mass of bodies moving back toward the German front, the wreckage of the forest sliced through their lines like a jackknife through cheese. George did his best to keep pace with the group, but by the time he emerged to the wheat fields, Philip was the only man by his side.

The stream led them to a shallow bunker that must have been dug out as a last-minute attempt by the men inside to take cover from the Germans along the hill. It was in shambles, and the men inside, part of a machine gun battalion, were all dead.

Across the stream, the outline of the forest was barely visible through the thick smoke and fog that hung low to the ground. It was a moonless night, so the fact that it was visible at all meant morning was approaching.

Philip took a Chauchat machine gun from one of the dead gunners, along with a few extra clips, before he climbed out of the bunker and stepped out into the fog. George did the same, slinging his rifle over his shoulder and holding the machine gun at his hip, trailing behind Philip and tracing his footsteps to the edge of the water. They'd barely crossed the stream when they spotted a German Howitzer mounted into the side of the hill. The men who were supposed to be manning it were spread out beside it, resting between the trees, listening to the far-off booms in the valley below. They must have thought their fight was over.

Philip struck first. He gave no warning before emptying his machine gun into the side of the hill. He didn't announce his intentions or enlist George's help, but George jumped up beside him, squeezing the trigger of the machine gun even though he knew, by the lack of kick, that it had jammed. By the time the last of Philip's shots echoed through the forest and into the valley, no one was standing.

George threw the machine gun down and swung his rifle from his shoulder as Philip used his bayonet to silence the few men who were still alive, and by the time the screams and moans had finally stopped, another round of German soldiers had crested the hill above them. It was hopeless; there was nothing they could do. The message to Colonel McAlexander had arrived too late.

"We need to get out of here!" George yelled, struggling to pull Philip from the three-and-a-half-ton Howitzer. If they'd had the manpower, they might have been able to turn the gun from the valley full of American soldiers below to the approaching Germans on the hill up above, but the other men who'd set out beside them from Colonel Mac's dugout were undoubtedly in their own fights for survival.

"Our orders are to take back this hill!" Philip fired his machine gun into the woods at the approaching Germans, calling for George's extra magazines. "If we can get this thing turned, we can drive them back. I'll hold them off, Mountcastle. You get reinforcements. We need more men!"

There were no reinforcements. Retreat was their only option. Philip must have known that, but the adrenaline pumping through his body wouldn't allow him to fall back, and George was running out of time to get him off that hill. The nausea hit him with a vengeance, and the pounding headaches that had been taunting him over the past few weeks trailed him into the scene that played out in his mind: Philip's body leaned against the Howitzer with bullet holes riddling his chest; dozens of dead Germans scattered across the forest floor, all reaching for the gun. George shook the vision away as Philip's machine gun kicked back into action.

It was time to move.

If he'd had any warning, Philip might have stood his ground, but when George took a running start and slammed the full weight of his body into him, they both went tumbling down the side of the hill.

"It's time to go," George yelled, pulling Philip to his feet and shoving him into the creek at the base of the hill. It wasn't until they emerged on the other side and stumbled into the wheat fields that he realized they'd finally reached the end. German soldiers screamed orders they couldn't understand and pointed rifles at their heads as they closed in around them.

George fell to his knees, his body racked with exhaustion and defeat, his hands raised far above his head, and as he waited for the bullet he knew was coming, he was saddened by the futility of it all. He didn't dare raise his eyes to the German soldiers screaming at Philip, who refused to drop to his knees. Instead, he stared at the cracked and trampled wheat beneath their boots, praying the end would come fast.

The bullet never came. When Philip finally dropped down beside him, and the Germans searched their empty pockets for weapons, George knew that his final resting place would not be the Surmelin Valley. They marched along the creek with guns to their backs and the sounds of the battle fading into the distance as the Germans pushed toward Paris.

George followed Philip's gaze to the side of Hill 231, where dawn was filtering through the treetops and scattering light onto an endless sea of bodies carpeting the meadow. It took him a moment to recognize the body that was draped over the remains of a half-exploded Howitzer to their right. A mostly unraveled bloody bandage hung from his hand where his two remaining fingers were just barely kissing the ground. His helmet and gas mask were still strapped to his head, and George had the sudden urge to remove them, to make Milo more comfortable in death, if that was possible.

By the time the Germans were ready to march their prisoners out, the sun was throwing its first rays over the valley, as if testing the view, not quite sure it was ready to peek its head out over the horizon. But the sun would have been wise to submit to darkness that day; it would have been wise to withhold its light from the once tranquil valleys and hills along the banks of the Marne River, because death was its only view.

part II

part II

chapter 9

MARCELLE

Jaulgonne, France
German POW camp
July 1918

Silence.

And chirping birds.

Those were the first two things Marcelle noticed when the shelling finally stopped. It was strangely unsettling. The thundering of artillery had become a constant in her life, and its absence felt like a void, a vacuum that needed to be filled. By what, she did not know, but there was no calm to the current of energy that pulsed through her veins.

The guards were restless, hastily delivering meals to prisoners before the sun had even crested the horizon. Erich brought Marcelle's, as usual, but he was distracted and edgy, not like the man she had come to know over the past couple of weeks. She would not have known how much time had passed since her capture if not for Erich. He was nothing like the other guards, and, while he insisted he was twenty-one years old, the same as Marcelle, the softness of his features suggested he had barely reached puberty.

For days after her capture, a man whose height was something out of a storybook interrogated her, his French so mangled that Marcelle couldn't be certain that it was, indeed, French. His frustration with her was evidenced by the number of half-burned cigarettes in the corner of the wooden hut, and, by the time his breaking point had been reached, Marcelle was surprised they hadn't all gone up in flames. Her answers to his questions were always the same:

I am Josephine LeBlanc.
I only speak French.
I was fleeing Soissons with my family when we were
separated in Montmirail.
A man I had never met offered me food to deliver a
book to the man beneath the cherry tree.

No one had mentioned the witch of the river, but Marcelle had to believe they were suspicious. By the time she was taken to the prison in Jaulgonne on the German-occupied side of the Marne River, she had learned from the guards, who were unaware she spoke German, that she would be the only female in the camp, and a new interrogator with a better grasp of the French language would soon be arriving. So far, that man had not arrived.

Erich's French was impeccable, but he was not an interrogator. He had tried a few times to direct their conversation toward espionage, but Marcelle knew he was only trying to impress his superiors, to prove his usefulness. As the son of a general, he had nothing to fear from the baseless threats of men who outranked him, but he seemed to take comfort in the familiarity of his role as subordinate.

Erich enjoyed her company. Not in the way other men did, but in the way a friend might find solace just by being in the company of another person. Until that morning, until the shelling stopped, he'd never invited fear into their conversation. But that morning, instead of a culinary review of the meal on her plate and a weather forecast of the approaching day, Erich placed her breakfast on the mattress beside her and glanced nervously back at the door.

"You should finish your breakfast today," he said, and, though his words were almost a whisper, when he continued, he leaned in and lowered his voice even further. "I do not know when your next meal will come. Château-Thierry has fallen and we will soon be marching to Paris. From what I have heard, there will be thousands of prisoners in camp tonight. French. British. Even American. I do not know what they will do with you, Josephine. I do not even know if I will be here to protect you."

"Where will they send you?"

"I do not know what my orders will be. But I know the general who is on his way to interrogate you, and he is not a reasonable man."

"What do you mean?"

Erich stepped to the door and glanced down the hall in both directions before rushing back to her side. "Just tell him the truth," he implored her. "He will get the information one way or another. He will figure out who you are and who you work for, and he will find the people you are protecting. I promise you that. And if you make him work for it, he will make you suffer."

～～～

The chaos started before the sun could form its first shadows. Marcelle had taken Erich's advice to finish her breakfast, but it was a choice she would come to regret in the coming hours. She had barely taken her last bite when the din of the outside world found its way into her room. French. English. German. There were other languages she didn't recognize mixed in there, maybe Russian or Polish, but the conglomeration of all the different accents and noises and guttural utterances was dizzying. The more she tried to force them from her mind, the more fervently they burrowed, until each individual word was like the buzzing of a bee and, together, they had swarmed into her brain. With her hands cupped around her ears, and the buzzing of the courtyard faintly muted, Marcelle began singing an old nursery rhyme her mother had taught her as a child. She had only gotten a line or two in when the boom of a rifle sounded from within the courtyard and the bees scattered.

"Tous les Français ici," a voice bellowed over the loudspeaker.

"Deutsche da rüber. British, American, and all English-speaking in the north tent . . ."

The prisoners were being separated according to their native languages. Marcelle lost interest after English. She couldn't understand the Slavic men, or the Senegalese, or any of the others. She had no windows, so she could only picture in her mind the battle-weary men shuffling in their respective groups, huddled together for safety. She wondered how many had been left to die in the trenches, and what they had done with all the casualties at the hospital. Was Rosalie out there? Did they imprison nurses, and ambulance drivers, and ordinary citizens? Were they destroying villages on their way to Paris?

These would end up being questions for another day. The footsteps that echoed down the hallway did not belong to any of the guards that Marcelle knew. They were not the heavy, shuffling thumps of mud-caked boots that she had grown accustomed to. These footsteps were far more deliberate, more refined, and even before she saw the boots that made them, she knew, despite the recent rains and the mud in the courtyard, they would be black, laced to the knees, and polished to a shine.

When the general entered her room, she could only stare at his feet. She was wrong. They had no laces. But Marcelle was certain that if she stood close enough, she would see her reflection in the spit-polished cowhide.

"Guten Morgen, fräulein." The general stepped further into the room, and, when Marcelle finally looked up at him, she was surprised to see such an aged man. She wasn't sure what she had expected, but it had not been the man standing before her with the jowls of a mastiff. His eyes and cheeks and neck sagged as if gravity had taken its revenge on him, weighing down each feature until he had the look of a melted wax statue. Marcelle was so distracted by him that she almost responded in German.

"Je parle seulement français," she said.

"Of course," he replied, switching to French. "You will have to forgive me. I forgot that you only speak French." He watched her for a moment from across the room, his index finger tapping against his lips as if he were truly pondering something. "If I may, though," he continued, crossing his arms over his chest. "I would like to offer you a tip. For the future maybe. In case you ever find yourself in a situation such as this again."

Marcelle watched him from the mattress, his rheumy eyes taking in the features of her face.

"Next time," he said, "do not try so hard. We are neighbors, fräulein. Surely you know a *little bit* of German?" He held his thumb and forefinger up in front of his face, almost pinching them together. "When you say you know so little, it makes me think you are lying."

He paused expectantly, but Marcelle maintained her silence. Silence was her only weapon, her only defense. She kept hearing Erich's words about how this man would make her suffer if she did not speak, but, so far, he was not the monster she had been expecting. She didn't realize it at the time, of course, but of all the men Marcelle would come across in her life, this man would be the most brutal.

chapter 10

When consciousness crept in, Marcelle found herself curled up on the mattress, barely able to breathe through the pain of her broken ribs. The smell of sweat and revulsion lingered in the air, and the pain that pulsed through her groin mocked her, hammering into her head that she was weak, and dirty, and worthless, that she had been branded with a shame she could never wash away.

At least she was still alive. Wasn't that worth the price she had just paid? Once upon a time she would have chosen death over rape, but that girl was long gone, and the one who had taken her place was being groomed into something Marcelle wasn't sure she wanted to see.

Her scalp burned from the strands of hair that had been torn rather than sheared from her head, and her tongue kept returning to the hole where her tooth had been knocked out. The blood was still oozing, and she briefly considered searching the floor for it, maybe forcing it back into place. Was that possible? Could a tooth heal itself?

She closed her eyes again, running her fingers over the gash in her cheek that hadn't yet stopped bleeding, and preparing herself for the next round of beatings. But when the general returned, he had other things in mind, and the wounds he would soon inflict would never scar over like the ones he'd left on her body. They would bleed for eternity.

His boots were the first thing Marcelle saw. One of her eyes was swollen shut and the other was struggling to stay open, but from her position on the mattress, she could see that his boots still held their shine. They were alone, but she could hear voices in the hallway. Maybe even a woman's voice.

"Marcelle Marchand." The name hit her with the same force as the wooden chair leg that had taken her tooth and left the gash in the side of her face. It wasn't possible. She was hearing things. Too many hits to the head. He couldn't have known her name. She hadn't talked. Through all the beatings, she hadn't said a word.

"The witch of the river," he continued in German as he stepped toward her. "You were a worthy opponent, fräulein, but it appears that when I took your beauty, your power went with it." Marcelle heard a gasp from the doorway as someone entered the room, and even before she could focus in on the woman's face, she knew who it was. "Your sister has been looking for you."

The breakfast she had forced down was already on its way back up, her broken ribs screaming as her body retched and heaved. Rosalie was almost by her side on the mattress when the general yanked her back by her hair.

"Marcelle and Rosalie Marchand," he said, his cheek almost touching Rosalie's as he forced her head back with a fistful of hair. His eyes darted from one woman to the other. "You are much prettier than your sister now," he whispered into her ear. "But that will change if she does not give me what I want." The pistol was pressed up against Rosalie's temple before Marcelle even noticed he had removed it from the holster, and when she heard it click into position, she dared not breathe.

"Bitte," she whispered, the memory of Soissons still fresh in her mind after all those years. The German soldier. The gun. The dead body. "I will do whatever you want. Please do not hurt her." She breathed the words out for fear that the weight of them, if spoken too loudly, would somehow nudge the finger that was fiddling with the trigger on the gun.

"Two lives, Marcelle," the general said. "Your sister's life is worth that much, don't you think? If you do not deliver them to me, she dies."

Marcelle didn't hesitate. How could she? How could she take the time to weigh the value of one person's life over another's? And who could compete with her sister? She kept her eyes on Rosalie so she wouldn't falter, so she wouldn't see the faces of the only two men she could offer to him.

"Joseph Granger," she said, knowing that Charles had probably already fled Montmirail and was halfway to Paris by now. Maybe he had even crossed the English Channel and was home free. "He stays at the men's boardinghouse on rue Maupassant in Montmirail."

"Yes, Marcelle. Now you understand the rules. Go on."

"Adrien Rousseau," she whispered, refusing to offer Pierre's name to this man. She finally dropped her gaze from her sister's face.

"His address?" the general said.

Marcelle shook her head, pulling in as much air as her fractured ribs would allow. "I do not know."

"I will not ask you again, fräulein. Your sister has five seconds."

"Montmirail. The basement apartment on the corner of rue de l'Église and rue Pasteur."

And that was how Marcelle Marchand showed death to the door of a man she had loved since she was just a child. The ultimate act of betrayal.

She didn't breathe out a sigh of relief when the general put his gun back in the holster. He ushered Rosalie out the door so fast she didn't have a chance to find out if he would be true to his word. Would her sister be released? Would she be tortured? Would she be killed? There was nothing to make that man keep his word. The only mercy was that she didn't have to watch Rosalie die in front of her.

Night came quickly. Marcelle couldn't fight off the fatigue, and it wasn't until Erich came to wake her that she realized she had slept at all. Her memory was clouded, and she thought perhaps she had dreamed her sister had been there until Erich promised her that Rosalie had not been harmed. She had no choice but to believe him; anything else would have broken her. He was trying to tell her something, to prepare her for what was to come, but the fog that hung over her mind was blocking out his words, and, before he could force her to hear the message, two uniformed soldiers came in and hauled her from bed.

They didn't try to balance her on her feet or take care to avoid the bruises and broken bones mapping her body. They dragged her from her room, and out the door, and across the courtyard before dropping her onto the ground, where she crumbled beneath the weight of her own body. She could hear the murmur of the men around her. There must have been thousands of them, prisoners of every color from every nation.

Their voices settled when the general arrived, and when he walked up to Marcelle, waiting for her to acknowledge him, she could only stare at his boots, strangely satisfied by the layer of dirt covering them. He stood over her, the weight of his stare boring into the back of her head, the expectation of submission so ingrained within him that he did not even fear retribution.

"This is Marcelle Marchand," he announced in German, and, though most of the prisoners could not understand his words, they must have been able to interpret the scene before them. "She is a witch. She is an enemy of the German Empire and a traitor to her own people. Let this be a lesson to you all. We will not tolerate insubordination from anyone. This is what will happen to those of you who refuse to ally with the Kaiserreich."

Marcelle prayed the end would come quickly. A bullet to the head. She couldn't take another beating. If she'd had the strength to pull herself from the ground, she would have considered lunging for the general's gun, but she feared she would only make it as far as his knees and that his boot would deliver another agonizing blow to her ribs.

It wasn't until the general crouched down beside her, took her chin in his hand, and forced her to see what was right in front of her that Marcelle noticed the two blindfolded men who were tied to the poles. One of them had a shock of red hair sticking up from his head, and the other was missing half of his right arm. The general nodded and the guards tore off their blindfolds.

"Bereit!" *Ready*

"No!" Marcelle cried out, her nails clawing at the ground as she tried to drag herself over the hardened earth.

"Zielen!" *Aim*

She pulled herself to her knees, struggling to bring her feet underneath her, just in time to hear the final word.

"Abfeuern!" *Fire*

Pierre and Charles both smiled at her before the guns exploded, before her own body crumpled to the ground as if a bullet had found her, as well. The courtyard descended into silence.

Or maybe Marcelle had just lost the will to hear, and to see, and to feel. Why was death mocking her? Why wouldn't it just take her, too?

When the guards came to drag her back inside, Marcelle didn't offer any resistance. She didn't flinch when they wrapped their arms around her broken ribs or pressed their fingers into her bruises. She hung like the rag doll her mother had given to her for her fifth birthday when she had thought the world was kind and beautiful and full of good people.

It wasn't until they crested the last step that Marcelle turned her head back to the sea of prisoners watching her from the courtyard. Her eyes stopped on an American soldier, the one she had met at the hospital the day she had been captured.

Did he remember her?

Even as she felt herself going under, the waters rising and the waves lapping over her face, she could feel him reaching out to her, making her a promise across the swelling seas that he would come for her, that he would save her. She didn't want his promise, though. She wanted instead to float away in her guilt and let it drown her; she wanted it all to end.

chapter 11

MARCELLE

Soissons, France
May 1991

"Papa."

Juliette's whispered word floated just beyond Marcelle's reach. Marcelle blinked away her tears as she struggled to blink away the image of her husband smiling back at her, their bodies both crumpling to the ground. She had to remind herself again that it wasn't real. It was a story that held no merit, and whatever Marcelle was feeling was just a manipulation of her emotions, a response to a *what if* scenario that had played out in her mind a thousand times over.

"Please tell me you didn't do it," Juliette cried. "Please tell me you didn't turn Papa in."

"How can you even ask this, Juliette? How can you think I would ever do something like that?" Marcelle fumbled with her words, desperate to convince both her daughter and herself that what she was saying was true, that she would never have betrayed Pierre. But the guilt was heavy, and she could feel the burden of it weighing her down. She could see it in the smile of her husband, she could hear it in the boom of the guns, and she could almost taste it in the swirling clouds of dirt beneath her broken body as it lay motionless in the middle of the courtyard. What wouldn't she have done to save her sister's life? "There was no prison in Jaulgonne," Marcelle muttered. "Don't you think I would have remembered something like that?"

"I'm sorry, Maman," Juliette replied. "Of course you would

have remembered that. And it couldn't have happened this way. Not to Papa."

Marcelle shifted her gaze from the journal in her daughter's hands to the rosebushes that were beginning to bloom against the stone wall in her garden. Juliette was right. It couldn't have happened this way. But why were the memories so clear in her mind?

"Why do you suppose this man wrote these things?" Juliette continued, before rifling through a few more pages in the diary. "Maybe he's mistaking you for someone else. Although some of the fact seems a bit too coincidental."

"It is not a mistake," Marcelle replied. "It is me. But his story is starting to veer from the truth." Marcelle didn't elaborate. She didn't explain to her daughter that she had flirted with an American soldier behind her father's back, or that she had snuck a peek at Charles's private correspondence in his boarding room, or that the man in the black beret had been waiting for her beneath the cherry tree. She had guarded those secrets for over seventy years. What need did she have to share them now?

"But why would he write these things about you if they weren't true?" Juliette asked. "Who was this man?"

"Perhaps he was a storyteller," Marcelle replied. "And perhaps I am just a character in one of the many tales he told throughout his life. I suppose we will never know."

Juliette opened the diary in her lap again and stared down at the words on the pages. This version of her mother, the one that George had known so well, had fears, and insecurities, and secrets that had been hidden for decades beneath a vibrant façade. This version of Marcelle had not been the mother Juliette had known since birth.

"Should we continue?" Juliette asked, running her hand over the open page before her. "Or is it too upsetting?"

"It is just a made-up story," Marcelle replied. "Let's read a bit more and see where it takes us."

chapter 12

GEORGE

Jaulgonne, France
July 1918

It lasted no more than a second.

It was just a fleeting glance, really, but in that moment, George felt a lifetime pass between him and the nurse from Montmirail, the one who'd been with him on the battlefield for weeks of sleepless nights. She was more than just a nurse, it seemed. Her eyes fluttered shut and her head rolled back as the guards hauled her away, but George was certain she'd understood what he'd been trying to tell her: He wouldn't leave her to die.

The guard trailing behind them into the barracks was nothing like the ones who were dragging her up the stairs and lugging her through the door. His face was soft, and his eyes full of mercy. Even when Marcelle's friends had been shot in front of her, he hadn't been able to watch.

"We have to save her," George whispered, but whether his words were meant for himself or the men standing beside him in the prison courtyard, he couldn't say. He'd simply felt the need to breathe life into his thoughts before reason and common sense could charge in and carry them away.

They'd arrived at the prison just hours earlier, shortly before the sun had set, and Philip still wasn't speaking to him. He'd wanted to be the hero, even if it had meant dying, and there was nothing George could say to convince him that his death would have been in vain if he'd stayed behind with the Howitzer, if they hadn't taken that tumble down the hill.

"She's not worth it," Philip mumbled, turning his back to George and the scene they'd just witnessed.

"Not worth it?" George said. "You can just watch a woman being beaten and tortured and then turn your back to her?"

"Yes," Philip replied, pouncing at the opportunity to let loose the thoughts that had been festering in his mind. "Just like you can turn your back on your country. We could have held that hill. You had no right to take that away from me. From all of us."

"I saved your life," George snapped, lowering his voice only when he noticed the crowd of men starting to gather around them. "The only thing that would have changed on that battlefield if I hadn't stepped in would be one more dead body. Yours."

"Well, aren't you a hero, Mountcastle?" After an overly exaggerated salute, Philip gestured toward the building where the nurse had been taken. "Show us how it's done, why don't you?"

If George had taken the time to think it through, if his mind hadn't been infected with turmoil and angst and rage from the recent battle, he might not have lunged at his friend for the second time in one day. He might not have tackled him to the ground, or shoved his face into the dirt, or pummeled his back with his fists.

It was a strange phenomenon, his body reacting faster than his brain. There was a monster who'd slipped into his skin and was driving him to do things he never thought possible. He was beating a man, and not just any man. He and Philip had walked through hell together; they'd survived impossible odds.

"What the hell is wrong with you two?"

Ace was the one to separate them. He pushed George aside as he pulled Philip off the ground, dusting the dirt from his coat. Besides Philip, Ace was the only man George recognized from the hundreds of American soldiers who'd been marched into the prison together.

"Mountcastle thinks he's going on a rescue mission." Philip nodded toward the barracks where the Germans had taken the nurse. "He's going to get himself killed."

"They just beat that woman half to death. And what do you think they're going to do to her in there?" The crowd was swelling around them as George and Philip squared off in the middle of the courtyard.

"She's already dead," Philip said, still wiping the dirt from his face and trying to spit it out of his mouth. "You need to learn how to pick your battles."

"It's not right what they did to that woman," Ace said, stepping between them and extending an arm toward George's chest to keep him back. "I'll give you that, Mountcastle. But you've gone plumb crazy if you think you're going to sneak into those barracks and rescue her. Foster's right. Let it go."

"I'm not asking your permission. I'm not even asking for your help. You two can rot in this prison for all I care. If I die trying to get her out, then it would be worth it."

"So, this is a cause worth fighting for," Philip said, "but your country wasn't?" He didn't wait for a response, or maybe he knew George was about to lunge for him again, because he stormed off in the opposite direction before it could come to that. Even through his rage, George felt an emptiness as he watched Philip disappear inside the tent barracks that had been thrown together for the prisoners. He hadn't meant for it to end like this, and he wondered if they would ever meet again, or if either of them would survive this prison.

"What's the plan, Mountcastle?" Ace was the only one standing by his side when George turned around, the other men having lost interest.

"Over there," George said, nodding toward the razor-wire fence behind the building where they'd taken Marcelle. "I think there's another entryway back there that we can't see. A couple of guards have come out from that direction, but not too many."

"And then what?"

"And then there's a certain guard I'll look for when I get in. I think I might be able to convince him to help me."

Ace's laughter didn't bother George. Like Philip, Ace was a man who solved problems with might, not words. It would never have occurred to him to navigate his way out of a situation like this without a skirmish. Besides his recent attack on Philip, George had spent his life avoiding confrontation. He'd survived by reading the people around him, watching for patterns, and calculating the cost of each and every action.

"And what if you're wrong about this guard?" Ace asked.

George shrugged in response. "Then I'm wrong."

They hadn't been in the prison long enough to establish a routine, so George didn't know when to expect shift change, or roll call, or anything else that might offer a distraction so he could make his way across the courtyard to the back of the building. Trains had been rolling by with increasing frequency on the tracks just outside the fences, and if the other prisoners were to be believed, they would all soon be loaded up and taken to a camp in Germany.

It was deep into the night by the time George decided to make his move. The prisoners were all in their barracks, and he'd been crouching in the shadows outside his own tent for so long that both of his feet were numb inside his boots. It couldn't have been more than fifty yards he had to cover, seventy-five at most, but George worried that when he decided to make his break across the courtyard, he'd stumble and be shot by the guard in the watchtower.

It was a cloudless night, the moon unnecessarily bright, and when he finally stepped from the shadows, he couldn't still his nerves as his mind jumped from one thought to the next, every step forward a reminder that it could be his last. The guard in the tower was facing the opposite direction, but George had only made it about ten yards when the lights hit him, and the blast of a horn shook his bones. The ground rumbled as the train rushed past the prison and rattled the fences, the razor wire wrapped atop it glinting in the glare of its spotlight. There was no hesitation. Even as his mind was questioning whether he should move forward or go back, George's body was already scrambling across the courtyard and ducking behind the building where Marcelle had been taken.

With his body pressed flat against the wall and sheltered from the watchtower guard, George gulped down shallow breaths of air as he waited for the train to pass, not sure if the pounding in his head was the thrumming of his pulse or approaching footsteps. Had he been spotted? Were they coming for him?

The tiny hairs on the back of his neck pricked at his skin as fear held him in place; he was certain someone was watching him. His eyes scanned the darkened woods beyond the razor-wire fence, out past the train tracks, and when the twig cracked behind him, he froze. He couldn't force himself to turn around, and, instead, waited for the German words, or the hand on his back, or the bullet to his head that he knew was coming.

But they never came, and when George finally gathered the courage to face the threat behind him, he was met instead by a man he would soon come to think of as a brother.

"I heard there was a damsel in distress," Philip said, smiling down at him.

"What the hell is wrong with you?" George glared up at his friend through the darkness even as relief flooded his body.

"You didn't think I was going to let you have all the fun, did you, Mountcastle?"

With a renewed sense of courage, George pulled open the door at the back of the building and stepped into a shed where moonlight spilled over a collection of outdoor tools: shovels, axes, mallets. Philip grabbed a pickax from the corner and nodded toward the door at the far end of the room before

George picked up a mallet and stepped up to it. There were no voices coming from the other side, and when George eased it open, they were met by an empty corridor in a mostly abandoned building.

Gaping doors lined the corridor, leading to empty and abandoned rooms, and it wasn't until they reached the far end of the hallway that they found any signs of life. Behind each bolted door they opened was a prisoner who'd been recently beaten, a man too weary to even raise his head. They had all but lost hope by the time they finally found Marcelle. It was the back of her head that George noticed first, the gentle curve of her neck leading his eyes to her bruised and bloodied scalp.

Philip shut the door behind them as George crouched down beside the mattress on the floor. He was scared to touch her, fearful he might further break her already fractured body, and he couldn't pull his eyes from the rise and fall of her chest, the only assurance that she was, in fact, still alive.

He was so disarmed by the frailty of her state that it wasn't until they heard the shuffling of boots outside the door that reality bit into him. Philip was already tucked into the wall, his hands wrapped around the handle of the pickax and ready to pounce the moment the door opened.

But the guard had already known they were there. His pistol was aimed at George before the door had even crashed into the side of Philip's face, and he was spitting out some combination of French and German that only added to the confusion. George raised his hands into the air, stuttering in English as his mind searched for words.

"No German," he said. "Only English. Please, don't shoot."

The man stepped into the room, nodding for Philip to drop the pickax, and waving him away from the door with the barrel of his gun. When he got the two of them together on the far wall, his pistol stayed locked on Philip. He was always the bigger threat.

"Amerikaner?" His eyes scanned over their uniforms before

settling on Philip, who nodded back in response. "What do you want with her?" he asked, gesturing toward the mattress.

This was the man George had been looking for, the guard he'd seen trailing Marcelle into the barracks after her friends had been shot in the courtyard. In the darkness, his features were sharp and angular, not quite as soft as George had remembered.

"Please," George said. "We're just trying to help her."

"You think I am going to let you take her from this prison?" The man's English was good, but the harshness of his German accent was a cold reminder that they were fighting two very different battles, and as much as George wanted to say *yes*, as much as he wanted to believe the man standing before them with the pistol in his hand would allow them to walk out of that prison with Marcelle, he knew the answer was no. Ace had been right to laugh at him; there was no talking his way out of this.

"Please," George said, nodding toward Marcelle with his hands still raised and taking a tentative step toward her bed. "May I check on her? I think she has stopped breathing."

The guard hesitated just briefly as George inched his way toward the foot of the mattress, reaching his hands out toward Marcelle's legs.

"Back against the wall," he snapped, waving the pistol between them, and giving George just enough time to jab his thumb into the side of Marcelle's ankle. Her body jumped in response, and when the guard turned his head, it gave Philip the split second he needed to pounce.

The gun skidded across the floor before George clambered after it, and by the time he had it in his hands and pointed at the German, Philip had already tackled him to the ground.

"Shoot him," Philip said, holding the man down and nodding up at George.

"I can't shoot him," George whispered. "Someone will come running if they hear a gunshot."

Philip's eyes darted around the room before catching on

the pickax he'd dropped by the door. "Hand me that," he said, but the man beneath him was not about to be hacked to death without putting up a fight.

"Hilf mir!" he screamed. "Geflohene Amerikaner! Hilf—"

There was only silence when George landed the side of the pickax against the guard's head and his body finally stilled. Philip felt for a pulse before he stood up and took the ax from his hands.

"He's still alive," he said, "but he'll be out for a while."

George nodded before tucking the gun into the waist of his pants. "What do we do now?"

"I don't know, Mountcastle, but you better think of something fast."

Their options were dwindling. They had tools to dig their way out, maybe even cut through the fences, but there was little cover from the patrolling guards, and dragging Marcelle's unconscious body through a hole in the fence and under rolls of razor wire would be a clumsy and dangerous affair. She would be shredded by the time they got her into the forest.

George stared at the unconscious guard on the floor as he considered their options. What had he expected to happen? Even if the guard had offered to help, did he think the man would have walked them out the front door to freedom? To Philip's credit, he somehow managed to keep his mouth shut while George ran over every possible scenario in his mind: digging, climbing, cutting, fighting. What else was there?

"I think I have an idea," George finally said, when he'd gotten to the end of their options. "We're going to walk out the front gate."

By the time Philip returned from the shed with a shovel, George was already stripping the guard of his uniform and finalizing the details of the plan in his mind.

"Help me with the pants," he said, tugging the boots from the man's feet before tossing his own filthy uniform into the corner. He was buttoning up the coat that was still warm from the guard's skin when Philip handed him the belt. The uniform fit well enough, and when George nodded toward Marcelle's seemingly lifeless body on the bed, Philip scooped her up into his arms. The sheet from her mattress was barely long enough to reach across her torso, but George made sure to cover her face before they stepped back out into the corridor.

"Ma soeur." They had only made it a few steps before Marcelle started tugging at the sheet and trying to pull it from her face. She was mumbling something that neither of them could understand. "Ma soeur."

"Shh." Philip squeezed her against his chest, but the more he tried to calm her, the more she struggled for her freedom.

"Rosalie," she said, her voice nothing more than a scratchy whisper. "Ma soeur. Où est ma souer?"

"What is she saying?" Philip whispered, as Marcelle finally freed herself from the sheet and glanced from one man to the other, her eyes darting back and forth between George's face and the German uniform he was wearing.

"I don't know," George replied. "I don't speak French." He shifted uncomfortably beneath the scratchy fabric, tugging at the sleeves before offering Marcelle a smile. "We aren't trying to hurt you," he said. "This is stolen." He pointed to the insignia on his coat. "I'm not a German. I'm an American, and we've met. We're going to get you out of here, okay?"

Marcelle didn't respond. Her face revealed nothing as she listened to his words, and when she finally pulled her gaze away from him, it landed on the bolted door behind them. "My sister," she said, her eyes slowly drifting shut again. "Please help . . . my . . ."

She was unconscious before the sentence found its way out, her body collapsing back into Philip's arms. The doorway behind them, the one Marcelle had been nodding to, was the only one they hadn't opened on their way to her room.

"You really think her sister is in there?" Philip asked.

George shrugged. His instinct was to move along with their

plan, but if Marcelle was right, what would happen to her sister when the injured German guard was found in the empty room next door?

George slid the bolt free with quiet hands, glancing back at Philip before easing the door open into the room. The face that materialized from the darkness was an eerily perfect match to the one he'd first laid eyes on at the train station in Montmirail, but the woman who wore it recoiled in fear at the sight of his German uniform.

"American," George whispered, holding his hands up and open so she could see he was unarmed. "We have your sister, Marcelle." George nodded back toward the door, motioning Philip in. "Are you Rosalie?" he asked, repeating the name Marcelle had called out before she'd sunk back into oblivion.

The woman nodded and stepped forward, gasping at the sight of her sister's limp and shrouded body. "Is she . . ." She couldn't force the words out and cried in relief when Philip pulled the sheet back to show her that Marcelle was still alive. "Where are you taking her?"

Rosalie listened quietly as George detailed their escape plan to her, seeming to understand there was no room for her in it and that her presence would put them all at risk. "We'll have to find another way to get you out," he explained, but Rosalie shook her head.

"No," she said, drawing the sheet back over Marcelle's body. "I will not put your plan in jeopardy. Please . . ." She nudged them toward the door. "Please take her to safety."

"I'll be damned if I leave you here to die." Philip shifted his feet to accommodate the weight of Marcelle in his arms. "If I have to carry you both out of this prison together or fight my way past the guards, I'll do it. But I'm not leaving you behind." If anyone else had said it, George would have called it grandstanding, but Philip meant it.

"You'll have to cut a seam through the fence," George said. "There are tools in the shed at the end of the hallway. I'll show you before we leave. We would go with you, but it would be too dangerous to drag Marcelle under the razor wire. That part will take some finesse."

"No," Rosalie argued. "If I am caught, it will only make your escape more likely to fail."

"Please," George said, glancing down at Marcelle's motionless body. "I don't know that we can survive on our own out there even if we do escape. We don't know the area or speak the language. We will need someone to guide us. Especially with Marcelle in this state."

It didn't take much to convince Rosalie. She said good-bye to her sister and followed George to the end of the corridor, where they rifled through the tools in the shed, searching for a pair of shears strong enough to slice through the metal fences. George offered what little he knew about the guards who patrolled on foot: They traveled in pairs, they always reeked of burning tobacco, and they moved like elephants. Stealth was not in their nature.

Rosalie was scared. They were all scared, but the trembling in Rosalie's arms as she reached for the rusted clippers was so obvious, George wondered if she would even have the strength to use them.

"Go," she whispered, clutching the shears in her hands. "Head north through the forest past the railroad tracks. I will meet you on the other side."

George nodded, taking only a few steps before turning back to Rosalie and asking her a question that would end up saving their lives.

"What is the German word for 'dead'?"

chapter 13

"Tot." *Dead*.

Was he saying it right? George waved the barrel of the gun toward Marcelle's veiled body and nudged Philip forward with his other hand, the one that held the shovel. The sweat from his back had already drenched the shirt against his skin, and he feared it was beginning to seep through the coat of his stolen German uniform. The scent of pine and moss swirled up from the forest floor on the other side of the fence, and the colors, though muted by the night sky, seemed to dance before George's eyes. His senses were so heightened that he felt he could almost understand the German words coming from the guard in the watchtower beside him.

"Was machst du? Wo gehst du hin?"

The man wanted an explanation, no doubt, a reason for burying the dead before the thought of dawn had even entered the sky's mind. George passed a glance toward the guard in the tower less than six feet away before nodding back to Marcelle. "Tot," he repeated, while grumbling indecipherably and doing his best to impersonate a beleaguered German soldier overseeing burial duty.

Chances for failure greeted them with every passing moment; if they didn't move now, luck would soon abandon them. George nudged Philip again, harder this time, causing him to stumble as he stepped forward and clung to Marcelle. If she chose this moment to stir, it would most certainly be the end.

"Wieso machst du das jetzt?"

George couldn't understand the man's words, but he continued to mumble under his breath, raising his hand to him without turning back as he pushed the gate open. He didn't wait for the gunshots, or the spotlights, or the security sirens. He forced Philip through the gate and nudged him forward until the man's voice began to fade. He didn't look back until they had crossed the train tracks and descended the embankment on the other side, until their steps had carried them into the enshrouding darkness of the forest. Even then, he pushed them forward until Marcelle's sister stepped into a moonlit break in the trees and George, whose nerves were on edge, almost shot her with the pistol that was still in his hand.

No one said a word. They stayed off the roads, sticking to the deep, overgrown forest where the light of the moon couldn't penetrate the canopy of leaves overhead, but they had no idea how far they'd gone or how straight their path had run.

Philip and George took turns carrying Marcelle, but Philip did the bulk of the work, his back spasming with each step. Even through his coat, George could see Philip's muscles tensing, but the dead weight of Marcelle in his arms was a burden he wouldn't dare bemoan. He walked through the night in silence. No stories. No jokes. No laughter. Rosalie stayed by his side. Marcelle's sister fed him sips of water from a canteen as they marched on. They stopped a few times to refill their bottles from a stream, but they never rested long, always feeling the Germans breathing down their necks.

It wasn't until the first hint of morning light filtered through the darkness that they saw it. A farmhouse sitting in a clearing through the woods. It looked like salvation, but they were all acutely aware that the risk of thinking such a thing could be death. The balance was tricky, salvation or death, and there was no one who could puzzle it out for them but Marcelle's sister. She was the only one not wearing an American or a German uniform, and she was the only one who could speak French.

Though she didn't balk, Rosalie was nervous. She tiptoed through the forest wall as daylight followed her into the clearing. Marcelle turned her head and moaned, as if she could sense her sister's fear, but her eyes didn't open. They fluttered beneath their lids as Rosalie approached the farmhouse, they rolled from side to side as her sister's knuckles rapped against the hardwood door, and they danced feverishly back and forth when a giant of a man swung the door wide. But it wasn't until her sister's body crumpled to the ground that they finally popped open.

No one moved—not George, not Philip, not Rosalie, whose body lay slumped on the ground—not even the man lumbering in the doorway staring down at her.

It wasn't until Marcelle gasped that the stillness around them fractured. She fought against Philip's best attempts to calm her, scrambling to her knees, and clawing for freedom when he set her on the forest floor. The panic coursing through her body was a veritable match to Philip's own brute strength, and when he tried to pin her to the ground, she slipped through his hands and rolled away.

"Shh!" he whispered, crawling after her over a carpet of dead leaves that crunched beneath his weight. "You have to be quiet."

It wasn't until George stepped between them that Marcelle calmed. Her eyes flashed between the two men as George knelt beside her, the terror slowly dissipating as her memory pulled forward his image.

"Do you remember me?" he whispered. "I'm George. I met you in Montmirail. At the train station."

"Give me the gun, Mountcastle." George didn't protest when Philip reached into his holster to remove the pistol and made his way toward the farmhouse. He sat by Marcelle's side, trying to calm her and assure her that Philip would bring her sister back.

Marcelle's eyes stayed locked on George, but whether it was affection or suspicion that kept her gaze from faltering, he couldn't say. He hadn't yet learned to interpret her emotionless expressions.

The air was warming, the chill of the night seeping into the forest floor around them. The swelling in Marcelle's face had worsened overnight, the area around her eye becoming distended and tight. But her cheek was the most worrisome. The gash that ran from the corner of her left eye to the corner of her lip was angry and in desperate need of stitches.

The sun had shifted in the sky by the time Philip returned, the shadows of the trees on the meadow floor already shrinking back into the forest. He walked out the front door of the farmhouse and strode back to Marcelle and George alone and unarmed.

"She's fine," he said. "She fainted. The big fella scared her half to death, but he seems like a decent guy. He invited us in."

With Marcelle balanced between them, Philip and George stepped from the forest edge and into the clearing beneath the sun. George's body tensed. He'd been hiding from the light for so long that the weight of it on his skin felt like an unfamiliar cloak.

"He knows we're Americans, right?" George asked.

"I think so."

"You think so?"

"I'm wearing an American uniform, Mountcastle. I'm sure he figured it out."

Marcelle struggled between them as they inched forward, George doing his best to respond to the give and take of her movements.

"And he said it was okay for all of us to stay?"

"I'm sure it's fine," Philip mumbled, shrugging off the question. "Stop worrying so much."

"Did you ask him?"

"Well, I would have, but he doesn't speak a lick of English."

When George's feet stilled, they were less than ten yards from the house and retreat would have been a monumental task. The panic that was humming beneath the surface of his skin was about to seep into his muscles and paralyze him when the front door flew open, and a hulking figure barreled out toward them.

"Viens! Viens!"

The man smiled and waved them in with his mitt-like hands, slapping Philip on the back like they were old pals and wincing at the wounds on Marcelle's body.

The aroma in the house was dizzying, the rich scent of chicken, and spices, and vegetables overwhelming George's senses and sending a message to his stomach, which growled in response. How many days had it been since their last warm meal? The man laughed and dragged George to the pot on the stove, before opening the lid and fanning the steam toward their faces.

"Soupe. C'est bon!"

His name was Maurice, and he was a widower. His wife had given up when their two sons had been killed at the front, and Maurice was living out his days in isolation. It was only a matter of time before the Germans came for his home and his farm, and since he had no intention of giving it to them freely, he was happy to offer the Americans whatever refuge he could provide.

Marcelle had been ushered to one of the bedrooms, and by the time George found her, she had slipped from consciousness again, her eyelids dancing beneath their lids as if fighting off the nightmares that were calling to her. The hazy glow of light that filtered in through the sheers was pulling out new shades of colors from the bruises around her eye. Mostly shades of purple and blue, but none as beautiful as the blue beneath her lids.

"She is badly injured." Rosalie stepped into the room with a handful of bandages and towels that Maurice had found for her. "She would not have made it much longer if Maurice had not offered us shelter."

"Will she be okay?"

It took her too long to respond. The answer should have been a quick and simple *yes,* but when this woman with Marcelle's eyes and hair and sloped-up nose hesitated, all George could hear was *no.*

"Marcelle is strong," she finally said. "If anyone can survive this, it is her."

When Maurice returned, he was carrying a pot of boiling water, a sewing kit, and a bottle of liquor, and when Rosalie shut the door between them, George was six years old again, watching the doctor call for more towels, and about to learn that his mother was dead.

The stars were out by the time Rosalie finished tending to Marcelle's wounds. George had spent the better part of the evening on the back step, watching the sun slip from the sky before disappearing beneath the horizon. Under the glow of the moon, Maurice stepped out to join him, dumping the dirtied water from the wash basin into the grass.

Dirt lined the creases of George's own body, as if it had been stitched into place, and the film of soot and toxins that coated his scalp was impervious to Maurice's homemade lye detergent. He and Philip scrubbed themselves until the water from the basin was black with sludge and slime, and then they scavenged through the old clothes in the back of Maurice's closet that he had offered to them.

Weeks passed before Marcelle was strong enough to take walks on her own. No one ventured far; they could feel the Germans pressing in around them and knew that time was not on their side. They would need to move on soon, find a more suitable place to blend in.

"We can go to Paris once Marcelle is better," Rosalie was saying as they all settled around the kitchen table one evening. Maurice was dishing out bowls of soup. "My parents are there. Papa will know what to do."

Maurice was already shaking his head before Rosalie could even finish her sentence. "Non pas Paris," he said, wagging his finger back and forth.

News from town was that the Germans had already marched into Paris. They were pushing north toward the coast now, east toward Tours, and south on their way to Moulins. No one knew the exact location of the front line because it spread wider each day, each hour. The British and Americans were fleeing with the French, abandoning supplies, artillery, and soldiers who got separated from their units, trying to regroup and re-join the fight.

Checkpoints had been set up throughout the country, and the Germans were taking the threat of an uprising by civilians very seriously. Orders to shoot on sight were rampant:

Anyone identified as a British, American, or Allied
   soldier was to be shot on sight.
Anyone harboring British, American, or Allied soldiers
   was to be shot on sight.
Anyone trying to flee German-occupied France was to
   be shot on sight.

Rosalie was still speaking when George stopped listening. People were scared, and when people were scared, they saw a monster with mincing claws and bloodthirsty fangs in the oversized shadow of a tiny mouse.

The Germans didn't have the might to barrel over the Allied forces and sweep through France unimpeded, and they weren't barbarians. Not all of them. What reason could they have for killing Allied soldiers on sight?

"Then we will go to Soissons," Rosalie said. "If my parents made it out of Paris, that is where they would go. And I can hide you there."

They spent two more weeks preparing for the journey, Marcelle's strength coming in waves that seemed to ebb less frequently as the days went on. Maurice had warned them of the perils they would face at the German checkpoints that were being set up along the roads, but the route would be straightforward. The Aisne River, just five kilometers to their east, would take them straight north into Soissons. If they could travel eight to ten kilometers per day, they would make it in just a few days.

The evening before their departure, they sat in front of the fire and watched the last threads of their identities go up in flames. Philip didn't stick around. He couldn't bear to see his uniform reduced to nothing but ashes, and when the fire lost its flame, Maurice retired to his bedroom, leaving George and Rosalie alone and transfixed by the smoldering embers.

Rosalie pulled out the cross that she wore tucked beneath her blouse and slipped it over her head, brushing the tip of her finger over the crucifix and rolling the beads through her hands in a gesture so often repeated that it was as natural to her as breathing.

"Why did you save her?" she asked, without looking up at George.

It was a difficult question to answer, the truth too complicated to put into words. How could he explain something that he didn't even understand himself? How could he describe the sensation of drowning in Marcelle's eyes as something so illuminating and beautiful that he would choose it over air every single time.

Rosalie nodded at George's silence. If anyone could understand the spells that Marcelle could cast, it was her twin sister. She sighed into the lifeless fire between them.

"That man," she said. "The German general at the prison, he called my sister *die Hexe des Flusses*. Do you know what that means?"

George shook his head.

"It means the witch of the river. They think that because Marcelle is a woman, she cannot be brave or clever or strong." Rosalie laughed. "She outsmarted them all, and, therefore, she must be a witch."

George smiled as she continued.

"You are brave like Marcelle," she said. "I do not understand that kind of bravery. I was so terrified when I snuck out of that prison. And when Maurice opened the door that night, I thought for sure he would kill me."

"You worked as a nurse on the front lines of a battlefield," George replied. "You can't tell me you're not brave."

"That is different." Rosalie paused as if she might not continue, as if her words held no merit. "I do what I am asked to do. When the sisters of the Croix-Rouge française pointed me toward the soldiers, I went. When my father insisted that I watch over my sister, I did my best. When my mother encouraged me to attend mass, I did not miss even one day. But it is not bravery that compels me to do these things. It is duty."

"Bravery is nothing more than a combination of duty and desperation and love," George replied, his eyes never leaving the ashes from the fire as his thoughts dragged him back to the battlefield. "Doing what needs to be done is brave. Sometimes simply surviving is brave."

Rosalie breathed out a regretful sigh and nodded her head.

"I suppose you are right," she said. "But I could not even do that on my own. I had no idea that Marcelle was risking her life for us. I thought God was rewarding us for doing His work. Providing us shelter and keeping us fed. So, I prayed day and night, thanking Him for protecting us."

She stared down at the rosary and closed her fingers around it, her ragged breaths turning into sobs. When she finally looked up at George, he was amazed at how unnervingly similar her eyes were to her sister's. And how vastly different.

"All that time, it was Marcelle," she said, tossing the rosary into the ashes before drying her tears. "And God was never even there."

chapter 14

MARCELLE

Soissons, France
May 1991

"The rosary."

Marcelle reached for the cross at her neck, the one Rosalie had given to her as a wedding gift all those years ago to replace the one they had lost during the war. The feel of it between her fingers was an instant comfort.

"You remember the rosary, Maman?" Juliette looked up at her from the diary. "The one Tante Rosalie threw into the fire?"

"Yes, but . . ." Marcelle's mind was playing tricks on her again. "That is not what happened to the rosary," she said, still running her fingers over her own necklace. There had been no Maurice, no farmhouse, no prison in Jaulgonne. None of that had really happened. The Germans had lost that battle on the Marne River, and they'd never made it to Paris.

"This story is getting more bizarre by the minute," her daughter said, closing the diary and slipping it beneath the chair before standing up and stretching her arms above her head. "Shall we take a break, Maman? Have a bite to eat?"

Marcelle wasn't interested in a break. She wanted to hear the rest of the story, but Juliette didn't wait for an answer. No one did that these days. They simply put her where they thought she should be when they thought she should be there and carried on as if that was a perfectly acceptable existence for a woman whose independence had once been the most valuable thing she'd owned.

Juliette locked Marcelle's wheelchair into place at the kitchen table before she smeared a few slices of bread with butter and filled their teacups with hot water. "I keep having to remind myself that none of this is true," she said, placing the tea bags into the cups, and slicing some cheese for their sandwiches. "It seems so odd to make up a story like this."

"The man in the black beret was true." The words slipped out of Marcelle's mouth before she could stop them. She could still see him standing beneath the cherry tree, his pipe glowing in the darkness. She shuddered as she reached for her sandwich, trying to shake the memory away.

"But the prison in Jaulgonne?"

Marcelle shook her head. "No," she said, running her hand over the wrinkled skin of her cheek, searching for a scar she felt certain lay just beneath the surface. "I already told you. There was no prison in Jaulgonne."

"Perhaps we should be done with the diary," Juliette said, taking a sip from her teacup and peering at her mother over the rim. "I don't want it to upset you."

Marcelle smiled back at her daughter. She knew better than to argue. Nowadays, when she stood up for herself, people called her combative and gave her a little pill to help "take the edge off." Aging was not for the weak. Of all the losses in Marcelle's life, the loss of her independence had been the most unanticipated. Balancing her emotions had turned out to be a full-time job. If she was too eager, they called her unsettled; too complacent, they called her depressed. Being agreeable had been her key to success in old age. Lowering her expectations.

"Maybe just a few more chapters," Marcelle suggested, washing down her sandwich with the rest of her tea. "I think I am up for a bit more."

chapter 15

MARCELLE

Soissons, France
August 1918

Soissons was in shambles.

Out of the dust and rubble, the cathedral tower reached up toward the heavens in a final plea for salvation, while around it lay the shattered remains of a civilization that had endured centuries of plagues and revolutions and countless wars.

The trek had taken them longer than they had anticipated. They'd followed the Aisne River, sticking to the west bank where the Allied trenches had been abandoned and the bodies of fallen soldiers stripped and looted. When the terrain had become too treacherous and the forests had threatened to slow their pace even further, they'd been forced onto the dirt roads with the other refugees, forced to lie their way through German checkpoints. The thirty-kilometer trip that should have taken them three or four days had ended up costing them an entire week.

Dusk loomed as they staggered into town, the barren streets like rivers of destruction sweeping them to where their house had once stood. A pile of stones that had long been looted and scavenged was all that remained.

Their father's store down the street had fared no better, and as Rosalie tunneled through the ruins, digging until her hands bled, the winds shifted as if to steer them away. But Marcelle was the only one listening. Philip and George dug beside Rosalie. She had come out of Maurice's farmhouse a more emboldened woman and had delivered them safely through checkpoints and roadblocks as promised to get them to Soissons.

By the time they uncovered the cellar door, all the light had been drained from the sky.

Marcelle descended the stairs into a dream, her feet touching the soft earthen floor and guiding her into a long-lost life, every detail frozen in time. Her grandmother's blanket on the mattress. The wine bottles stacked beneath the table. An empty box of matches beside a broken gas lamp. The only evidence of her existence lay entombed beneath a shattered city.

Threads of dust danced through the beam of Philip's flashlight as he shined it into the corners and over the mattress Pierre's family had once shared. George pulled the cellar hatch closed behind himself as Rosalie enlisted Philip's help to move the wine bottles and the wooden table away from the wall. Marcelle had never noticed the boulder they rolled from the surrounding stones, and when Philip shined his light into the hole behind it, she couldn't quite wrap her mind around what she was seeing.

Her mother's jewelry box.

"What? How did you . . ." Marcelle's words evaporated between them as her memory pulled forward the image of her mother's jewelry box sitting on the wooden table as her father and Rosalie stacked the wine bottles beneath it.

It had always been Rosalie.

Her father's chosen one.

"Papa told me it was here," Rosalie said, an apology buried in her words. "He wanted one of us to know just in case we ended up in a situation like this."

How could her sister have kept this from her? Why had her parents not entrusted her with this secret?

The footsteps that shuffled on the floor above their heads took precedence over her wounded ego, though, and when Philip switched off the flashlight, Marcelle could hear the thump of the boulder as someone rolled it back into place. There was no time for clinking wine bottles or shuffling tables. There was just enough time for them to pile into a far corner atop a thin and mildewed mattress before the hatch door opened and light flooded the cellar.

Marcelle didn't move. She didn't flinch or blink or breathe. Even when she heard the cock of the pistol and saw the boot as it landed on the first step, she stared straight ahead, fighting to banish the general's voice that echoed through her head. *Guten Morgen, fräulein.* Had he found her? Was he even looking for her? He spent each night haunting her dreams and each day whispering to her from the shadows of every corner. When would he come?

"Qui est là?" *Who is here?*

The voice belonged to a girl, though her words were spoken with the authority of a woman.

Still, no one moved.

"We know you are here." She swung the light into the cellar from the top step. "We saw you come in. This is private property. It does not belong to you."

Marcelle waited for her sister to do something, to step in and save them like she had done every step of the way from Jaulgonne. But no one moved. Before reason could dilute the courage that was pulsing through her veins, Marcelle stepped forward into the glow of the oil lamp.

"It does belong to me," she said, taking a cautious step back when the woman with the light gasped and stumbled the rest of the way down the stairs.

"Marcelle Marchand?" It took her a moment to run her gaze down the entire length of the scar on Marcelle's cheek. "What did they do to you?"

Lina Fournier.

Pierre's little sister had been just a child when they had left for Paris all those years ago, quiet as a mouse and hiding in her mother's skirt. Not at all like the wiry teenager standing before her with the pistol in her hand.

"Their best," Marcelle replied, hugging the girl who would have been her sister by now if she would have just said yes to Pierre in his basement apartment. Would he still be alive now? "Is your mother here? And your sister?"

Lina stepped back and shook her head. "Maman passed last year. Grippe. Marie and I stayed with your parents after that. Until Paris was bombed."

"Where are they now?"

When Rosalie stepped out of the corner, Lina glanced from one sister to the other, her voice hesitant and her words distant.

"Your parents never made it out of Paris," she said. "I am sorry. They did not survive the bombings."

Time circled back and caught Marcelle unprepared. She was in the cellar, seventeen years old, her mother handing her a slice of apple, her father sending Rosalie out to the wolves, Lina sobbing in the corner. She glanced back at the mattress Lina had been sitting on when she had delivered the news of her father's death. Fate was playing a cruel game, it seemed.

Marcelle held her sister, their bodies pressed so tightly together that Rosalie's sobs racked them both. She took comfort in the steady rhythm of their hearts beating in time, but she did not weep for her parents. She couldn't remember the last time she had wept. The tears just wouldn't come.

"And your sister?" she asked, glancing at Lina over Rosalie's quivering body.

"She died with your parents."

"I am sorry, Lina," Marcelle replied, still clutching her sister, the person for whom she had traded Pierre's life. "You have lost everyone."

"Not everyone. I found my cousin Roland when I got here last month. We stay across the street in an abandoned apartment with another boy we found wandering around town and scavenging for food. You are welcome to join us. The Germans have no use for this section of town, so they do not bother us much."

"We are not alone." When Marcelle switched from French to English and called George and Philip from the corner, Lina's eyebrows shot up in surprise. She stared up at Philip, whose head bumped the ceiling when he stood upright.

"Do you know the penalty for hiding American soldiers?" she asked, her English as fluent as her brother's had been.

"Yes," Marcelle replied. She scanned over the men's ragged clothing, the outfits that had been scavenged from Maurice's closet before their uniforms had been burned. "But how do you know they are American?"

"They just look like Americans," Lina laughed, waving away the question. "I can see you have not changed, Marcelle. You are as daring as ever."

Marcelle didn't share in her laughter. She couldn't remember the last time she had laughed, or even smiled. The tug across her cheek was a constant reminder that she didn't have anything to laugh about, and the missing tooth was a good enough reason not to smile. On top of that, she didn't understand Lina's words. She had been weak and naïve when they had last been in Soissons. Had she not changed?

Lina guided them back out onto the street where a single apartment stood tall, a lone survivor of the bombings. Was it Monsieur Barnard's clothing shop? Hadn't that been across the street from her father's store?

Marcelle couldn't remember. Without the other shops around it and the mannequins in the window, it was as unfamiliar to her as a storefront in Paris. Walls had been blown out in some sections, and where the front door had once stood lay a mound of stones. When Lina swung her light toward the wreckage, a young boy scurried from the rubble and into the apartment.

"That is Paul," she said. "He does not talk much, but do not let him fool you. He sees everything."

They climbed over the pile of stones and bricks, following the boy into the apartment, where a treacherous staircase led them to the living quarters on the second floor. If George hadn't been by her side, Marcelle would not have had the strength to make it over the sections of blown-out stairs.

Lina turned the gas lamp off when they entered the apartment, and when Marcelle's eyes adjusted to the muted glow of the candle in the middle of the table, she noticed the boy who had hurried in before them crouching on the floor in the corner. His arms were wrapped around his folded-up knees, and his body rocked back and forth to a soothing rhythm.

At the table, behind the soft candlelight, sat a man whose features tugged at a place in Marcelle's memory that hadn't been visited in many years.

"Roland." She breathed out his name. He was the boy with whom she'd had to share Pierre. His cousin and best friend. Whatever secrets had floated between Marcelle and Pierre had always managed to find their way to Roland's ears.

"Marcelle." He stood when he saw her, the pant leg that had been folded up around the stub of his right leg unraveling to the floor. Marcelle pretended not to notice as she self-consciously ran a finger along the scab on her cheek.

"You survived," she whispered, seeing him in perfect formation beside Pierre and her brothers as they had marched out of town four years earlier, and recalling how she had thought only of herself and the proposal she knew would be coming by Christmas. "They said no one survived."

"I am sorry, Marcelle." He hopped forward, balancing his weight on the unsteady table between them. "I do not know what happened to the rest of them. Pierre or your brothers. I woke up days after the battle, surrounded by the dead."

"We have not heard of any other survivors from their unit."

Lina was pulling the settee from beneath the window up to the table. "Sit here, Marcelle. The other chairs will break your back."

Break her back. Break her ribs. Break her soul. What difference did it make? And how did Lina know she was already so broken? Could she see through Marcelle's dress and beneath her skin to each faded bruise, half-healed fracture, and budding scar on her body? Could she hear the crack of the rifle that echoed through Marcelle's thoughts and preyed on her each night, reminding her that she had sent Pierre to his death? What would she do, and what would Roland do, if they knew what she had done? Marcelle eased onto the cushioned chair, Rosalie sliding in beside her before they noticed the chatter from the corner.

"Américains, Américains, Américains . . ." The boy rocked to an endless and steady rhythm that only he could hear, one hand squeezing and twisting the fingers of the other to that same constant beat. He was not a young boy after all, as Marcelle had first though, maybe twelve or thirteen. Despite his small size, his face was already starting to sharpen into that of a man's, and his features were so strangely familiar to Marcelle that she found it difficult to pull her eyes away from him. Had she once known him? "Américains, Américains, Américains . . ."

"What now, Paul?" Roland slumped onto one of the unbalanced wooden chairs around the table and breathed out a hefty sigh. "That kid is going to get us killed."

"We do not see too many Americans this far from the front," Lina explained in English, gesturing for Philip and George to join them at the table. "Paul is just excited."

"Americans?" Roland pointed what looked like an accusatory finger at the two men sitting across the table from him. "You are Americans?"

"Yes," George replied. "And we're sorry to put you in this situation. We know it's dangerous, but we had nowhere else to go, and Rosalie . . ."

When he nodded toward Rosalie and let his words trail off, Marcelle couldn't help but finish his sentence in her mind.

. . . and Rosalie promised to help us if we saved her sister.

Was that it? Until that moment, it hadn't occurred to her that George and Philip were awaiting payment, cashing in on a debt. How could she have been so blind? In her mind, it had been George who had come for her, George whose eyes had made her a promise as she was being dragged from the courtyard:

I will save you.

And he had. They had all worked together to save her. It just hadn't occurred to her that Rosalie might have been the one to coordinate it all, that she had promised them safe passage for her sister's life.

"There is no need to apologize to us." Roland's Cockney accent was a near perfect match to Pierre's. The last time the cousins had been together, Marcelle had been unable to understand the secrets they'd passed to each other in English. "We are not scared of the Germans," Roland said. "And I am proud to help Americans. You traveled across the sea to help us. The least we can do is keep you safe until we can get you back to your troops."

"We heard rumors that the Americans had withdrawn with the Allies and left everything behind." Philip was restless to join the conversation, his energy spinning through the air around them. "It's not true, is it?"

"It is true," Roland replied. "But there is word they have rejoined the French units south of Moulins. The Germans have not pushed past Moulins even though there has been little resistance. We think they are running out of steam and supplies. They are spread too thin. It would be the perfect time for the armies to regroup and come in from the south."

"Then we need to get to Moulins," Philip proclaimed. He was a soldier. He was the type of man who would charge headlong into battle for a land whose language he couldn't even speak, simply to be a part of the action.

"Moulins is very far from here," Roland replied. "It would take weeks and weeks to get there."

"Is there another direction to go, then?" Philip's enthusiasm was made more obvious by George's silence. Marcelle was intrigued by George's silence, if not impressed by it. His emotions didn't rule him. He listened pensively as Roland explained there was nowhere else to go. Soissons was so far north that Belgium was just a one-hundred-kilometer trek to the northeast while Paris was an equally short trek to the southwest, but both were heavily fortified with German troops, and neither would be safe for an American. Getting to the English Channel might offer them a chance to enter Britain, but it had already been peppered with mines and crossing would be a risky endeavor.

George was impervious to the excitement that Roland and Philip shared. Maybe he didn't want to rejoin the fight. Maybe he didn't think France was worth saving. Marcelle couldn't read his expression and blushed under his gaze when she caught her trying. She lingered in her embarrassment for so long that by the time she rejoined the conversation, they had moved on to other matters, and Lina was explaining the German system of recordkeeping.

The Americans would need identification cards to travel through France, but obtaining them would be tricky. Along with ration cards, they were given only to residents whose names were in the civil records books.

"There are plenty of names to choose from," Roland said. "Most of the men from Soissons will not be returning. But the Germans will wonder why two young and healthy men are not fighting with their troops at the front or rotting in one of their prisons."

"Captain Neumann will be our best option," Lina said. She and Roland were discussing strategies in French when the boy in the corner started his rocking again.

"Max Neumann, Max Neumann, Max Neumann . . ." He

didn't flinch when Roland slammed his hand onto the table and barked at him to be quiet. The rocking and chanting continued until *Max Neumann* faded into the background.

"Leave him alone, Roland," Lina said. "We have other things to worry about right now."

"He is going to get us killed," Roland snapped, before Lina turned her back to him to address Philip and George.

"Max is one of the German officers who does not speak French," she said. "He just takes names and hands out cards. I have never seen him ask questions. I do not know what he will do with you two, but I still think he will be our best option."

Lina's gaze lingered on Philip. He was a handsome man, taller than anyone Marcelle had ever met, and she wondered if perhaps that was how Lina had identified him as an American.

George would be fine. Marcelle had watched them on the road to Soissons, and he was a natural Frenchman, devouring the few phrases she and Rosalie had taught him and repeating them with a confidence that infused the very air around him. He'd passed off his ignorance of the language as pretentious indifference to the German soldiers at the checkpoints, and not once had he been questioned.

Philip, on the other hand, had no natural ability to blend in with anyone. It wasn't just his height that made him stand out. It was his sheer mass. Even the Germans didn't measure up to him, and they were endlessly suspicious of the giant who came lumbering through their checkpoints. If not for Rosalie's quick thinking, they would never have made it to Soissons. There was only one way to get Philip past the Germans: make him stand out.

"Philip will be questioned," Rosalie said, as if answering Marcelle's thoughts. "We had to pretend he was deaf and dumb to get him here. It was the only way they would allow him through the checkpoints. And even then, they were always suspicious of him."

A silence fell over the group, the excitement that had been

swirling through the air moments earlier being pulled away with the draft through the cracks in the walls. It was a dangerous game they were playing, a game of life and death, and Marcelle hadn't even shared with them the most worrisome news, the part that would put them all at risk.

Would the general be searching for her? It was a burden she had lugged with her all the way from the prison in Jaulgonne, and though no one spoke of it, it had grown into a monstrosity Marcelle could barely contain.

"I have an idea," Lina announced, the flicker of the candlelight dancing across her face revealing a rueful smile. "But we are going to need some blood."

chapter 16

Philip retched in the corner.

Lina had found the blood behind the butcher's shop, and the bandages she'd cut into strips from an old sheet had been soaking in it all night. Rosalie did the wrapping. She and Marcelle were the only two with experience dressing field wounds, but Marcelle couldn't stomach the scent of congealed blood. When had she become so weak?

It was a masterpiece by the time Rosalie was done. One could only guess what was beneath the bandage. A missing eye? A piece of brain? And the stench, which could only have been rotting flesh, was so distracting that Philip couldn't even remember the name he'd been given, the one he'd been practicing all night:

Joseph Marchand.

Joseph and Henri were the brothers Marcelle had waved off to war four years earlier. Giving away their names felt like a betrayal, like a curse that might seal their fates and prevent them from ever returning.

"This isn't going to work." George stepped around Philip, surveying the bandage from every angle as if critiquing a sculpture. He was a man who seemed to live his life in silence, always observing. He didn't speak unless he had something important to say, and Marcelle found herself always listening. "You've done a great job," he said, looking back at Rosalie.

"And I don't think you'll have any trouble getting Philip a card. But there's no way we can pass for brothers."

"It will be fine," Roland replied. "The Germans don't want any trouble. Just give them a name on the register and they will give you a card."

When Lina stepped up beside them, tilting her head back and taking in the physical differences between the two men, Marcelle could almost see her brother in her: the long eyelashes, the aquiline nose, the wide face with the prominent cheekbones.

"I don't know," she finally said. "I think George might be right. There is no reason to push our luck."

"Well then, who is he going to be?" Roland asked.

"George will be Pierre." Lina glanced back at Marcelle as she offered up the name. Marcelle's body tensed at the sound of it, seeing so clearly the fresh-faced boy who had stolen kisses from her when they were young and untarnished. She jumped when Lina placed a hand on her back. It felt like a betrayal, gifting Pierre's name to another man who made her heart flutter.

"Pierre is very important to all of us," Lina continued, her hand still on Marcelle's back. "He was my brother. And he and Roland were not only cousins, but also best friends. And, if he had survived, he would have been Marcelle's husband by now."

Marcelle couldn't read George's expression when his gaze settled on her face. He was a mysterious man. Dark. Quiet. Contemplative. She missed the man who had flirted with her in the Montmirail hospital. Was she too tarnished for him now? Already promised to a dead man, and already taken by a monster.

"Thank you." George nodded to Lina and Roland before he returned his attention to Marcelle. "I would be honored to carry his name."

"There is no time to dwell on the past today." Roland slapped George on the back before winking at Marcelle. "Pierre would be proud for you to take his name. We will tell you all about him tonight as we celebrate with one of those bottles of wine the Marchand sisters are hiding in their cellar."

"Yes," Lina replied. "Stories for later. For now, Rosalie and Marcelle need to listen up. Today is ration card day, so there will be hundreds of women out there. Your job is to blend in. There is nothing more dangerous than being noticed by the Germans. It will be difficult because Philip will draw attention to you, but being forgettable is an invaluable tool. Remember that. And not just for today."

Marcelle nodded along to her words. *Go unnoticed.* Could she ever really go unnoticed again? Could anyone ever forget her face?

They waited until mid-morning, until the ration card lines were at their peak. Three snaking lines wound their way from three different German soldiers who sat behind makeshift desks and scratched down names onto cards, each less interested than the next. No one wanted to be there, it seemed. Perhaps Roland was right, just give them a name and move on.

Lina directed them to the line headed by Max, the German officer whose indifference to the people of Soissons made him less of a threat, or so they thought. But Marcelle knew all about misinterpreting unassuming men. That was a lesson that would live inside of her until the day she died.

Max's line was longer than the others, but it moved fast, half the women forfeiting their spots just to escape the stench of Philip's bandage, and within minutes, they were standing in front of the German captain and watching him gag.

"Du stinkst. Geh weg." He held his nose with one hand and waved them away with the other.

"S'il vous plaît, monsieur," Marcelle replied in French. "We need our cards."

"Next!"

The woman behind them scurried up to the table, pushing her way past Marcelle and Rosalie before the captain could repeat himself. Marcelle became flustered as they were shuffled to the back of the line by the women behind them, worried they would lose their chance if she didn't step forward and take charge. She had to do something. She had to fight back, or risk being swallowed up by the crowd.

"Ich bitte Sie," she said, pushing her way past the woman who had taken their spot, before continuing in flawless German. "Please don't send us away. My brother has a severe head injury that we are treating, but we haven't the supplies to clean it because we have been traveling for weeks to get here. Please. Now that we are home, we will get him cleaned and taken care of."

A muttering of voices washed through the crowd before the silence swept in, and when Max leaned back into the chair with his arms crossed over his chest, his eyes instantly found the clumsy suture scars that held Marcelle's cheek together. She could feel them bouncing between the jagged stitches, zigzagging back and forth over the scabbed incision like a drunken man hobbling down a flight of stairs. Did he know about the witch of the river with the scarred face?

"Your German is quite good." He waved off the woman who had jostled her way to the front, before his gaze landed on Rosalie. "Does anyone else in your family speak German?"

Marcelle shook her head. "Just me, sir."

He nodded, and when he pulled himself forward at the table and picked up the pen, the cord of tension threading through the crowd seemed to slacken.

"I need names and birthdates."

"Rosalie and Marcelle Marchand. August third, 1897. And this is my brother Joseph Marchand. January fourth, 1892."

If Marcelle hadn't been paying attention, she wouldn't have noticed that the captain didn't even search for their names. He opened the civil records book to a random page and ran his finger halfway down to some names that had been scratched into it decades earlier, and then he nodded his head and threw the book back under his chair.

"If he does not die," he said, pointing up at Philip as he handed their identification and ration cards to Marcelle, "he will be expected to report for duty as soon as he has recovered."

Marcelle nodded and motioned for Rosalie and Philip to follow her before a flurry of movement caught her eye. It was a mop of brown hair bouncing atop a boy's head as he skipped to the front of the line.

"Max Neumann, Max Neumann, Max Neumann . . ."

Marcelle froze, her breath catching in her chest and her eyes searching for Lina amongst the crowd of people fanning out from the tables. Paul bounced closer and closer to the German soldier, and by the time she spotted Lina and George in the middle of the line, he was standing in front of Max and laughing at something the man was saying. He jumped at the ration card that was being held just above his head and basked in the glow of the captain's praises when he was able to snatch it from his hand. It wasn't until the boy turned back to her, and the dimpled smile spread across his face, that she realized why he had looked so familiar to her the previous evening, and who he was.

Paul Bauer.

Her German teacher's son.

Just as this was dawning on her, a commotion from the center of the line pulled Marcelle's attention away from the boy and back to the spot where Lina and George were waiting their turn.

"Why are you here instead of out there fighting with the other men?"

The woman poking at George's chest did not suffer from hunger. Compared to the women around her with their sallow and hollowed-out cheeks, she was almost portly, her skirt swishing and rustling over the cobbled street as her hips shimmied beneath it.

"Be quiet," Lina hissed under her breath, forcefully pushing the woman's hand away. "He has been out there fighting for four years."

"You disobedient child!" The smack across Lina's face echoed through the square. "You bring this man here to take food from women and children and old men. You should be ashamed of yourself."

"Es reicht!" *Enough!*

With one finger, Max singled out George and Lina before pointing to the ground in front of his table. They stepped up obediently, Lina doing her best to explain the situation to a man who couldn't understand her French words.

"My brother has been gone for four years and has come back to me shell-shocked," she said. "He is out of his mind."

"Es reicht!"

If not for the crowd parting beside her, Marcelle might not have noticed Max's eyes following her, or that he was already aiming his finger in her direction. She did as he instructed, stepping up beside George, who stood silent and unflinching. Despite the chilled air sweeping over their skin, the smell of sweat and fear radiated from them all.

"What is this girl saying?"

Marcelle hesitated, glancing from one face to the next. Max, George, Lina.

"Well," she finally muttered. "The woman back there . . . she is upset because . . . well . . . she says that this man is taking food that could go to women and children." Marcelle cleared her throat before she continued. "But this man has—"

"Enough of this!" With a wave of his hand the captain cut off Marcelle's words. "You French are too emotional. How can we get anything done with all these hysterics? What are their names?"

"This is Lina Fournier. And her brother, Pierre."

His hands were deliberate and precise as he slowly pulled two ration cards from the stack and balanced his pen above them.

"And how do you know them?"

"We were in school together," Marcelle replied. "Before the

war. Soissons is not such a big town. Most of us know each other."

"I see." With his pen still hovering above the cards, he slowly pulled his gaze from Marcelle and settled it upon George's face before asking in broken French, "How to spell name?"

George gave no response, of course. He had no idea what the man was asking. When Marcelle began to spell out Pierre's name, the captain cut his eyes her way, silencing her without so much as a word.

"Surely the man knows how to spell his name," he said, turning back to George. "How to spell name, monsieur?"

Marcelle had been in this place before, this moment of suspended possibility, where one wrong step was the difference between life and death. One word. One blink. One breath. The heaviness swelled around them, growing and filling the space between their bodies until Marcelle could feel the force of it upon her skin, compressing her limbs until she was immobilized by it. Almost paralyzed.

George stood impossibly still beside her, staring straight ahead, past the German soldiers, past the bombed-out cathedral, past the invisible boundaries holding them to that moment.

"Sir," Marcelle whispered in German, not daring to look the man in the eye. "This is Pierre Fournier. He is well known in town to have fits." She tapped her finger to her head. "Epilepsie," she said, hoping George would understand the word. Then she turned to Lina, switching to French. "Is your brother having one of his seizures?"

"Oui," Lina replied without hesitation, before stepping in front of George and rubbing his face. "Shh, it is fine, Pierre. The man is just asking for your name. We will be home soon."

"Well, aren't you helpful, fräulein?" Max smiled. His eyes were a piercing green, a color that had no name because there was nothing in nature that could match it. A color that could hypnotize you if you stayed too long in it. He wrote down the names as Marcelle spelled them out for him, then handed the cards to her without looking back at Lina or George.

"I believe we might have some work for you in the occupation administration office," he said, before dismissing her with a nod. "We will be in touch."

chapter 17

"That was foolish."

Lina's words were razor sharp. On the surface, she looked much like the child Marcelle had left in Paris all those years ago. She was sixteen now, but years of starvation and hunger had stunted her growth, leaving her forever twelve. Hunger was like fire, though. In the right hands, it could forge steel into a mighty weapon, and Lina had come out sharpened and polished, ready to fight.

"She got us our cards," Rosalie snapped back, placing herself between the two women in the cramped space that had become their shared bedroom. The apartment was similar to the one Marcelle had grown up in, if not a bit smaller. Monsieur Barnard and his family would not be returning, but Marcelle still felt like an intruder as she slept on his bed, and wore his daughter's clothes, and cooked in his wife's kitchen.

"She put us all in danger," Lina said, and Marcelle could almost see Pierre standing there in front of them, the same squint in his eyes. "I would have gotten the cards for everyone. I would have taken care of it. You both need to learn how to stay invisible if we are going to survive this. I have enough on my plate trying to keep Paul out of danger. He doesn't know better. But the rest of us do."

"I am sorry, Lina," Marcelle said. "You are right. Paul was just a child when we fled Soissons, maybe seven or eight. And

Monsieur Bauer was always very good to me, so it means a great deal that you took his son in. I will be more careful."

"Paul is very important to me," Lina replied. "I have protected him for many years."

"Years?" Marcelle couldn't make sense of Lina's words. She had only returned to Soissons after Paris had been bombed, after losing her mother and her sister. Barely a month had passed since then. "Did you know the Bauers before we left Soissons?"

Lina shook her head. "The timeline of my life is a bit different than yours," she replied. "I will explain it to you someday, but first we have other things to discuss."

Marcelle looked to Rosalie for an answer, but her sister simply shrugged back at her. Lina was an enigma to them both with her uncanny instincts and prophetic comments, but the question to come would outdo them all:

"Have you told your sister yet?"

"How could you . . ." Marcelle's hands instinctively followed Lina's gaze to her belly as questions tumbled through her mind. How could Lina have known? Not even two months had passed, not enough time to be sure that her missed monthly bleeding was from a baby growing inside of her or simply starvation.

Lina was right, of course. But how she could have known, how she could have seen that far into the distance when the others could barely see past their own noses, Marcelle would never fully understand. What else did Lina know? Did she see the general from Marcelle's nightmares? Was he looking for her? And if he found her with a baby, would he take the child? Would he kill it? Or worse, would he raise it to be like him?

"What are you talking about?" Rosalie's attention bounced between the two women before settling on Marcelle.

"I'm pregnant," Marcelle said, and when her sister pulled her into an embrace, unable to hold back her sobs, and ran her hands over the chopped and uneven locks of Marcelle's hair, it felt almost as if her mother had returned.

"Oh, Marcelle," Rosalie said. "What do we do?"

"We have to get rid of it," Marcelle replied, pushing back from her sister's embrace. "I will need your help, Rosalie. I cannot bring this baby into the world and look at its face and see . . ." What would she see? She still wasn't sure who would be staring back at her.

"No." Rosalie's eyes were panicked as she wiped the tears from her cheeks. "You cannot ask this of me."

"Please, Rosalie."

Before Rosalie could answer, Lina was standing above them at the edge of the bed and studying the scar that tracked down the side of Marcelle's cheek. The stitches had been removed weeks earlier, but it was still in the early stages of healing.

"What happened to your face?" she asked. "You did not have that scar last time."

"What are you talking about, Lina?" Marcelle ran her finger over the raised tissue on her cheek, the skin beneath it tingling. She had never spoken of the general from Jaulgonne, and, while the others knew all about him, Marcelle worried she would somehow summon him if she mentioned his name.

"Things are different, but somehow . . ." Lina's eyes landed on Marcelle's belly, which didn't yet show the first signs of pregnancy. "Somehow they are also the same. You must have this baby, Marcelle. He will be healthy and happy. And we will all love him."

"She is right," Rosalie said, squeezing her sister's hands between her own before placing a kiss on her forehead. "This child is already a part of us now. A gift in the midst of this horror. And I will be here with you. We will get through this together."

"I will be here too," Lina said, joining the sisters on the bed. "I was so excited the day Pierre said he was going to marry you and that you would be my sister. You were always so brave and strong. And when you went out to find Rosalie the day my papa was shot, I knew then that I would do anything to be just like you. You made me a stronger person, Marcelle, and I will do everything I can to help bring that strength back to you. But you must promise me that you will have this child."

chapter 18

"Bébé, bébé, bébé . . ."

Paul was rocking in the corner as Roland and Philip sat at the kitchen table devising strategies to get across the German front at Moulins. They'd been at it for the better part of an hour, but they still hadn't come up with a solution. Roland had been a wealth of information. He was a trusted contact of the underground runners who passed reports along a route that spread like a spider's web throughout the villages of occupied France, and the latest news was that the Germans were still dug in at Moulins. Reports were always a month old by the time they got to Soissons, though, and their accuracy could never be validated.

Rosalie would be their escort. She'd already laid out their plans for the four-hundred-kilometer trek: They'd travel during the day—only people who had something to hide traveled under the cover of darkness; they'd stick with the refugees on the roads, bartering her mother's jewelry from the cellar for rides on wagons or trains; and they'd go with the deaf-and-dumb routine for Philip, maybe a bloody bandage thrown around his head for good measure. It was getting them across the front, when they finally found it, that had them scratching their heads.

"Maybe you can get your hands on some German uniforms," Roland suggested.

"I like that idea," Philip replied. "Hiding in plain sight."

"Yes, then you won't have to—"

The scream that silenced Roland's words pulled them all from their chairs and knocked them off balance. George was the first of the men to the bedroom, the first one through the door to see Marcelle clawing at her sister and screaming words in French that didn't need translation.

"N'approche pas! Arrête!"

What else could they be but pleas for help?

"Marcelle, c'est moi." Rosalie was trying to coax her sister back from whatever world she'd disappeared into, but Marcelle could no longer see her sister or Lina in the faces of the women beside her as she scampered across the floor to the other side of the room.

"What happened?" George stood at the door, the other men beside him peering over his shoulder at the three women.

"She had a bad dream," Lina replied. "She was taking a rest and . . ." She glanced down at Marcelle, who was trembling in the corner, and then back to the men in the doorway before she lowered her voice. "She has been through a lot. It will take some time."

George eased down onto the floor beside her, his hands open in front of him, before scooting back against the opposite wall. When Marcelle looked up at him, George knew she could only see the general from Jaulgonne in his face. The man who'd finally broken her. The man who would haunt her dreams for years to come. He gestured to the open door, an escape route if she needed it, and as her eyes followed him, whatever hold that man had on her started to loosen. "He's gone," George said. "And he's not coming back."

Marcelle had been unraveling since talk of her sister leaving for the front with Philip and George had begun. There was no one else to make the journey with them. Roland and Paul were out for obvious reasons, Marcelle still lacked the strength to make the round-trip journey herself, and Lina, who would have been the likely choice, couldn't leave Paul. So that left

Rosalie, which had sent an already frazzled Marcelle into hysterics.

She couldn't lose her sister. Her world was still spiraling out of control, all of it set in motion by the German general at the prison who'd spun her like the toy top George had played with as a child. She was still dizzy and wobbling and unbalanced, waiting for the momentum to stop so she could finally come to rest, and realizing when she came to her senses, everyone she loved would be gone. Her parents, her fiancé, and now her sister.

"But she is leaving," Marcelle whispered. "She is leaving me, and I will be all alone. How can I bring a child into this world without her?"

It wasn't until Roland gasped from the corner that George remembered he was standing there, Philip at his side and Paul hovering in the background.

"Bébé, bébé, bébé . . ."

Baby.

Marcelle was pregnant, and somehow Paul had already known. Lina was right. He was always listening, always seeing, always knowing.

"Roland, can you please take him?" Lina nodded toward Paul, who rocked back and forth over a squeaking floorboard that whined like an out-of-tune banjo. When they left for the kitchen, she shut the door behind them.

"You are not alone, Marcelle." Rosalie wrapped her arms around her sister in an unreciprocated hug. "I will find my way back," she said. "I promise."

"She is right," Lina said, joining the women on the floor. "You will see. We are all a family now. Me and you and Roland and Paul and Rosalie." She paused as she nodded toward Marcelle's belly. "And the baby."

"And me."

The words slipped out as effortlessly as water through his fingers, and George was just as surprised as the women around him when he heard them drifting through the air. He hadn't planned them, or even thought them through. They'd come from a place where ration and reason and logical thought didn't exist. It was the same place he'd been the night he'd walked into the barracks to find Marcelle at the prison.

It was a foreign place, and the man sitting beneath his skin was a foreign man. Because George was a sensible man, so unlike Philip, who cracked jokes under pressure and jumped into danger with both feet. George was the kind of man who took calculated steps and made well-thought-out decisions, the kind of man who didn't go into rescue missions unprepared or offer to risk his life for people he barely knew.

Only Marcelle could do this to him.

She was like a tonic. Hypnotizing him, entrancing him, enticing him to do things he would never otherwise consider. She smiled back at him with the tight-lipped smile she reserved for strangers.

"You've done your part, George," she said. "You deserve what you were promised."

What had he been promised? When he looked to Rosalie and Lina for an answer, they both shook their heads in response, neither seeming to understand the meaning of Marcelle's words.

"What was I promised?" George finally asked.

"Safe passage for rescuing me from the prison."

Marcelle's response pushed George back onto his heels for a moment, forcing him to question what he thought he knew. Had he been promised safe passage? Was this something Rosalie and Philip had worked out?

"I don't understand . . ." He let his words trail off as he once again looked to Rosalie for an answer. "Did you promise Philip something?"

"I did not promise anyone anything," she replied. "What are you talking about, Marcelle?"

"Didn't you plan my escape?" She pulled away from Rosalie's embrace so she could see her better. "I thought you promised George and Philip safe passage if they helped you get me out of the prison."

Rosalie's smile was everything Marcelle's wasn't: bold, bright, and uninhibited. "I wish," she said. "I wish I could take credit for saving you. I should have been the one to get you out of there." She shook her head and nodded at George. "But he is the one who did it."

When Marcelle looked at him, George was back at the prison the night he'd watched her being dragged from the courtyard, the night he'd stumbled into the barracks to be with her.

"I saw you." Her gaze was steady on George's face. "When the guards took me inside. And you promised me . . . I mean . . . you didn't promise me anything . . . but . . ."

George nodded.

"I promised you," he said.

"With your eyes."

"With my eyes."

Something divine was at play, something mysterious and beautiful, and George understood with a conviction he'd never known that every second of his life, every seemingly inconsequential decision and action, had led him to this moment with Marcelle. Every triumph and tragedy had been its own lighthouse guiding him to her shore.

"Why?" she whispered. "Why did you save me?"

"Because I love you."

He'd never seen Marcelle cry. He'd never comforted her, or laughed with her, or known anything about her. But on the floor of that bedroom, as she melted into his arms, he knew their story hadn't begun at that tent hospital in Montmirail. He'd known Marcelle forever. She'd always been a part of him. In every breath and heartbeat and sleepless night, she'd been there.

"You don't have to do this." Sobs racked her body and her breath hitched as she gulped the air between them.

"Please," George whispered, leaning in and brushing his lips across hers, tasting the salt from her tears. "Please let me do this." He'd forgotten they weren't alone until the door shut behind Rosalie and Lina. "Marry me, Marcelle."

He pressed his forehead to hers and slipped his hand over her belly. She never answered him, but there was no need. When she slid her hand over his and tucked her head into the curve of his neck, he knew the answer was yes.

chapter 19

"To the proud papa!"

The glass shattered against the cellar wall when Philip raised the wine bottle in a mocking and exaggerated toast. He was drunk. He was slumped against the wall at the bottom of the cellar stairs, and through the dim glow of the candlelight, George could see the red wine trickling down the stones beside him. The glass from the bottle sparkled around him as the flame cast a dancing shadow across it, but Philip didn't seem to notice it, or care.

George knew better than to open another bottle, but he still grabbed one from beneath the wooden table and joined his friend on the dirt floor. He'd never been a drinker. He'd never had the urge to numb his senses or lose control or forget. But that was all he wanted now: oblivion.

As much as he believed he was in love with Marcelle, he was also afraid he would fail her. He was grossly unprepared and unqualified to be a husband or a father, and how would he pull it all off under the noses of the Germans?

He struggled with the wine bottle, digging the double prongs of the rusted opener into the crumbling cork, twisting and pulling until it finally popped out and wine splashed over his hands and onto his shirt. Philip was already reaching for the bottle, and George had to swat his hand away so he could get a taste.

"What the hell is wrong with you?" He took a swig before

giving it to Philip, who chugged it like a dying man in the desert. Half the bottle was gone by the time he wiped the dribbles from his face with the back of his hand.

"Bon vin!" he exclaimed, shoving the bottle back into George's hands. "If nothing else, that right there is worth fighting for." He pointed to the wine before draping a heavy arm around George's shoulders. "I'm so glad you joined me, Mountcastle. I was just trying to decide what to get you for a wedding gift. Anything in particular for you and the missus?"

"You're an ass. You know that?"

"So I've been told," Philip laughed, snatching the bottle back from George's hands.

"What are you doing down here, anyway?" George asked. "Shouldn't you be planning your escape with Roland?"

"I'm practicing my wedding toast. I can't seem to get it just right. You see, my best pal has apparently lost his mind and proposed to a woman who is pregnant with another man's baby. And he's somehow forgotten that he's an American soldier living in France with a bunch of Germans who want to kill him. I'm trying to figure out how to work all of that into my toast without stepping on any toes."

It had been so long since George had seen the Philip beside him, the one who had a joke for every occasion, that he couldn't even find it in himself to be offended by his words. He'd missed that man.

"No one is stopping you from leaving," George replied. "Rosalie will still take you to Moulins. Just because I'm staying doesn't mean you can't get back to the fight."

"You're just going to send me out there alone, huh? After all that shit we went through together?"

George took the bottle from Philip's hands and drank until his stomach burned and the wine tried to force itself back up. He'd been nothing but a liability to Philip, slowing him down at every turn.

"Think of how much easier it will be without me tagging along," he said. "All I've ever done is slow you down. On the battlefield. On the trip to Soissons."

"Listen to you." Philip laughed under his breath. "That's not the way I remember it."

"What are you talking about?"

"I'm a fighter, Mountcastle. That's what I do. Stick me on a battlefield and put a gun in my hand and I'm your man. But you . . ." He pointed a drunk and clumsy finger at George. "You're a survivor. You're the one who watches and waits and studies. I followed you at the prison because I knew you'd figure a way out. And I couldn't have gotten through those checkpoints without Rosalie. But you don't need anyone. You figure things out faster than anyone I know."

George didn't recognize the man Philip was describing. His head was swimming, and his memories were disjointed, but it didn't sound like any version of himself he'd ever known. He'd never thought of himself as anything but weak, and as he watched the shadows from the candle leaping across the cellar floor, he wondered if perhaps he'd judged himself too harshly.

"You love her?" Philip asked.

George nodded into the darkness between them, but Philip didn't appear to be paying attention. His mind was somewhere else, worlds away from that musty, damp cellar in the middle of France.

"I was in love once," he finally said, and, if George hadn't been drunk off the wine, he might have been able to disguise his amusement. He couldn't match the vulnerability of love with the man beside him who was anything but vulnerable. The image of Philip holding a woman's hand, and whispering into her ear, and handing her flowers played over in his mind until he couldn't contain the laughter that spilled out between them.

"What the hell's so funny about that?"

"I'm sorry," George said, barely able to get his words out through fits of laughter. "I just can't picture it. I just assumed there were lots of women. Not just one."

"Well, it's true, Mountcastle. I have loved lots of women." Even Philip couldn't hold it together, following George into the circus of drunken laughter. "And lots of women have loved me."

"I'm sure they have," George replied as they cackled at jokes only wine could make funny.

"It's my charm they can't resist."

"And your jokes."

"Yes, my jokes. And my legs. They love my legs."

"Well, that goes without saying."

Philip sighed as their laughter died down, then pulled out a tattered photograph from the front pocket of his pants and held it out to George.

"She's prettier than she looks in the picture," he said.

George turned the photograph over in his hand. It was cracked through the middle, making it difficult to appreciate, but when he tilted it toward the candlelight, he could see the mischievous smile that played across the woman's face. She was posed on a chair, a vase of flowers by her side, and an arm casually draped across the table in front of her. She didn't share Philip's film-star handsomeness, but there was a confidence behind her smile that made her interesting.

"I think she looks just fine," George said. "It's impossible to know if someone is beautiful without meeting them. Look at Marcelle. If you only saw a picture of her, you'd never know that, even with all her scars, she's still the most beautiful woman in France."

"Listen to you. When are you going to teach me how to talk like that, Mountcastle?"

"There's no hope for you, my friend." George held the photograph up between them. "What's her name?"

"Dorothy." Philip took the picture back and ran his finger

over the crack, trying to straighten it out. "Back in Château-villain, when we first got to France, a couple of the guys found her picture and I told them she was my sister. I can't believe I did that now. Everyone assumes I'll marry the beauty queen. But Dorothy's the one I love."

George couldn't find any sympathy for him. No one had ever assumed anything of him, and there were certainly no beauty queens waiting for him back home. Farm work was lonely business, and he'd always figured he'd be a lonely man until a lonely woman came along looking for a husband. Then he'd get married, have a couple kids, and die. Except for the dying part, that's what his father had done.

When Philip tucked the photograph back into his pocket, George tried to get a peek at his watch. "What time is it?"

"Just shy of five in the morning."

"It's not five in the morning. There's no way we've been down here that long. You didn't even look at your watch."

"See for yourself." Philip held up the cracked watch face for George to see. "It's a Hamilton. They're never wrong."

"Must have been a nice watch."

"My grandfather gave it to me before I left for training last year. My kid brother was so jealous he almost joined up just to get one too. I kind of wish I'd left it with him. It broke when we went tumbling down the hill that night."

That night.

They never talked about that night. He knew it still haunted Philip, because he heard the screams that woke him from sleep, but what was there to say about it? They'd survived. Most of the men hadn't, but for some reason, they'd found a way out.

"Do you think we could have taken that hill back if we hadn't run?"

It took George a moment to respond. Of all the dreaded minutes of that interminable night, the ones on the side of the hill were George's proudest. If ever he could have been credited with saving Philip's life, it was in that moment when he'd pushed him down the hill away from the approaching Germans.

"We didn't stand a chance," George finally replied. "It was already over by that point. There was nothing that would have changed the outcome of that battle."

"I don't know. It felt . . ." Philip hesitated, running the tip of his shoe through the dirt of the cellar floor. "It felt right being there. Like I was *supposed* to be there behind that gun."

"You'd have been killed if you stayed."

Philip shrugged. "Maybe," he said, reaching for the empty wine bottle before dragging himself to his feet. "But something about being here just doesn't feel right. It's almost like I skirted my destiny out there on that battlefield. Like I was never supposed to leave it."

A dull ache was winding its way around George's head as he pulled himself from the ground. His mouth felt thick and parched; alcohol was not his friend.

"I don't know," George said. "But maybe when this is all over, I'll bring Marcelle back to America and we'll come find you in Pennsylvania." The candle had almost burned down to the table when George picked it up. "You and Dorothy."

"I'd love that, Mountcastle. If she'll still have me." Philip draped his arm over George's shoulders as they headed for the stairs, two vastly different paths awaiting them. Two different dreams. Two different futures. Two different lives.

"Meadville, Pennsylvania," Philip said as they emerged through the cellar hatch into the crisp night air. "If you can find your way to the Meadville Market House, I can pretty much assure you I'll be there. It's been in my family for over forty years."

The stars were sprinkled across the black sky like tiny grains of salt. No order. One here, two there. Stuck wherever they landed. Just like people, George supposed, as he wondered where they would all land.

Would Philip make it to Meadville? Would he and Marcelle ever visit him? Would they ever see each other again?

He didn't know it at the time, but George would come to find the randomness of the stars a comfort to him, a place he would visit when he missed his friend and didn't want to be alone. It would be a refuge, steady and consistent and timeless, and Philip would always be there.

chapter 20

"Will you at least drink some tea?"

Marcelle ignored him. She was bundled beneath layers of clothing—jackets, hats, scarves—everything she could find to keep herself warm. George was so used to her silence that he no longer repeated himself. When she'd first started ignoring him, he wondered if maybe she was losing her hearing from the beatings in Jaulgonne. Then he wondered if maybe she was just too lost in her sorrow to care. But now he understood that she was trying to save his life. If he couldn't speak French, how could he pass as a Frenchman?

"Thé?" He pointed to the mug of now cold tea in his hand, but Marcelle rolled her eyes and looked away. "Vouloir thé?"

"Voulez-vous du thé?" She enunciated each syllable as if she were speaking to a toddler, but George just smiled back at her. She'd shown so little interest in anything since Rosalie and Philip had left three months earlier, so he took her irritability as a sign that she was on the mend. Her hair was finally growing in, and the last of the scabs from the wound on her cheek had fallen off. A thick, pink line of scar tissue tracked from just below her left eye to the corner of her mouth, and while George thought it did nothing to detract from her beauty, he was thankful there were no mirrors in the apartment. The missing tooth was her greatest insecurity. It was on the top row, not even one of the front four, but when she smiled, which she rarely did, she always covered her mouth with her hand.

He offered her the tea again, repeating his words in French. She was bone thin, having lost even more weight since their arrival from Jaulgonne, and he wondered how the baby inside of her was surviving. She never talked about it, never even acknowledged its existence, and it wasn't until the slight bulge had started to bloom from beneath her dress that George had known it was still alive. She took the tea from his hands and mumbled a thank-you before turning back toward the window.

She spent hours in front of that window, sometimes entire days, and George often wondered what she saw out there. Was it the town she had once known, the one she had described to him in detail with the narrow cobblestone streets that wound through rows of quaint homes, each with its own overflowing window box? George had never seen that version of Soissons. All he'd seen when they'd arrived was miles of overgrown fields leading to a devastated town where the highest structure was the spire of a bombed-out cathedral. The streets had been empty, and remained so, too many of its citizens having been lost to the war. Those who persisted made themselves scarce.

Despite the barrenness, Marcelle was diligent in her surveillance, sitting in the window day after day, though George wasn't sure who she was waiting for. Was it Pierre? Or Rosalie? Or the German who'd carved up her face?

No one knew for certain what Marcelle had done to warrant the beatings she'd taken at that prison; she refused to discuss it, even with her sister. But they all knew she was expecting the man who'd delivered them to show up any day. She rarely left the house, and when she did, she hid her face from the Germans who patrolled the streets and kept order. George had tried to reassure her that he would protect her, flee with her if necessary, but Marcelle would never leave Soissons without her sister.

Winter was upon them, Christmas in a few short days, and

the absence of Rosalie had become an uninvited guest that took up too much space in their tiny apartment. No one acknowledged it, but it fed on their fears and grew larger each day. Marcelle denied any concerns, maintaining that her body would know if her sister was gone, and that she didn't need to wait by a window to mark her return.

The hours passed slowly for them all. They took turns waiting in queues and had learned to spread their rations over far too many days. Lina had left the apartment at dawn that morning, on the hunt for food. She ran most of their errands since she somehow always managed to secure more than the others.

"Voulez-vous du pain?" George pulled an old piece of crust from his pocket that he'd saved from dinner the previous evening. It felt like a stone in his hand, but he offered it to Marcelle, who, of course, turned it down. "The baby deserves a chance, Marcelle. He won't survive unless you feed him."

She watched him, unblinking, for so long that, if it had been anyone else, the moment would have become uncomfortable, but Marcelle felt like home to George. Her yearnings, her insecurities, her sullenness.

"He?" she finally replied in French, without pulling her gaze from George's face.

"Or she," he replied back in English. "Does it matter?"

"You are going to get yourself killed if you refuse to speak French." She turned her attention back to the street where they both watched Lina scurrying through the shadows with a package tucked under her arm.

"How am I supposed to speak French when no one will teach me?"

He sat down beside her on the settee that was pushed up against the window. The scar on her cheek softened when she turned to look at him. He was still learning the intricacies of her face. How her eyebrows shot up and her forehead crinkled when she was excited. How her teeth worked over her bottom lip when she was scared. How the scar on her cheek relaxed when she gave him her full attention. She was a beautiful woman. Most men, and women, would agree on that. But, to George, her beauty didn't come from any God-given features. It came from the way she loved and hated and mourned and celebrated. She was so true to her emotions that it was almost painful to watch. Nothing could detract from that beauty.

When he leaned in to kiss her, she tilted her chin back, welcoming his lips to hers. He hadn't yet figured out what they were to each other. *Husband and wife* wasn't exactly right. There had been no wedding, no certificate, no shared bed. But Marcelle was his soul. He didn't need a certificate to prove his devotion to her. He ached for her touch, hungered for the feel of her breath on his skin. But there were always those same men standing between them, holding her hostage, unwilling to let her go. Pierre and the general. He was constantly fighting them for her attention.

By the time they noticed Lina had come inside, she was already at the cupboard, sliding the package she'd been carrying onto the shelf. She grinned when she looked back at them, and George could almost feel the heat radiating from Marcelle's cheeks.

"Marcelle is teaching me French," he said.

"Is that what she's doing?" Lina laughed as she pulled a chair from the table and collapsed into it. "And how is the lesson going?"

"Very well," George replied. "Would you like to help?"

"I would love to," she sighed, "but I heard there is meat at Monsieur Martin's, so I must run along and get us a delicious Christmas meal." She nodded toward Marcelle before heading toward the door, her smile widening. "But I leave you in very capable hands."

~ ~ ~

The tree was George's contribution. It was a long-dead sprig that sat in a lonely corner of the apartment, absent any decorations.

It added no warmth to their Christmas celebration, but the others pretended to love it, knowing that George had brought a tiny bit of home to their apartment.

Everyone had contributed something. Paul had lined all their shoes beneath the settee near the window, two rows of tattered and worn-out leather, awaiting Father Christmas. No one knew where Roland had come up with the cigarettes he'd placed in the shoes, but there was one for each of them. And Marcelle had brought a bottle of Bordeaux up from her father's cellar.

Lina, as usual, had outdone them all with a Christmas Eve dinner that was cooking on the stove and stirring up a hunger in George that he didn't think could ever be sated. It was the scent of onions and meat that ensnared him, the fat and gristle popping on the stove. His eyes watered, and his mouth salivated.

Roland and Paul were already at the table, both freshly scrubbed and wearing shirts that Marcelle had recently mended and ironed. She'd decorated the table with a curtain she'd found buried beneath some rubble after spending the greater part of the week washing it and sewing it up. Under the glow of the candles that sat atop it, the tiny stitches holding it together almost disappeared.

"Come sit down." Roland waved George over to the table, eager to discuss the latest musings of *la résistance*. He had joined a group that was sympathetic to the Bolsheviks who'd recently replaced the monarchy in Russia, and Lina didn't want any part of it in their home. She ardently disapproved of Roland's association with them.

Roland was a revolutionary, though. He was young and idealistic and impressionable. He wanted everything he'd lost to be worth something, and as long as German was spoken in the streets, that fire would burn inside of him.

"Have you heard the news, George?"

George shook his head no as he took the spot beside Paul.

The only news that found its way into their lives was through Lina and Roland, and Lina's news was rarely about Russians.

"Lenin and his men have moved into Germany."

"Assez de ces absurdités." As Lina scolded Roland from the stove, George tried to translate her words. *Enough absurdity.*

"This is important, Lina. This is our country. Our home. Don't you want the Germans out?"

"Of course I do," Lina hissed. "But you need to keep your voice down. You don't know who is listening."

"No one is interested in us," Roland replied. "When have you ever seen a German on this side of town?"

"Exactly. They leave us alone. So why do I want someone else to come in and make things worse?"

"They are our allies, Lina. We are fighting this war against Germany together."

"They are not our allies," Lina spat back. "They signed a treaty with Germany behind our backs, and now they are taking advantage of Germany's weakened position at their border and pushing toward France. What do you think they will do when they get here?"

Roland and Lina went back and forth, seamlessly slipping between English and French, neither willing to compromise their position. Roland sang praises to Lenin and his Bolsheviks, glorifying the awakening that was spreading through Europe. But the truth, Lina insisted, was muddled and vague. There was no honor among thieves. The ink hadn't even dried on the treaty the Russians had signed with the Germans when Lenin had led them through the eastern front like water through a sieve. They'd waited only long enough for the Boche to shift their troops from the Russian front to the French one, and then they'd simply walked across the border and promised food to the hungry, rest to the weary, and riches to the poor.

Wherever Lina got her information was a guarded secret, but she didn't come to the conversations unprepared.

"You think Lenin is a good man, but is he not a conqueror?

Is he not trying to take our lands? You will be sorry if he shows up at your door. Mark my words, Roland."

"He's not conquering people or taking lands," Roland rebuked. "He's spreading communism, *equality*, to people who wouldn't have it otherwise. He's taking excesses from the ruling class and redistributing it to the working class. And stop pretending like you know what will happen."

"I *do* know what will happen if they reach France," Lina replied, spinning around and tapping the wooden spoon to her temple. "I have already seen it."

Lina considered herself somewhat of a prophet, and while her ramblings put the others on edge, particularly Marcelle, they were typically accurate.

"Meurtriers, meurtriers, meurtriers . . ."

Paul had been sitting so quietly that George had almost forgotten he was there. The rocking didn't start until his words were moving through the air, and, while George didn't know the exact translation of *meurtriers*, he knew it had something to do with death.

"That is right, Paul," Lina said, placing the tray of meat onto the table between them before tousling Paul's hair. "Meurtriers. They are murderers."

"You don't really believe they kill people just for not agreeing with them, do you?" Roland asked.

"I believe what I have seen," she said. "And I am tired of people telling me what to do. And I am tired of this conversation. So, let's eat a delicious dinner of rationed meat and onions that our *current* occupiers think is worthy of a Christmas meal."

It was unlike any Christmas George had ever seen. The flames of the candles sputtered beneath the drafts that stole through the cracks in the walls, and the plates were all but empty before the meal had even begun—no heaping potatoes or gravy or ham. The faces around the table were weary and starved, but as George raised his glass of wine to propose a toast, looking from one friend to the next, he knew that he'd never seen a more beautiful celebration.

"À la famille!" he said, and when everyone, including Paul, repeated his toast in unison, the warmth and laughter and chatter that filled the room drove out the darkness they'd become so accustomed to.

"It's so good to eat meat again," George said, biting through the gristle and fibers of the beef or chicken it had come from. "This is delicious, Lina. What is it?"

Marcelle slipped her hand over her mouth as Roland snickered under his breath.

"What's so funny?" He paused with his fork halfway to his mouth. "What is this?"

Lina shrugged. "Cheval?"

"Chicken?"

Laughter spilled from the table and filled the corners of the room, seeping through the cold stone walls and rising into the night sky.

"It seems your French lessons are not working," Lina said, winking at Marcelle, whose hand had fallen from her mouth and whose laughter was so beautiful George didn't even mind that it was at his expense.

"Is someone going to tell me what cheval is?"

Paul's body rocked with excitement as he clapped his hands in front of his face.

"Neigh, neigh, neigh . . ."

chapter 21

MARCELLE

March 1919

"Breathe."

Lina's voice was beginning to wear on her, and because nothing could ease the pain, Marcelle panted even faster just to spite her.

"You need to slow your breathing down, Marcelle."

"Go away, Lina!" Marcelle snapped back at her, unable to heed even the simplest of Lina's commands.

Lina wasn't going anywhere, though. She was the only one in the apartment not panicking. Roland had finally taken Paul outside when his rocking had turned into head banging and the volume of his *bébé, bébé, bébé* had begun to rival Marcelle's screams. And George was his own mess of emotions, pacing in the hallway, pulling promises from Lina every five minutes that Marcelle would survive childbirth.

Lina, calm as ever, went about her work, assuring him repeatedly that Marcelle would soon deliver a healthy and robust baby boy. How she could make those promises, Marcelle didn't understand. She was certain she was dying. It didn't seem possible that anyone could survive this kind of trauma to her body.

"He has a very large head, Marcelle." Lina was trying to wipe the sweat from her forehead as Marcelle batted her hands away. "But once you push through it, it will all be over."

"It is not a *he*," Marcelle growled back at her. "Stop saying that."

But Marcelle knew as well as Lina that the baby inside of her was a boy, even if she still prayed for a girl. She wasn't ready for him to come out; she was scared to see his face. What kind of a mother didn't want to meet her son because she was scared to look at his face? But who would she see there?

"Marcelle, you must listen to me now." Lina's tone was suddenly more serious, but Marcelle couldn't focus. She just wanted it to end. She wanted the pain gone; the baby gone. She wanted to rewind her life and make different choices.

"Please, Lina," she begged. "Just make it go away."

"That is not how this works," Lina replied, peeking beneath the sheet covering the bottom half of Marcelle's body and nodding to herself. "It's time. I will be right back."

Marcelle could hear George's muffled voice from the hallway as Lina made him promise that, regardless of the screams and cries coming from the bedroom, he would not enter until she gave him permission. He seemed to acquiesce, although somewhat reluctantly. Lina was ready when she came back in, having gathered a pile of blankets and a pot full of boiled water that had cooled just enough for her touch. She soaked a towel in the water before placing it between Marcelle's legs.

"This will help prevent tearing," she said, and while Marcelle couldn't fathom how Lina would know such a thing, she didn't question her. The warmth of the towel felt nice. She was between contractions, but they were coming so fast, there was little time to rest and gather strength. Lina was right; her body was fatiguing, and she needed to get the baby out.

"I am scared," Marcelle cried. "What if I cannot do it?"

"You must," Lina replied.

The inevitability of it loomed over them, a ticking clock in the background, offering no respite from time. But there was a certain catharsis in giving voice to her fears. Even as Marcelle said the words, *I am scared,* she could feel her own doubt chipping away, cracking from the surface of her skin as if she was emerging from a cocoon.

The final contraction came faster than she had anticipated,

and Marcelle didn't recognize the bellows and moans that escaped her body. They thundered through their tiny apartment, and when they finally ceased, they were replaced with the wailing cries of a furious baby boy.

His howls intensified as Lina rubbed his little body vigorously before placing him on Marcelle's chest. His fists were balled and shaking, and when he turned his head up toward Marcelle, she gasped in awe. He was the most beautiful thing she had ever seen.

"He doesn't look like anyone," she marveled, staring at the scowling red face that was starting to blur from the tears in her eyes. "He just looks like a baby."

George was already by her side, having ignored Lina's orders to wait for the okay. Marcelle didn't know when he had barged through the door, but she was thankful to have him there. "Marcelle, he's perfect." George placed his hand gently over the infant's heaving chest before pulling the blanket around him. "May I?" he asked, and when Marcelle nodded, he lifted the baby into his arms.

"Hello, my boy," he said, rocking the infant and pacing the room. "I am your . . ." He paused before glancing up at Marcelle, suddenly aware of his boldness and the emotions that had begun to carry him away. But Marcelle simply nodded back at him and smiled.

"I am your papa," he said, and as the words came out, the baby stopped fussing and settled into George's arms. Every day, he did something to make Marcelle love him even more, and every day, she felt unworthy of him.

"Thank you, George," she whispered, trying to swallow down her tears.

George placed a kiss on Marcelle's forehead before he smiled down at the baby in his arms and laughed. "What is your maman thanking me for?" he asked the child. "I should be thanking her."

"Come," Lina said, taking the baby from George's arms.

"Let me get him cleaned up so Marcelle can start nursing him." As she walked toward the door, Marcelle could hear her whispering into the baby's ear. "Gabriel, my sweet nephew. You will be a little rascal one day."

"Lina, wait." Marcelle lacked the strength to pull herself up but tilted her head toward the door so she could see the baby. "How did you know . . . well . . . Gabriel was my father's name, and I thought . . ." She paused, trying to remember if she had mentioned her intentions before that moment, but she was certain she hadn't.

"Gabriel is a fine name," Lina replied.

"But how did you know I would name him that?"

Lina simply shrugged and smiled down at the baby. "Look at him," she said. "He just looks like a Gabriel."

chapter 22

June 1919

"Why was I summoned?"

The woman sitting at the front desk of the occupation administration office had no interest in Marcelle, or answers for her. She fidgeted with the curls of her flaxen-colored hair and pinched a rosy blush into her cheeks with her fingertips before she pulled out a handheld mirror and dabbed some color onto her lips.

"Captain Neumann told me to be here first thing this morning. Is he here?" Eliciting a response from her was akin to pulling French from George's mouth. Marcelle had rephrased the question at least five different times before the woman finally nodded to the lone chair sitting against the wall across the room.

"You can wait there if you would like." She was a beautiful woman. There was a softness to her features that Marcelle imagined most men found particularly attractive, a plumpness that was so rarely seen these days. At least not in Soissons. It was likely the reason she was sitting in an office run by German men.

"Should I wait for him?" Marcelle asked, and for the first time in their brief encounter the woman's eyes finally stilled on Marcelle's scarred face.

"It depends," she answered.

"On what?"

Her eyes were so fast when they flashed to the door that

Marcelle wasn't sure if she had just imagined it. "On what you are hiding."

Hours ticked by. Marcelle sat in the lonely chair by the wall and watched the shortening of the noon shadows through the window as she thought about what she was hiding, the secrets that could get them all killed. If Max had known about them, wouldn't he have arrested them already? He had summoned her the previous day when she had gone to pick up her ration card.

Report to the occupation administration office first thing to-morrow morning.

That was the extent of the conversation. She had nodded, taken her card, and walked away. The rest of the day and half the night had been spent lying awake in bed and thinking about the general from the prison in Jaulgonne. Did he know she was there? Had he told Max to summon her? He would always be the wolf that stalked her in the night. She was so certain he would show up one day looking for her that his voice woke her from sleep each morning and the scent of him found her as she slipped into her nightmares each night.

By the time the door opened, Marcelle's fears were refreshed and emboldened, her senses sharpened. But it was not Max. It was a German officer she didn't recognize, whose eyes barely swept over her on their way to the woman across the room. She stood to greet him, her sweater tugging at her curves as she offered him a poorly enunciated *guten Morgen* with a smile that transformed her into the picture of Nordic perfection. Her rouge-kissed cheeks dimpled and her teeth sparkled beneath freshly painted lips. The man made no effort to disguise his desire, leaning onto the desk and whispering something into her ear before placing a box into her hands. She giggled as she pulled the top off to reveal an assortment of chocolates before sending him off with a kiss.

When he disappeared to the back of the building, Marcelle ran a finger along the ridge of her own scarred cheek. Five years she had suffered while this woman had been eating chocolates. She'd been starved, beaten, raped, and tortured, stripped of her beauty, and not one bite of chocolate. Her pride had cost her a hefty price.

She didn't notice when Max walked through the door. It wasn't until the woman behind the desk tempered her smile and dropped her eyes, and the light around her dimmed, that Marcelle realized he was standing there. Watching her.

"You want what she has?"

Marcelle followed his eyes back to the front desk, shaking her head and muttering something about being pleased with everything the Germans had already provided for her, but Max only laughed at her response.

"It was not a test, mademoiselle. But trust me, you do not want what she has. It makes your urine burn."

Marcelle's cheeks flamed. She had no need of a mirror to know that her skin was the color of fire. She offered an apologetic smile to the woman behind the desk that Max was too keen to miss.

"No need to apologize to Jeanne," he said. "She cannot understand us. *Guten Morgen* is the extent of her German, yet she is somehow the secretary of the occupation administration office." He folded his arms across his chest and stepped up to the desk, tilting his head as if studying the woman's face before turning back to Marcelle. "I wonder how she got that job. What do you think, Mademoiselle Marchand? Do you think it was her exceptional transcribing abilities?"

"I do not know, Captain Neumann," Marcelle whispered, unable to hold his gaze without getting trapped in his eyes. The urge to bolt was overwhelming, its viselike grip drawing her toward the door even as fear fought to pin her in place.

"Would you like that job, mademoiselle? It really should be yours."

Marcelle's eyes darted from Max to the chocolates on the desk to the woman who sat behind it. Her face had been drained of its rosy sheen, and, while she may not have understood their words, she knew there was danger in them.

"Unfortunately," Max continued, "I do not have the authority to replace her. But that is not why I called you here today. I have a special job for you. I need a translator."

Marcelle gave him no response. What could she say? No thank you? It was not a request. She had no choice in the matter.

"You can start next week. But first, I would like for you to join me at my home for dinner tomorrow night. Just so we can get to know each other a bit better. Does that suit you?"

"Of course," Marcelle mumbled. "Should I bring my husband?"

She regretted the words the moment they left her mouth, but how else could she save herself from this man's bed? She would not make it easy for him; she hadn't yet shared a bed with the man she called husband. George spent his days stealing kisses from her and wanting her with an urgency that she could feel through every touch and whisper. Day and night, his hands wandered over her body, searching for new places to explore, needing her more and more. It always ended the same: tensed muscles, a searing panic filling her chest, and George's face transforming into nothing but jowls and sagging skin.

"I did not realize you had a husband," Max said, and when his eyes dropped to her belly, Marcelle had to fight off the shame that was endlessly trying to wrap itself around her. She had burned under the judgmental gazes of her neighbors as her belly had grown larger and larger over the months. She'd heard their whispers. Rape or promiscuity. It had made little difference to them, both equally egregious sins in their eyes, and it wasn't until her belly had shrunken away again that the rumors had ceased.

"I apologize," Max said, pulling his eyes back to her face. "Of course you have a husband. I just assumed he was off fighting."

"He has an epileptic disorder."

It took Max a moment to match Marcelle's words to the man he saw standing beside her every month in his ration card line. The man who never spoke.

"Pierre is your husband?"

"Yes, Captain Neumann."

"I see." Marcelle dutifully avoided his gaze as he considered her words. "Of course, then," he finally said. "Bring Pierre. I would like to get to know him better, as well."

~ ~ ~

Fille naïve.

She had been a foolish girl to bring George into that conversation.

Marcelle leaned back against the door of the empty apartment, wishing she could take back her words to Max. Would he have expected something from her? Was that not the reason men called women to the occupation administration office?

Where was everyone?

She peeked her head through the door of the empty bedroom she shared with Lina before returning to the kitchen. When she jiggled the handle to the back door, the tricky one that always stuck, it almost came off in her hand before popping free and leading her to the rickety staircase George had fixed for her.

Marcelle stepped into the blinding sun of the courtyard, where wildflowers flourished around her in a blanket of dazzling colors. The laughter spiraling through the air was the most beautiful thing she had ever heard.

Gabriel's chubby hands were reaching for her when Marcelle's eyes finally adjusted to the light, his fingers opening and closing as he gurgled with excitement, and when George planted a kiss on her cheek and the baby in her arms, she smiled. He was a hefty three-month-old. Despite their rations, he was thriving. He was alert and jubilant, and both Marcelle and George were certain he was the smartest baby who had ever been born.

"What did he want?" George asked, and as Marcelle painted the picture of her day in the occupation administration office, and the invitation to dinner that she couldn't refuse, George nodded along, seemingly unaffected by her words. "It'll be fine," he said, running his hand down the length of her arm. "We'll get through it."

"And what if we don't?"

"Then I'll pack you and Gabriel up and take you somewhere safe. I won't let anything bad happen to you, mon amour. You know that, right?"

Marcelle nodded. She loved that George was always throwing French words into his English. He worked hard to blend in, and he loved her like a husband *should* love a wife, even if that wasn't what they were. When they'd first arrived in Soissons, it had been difficult to parse out her feeling for him: She loved him for staying by her side; she loved him for promising to protect her; she loved him for adoring her son. But after getting to know him, after really seeing him for who he was, she realized that she just loved him.

Marcelle's gaze swept over her tiny garden. She spent hours out there every week, tending to her roses and trimming back her rosemary bushes. George had insisted on planting a few vegetables out there, as well, even though it was forbidden by the Reich. Farming was in his blood, and the tomatoes he grew in their shabby garden were some of the plumpest and most delicious Marcelle had ever eaten. She couldn't fault him for the simple risks he took. She understood the need to own some small portion of his life. She had the same need. It was the reason she had insisted they turn the apartment into a proper home. No one had argued with her. Lina had scavenged for furniture. George and Roland had cleared the debris from the front entrance and affixed a new door that didn't fit quite right but served its purpose. Paul had even gotten involved, assisting George with the staircase, and building up the fallen brick wall so the Germans couldn't see the vegetables he was growing.

Would they be forced to flee this life they had built for themselves together?

When she looked back at the garden, Marcelle could almost see her mother walking away from her own life all those years ago. Had she known she would never return? Would she be proud of the life Marcelle had laid down with her unconventional family? She missed her mother. Not in the way she had missed her when they were separated only by miles, but in the way a soldier missed a limb that had been left on the battlefield. The way Roland was convinced he could sometimes feel the leg that had not been a part of his body in over four years. She could still feel her mother beside her in her quiet moments, especially the ones she spent in her garden. She could still hear the melody of her voice and see the crinkles in the corners of her eyes; she could still smell the rose petals she had once rubbed over her skin.

Marcelle had no desire to be uprooted again. She wanted to see her sister. Nine months had passed since she and Philip had left for the front. She longed to see the expression on Rosalie's face when she walked through the front door of their home, laid eyes on her nephew for the first time, and learned that he'd been named after their father. Would her father have been honored? Would he have loved his grandson, even after knowing what he'd been born from? Would he have been proud of Marcelle for everything she had endured? For leaving the silly girl with her head in the clouds far behind?

She couldn't flee Soissons. Rosalie would return. She knew that with the same certainty that she knew the sun would rise each day. She saw the worried glances over the dinner table when she mentioned Rosalie's name; she heard the hushed whispers when they thought she wasn't listening. But she let them fret. What else could she do? There were no words to explain how she could feel Rosalie's heart beating inside her own chest, or how she could hear Rosalie's words whispering to her through the wind, or how she could see Rosalie's smile in the face of her son.

Rosalie would return.

Marcelle just needed to be there when she did.

chapter 23

The lion didn't flinch. He stared back at her with his teeth clenched around the brass ring as Marcelle tapped it against the door. He had been polished to perfection, his mane flowing in golden waves around his face, and Marcelle felt a tug of jealousy at the door knocker as she reached up and tucked a few stray hairs into the clip that Lina had given to her. Her hair had barely grown since Jaulgonne. Starvation was the culprit. It was like a thief, already robbing her of beauty and dignity and time. She smoothed her hands over her skirt one last time, wiping away the wrinkles.

"Stop fidgeting," George said.

"En français," Marcelle snapped back, refusing to look at him.

George was nervous. They were both nervous. They had spent the afternoon bickering at each other, Marcelle scolding him for repeatedly slipping back into English and George endlessly frustrated with her edginess. Stress pulled them each in opposite directions, and George's suggestion that he take the lead during their dinner with Max, since, as he stated, he could calm even the most agitated of mares, had left Marcelle fuming. She hadn't uttered a single word since that conversation. She did not appreciate being compared to a horse.

But the silence was lonely, and the walk was long. The chateau that Max inhabited was on the outskirts of town and one that

Marcelle had only seen from a distance when she was a child. Somehow, despite all the destruction to the rest of the town, the Germans had managed to preserve the homes that would afford them the most luxury and elegance and discretion.

George slipped his hand into hers just moments before the door opened, just moments before the panic that had been rising from within her gut was able to claw its way out. His hand was cool and dry in hers, making the contrast of her warm and clammy skin more obvious. Maybe he was right. Maybe she was like one of his horses, panicked and untamed.

The woman standing in the doorway wore an unwelcoming scowl. Marcelle recognized her as a local from Soissons, one of the many women to have been offended by her once swollen belly. Marcelle could still hear the muttering of their disparaging comments and the clucking of their tongues whenever she and George joined the ration card line. They all knew that George was not a local, that he was not Pierre.

They followed the woman through the house, which was both stately and warm. The walls were adorned with bronze sconces that each burned a paraffin gas lamp and led them to the living quarters, where rich tapestries were laid out on the floors and above the mantel of the fireplace. Matching sofas sat like bookends on either side of a massive hand-woven rug that would have covered the entirety of George and Marcelle's apartment. And the aroma from the kitchen was almost unbearable. Marcelle had no control over her body's reaction to it, her mouth salivating, her stomach groaning, her hands trembling.

"Welcome, Marcelle!" Max's booming voice found them before he did. When he rounded the corner, Marcelle was surprised to see him in his uniform, a pistol holstered at his waist. "And Pierre. Welcome to my home."

Max welcomed George with a handshake and Marcelle with a kiss on the cheek before gesturing to the sofas.

"Pierre does not speak German, Captain Neumann." Marcelle stepped over the fleur-de-lis design that had been woven into the rug at her feet and settled onto the sofa beside George.

"Ah, well, I guess you will have to teach him. Pretty soon everyone will be speaking German. But in the meantime, we must find a way to communicate. Pierre, do you speak English?"

Marcelle's smile slipped as she considered the question. Max's English was both articulate and precise, a subtle British inflection threading its way through his German accent. He was an educated man, a dangerous threat.

"A little." George's response was equally shocking, his fake French accent almost comical. If anyone but a German had been listening, they would have found it humorous, or perhaps offensive.

"And Marcelle? English?"

Marcelle nodded.

"You are a curious woman, Marcelle," Max continued. "French, German, English. Full of surprises. You would make the perfect spy."

Marcelle froze, the air suddenly heavy and forcing her down with a weight she was certain would soon crush her. Her mouth was parched, and her throat was dry, and when she swallowed, the gulp was audible through the silence. There was no panic reflected back at her from George's eyes though when he turned to her with a puzzled expression on his face.

"Quel est ce mot?" His French was perfectly timed and impeccably spoken, before he switched back to English. "What is meaning? This word? Spy?"

Quel est ce mot?

How many times had she asked this question of him?

What is this word?

Marcelle responded in French with words George had never heard until that moment. He nodded along and smiled, as if he could understand them, waiting until she finished her explanation, and then collapsed into laughter.

"A woman spy?" When he pointed his finger at her, Marcelle could feel the heat rising into her cheeks, but she wasn't certain if it was humiliation or anger that she felt. George repeated the question, looking to Max for comradery, inviting him to join in. Which he did, with gusto, slapping his leg with his hand and roaring with laughter, as if it was the most ridiculous thing he had ever heard. Tears were streaming down both of their faces by the time they had worn themselves out, and Marcelle glared at them openly, somewhat surprised by the sudden attraction she felt for George.

He had made an alliance with Max. Against her, true, but it was a brilliant move. He played this game better than anyone, and for the first time since Jaulgonne, she felt a stirring inside herself for the touch of a man. For George.

When the maid returned with a tray of wine and hors d'oeuvres, Max was the only one who ate. There were plates enough for all of them, but Marcelle and George dared not reach for them. Max picked a thin slice of salted ham from the tray, the smoky aroma infusing Marcelle's senses, and she could almost feel the texture of the salt on her tongue when he placed it in his mouth.

"Has Marcelle shared the exciting news, Pierre?" he asked as he chewed the meat and swallowed it down. "She's going to be my personal interpreter."

"Yes," George replied. "Very good news."

"Very good news, indeed. In fact," he said, winking at Marcelle before continuing, "with her background as a spy, we might have other uses for her as well. I hear that spies, especially beautiful French ones, are very good at getting information from prisoners."

Marcelle tried to smile, but her lips twitched and the heat that was spreading through her body was threatening to boil over, and it wasn't until Max turned his attention back to George that she allowed herself to breathe again.

"Tell me, Pierre," he said, as Marcelle wiped the sweat from her upper lip and tucked her trembling hands beneath her thighs, "what work are you doing for the Reich?"

"No job," George replied, pointing to his head with the tip of his finger. "I have disorder and no skill."

"No skills? That cannot be true. Marcelle would not have married a man who had no skills. What did you do before the war? You must have worked, no?"

George turned to Marcelle. The question seemed to knock him off balance, and she knew he didn't have an answer. She slowly translated the question into French words that George couldn't understand, giving him time to formulate a response and trusting him to save them, to charm his way through this interminable night.

"Farmer," he finally replied, coughing into his fist. "I was farmer before war. And horse trainer."

"A farmer? And how does a farmer with no skills learn English?"

"My wife, of course," George laughed, turning to Marcelle with a smile. "The spy."

"Ah, yes, of course! Well, I am glad I got to see you, Pierre, because there is a punishment for all able-bodied men not assisting the Reich. But not to worry. I can get you work. If your English was better, perhaps office work, but with your farming background, I'm afraid it will probably be field labor. Unless your horse skills prove to be superior to our current stable master's. He doesn't seem to know the first thing about horses."

"I know horses," George replied. "I can try."

Marcelle ran her fingers along the scratchy fabric of the couch as George nodded along to Max's words and thanked him profusely for his generosity and kindness. She tried to envision the family that had once sat in this room, upon these couches, beneath the glow of the sconce lights. Had they watched from afar as their home had been taken, or had they fought for it despite the inevitable outcome? It wasn't until

George nudged her leg that she realized Max had been talking to her, asking about her brother.

"The one with the bandage? What ever happened to him? And your beautiful sister?"

Dead? Should she pronounce Philip dead? Tell him the infection from his wound was too far along to be stopped? But then, what of Rosalie? Where would her sister have run off to all alone?

"They went back to Paris to look for our parents." Marcelle folded her hands together in her lap and stared down at them. "We all fled to Paris when Soissons was first taken, and then were separated during the recent bombings. The three of us came back here thinking they would do the same, but, so far, we have heard no news of them. They should have returned home by now."

"I am sorry to hear that. I have heard that Paris was heavily bombed. I hope they have luck."

"Thank you," Marcelle whispered, slightly thrown off by the sincerity in his voice. As the evening had worn on, she had found herself wanting to stay; wanting to take comfort in the deep timbre of his voice; wanting to be consoled by someone who didn't need his own consoling. He reminded Marcelle of her uncle, her mother's younger brother who had always been asking her about school, and friends, and boys. But Max was a dangerous man, and Marcelle was falling into a dangerous trap.

"What about you, Pierre?" Max nodded to George before he sipped on his wine. "I know you have your sister, Lina. But are there other brothers and sisters? Or parents?"

His eyes were like a serpent's, fixed on George even as he reached toward the tray for a bite of cheese. Was he baiting them? Did he already know the answers to these questions? He must have seen hundreds of faces per week, yet he knew the details of both George's and Marcelle's lives so intimately, it almost seemed he'd been studying them.

"My parent die in Paris," George replied. "My sister and me, we come back here."

"Ah, well. I am terribly sorry for you both. So much loss. But you have Marcelle now. And your beautiful son, Gabriel. So fair. He must get that from Marcelle."

"Yes," George replied, smiling at Marcelle. "From his beautiful mother."

"A toast to Gabriel, then." Max picked up his wineglass and held it high in the air before noticing neither of them was drinking. "You haven't touched your wine."

Marcelle reached reluctantly for one of the two glasses that still sat on the tray between them, unable to still the fine tremor in her hand as she lifted it into the air. How did he know her son's name? How did he know everything about them? When she turned to George, he was tapping his finger to his head and sighing in mock exaggeration.

"Not for me. Bad fits with wine."

"Ah, yes, of course," Max replied. "But surely just one sip will not cause problems? We must toast your new arrival."

George nodded as he reached for the last glass on the tray and then held it up triumphantly between them. "You are right," he said. "One sip. For my son."

When they clinked their glasses together, Marcelle understood that there was a certain significance to the moment. There was a thread, however delicate, that now bound them together. What she couldn't know, what she wouldn't find out for years to come, was the circuitous route that thread had taken to ensnare them.

chapter 24

September 1919

It was well into September when Marcelle finally got the message she'd been waiting for. The radio hadn't stopped buzzing since early morning, and while most of the correspondence didn't concern them in Soissons, she was always tuned in to the traffic across the airwaves. Of all her responsibilities at work, manning the radio was Marcelle's favorite. It was a mindless job, placing her in a back room of the occupation administration office where she transcribed messages from across the country. Most of the transmissions came from the front, and they were invariably about supply trains or prison transports that would be coming through Soissons and other towns on their way to work camps in Germany. Nothing top secret and certainly nothing that couldn't be trusted to local Frenchwomen who could speak German.

Marcelle's least favorite job was also the one that made her rather unpopular with the locals: interrogator. Max would often send her in alone to gather information from prisoners, especially French ones, and it was a constant balancing act. She couldn't emerge empty-handed; he'd made it clear that if she couldn't produce information for him, she would be as useless as the secretary at the front desk with the tight sweaters. She did her best to keep her countrymen safe, often omitting information that could get them tortured, or worse, but she was a villain either way. When a prisoner was beaten, it didn't matter if she had saved his life by risking her own, that his response would have gotten him killed if it had been accurately translated. She would always be a traitor in their eyes.

Marcelle had other things to worry about, though. What were whispers and rumors when the general from Jaulgonne was still out there looking for her, offering a handsome reward for her capture? With each disbanded resistance cell, she heard the chatter over the radio:

> *Was the witch of the river among them?*
> *Had she been recaptured?*
> *Had she already vanished into thin air?*

Everyone wanted to know about *die Hexe des Flusses*. Chains around Marcelle's wrists would have offered no better control than what Max already had on her. Fear was an effective restraint. He'd been sitting by her side the last time her description had been broadcast over the radio, and while he'd at least had the decency to turn it off shortly after they got to the part about the scar running down her left cheek, he'd made it clear that her protection was dependent on her usefulness to him.

Marcelle turned up the volume on the receiver as she jotted down the information that was being transmitted, the news coming from the front that had piqued her interest. It wasn't intended for her. It was being dispatched from Moulins and directed to a radio operator in Paris. A resistance group had been disbanded and there was a female among them. In the three months she'd been tracking prisoner movements, Marcelle had only come across a handful of females, and they'd all been part of the resistance, sent to a facility outside of Paris for questioning.

None of the previous women had fit Rosalie's description, and while Marcelle doubted her sister would have gotten involved with the resistance, she always paid attention. There hadn't been word from Rosalie or Philip since they'd left for Moulins almost a year earlier. Marcelle knew her sister was still alive, but what she feared, more with each passing day, was that some sort of tragedy had befallen her.

"Approximately eight kilometers north of Moulins. Five males. All early twenties. French." The transmission was peppered with static, but Marcelle frantically jotted down each word she could understand. *"One female. Early twenties. French. Transport scheduled for tomorrow. Await transport time."*

Marcelle's pulse was thundering through her head by the time the radio went silent. Could it be Rosalie? She reached for the transmitter just as a blast of noise erupted from the radio, startling her. She'd forgotten to turn the volume down, and as she listened to a transmission between Tours and Reims about a supply train, she worked out the details in her mind about the call she was about to make. If it was indeed Rosalie, she'd need a plan to get her back to Soissons.

"Soissons to Moulins." Marcelle's voice cracked as she spoke into the transmitter.

"This is Moulins," a woman replied.

"I have a request from Hauptman Neumann for information on two of your resistance prisoners being transported to Paris in the morning. Could you please call over the telephone wire when you have a moment?"

There was no response from Moulins, and Marcelle wondered if she'd somehow made a blunder with her request. She'd heard other radio operators request wired telephone calls in the past, so she knew it was done, but she'd never made one herself and if there was a protocol for it, she didn't know what it was. She imagined the other women sitting by their radios and cringing at her ignorance. She startled again when the phone beside her buzzed in two rapid successions.

"Soissons," she answered.

"This is Moulins. You requested a call?"

"Yes, thank you," Marcelle replied, infusing her voice with a honey-laden sweetness, and switching from German to French, a small reminder to the woman on the other end of the line that they were, in fact, on the same side. "Captain Neumann has been trying to locate two locals from Soissons, a brother and sister who left town last year. He asked me to reach out to see if they were among your prisoners being transported to Paris in the morning."

"Of course," the woman replied in French. "Do you have their names?"

"Joseph and Rosalie Marchand."

Marcelle could hear the rustling of papers on the other end of the telephone. "Give me just a moment," the woman mumbled. "I have the transport orders here somewhere."

"It sounds like you are busy down there," Marcelle said, thickening the sweetness of her words and inflating her praise even as she struggled to calm the hammering of her heart inside her chest. "I cannot imagine working near the front. You must have nerves of steel."

"It is not as exciting as it may seem," the woman laughed. "Just busywork, really. Here it is. Yes. Your captain is correct. Joseph and Rosalie Marchand."

The woman kept talking, but Marcelle could no longer hear her words. She couldn't quite grasp the information she was receiving. After all this time, she'd finally found her sister. But in a resistance group? If Rosalie got off that train in Paris, it wouldn't be long before the Germans would figure out who she was and the general would be knocking down Marcelle's door. She had to get them rerouted; she had to somehow convince this woman that, come morning, Joseph and Rosalie Marchand needed to be on a transport to Soissons.

"Captain Neumann has a request for those two particular prisoners," Marcelle said, tempering the panic she could hear threading its way through her words. "He would like for them to be rerouted to Soissons. Is that a request that I can make through you?"

"I will need permission to reroute them," the woman replied. "I will have Major Beck contact Captain Neumann this afternoon. It should not be a problem."

"Oh dear," Marcelle lamented into the phone. "Captain Neumann is gone for the day. He will be so angry if I cannot get this done. I suppose I should have anticipated this. He asked me to get them rerouted, and I did not realize . . ." Marcelle sighed, letting her words drift off and welcoming the uncomfortable silence between them. Very few people could tolerate that silence.

"Well, I suppose . . ." The woman hesitated before she finally relented. "I suppose I could try."

"I hate to ask that of you," Marcelle continued. "But I don't know what else to do. Do you think you could talk to your major? Captain Neumann will not be very forgiving of me if those prisoners are not rerouted."

"I cannot make any promises," the woman said. "But I will see what I can do."

Max was already in the office when Marcelle arrived to work the following morning. That rarely happened. She had spent the previous night chasing her thoughts through a labyrinth of scenarios from which there was no escape, and when she had finally dragged herself from bed at the first hint of dawn, she was no closer to a solution. She was in quite a predicament. Whether or not Rosalie was on that transport from Moulins, Marcelle's day was about to get complicated.

Max didn't look up at her from his desk where he was signing orders but gestured to the chair across from him with his hand. Marcelle sat, her movements quiet and tamed as she folded her hands together in her lap and stared down at them.

"Did you forget to relay a message to me yesterday?"

The question hung between them as Marcelle considered a response. There were no alternate routes through this mine field, no way for her to get her sister back without Max. When she finally looked up at him, she was surprised by the lack of anger in his expression.

"Yes, Captain Neumann," she whispered, before dropping her gaze back to her hands.

"Imagine my surprise when Major Beck approved my request for the rerouting of two resistance prisoners." When Marcelle didn't respond, Max simply laughed. "You are a different breed of woman, Marcelle. I think I could study you forever and never quite figure you out."

Was she? Was she any different than any other mother or wife or sister? Didn't they all do what needed to be done to protect the ones they loved?

"Are you really a witch?" he said, and when Marcelle didn't respond again, he slammed his hand onto the desk between them. "Look at me!" There was still no anger in his eyes when she met his gaze. Frustration, maybe. Annoyance. "How do you do it?" he asked. "How do you seduce people into doing what you want?"

Marcelle didn't have an answer for him. It wasn't a skill that could be taught, and it wasn't exactly seduction. She only ever asked people to do what she knew they wanted to do. That was the only magic involved. If the woman on the other end of the line had wanted to be praised for her discipline to the Reich, Marcelle would have spoken to her in German and suggested they figure out a way to go through the proper channels. But she hadn't wanted that. She'd wanted to be Marcelle's savior. She'd wanted to seem important and brave and in charge. So Marcelle had given that to her.

"I do not suppose I will ever understand you," Max sighed, before returning to the orders on his desk. "Your sister will be here this afternoon. She will be released to your custody, along with the man whom you claim to be your brother."

"Thank you, Captain Neumann," Marcelle gushed, and though she tried to maintain her composure, she couldn't temper her excitement.

Max paused, his pen hovering above the order he was about to sign as he considered his next words. "I can see why you think this is a good thing," he said. "But do not allow your emotions to cloud your judgment, Marcelle. You have put yourself in terrible danger. Your sister and brother will be watched closely. They will be under constant surveillance and one wrong move from either of them will be on your head. Every choice they make puts everyone in your house at risk. Including your son."

The excitement she'd felt just moments earlier had been replaced with an equal amount of dread. What had she done? Max was right; she didn't even know Philip. He was likely planning his next escape attempt at that very moment and wouldn't think twice about leaving them behind.

"But I cannot control what they do," she stammered. "Surely you cannot expect me to be their warden. I barely even . . ." *I barely even know him* was the thought she managed to keep from spilling out between them. Did Max already know that?

"Actions have consequences, Marcelle," he replied, turning back to the orders on his desk. "You of all people should know that."

chapter 25

GEORGE

September 1919

"I knew you'd miss me."

Philip was back. News from the front was grim. The Germans had created a new system of elaborate trenches that had been matched by the Allies, and both sides were dug in again.

The Americans were still in the fight, but with the recent upgrades to the German warplanes, the additional Allied troops had little effect. George could still see the giant Albatross planes in his sleep, drifting overhead and blocking out the sun. He couldn't imagine what they had been turned into. How could such a machine be upgraded?

Philip and Roland's plan to snag a German uniform had turned out to be a dead end. According to Philip, they weren't the first ones to come up with the idea.

"Even if I could have gotten my hands on one," he said, "I'd have never made it through. Everyone was checked and questioned. There were a lot of Americans and Brits stuck on this side after the battle, and they were all trying to get back to their units. The Germans were expecting us."

The room felt infinitely smaller in Philip's presence, but there was also a familiarity to his company that George hadn't realized he'd missed. And to Rosalie's. There was an easy connection between her and Philip now, the way they communicated without words and caught each other's eyes from across the room.

"The Germans won't last long," Roland grumbled, shrugging off Philip's news. "They can sit in their trenches and think they've won, but when the Bolsheviks come in, we will send them home. Or, better yet, destroy them all."

Roland's radicalization was escalating by the day, and his hatred for the Germans was putting them all at risk. He and Lina could barely tolerate being in the same room together anymore. Lina left home every morning, Paul by her side, and didn't return until almost dark. No one knew where they went, but they almost always returned with something useful. Flour, paraffin, fabric.

"You better be careful, Roland," Philip said. "The checkpoints throughout the country are heavily guarded, and they're sending in the shock troops to deal with uprisings throughout the occupied territory." He nodded toward George. "You remember those troops, right, George?"

Sturmtruppen.

If Roland had faced off against the shock troops on the battlefield like they had, Philip's words might have had more sting. The Sturmtruppen were the same elite forces they'd battled along the Marne River the summer before last.

It was strange to imagine Philip and Rosalie had been out there all this time. George had buried Rosalie in his mind months ago, certain she was dead. They all had, except Marcelle. Marcelle had welcomed her sister home with a kiss on each cheek and a brief but firm hug before sitting her at the table and heading to the stove to boil a pot of tea.

Gabriel loved the commotion in the house. New faces, new voices, new smells. He laughed and drooled, showing off the two bottom teeth that had just popped up over the last few weeks, as Rosalie bounced him on her lap.

"Mon ange!" Rosalie was already enamored with her nephew, not even allowing Marcelle to take him when he fussed. "Gabriel," she said. "Papa would have been so proud, Marcelle."

"Would he?" Marcelle's eyes dropped to her son as she set

the tea in front of her sister and slid onto the chair across from them at the table.

"Do not talk like that. You should be proud of the way you have survived this war. Look at this home you have made for yourself and your son. Your garden is as beautiful as Maman's."

"We have all done it together. Lina and Roland and even Paul. And George, of course. I would not have survived without him."

George was eavesdropping. Marcelle and Rosalie never spoke to each other in English, so he'd never been privy to their conversations, until today. He'd worked hard on his French lessons, and, while he couldn't quite pass for a Frenchman, not much got by him these days.

"And how is married life?" Rosalie sipped her tea and eyed Marcelle over the rim of the chipped ceramic mug. "What is it like going to bed with a husband every night?"

"Maybe you should ask my husband." Marcelle's eyes flashed over to George, who gave her a knowing smile.

"C'est fantastique," he said, winking at Marcelle and making her cheeks flush.

"Mon Dieu!" Rosalie exclaimed. "This house will be filled with babies soon."

Marcelle's laughter was as sweet as the day George had met her in the Montmirail train station, the girlish lilt bringing him back to the confident and carefree woman who hadn't feared anyone or anything. He had tried so hard to give that back to her, but, all this time, it was Rosalie she'd needed. She had so rarely talked about her sister that George had unwittingly overlooked her importance. He wouldn't make that mistake again.

"The Bolsheviks are coming." Roland hadn't given up yet, still trying to sell communism to Philip and recruit him to their next meeting. "Even the Germans are welcoming Lenin with open arms. They are starving with the rest of Europe."

"I guess if they can figure out how to keep everyone fed," Philip replied, with a shrug. "What's the harm in trying?"

"But the problem is that the Germans are forcing us to fight with them," Roland continued. "I have been ordered to report for training next month. Can you imagine? First they take my leg and then they want me to fight with them? I would rather die. Even Paul has been summoned."

As if on cue, Paul came bustling through the front door with Lina, who almost dropped the package in her arms at the shock of seeing Philip in her living room. Lina, who guarded her emotions with the skill of a sentinel, couldn't even find the words to welcome Rosalie home. She tucked the package into the pantry in the kitchen before offering Rosalie a quick peck on the cheek and Philip a nod. Paul, ever tuned in to Lina's emotions, rocked silently in the corner.

"You don't look happy to see me, Lina." Philip winked at her from across the room.

"What girl would not be happy to see your handsome face?" Lina sank down onto one of the chairs beside him at the table and pulled out a stub of a half-smoked cigarette. "But your handsome face sitting in my living room tells me that things are not good at the front."

"It depends what you mean by good," Philip said, striking a match and holding the flame between them as Lina leaned in and lit the end of her cigarette. "Things are very good for the Germans."

"Yes, well, at least someone is having a nice year." She blew a curl of smoke into the air that hung over them in a thick cloud.

"The Germans will be gone by this time next year," Roland said, reaching for Lina's cigarette and taking a quick puff before she could snatch it back from him.

"Get your own cigarettes," Lina said.

"I would. But then I would have to collaborate with the enemy."

"Do not listen to him, Philip. He will have you speaking Russian in no time."

"It is better than German," Roland snapped back at her.

Evenings were unpleasant, to say the least. They devolved rapidly into a back-and-forth between Lina and Roland that persisted until one of them, typically Lina, finally walked away. In front of Philip and Rosalie, Lina once again proved herself the bigger person by not taking Roland's bait. She shrugged off his words and took another puff from her cigarette before blowing out the smoke between them and glaring at him through the stagnant air.

"I suppose we will have to wait and see."

chapter 26

"What month do all soldiers hate?"

George was trying to ignore Philip as they hauled water from the well to the horse corrals. Philip had somehow managed to stick to his deaf-and-dumb routine to avoid being summoned for military training with the Germans, and George had gotten him work at the corrals, insisting his brute strength would be ideal for hauling hay and water and supplies. Max had signed off on the request without question. George hadn't lost one horse since he'd become stable master, and Max was constantly being praised for his ability to supply the Reich with the most obedient and fit steeds to ride into battle. The horses were doomed either way, and George struggled daily with his predicament: let the horses starve to death or prepare them for war.

"March."

George didn't laugh. He never laughed at Philip's jokes, even the funny ones. Philip was getting him into trouble at home, sneaking off to the cellar across the street from their apartment with Rosalie each night. Neither Marcelle nor Lina approved of the situation, and they put it on George to handle, but what could he do? Philip and Rosalie were grown adults.

Marcelle was constantly on edge, waiting for Philip to make a break for it. But Philip wasn't that kind of man. He had given Marcelle his word that he would behave, and Marcelle reluctantly kept her mouth shut when he slipped off with her sister each night after the sun went down.

They'd been in France for almost two years now, and George was beginning to wonder if they would ever make it back home. It wasn't until Philip and Rosalie brought news back to Soissons from the front that he'd really considered he might never leave, that he'd really let it sink in. It was only then that he'd realized how badly he wanted to go home.

"You ready?"

Philip was standing over him, blocking out the sun behind him like an impenetrable and slow-moving cloud. George finished clipping the wire fence he'd been mending before dropping the tools back into the shed and following Philip toward the walking path.

"Did you hear the one about the tank that ran over a box of Cracker Jacks?"

He couldn't even offer five minutes of silence. Talking was as vital to Philip as breathing, and though he'd learned a good bit of French while in Moulins, he almost always conversed with George in English. George glanced around to make sure they were out of earshot before shaking his head.

"Killed two kernels. God rest their souls."

"That was horrible. Did you come up with that one all by yourself?"

"All originals, my friend."

They were almost to the cathedral when George slowed his pace, trying to find the right words to start a conversation that he was reluctant to bring home to the others. It was an idea that had been floating through his thoughts, but he hadn't yet figured out how to turn it into a plan. Marcelle was probably better suited for strategizing than Philip, but George suspected she would have shut this idea down faster than the Germans had barreled through Soissons.

"What do you think about Max?" he asked.

Philip didn't answer. He just shrugged his shoulders and

kept on walking, his boots shuffling over the uneven cobbled stones leading from the horse corrals on the edge of town.

"Do you think he's a decent guy?"

"I think he's a German," Philip replied.

"Well, obviously he's a German. But he seems like a nice enough guy. What if we could convince him to help us get out of this place?"

"Out of what place?"

"France, of course." George stopped walking and glanced back down the path to make sure it was, indeed, empty. Part of the reason Soissons stayed so peaceful was because its people were adept at making themselves invisible. "What if he was willing to help us?"

"The problem with you, George, is that you have no respect for your enemy."

"What's that supposed to mean?"

"It means that Max is not your friend. He's a lonely son of a bitch who keeps you around for his entertainment. And because you make him look good with the horses. He just dances you around like a puppet, pulling your strings."

George tried not to laugh as Philip hopped from one foot to the other and dangled his arms like a puppet's. For all his bravery, Philip was not a strategist. George should have known better than to pull him into this.

"What do you know?" he mumbled, moving along the path as Philip continued to dance around him. He should have just kept his mouth shut. He should have known that Philip would have no inclination to ally himself with a German, even if it meant escaping France. Max would be his own puzzle to work out. Intuition was a tricky thing though, just a guess really, a game of equal odds. If he was right, Max could end up being the key to unlocking their freedom. But, if he was wrong, the consequences would be as far-reaching as they were severe. No one he loved would be left untouched.

"I know that Max and I have a mutual understanding," Philip

said, finally settling down. "I don't trust him, and he doesn't trust me. I keep up my imbecile charade, and he pretends he doesn't know any better."

"We need to be thinking about how to get out of here."

"It's not as easy as you think," Philip said. "Moving around the country is tricky. Especially when you don't speak French well. The resistance group we joined couldn't do anything to get us across the border, and by the time Rosalie and I decided to come back to Soissons, it was impossible to get through the checkpoints. I don't know that I would have made it back here if we hadn't been arrested and Marcelle hadn't worked her magic." Philip kicked at a rock on the ground and George's eyes followed it as it skipped into the weeds. "It all seems kind of pointless now anyway."

"What do you mean?"

"I don't know," Philip replied. "It's hard to explain. But it's almost like there's no point in fighting anymore. It's like we lost our chance, and we can't win. And I know you don't agree with me, but I still can't shake the feeling that I was meant to defend that hill on the side of the Marne River during that battle with the Germans. And everything that's happened after that moment is just . . . I don't know . . . *off* in some way."

"You're still thinking about that?" George would never admit it, but he'd been dreaming about that battle recently. In fact, just the previous night, he'd woken in quite a state, sweating and trembling. But this time, instead of pushing Philip down the hill and saving him from the approaching Germans, he had left him there to die. He hadn't even told Marcelle about it. She had her own nightmares to battle, and he certainly didn't want Philip knowing he spent any time dwelling on the choices he'd made that night.

"It was my destiny," Philip continued. "And I didn't do it. And now, no matter what I do, it won't make any difference, because I've already failed."

"You didn't fail. You survived."

"You don't understand."

"I do understand," George replied. "You wanted to be the hero. But you still can be. You can still fight against the Germans in other ways, free yourself from this place and even have Rosalie by your side."

"I don't want Rosalie."

Philip's voice echoed through the empty cathedral square. George hadn't realized they'd already reached it. They were just a couple of blocks from their apartment now, and he glanced down the empty streets to be sure no one had heard Philip's words.

"Look," Philip sighed. "I care about Rosalie. I really do. She's a wonderful person and I don't want to hurt her. But my heart will always be with Dorothy. I'm not here to fall in love. I've already done that. And I'm not looking to be a hero. I wasn't supposed to come out of that battle. I wasn't supposed to end up here in Soissons with you and Rosalie and Marcelle. And, no matter how much I love her, I wasn't even supposed to return home to Dorothy."

The house was quiet when George opened the front door. He'd left Philip with Rosalie by the cellar before making his way across the street to their apartment, where Lina was at the stove stirring whatever was left in the pot from yesterday's supper. Paul was sitting by the window, rocking, and staring out at the street below. No one else was home.

"Where is Philip?" Lina asked, before glancing back at George and reading his expression. She sighed into the soup and shook her head. "They are like rats hiding in that cellar. I would never allow Philip to do that to me."

"They're in love," George replied, sinking onto one of the chairs at the table. "Love makes you do desperate things."

"They are not in love." Lina pulled out a nub of a cigarette before taking the spot across from George. "Dorothy is the only woman Philip has ever loved."

"Philip told you about Dorothy?" Lina was right, of course, but how could she possibly have known that? She took a puff from the cigarette before handing it to George.

"Not yet," she said. The cigarette burned George's fingers as he tried to take a puff before Lina took it back and stubbed it out. She added whatever was left of it into her tobacco pouch and placed it on the shelf above the stove. "Philip and I used to be lovers," she added nonchalantly. "So I know all kinds of things about him."

"What are you talking about?" George choked out the words, coughing into his fist and pounding on his chest. "When? I can't believe he didn't tell me this."

Lina laughed as she went back to the pot on the stove. "He would not remember it," she said. "It was a long time ago."

"You can't say things like that, Lina." George continued to pound on his chest, struggling to catch his breath. "You're going to get him into trouble with Rosalie. How do you know about Dorothy, anyway?"

"I already told you," Lina said. "Philip and I were lovers the last time we were here. Rosalie was much more pious back then. She would never have snuck off to a cellar, married or not."

"What do you mean, *the last time we were here*?"

"How do you think I know so much about surviving this world? I am not yet even eighteen, but I know where to find food and cigarettes when the rest of you do not. I know how to outsmart German soldiers. I know how to deliver a baby. Why do you think I know these things?"

George didn't have an answer for her. She was right. She was far savvier than the rest of them, and if not for her, they probably wouldn't be thriving as they were.

"Are you saying you've already been through all of this before?" Lina smiled in response, but even as George considered it, he knew it wasn't possible. "I think maybe you've lost your mind," he said. "Is there some reason you're telling me all of this?"

"Because you are different from the others, George. I tried talking to Roland when I first came back, but he thinks my mind is gone from the stress of war." Lina stepped up to Paul, who was still sitting in the window, and ran her hand through his hair. She was the only one who could touch Paul's head without him throwing a fit. "And I am worried about you. I think perhaps you are getting too close to Max."

"What do you mean?"

"Max is the one variable I cannot control," Lina replied. "I don't know what he will do or how he will react in certain situations, because he was not here last time."

"Where was he?"

"I let him die," Lina said. "The first time I was here, I let him drown in the river."

George leaned back into his chair, almost embarrassed he'd let the conversation go on as long as it had, ashamed that he'd encouraged it in any way. Lina had been through a lot; it was no wonder she was a bit unbalanced. Roland had been trying to convince them that something was wrong with her, but, since he and Lina were constantly bickering with each other, and each endlessly trying to win the group's favor, he'd shrugged it off as petty jealousy.

"Let's talk about something else," George said. "There's been too much talk of Max already today."

"I don't know what your intentions are with Max," Lina continued, ignoring George's request. "But I am worried that you and Marcelle are spending too much time with him. That you are too trusting of him."

"What are you talking about?"

"Shortly before you and the others showed up in Soissons, I rescued Max from the Aisne River. He'd been thrown from his horse on one of the footbridges, and I ran downstream with a branch to save him."

"And what does that have to do with me and Marcelle?"

"Max owes me," Lina replied. "And he is the one who gets me my supplies. But what he doesn't know is that the first time we were here, I let him die. I let him drown because he was a German."

"So why did you save him this time?"

"I don't know why I saved him," Lina sighed. "Before I died and came back, I kept having dreams about him, about saving him in the river. And I just knew, when I woke up here, that I was sent back to do it." She glanced back at Paul to make sure he wasn't paying attention to their conversation before lowering her voice. "I couldn't keep Paul alive last time," she said. "I think that might be the reason I was meant to save Max this time. I think he is the one who will help me change Paul's destiny."

"You think you died and came back to life?" Maybe Roland had been right. Maybe the stress of war had taken a heavy toll on Lina, and the others had failed to notice because they were too busy with their own traumas.

"I don't expect you to believe me, George. But you need to understand what it means that I saved Max's life. He is indebted to me now. The way he sees it, he owes me for his life. But he is still a German. He still has the potential to be a very dangerous man. I don't know if he is helping me out of graciousness or gratitude, but either way, he is not someone to be trifled with. You must be careful with him, and you must never let him know that you are an American."

chapter 27

"Why won't you listen to me?" Gabriel was propped upon Lina's hip as she trailed George through their tiny apartment and battered him with questions that sounded more like accusations. "Why are you going to his house again?"

"Because he's Marcelle's boss," George replied, struggling to mask the ire that was stabbing through his words. "And he invited us. And he can have us killed if he wants to for nothing more than not showing up."

Gabriel was whining. It was his first birthday, and he wanted to be in the kitchen with his tante Rosalie baking a cake with the extra flour and butter rations that Lina had secured. He reached his hands out to George, wiggling his way out of Lina's grasp.

"Viens, mon chou." George lifted him over his head and tossed him into the air, the sound of his laughter luring his mother out from the bedroom.

Spring was stunning on Marcelle, the sun still flush in her cheeks from her morning in the garden. Her curves were beginning to soften with all the extra rations Max passed on to them, and, while Marcelle avowed herself a traitor for taking them, she never said no. "When are you going to say *papa*?" George whispered into Gabriel's ear. "Hmm?"

"You are trying too hard," Marcelle laughed, and at the sound of his mother's voice, Gabriel started his squirming again, his squeaky voice calling out for his maman.

No one could compete with Marcelle. He'd been saying "maman" for weeks, and George had been in a constant battle with Lina and Rosalie to be next, none of them above bribery. In truth, he wouldn't have been surprised if the next word out of Gabriel's mouth was "Paul." He loved Paul and could oftentimes be found rocking beside him on the floor, the two of them chanting in perfect harmony.

Maman, maman, maman . . .

"Gabriel." Lina was trying to lure him into the kitchen. "You want a taste of sugar from your tante Lina? Can you say *Lee*na?"

Marcelle was almost jubilant on the road to Max's house, pointing out all the varieties of flowers that were in bloom and enunciating them with such clarity that George wondered if he might be quizzed on them later.

Max was a lonely man. Philip had been right about that. He was frequently inviting Marcelle and George for lunch or dinner or an afternoon cocktail, but Marcelle, like Lina, was endlessly suspicious of him. Max was the enemy. It made no difference that he adored Gabriel and gifted them with all the excesses he was granted simply for being a German. No one trusted him.

"Where is my Gabriel?" Max stepped out onto the landing to greet them. He'd given his maid the day off and welcomed George and Marcelle into his home with a handshake and a kiss on the cheek. Not the scarred cheek, of course. Marcelle never offered that one to anyone, except George. "I haven't seen that boy in weeks. Why don't you ever bring him around?"

"He is at home with his tante Rosalie," Marcelle replied. "Baking a cake for his birthday."

"His birthday? Today?"

Marcelle nodded as she and George stepped into the house. The windows were open, an unseasonably warm spring breeze sweeping a bouquet of aromas through the sunlit rooms. It was a beautiful house; the kind of home George would have liked to provide for Marcelle and Gabriel.

"We must throw him a party. Why don't you bring him over today?"

"That is very kind of you," Marcelle replied. "But we are just having a small gathering at the house."

"Well . . ." Max hesitated in a rare and uncomfortable moment of indecision. "I would love to join the celebration if that would suit you?"

Max didn't know Marcelle well enough to know that she felt trapped by his suggestion. That her tight smile, the subtle tilt of her head, and the twitch of her fingers were all tells that she would rather have been anywhere in that moment than under his gaze and having to submit to his biddings.

"Our home is not so nice," she replied. "I would be embarrassed to have you see it."

"Nonsense. I am certain you make a beautiful home, Marcelle. I would be honored if you would allow me to attend Gabriel's party today."

"Of course," George said, reaching out for Marcelle's hand. "Willkommen zuhause."

"Ah, very good, Pierre! We welcome you to our house. You have been practicing your German."

There were few things Max enjoyed more than spreading German culture, whether it be with language lessons, culinary lessons, or history lessons. He lit up when George pretended to be fascinated by his teachings, and he couldn't seem to understand why no one in Soissons had any interest in Germany.

"Did I say that correctly?" George asked. "Willkommen zuhause?"

"Yes, yes, very good, Pierre. Danke, danke schön. I can't wait to see Gabriel. I have the perfect gift for him."

———✦———

"He was saying *lee* for *Li*na. It was very clear."

"No, no. It was *lee* for Rosa*lie*."

"If he was saying Rosalie, he would have said *Ro*sa. Not *lee*.

It was obvious he was talking about his tante Lina. Isn't that right, mon bébé?"

Gabriel ignored them both when he noticed Marcelle standing in the living room, and scooted across the floor to her feet. She bent down and picked him up, kissing the top of his head and letting her face rest in his downy hair, inhaling the scent of him. Marcelle's moods could be parsed by the way she held their son. George had learned this within a week of his birth. Cheek to cheek meant she was content. Forehead to forehead, cautious. But what she did now, with her eyes shut and her nose buried in his hair, was a sign that fear had snaked its way into her body and was about to take over.

"You're home early." Lina watched them from the table, Rosalie by her side, as they passed a cigarette back and forth. "Everything all right?"

"Max is coming for Gabriel's birthday," Marcelle replied. "He should be here soon."

"What?" Lina gasped, pushing herself back from the table and almost toppling her rickety chair. "Why would you invite him into our home? This is not wise, Marcelle."

"Don't you think I know that?" Marcelle handed the baby to George and stepped around the table until she and Lina were almost eye to eye. "Do you think I invited him? That I have control over what this man does? Control over what any man does? Men do what they want, Lina. They come and go as they will, take what pleases them. Have you not learned this yet?"

"That's not what I—"

"No." Marcelle held her hand up between them to stop Lina's words. "I know what happens when you don't give them what they want. So do not lecture me about making poor decisions or question what I have done to keep my family safe. Just because your face is unbroken does not mean that your hands are clean. I do not know where you get your cigarettes or your flour or your sugar, but I do not question you or judge you for it. At least extend the same courtesy to me."

Lina didn't respond. George couldn't read the expression on her face when she turned away from Marcelle and faced the stove where the cake was baking. He didn't know if it was anger or sorrow or pride, but he knew that Lina was terrified of losing Max as an ally and that she would do anything to keep him on her side.

No one spoke for some time. Even Gabriel had enough sense to keep quiet as they all scrambled around the room picking up dishes and hiding the extra rations in the pantry, before Rosalie and Philip left for the cellar across the street to stay out of the way.

"What if he sees the vegetables in the garden?" Marcelle asked, but the knock on the door came before George had a chance to answer her, a chance to assure his wife that he would take care of it.

Within the ever-tightening radius around them lay any number of things that could get them arrested, or even killed: the ripening vegetables in the hidden garden; the German pistol tucked into the mattress; the American identification tag with George's name on it that he'd stashed in the far corner of the dresser drawer. There was danger everywhere.

"This is too much," George said, accepting the armful of gifts Max had brought for them. Cigarettes, wine, sugar. Excesses. As people around them starved, Max provided a comfortable life for their family. They didn't worry about starving. They didn't even notice the complacency that had allied itself to their contentment.

Max saved Gabriel's gift for last. From his coat pocket he pulled out a red bound book embossed with black letters and presented it to Marcelle.

"For you, madame. Every man should hear his mother's voice when he rereads these fairy tales from his youth. I want Gabriel to have nothing less."

"Merci," Marcelle whispered, her hands shaking as she reached out for the book. She ran her palm over the cover before opening it with tentative fingers, the aged spine creaking in protest.

"Can you translate one into German for me? Or maybe English so we can all understand? It has been too many years since I have heard a fairy tale."

"Of course, Captain Neumann." Marcelle stared down at the open page before her. "Le Petit Chaperon Rouge," she said, looking up at Max before continuing. "Little Red Riding Hood."

Max was right. Having never been read fairy tales by his mother as a child, "Little Red Riding Hood" was a tale George would come to memorize in Marcelle's voice. The first drawn breath heightening his anticipation. The exact inflection of her voice carrying each word to the next. The expectant pauses trapping him inside the story.

> *"Little girls, this seems to say; never stop upon your way.*
> *Never trust a stranger-friend; no one knows how it will end.*
> *As you're pretty so be wise; wolves may lurk in every guise.*
> *Handsome they may be, and kind; gay and charming, never mind.*
> *Now, as then, is simple truth: the sweetest tongue has the sharpest tooth."*

Max was the only one clapping when Marcelle finished, praising her beautiful translation and enunciation. He didn't seem to understand his role in the story, or perhaps he delighted in being the wolf. He laughed as Paul rocked back and forth repeating: *méchant loup, méchant loup, méchant loup.*

Bad wolf, bad wolf, bad wolf.

"Very good, Paul. Bad wolf." Max's eyes followed Lina to

the stove, and when she opened the oven door, he stepped forward to see what was inside. "Lina, your cake smells delicious."

"The coals went out earlier," Lina said, checking to make sure they were still lit. "It would have been done by now if I had been paying attention."

"If you need more coal—"

"No, no." Lina waved away Max's offer, and it wasn't until she heard Marcelle's subtle gasp from across the room that she seemed to remember her uncommon relationship with the German officer standing in their kitchen was not common knowledge. "I'm sorry," Lina said, turning back to Max. "I should not have interrupted you. Thank you for your offer, Captain Neumann. But we have plenty of coal."

The tension binding Marcelle in place was as real as the threads that held her dress together. George could almost see it winding itself around her as she waited for Max to make his next move.

They had all been so focused on him, no one had noticed Gabriel crawling across the kitchen floor and pulling himself up to grab hold of the wobbly handle of the door leading to the garden. Max was the first one to him when the knob came off in his hand and he fell back onto the kitchen floor in tears.

Marcelle scooped him up into her arms as George tried to take the handle from Max, mumbling something in French about fixing it later.

"Maybe I can fix it for you," Max replied, and, when he slid it back into place, the door popped open to reveal the secret staircase to the courtyard.

"Jardin, jardin, jardin . . ." Paul clapped his hands in front of his face and skirted past Max, down the stairs, and out the door.

"A garden?" Max trailed Paul down the stairs, and George could do nothing but watch his silhouette from above against the harsh contrast of the blinding sun from below.

"How wonderful," Max exclaimed as George joined him in the courtyard. "Who is the gardener?"

"I am," George replied, glancing up the stairs to see that neither Marcelle nor Lina was following them.

When Max's eyes caught on the rows of ripened tomatoes and cabbages, and he didn't react, George wondered if this might be his chance, his moment to enlist Max's help. Time stretched between them as Paul rocked back and forth by the little blue flowers that grew against the stone wall, and it was as if each was waiting for the other to speak. For years to come, George would often wonder if that day might have ended differently if he had just spoken first.

"Do you think I am a fool?"

"Of course not, Captain Neumann." The ground shifted beneath his feet as George struggled to steady himself, to prepare himself for what was to come. "Of course I know you are not a fool."

"Then why do you treat me as such?" Max opened his arms and gestured to the garden around them. "This makes me look like a fool. When people disobey ordinances right under my nose, it makes me look weak."

"Please," George begged. "It was me. Marcelle and the others had nothing to do with this. If anyone should be punished, it is me."

"What else are you hiding inside your home?" Max's voice thundered through the courtyard as he bounded up the stairs to the apartment. George followed closely behind, but his pleas were ineffective, falling on deaf ears. Marcelle was at the top, holding Gabriel, who was crying and squirming at the unexpected commotion.

"Do you know why you have not been sent to a work camp in Germany?" Max continued, as George stepped in front of Marcelle, tucking her and Gabriel behind him as best he could. "Because I have been protecting you. I have gone out of my way for you and Marcelle, yet you continue to lie to me again and again. Do you think you cannot be replaced?" He turned to Marcelle, who froze beneath his glare. "Do you think I don't know who you are? And you," he seethed, pointing at George. "I know you are not Pierre. And I know that other man is not who he says he is. But I will find out who you are. Both of you."

He tore through the pantry, pulling sacks of flour and sugar and potatoes from the shelves before toppling the settee beneath the window and rifling through the bin of clothes Marcelle had pulled from the line and folded earlier in the day.

Then he moved on to the bedroom.

He ripped the mattress from the bed and emptied the boxes Lina had stacked in the corner. Yarn, shoes, candles, matches. All the treasures she had collected over the months. When he tossed them aside and turned to the dresser, George froze.

In the top right drawer of the dresser, beside the rosary that he'd rescued from the smoldering ashes, the one Rosalie had tossed into the fire on their way to Soissons, lay George's army identification tag.

"Max, please." Lina was standing in the doorway. George hadn't even noticed she was there until she spoke, and when Max turned around to face her, he almost seemed to hesitate before heading back to the dresser. He rummaged through the drawers, pulling out shirts and linens and blankets, and when his hand reached for the handle of the top right drawer, George knew they were out of time. There were no other options.

He fumbled with the mattress at his feet, his fingers trembling and clumsy, before he got it unbuttoned and pulled out the pistol he'd taken from Jaulgonne. As he pointed it at Max's back, he walked himself through the next steps.

They would bury him in the garden. Marcelle would show up to work in the morning as if nothing had happened and they would carry on doing whatever needed to be done to survive this life. His hands shook as he pressed his finger against the trigger. Deep breath. He blew it out slowly, anticipating the moment the bullet would discharge and Max's body would fall to the ground.

Just as Max was pulling the rosary from the drawer, Lina stepped in front of the gun. Her eyes were wide as she wrapped her hands around the barrel, shaking her head in silence. It wasn't until Max slammed the drawer shut that she shoved the pistol into the front of her skirt and spun around to face him.

Max's eyes jumped between the two of them before settling on Lina, the handle of the pistol barely visible above the waist of her skirt. When she moved her arm to cover it, his gaze followed. He should have killed him. George should have shot him when he'd had the chance.

He was no match for Max, and they would all soon be arrested and imprisoned, sent to work camps in Germany, or worse. That was the scenario that played out in George's head, but it was not the one that played out in their apartment that day. Max didn't arrest them. He didn't move to take the gun from Lina or tackle George to the floor. He didn't do any of the things George had prepared himself for; he simply stared at them through the silence until the moment became almost unbearable, and then he walked out the door.

George waited until he heard the slam of the front door before he stepped up to the dresser and slowly pulled the top right drawer open. The rosary lay at the bottom of it, a heap of metal and beads tangled and twisted together. But no army tag. He slid his hand toward the back of the drawer, under the clothing and linens, the wood rough beneath the pads of his fingers. No army tag. He shook out each sock and hat and scarf, the yarn unraveling in his hands, but, still, no army tag. He clutched the rosary in his hand as he pushed the drawer shut and, at the sound of Lina's voice, spun around to face her.

"Are you looking for this?"

The silver disk glistened in the light as she swung the necklace from her fingers. When George stepped forward, and she placed it in his hand, he couldn't stop seeing the image of her stepping in front of the gun. She was so certain that Max would be Paul's savior, that she was even willing to give her life for it.

chapter 28

MARCELLE

April 1922

"You better hide that rosary."

Max's office was in disarray. The whole administration building was being turned upside down, and Marcelle couldn't get Max, or Gabriel, to listen to her. Her son's feet pattered over the papers littering the floor as he flew the toy airplane Max had given to him around and around the desk.

"Shoom. Shoom. Shoom."

"Gabriel, please!" she admonished.

Paul was rocking in the corner, his fingers working over the beads of the rosary with the deftness of a Benedictine monk. It was the one George had given to him. The one Rosalie had tried to burn. The one Max had pulled from the back of their dresser when he'd ransacked their house two years earlier. No one ever talked about that day, not even Max, except to acknowledge that he had quite a temper. Marcelle had shown up to work the following morning, upon Lina's insistence, and, after some time, the certainty that the burlap bag would be slipped over her head at any moment began to fade.

For months they'd lived in a perpetual state of fear. Every creak of a floorboard at night, every lingering stare of a German by day was the end; it was always the end. But the soldiers never came. The pistol, now buried in the garden, was never seized. They'd seen the last of Max's beautiful home and eaten the last of his delectable meals, but at least they were still alive.

"There is no reason to scold him, Marcelle. He is just a boy."

Gabriel was an active three-year-old boy, and clever enough to know that his mother never questioned or overruled Max's authority. He was particularly ill-behaved around German men, which was one of the reasons Marcelle rarely brought him out. Today was different, though. Max would be gone by the afternoon.

The Germans were done with Soissons.

"It is Paul you need to worry about." Max nodded toward the rosary in Paul's hands. "Communists do not tolerate Christianity."

The Russians had been trickling into Soissons over the last few months. Lenin had signed a treaty with Germany, giving the Russians control of certain areas of Belgium and northern France, and in return, they had agreed to rejoin the war effort—only this time, against France. Soissons would be under Russian control, and while Marcelle was ready for a change, she was leery of the Bolsheviks. They were hungry-looking men, and not necessarily for food.

But Marcelle had little to base this on. In truth, she didn't know what to think about the communists. Lina and Roland's ceaseless bickering only made them more of an enigma to her. According to Lina, they were like vultures, waiting, circling, and biding their time, surviving off the dead. But if Roland was to be believed, France would soon be free again; the communists would bring her into a new age. They would create a world where the people were the ruling class. They would all survive, or they would all go down, together.

"Maman! Dies ist Albatros!" German. Gabriel was a clever child. He spoke only German when Max was around, knowing he would be praised and rewarded for it. He held the plane up for Marcelle to see. It was German, too, of course. Marcelle had been a reluctant teacher, but George had insisted Gabriel grow up speaking both French and German.

"Un Albatros," she replied to her son in French, knowing

Max would not approve. "That looks like a very fine plane." If it weren't for trivial victories, she'd have none at all.

But Max was too busy packing boxes and sorting documents to worry about what language Marcelle was speaking. He didn't even notice when Lina walked through the door, flustered and agitated. She looked out of place standing in Max's office, in a building she'd likely never stepped foot in before. Why would Lina seek her out here in the middle of this chaos? Was it George? Or Rosalie? Something must have happened to one of them for her to show up there. But before Marcelle could formulate her thoughts into words, Max turned around and everything she thought she knew about this man she had believed was a wolf in sheep's clothing was proven false.

"Max, please," Lina begged. "What am I going to do?"

"I can't, Lina. You know I can't. He is a teenager now. If there was any way I could make it work, I would take him. But he is safer here with you."

Marcelle struggled to follow the course of their conversation. Were they talking about Paul? Was this something they had already discussed before today?

"You can have two of these," Max said, pulling a box from the closet that overflowed with all the things Lina would fetch throughout the week and bring home to their apartment; all the essentials for survival: candles, paraffin, coal, matches, flour, sugar, potatoes. There was enough in there to last them at least a couple of months. Max had been Lina's supplier all along. How had Marcelle missed this?

"The rest are for other families that will also be needing assistance," Max continued. "Marcelle will have to help you carry them. I suggest you dig out more space in the cellar. But make sure Roland doesn't know about it. I have already seen him out there with the *russkiye*. He thinks he is one of them."

Marcelle couldn't focus; time was moving at a cumbersome and sluggish pace: Paul rocking in the corner, Gabriel bounding across the room, Lina fussing with the chair so Marcelle wouldn't collapse onto the floor.

And Max.

"I didn't know," Marcelle whispered as she sank into the chair. "I am sorry, Captain Neumann. I thought . . ."

"You thought I was a monster?"

Marcelle nodded and looked up at Lina beside her. "Why didn't you tell me?"

"It was safer this way," Lina replied. "I saved Max's life at the river shortly before you and the others returned to Soissons, so he has gone out of his way to help me, but we didn't want anyone to know what he was doing. It could have gotten us all into trouble. Including Max."

"Yes," Max agreed. "Lina did save my life. So, of course, I am indebted to her. But I also made a promise to Paul's father many years ago that I would take care of his son if something should happen to him and his wife. And then when Gabriel came along, I knew you would need help with him too. It is difficult to care for a child in times like these. There are other families, as well."

"What?" Lina staggered back a step or two before she caught herself on the desk. "That is why you helped us? Because you made a promise to Paul's father?"

"Yes," Max replied. "He was my translator before he and his wife were killed. But he was also my friend."

"He was a good man," Marcelle said. "I was always very fond of Monsieur Bauer."

"And he of you, Marcelle. We talked quite often about his family and his work. His favorite pupils. He always knew you would return. The girl with the gift for language, he called you. He said I would know you when you returned because you would be speaking flawless German and you would be looking for your fiancé, Pierre, who was killed at the front with the rest of the young men from Soissons."

"You knew about Pierre, as well?" Lina asked.

"I knew the day Marcelle first stepped up to my table in the ration card line," Max replied. "A young Frenchwoman speaking nearly flawless German and introducing the man beside her as Pierre Fournier. A dead man."

"Why didn't you tell us?" Marcelle asked.

"I needed you to stay vigilant. I could not have you letting your guard down around me or anyone. There were too many people in your house. Too many chances that something might go wrong. I have a bit of a temper, unfortunately, and lost my composure at Gabriel's birthday party, and I knew, after that, I had to keep my distance. But I should have known better earlier. I shouldn't have been inviting you all to my home and befriending you and your family."

Paul's rocking continued in the corner, but Gabriel had abandoned his plane on the desk and was trying to pull himself onto Marcelle's lap. Despite his raucous ways, he was a sensitive child, always able to sense the shifting of his mother's emotions. Marcelle could feel Max's eyes on her as she ran her finger along the ridge of scar tissue on her cheek. How many times had she thought the general from Jaulgonne was on his way? "You were never going to turn me in, were you?" she said.

Max shook his head. "Fear keeps us sharp," he replied. "We all have our vulnerabilities, Marcelle, and complacency makes us sloppy. I have done my best to keep you and Gabriel safe, and I am going to offer you something that might seem like it will break you, but I want you to consider it carefully. The offices will shut down in less than an hour, and our transport will be coming soon after, so you don't have long to make your decision. But it is a vitally important one."

Marcelle wouldn't need any time to consider the offer Max was about to make. There would be no hesitancy, no uncertainty to her response. The answer would be no.

Let me take Gabriel to Germany and raise him as my son.

"No."

It was an instinct so primitive and reflexive that Marcelle hadn't known it existed inside of her until she was gripping her son in her arms, terrified he would be ripped away from her, and certain she would not survive the wound that would be left behind.

"I won't let you take my son."

"Send him." Lina knelt beside her, their faces so close that Marcelle could feel her frantic and uneven breaths on her cheek. "Gabriel will be safe with him in Germany. We cannot keep him safe here without Max. We have no one to rely on."

When Max tried to pull her up, Lina gripped at Marcelle's arms, digging her nails into the soft skin around her wrists, forcing her to cling more tightly to Gabriel. But Marcelle would never let go. They would have to rip her body apart to get to her son.

"You don't understand what is coming, Marcelle!" Lina fought against Max as he pried her fingers from Marcelle and dragged her off the floor. "I begged him to take Paul. We cannot keep them safe anymore."

"Enough, Lina," Max said. "I know this is not what you want, Marcelle. No mother should be forced to make this choice. But my wife will raise Gabriel as her own. I have already corresponded with her about it. We have a little girl who is five now, and I can promise you that he will be an adored little brother. He will be safe in Germany, protected and loved."

Had Max been planning this all along? Had he been grooming Gabriel to be a German, knowing the time would come when he would leave, and Marcelle would be too weak to care for her son without him?

"He is not German," Marcelle cried, nuzzling her nose into the hair on the top of her son's head. "He does not belong in Germany."

"Of course," Max replied, too gracious to point out what everyone in Soissons thought they knew about her son. "But he could pass for German. And that is all we need. No one will question me returning with a son. And I swear on my life that I will take care of him as if he were my own. I will provide him a good life, Marcelle."

What kind of a man would ask a mother to give up her son? What kind of a mother would not give up her son for a better life? Marcelle didn't know anything about Max. Until that moment, he'd been unmarried, childless, and alone. He hadn't been making sacrifices to be in Soissons; he'd just been living in a beautiful home with all the luxuries and amenities that hadn't been afforded to anyone but the Germans. He'd been the oppressor. She hadn't considered that, perhaps, he'd never wanted to be there, that he'd wanted to go home to his family. Or that he'd even had a family to go home to.

"What about my husband?" Marcelle said. "I cannot take him away from his father."

"You know what he would do, Marcelle." Lina's voice was leaden with defeat, and as they both watched Max pull more provisions from the closet, more boxes destined for other vulnerable families, Marcelle considered Lina's words. Max had bought them six months, maybe seven if they were frugal. But what would happen after that? When the supplies ran out, who would they turn to? How would she keep her son alive?

Lina was right; Marcelle did know what George would do. George was a man who didn't shy away from sacrifice. He was a man who made selfless decisions for the people he loved. He would choose to send his son away to give him a better life. She knew this with unfaltering certainty, which was why she could never let him find out about the offer.

chapter 29

GEORGE

"What happened?"

Marcelle was sobbing. She'd carried a box of supplies through the front door and had dropped it onto the floor before breaking down into tears beside it. George had returned home early from the stables, having been excused from duty permanently by the new Bolshevik regime, and he'd spent the better part of an hour pacing by the window and waiting for Marcelle to return. He'd been expecting her earlier, since the occupation administration office was changing hands, but he was thankful to see her now. The Russians had arrived in droves, outnumbering the German soldiers at least three to one, and they were not a welcoming bunch.

"Tell me what happened, Marcelle." George glanced down the empty stairwell behind her. "Where is Gabriel? Did something happen to him?"

When the door opened at the bottom of the stairs, and Gabriel's tiny voice carried up through the hallway, Marcelle's sobs intensified. Lina was behind him with Paul in tow, another box of supplies in her arms.

"What is all this?" George asked as Lina stepped into the apartment. "Where did you get this?"

"Max." Lina didn't elaborate. She placed the box on the table and knelt down beside Marcelle. "Get it out," she said, placing a hand on Marcelle's back. "And then be done with it. You haven't the time nor the energy to wallow in this. It is over."

"What is going on?" George stood over them as Marcelle breathed in a few final ragged breaths. Something was off, aside from his wife sobbing on the floor. The energy in the room felt heavy and unbalanced.

"Max gave us these supplies," Lina said as she helped Marcelle onto a chair. "You were right, George. He wasn't helping me because I saved his life. He's just a decent man."

"Where is he now?" George slid onto the chair beside Lina. "Maybe he can help get us out of here. Or at least the children. The Russian soldiers are everywhere. They've been marching up and down the streets all day."

"No," Marcelle said, fear spreading through her eyes like a sickness, like something so attainable George felt he could reach out and touch it, become infected by it. "There is nothing he can do for us."

Lina placed her hand over Marcelle's, whether to stop her or comfort her, George couldn't say, but there was something buried between them, something neither was willing to dig up and offer to him.

"He's gone," Lina said, and when George followed her gaze to Paul, who was still rocking by the window, he felt the imbalance of the room again. "The Germans left with their convoy an hour ago. I tried, George. I promise you, I tried." She hesitated before she pulled her hand from Marcelle's and stepped up beside Paul to see what he was looking at. "There was just nothing he could do."

As Lina watched the Russians on the street below, George could hear the steady beat of their footsteps, and he knew it was no longer safe to venture outside. For almost four years they'd lived in obscurity, an oasis in the midst of deserted streets, forgotten stores, and fallen homes. Max was the only German who'd ever visited them, and just that one time, but the Russians had already been up and down their street at least five times, pilfering through the rubble of downed houses and long-ago-abandoned stores. They were scavengers, so unlike the Germans who found foraging uncivilized.

"Roland." The name came out as a hiss when Lina spotted him amongst the Bolshevik troops outside their window. "That bastard!"

The cellar.

George knew Lina's intentions before she had even made a step toward the door, but he wasn't fast enough to stop her as she bounded down the stairs and across the street with the grace of a gazelle. She was almost upon Roland by the time the Russian soldier spotted her, but he, too, was quick and agile, with predatory-like reflexes that landed Lina on the street when the butt of his gun smashed into her face.

George got to her side just as her body stilled, and though he knew it would take more than that to kill Lina, he leaned in close to her mouth to make sure she was still breathing. Roland took a step toward them, stopping only when the Russian soldier who'd put her there shook his head. As he gazed down at his cousin's bleeding face and broken nose, George had to wonder if regret had already found him.

The Russians moved like ants, back and forth, up and down, lugging four years' worth of supplies from the cellar: wine bottles, sacks of flour, candles, blankets. By the time they'd cleaned out the cellar, Lina's eyes were fluttering open and immediately seeking out Roland. He was standing beside a group of soldiers who were pointing up toward their apartment.

A dozen sets of eyes were turned up toward Marcelle as she gazed down at them from the window, Gabriel on her hip and Paul rocking by her side. George didn't wait for the soldiers to move. He darted toward the door of their apartment, ignoring whatever orders were being shouted at him from the men on the street, and raced up the stairs.

Marcelle was on her hands and knees, furiously mopping away the pile of flour that had spilled from a sack that was conspicuously absent. The boxes she and Lina had brought home from Max's were nowhere to be found, but when George noticed the missing handle to the door off the kitchen, the one that led to the garden, he knew what she had done with them.

He'd barely pulled her from the floor and dusted the flour from her face when the front door slammed open against the wall, and the Bolshevik soldiers flooded into their tiny apartment. Marcelle swung Gabriel up onto her hip, as George backed them into the far corner where Paul rocked and mumbled and fiddled with the rosary.

The soldiers were already rifling through their cabinets and collecting anything of worth—food, blankets, paraffin—when Roland came hobbling in behind them.

"Roland, please," Marcelle whispered as she stepped toward him. "Think about what you are doing."

"This is what is best for everyone, Marcelle. I am trying to help us all. It may seem bad now," he conceded, "but it will get better. You will see." But this was not the passionate and confident Roland who had stood in this same apartment blasting the Germans and pining for the day the Bolsheviks would come marching into town. These were not the communists Roland had been expecting. These men were far worse than the ones they'd driven out of Soissons, and if George had thought escape from France was vital when the Germans ruled, under this new Bolshevik regime, it was dire.

"You are not a man, Roland," Marcelle jeered back at him. "You are a coward."

Even as George tried to calm her, he watched the soldiers struggling to get the door to the garden open without the handle. When they turned to Roland for assistance, he had no choice but to confront Marcelle.

"Please, Marcelle," he begged. "Give them the handle before something bad happens."

But Marcelle was stubborn, and as she and Roland watched each other through the mounting tension, the man in charge raised the stock of his rifle and stepped toward them. By the time Marcelle pulled the handle from her skirt, it was too late, and she had only enough time to turn her body away from him, sheltering Gabriel from the blow.

The last thing George heard as he pushed his wife and son out of the way was the thud of the door handle as it landed on the hardwood floor, and the last thing he saw was the butt of the gun as it came crashing down onto his face.

chapter 30

MARCELLE

Soissons, France
May 1991

"Mon Dieu!"

Juliette pulled her reading glasses off before placing the diary onto the table and collapsing back into the sofa beside Marcelle. They'd moved to the living room when the light had begun to fade outside, and the mosquitoes had begun to bite.

"Did the Bolsheviks . . ." Juliette paused for a moment before rephrasing the questions. "I cannot seem to remember my history now . . . but . . . did this happen?"

Marcelle shook her head. "I remember 1922," she said. "It was the year before you were born. The war had been over for years by then, and there were no Bolsheviks in France. At least not in Soissons."

"Do you think *I* will be a part of this story, Maman?" Juliette didn't wait for Marcelle to answer as she reached for the box from America that was sitting on the table before them. The photograph that had been labeled *Philip Foster* was resting on top. "I don't think George got Tante Rosalie right in his story," she said, studying the photograph. "I cannot imagine my chaste aunt with this man. Although he is quite handsome."

Marcelle smiled at the thought of it. Rosalie had never been one to sneak off to cellars with men, but they'd all had their secrets, hadn't they? She could almost picture the two of them together, Rosalie and Philip, laughing and dancing. She blinked away the image, surprised by the clarity of it in her mind. She had never even met the man. Had she?

"What about Lina?" Juliette continued. "And the German? Do you think Tante Lina really rescued that man from the river?"

Marcelle couldn't keep her memories straight, the story from the diary threading its way through the real story of her life. "I seem to remember something about that," she said. "Something about Lina rescuing a man at the river when she was just a child, a teenager maybe, near the end of the war."

"How interesting," Juliette remarked. "Was he a German?"

"That I can't remember. But perhaps no one talked about it much because of that." *Or perhaps because it didn't happen*, Marcelle thought.

"Well, I for one am fascinated by this story," Juliette said, rising from the sofa. "But it is getting late. I think we should get some rest. Shall we finish it tomorrow?"

Marcelle would have read through the night if it was up to her, but she knew better than to suggest such a thing at her age and didn't argue when Juliette helped her into the wheelchair and got her into bed.

Marcelle clicked the bedside light on before reaching for her strongest pair of reading glasses, knowing they wouldn't do much good. "Could you bring the diary in here?" she said. "And the box? I just want to take a peek."

"Yes, of course," Juliette replied, but when she returned with the journal, she was reluctant to hand it over. "I was actually thinking about reading through it tonight after you went to bed," she said. "Would that be okay with you? I am so curious to find out how it ends."

Marcelle smiled up at her daughter, remembering the time between Juliette's entry into adulthood and her own descent into old age, a time when neither had needed anything from the other but companionship, a time when staying up all night to read someone's diary together would have been the highlight of their week.

Juliette smiled back at her and crawled into the bed. "I suppose if you're not too tired," she said, fluffing up the pillows behind her back and getting comfortable, "we could read a bit more."

chapter 31

MARCELLE

November 1923

The baby sounded like a kitten.

Her cries were soft and weak, but Marcelle had no doubt she would survive. Her eyes matched her father's in both color and unfaltering determination. There was a depth to them that was impossible to fathom, a darkness that bled out from the pupil and into the surrounding mahogany-colored iris.

She was nothing like her brother, who had come into the world pink and plump and angry, howling at the top of his lungs. Juliette had known from the start how to survive. She'd entered the world in silence, her dark eyes darting around the room as Lina had cleaned her off. She never cried for Marcelle's breast. She took it when it was offered, drinking whatever Marcelle could produce, and never fussed when the milk ran out.

She was a wise baby, if that was possible. An old soul, perhaps, especially when compared to her brother's childish antics. At four years of age, Gabriel was still prone to toddler-like fits, throwing himself on the ground and screaming until his voice was hoarse and scratchy. Marcelle was starting to worry he would never outgrow them, and she often wondered what kind of a boy he would have been if she had allowed Max to raise him in a world where toys, treats, and three meals a day weren't considered luxuries.

When the Bolsheviks had come into power, they'd stripped everyone of everything. Homes, food, valuables. Even basics like utensils and clothing had been taken to be redistributed equally amongst all the citizens. Marcelle and her family—including Lina, Paul, Rosalie, and Philip—had been assigned the bottom floor of a house in the center of the city, just steps from the cathedral square, where the Russians could keep an eye on everyone. Their new housemates, a group of middle-aged sisters who lived on the top floor, made no effort to hide their disdain, banging on the floors and yelling obscenities down the stairwell when Gabriel started up. The house had belonged to the sisters until Marcelle and the others had been moved in a year earlier, and they still thought they were in charge.

"How is my little kitten?"

Lina leaned over and landed a kiss on the top of Juliette's head. She and Rosalie were just returning from the field, and Marcelle would rejoin them in less than a month, Juliette swathed to her side and Gabriel darting through the cabbage rows. Everyone, without exception, was expected to contribute. The women worked the fields, and the men, for the most part, worked in a metal-making factory.

The work was difficult, the walk to get there strenuous, and the reward for their labor almost negligible. They were starving, their bodies nothing but skin and bones. For all the food they produced in the vast countryside outside of Soissons, they received virtually nothing with the ration cards that were distributed to them each week. It didn't matter that the card said Marcelle was due ten ounces of meat for her family; the butcher had nothing to give her. She hadn't eaten meat in almost six months.

She had only thought she'd understood hunger before the Bolsheviks arrived. Gabriel had stopped growing. He wore the same clothes he had worn on his third birthday, and he was now four. No one knew where the food went. Severe punishments were doled out for questioning the system. Little else was deemed worse than going against the machine of communism, expecting more from your country than you were willing to give in sweat and blood.

The leadership of the regime would be changing hands soon. Lenin was either sick or dead and a new man was about to take the reins. Stalin was his name. Lina had shared the news at dinner the previous evening, but no one knew where she got her information. Russian propaganda newspapers were released every few months, but nothing had been circulating recently. Marcelle was cautiously optimistic about the news. Maybe Stalin would offer new hope to the French.

Roland was no longer welcome in their home. They would see him amongst the troops, on occasion, flaunting his Bolshevik uniform and marching along with his carved and polished wooden crutches. He was thriving, but Marcelle hadn't spoken to him since the day of the Bolshevik takeover in their old apartment. Without fail, he would look away when he noticed her, and Marcelle often wondered if it was remorse that made him do that, or maybe shame.

"The men are not home yet?" Rosalie stirred the soup on the stove, a days-old watery broth with a handful of potatoes, onions, and cabbage thrown in.

Marcelle shook her head and handed Juliette to her sister. "Will you take her, Rosalie? I think the bread is done."

The loaf in the oven had barely formed a crust, but Marcelle closed the damper to the fire box to extinguish the flame. Everything in her life was just enough. Just enough flour in the dough to call it bread. Just enough fuel in the oven to call the bread baked. Just enough bread in the body to call it alive.

Marcelle smiled when she heard the front door open. There was always cause for celebration when George returned home from the factory each day; many men didn't. The prisoners who had been released from the German prison camps had been trickling back to their homes recently, perhaps twenty or thirty of them from Soissons. The Russians reserved their prisons for the most violent offenders, so when they'd taken control of northern France, they'd cleared out the majority of the camps and sent the prisoners back to their homes to work in the factories. Cities were essentially run like prisons. Blocks of streets were sectioned off for the citizens, areas where the Russians could keep close tabs on the locals and squash an uprising at the first sign. There was little time for an uprising. All the men in town, from the teenagers to the decrepit, were forced to work at the metal factory from sunup until sundown; they didn't have the time or the energy to plan an overthrow.

Les soeurs.

When Marcelle turned around, she was disappointed to see the sisters from upstairs returning from work instead of the men. They had taken to calling them *les soeurs* because no one had bothered to learn their names. "The sisters" had taken on a frightful but comedic connotation in their little apartment, and Gabriel was known to tremble at the bedtime fairy tales Marcelle and Rosalie created about the women who lived at the top of the stairs.

Unfortunately, the only staircase to their apartment started in Marcelle's living room, so there was no way to avoid their condescending glances and disparaging murmurs about her ever-growing brood.

She cannot even feed her children . . .

The baby will not survive . . .

The boy is a German . . .

Their words didn't trouble her, though. She often had the same thoughts. This was not the time to be having babies, but Marcelle hadn't realized she could even *get* pregnant. She hadn't had her monthly bleeding for over a year, and because Juliette had known to conserve her energy, there hadn't been a flicker of movement inside her belly until she'd been ready to come out. Marcelle had only figured out a couple of months before her birth, when her belly had started to bulge and round out, that she was pregnant.

The youngest of les soeurs offered Marcelle a covert glance

over her shoulder and a discreet smile as she ascended the stairs behind her sisters. She was darker than the others, and far prettier. There were four of them in total, likely in their thirties and forties. They acted like old maids, too pious for their own good.

The draft from outside, the one the sisters had brought in with them, hadn't even settled before Philip came through the door with Paul in tow. Paul was a man now, still with a child's mind, but if he kept his mouth shut and his body quiet, no one was the wiser. George was not with them. It was the third time this month he had been late from work.

"George is coming," Philip said, seeing the panic on Marcelle's face. "He's just a couple minutes behind us."

Marcelle tried not to fret about it. George had recently been promoted to section leader at the factory and had assured her that if he was a little late on occasion it was no cause for alarm. Marcelle didn't like it—the promotion or the late nights—but no one else seemed concerned. Philip had a supreme confidence that George could finagle his way out of any situation.

"Papa!" Gabriel darted from the kitchen table and launched himself into George's arms when he walked through the door. "When do I get to work at the factory with you? I want to make guns."

"We don't make guns." George carried Gabriel into the kitchen, giving Marcelle a kiss on the cheek and glancing into the pot on the stove.

"Tanks!"

"We don't make tanks."

"Airplanes!"

"We don't make those either."

"Then what do you do all day?"

George laughed as he set Gabriel onto the floor before peering into the bundle of blankets in Rosalie's arms.

"Bonjour, mon chaton," he whispered as he pressed his nose against Juliette's cheek. She was *kitten* to all of them. "We make parts."

"What are *parts*?"

Gabriel was getting bored with the conversation and was no longer listening to his father, who didn't bother explaining to his four-year-old son that the French could not be trusted with weapons in their own country. They made parts for weapons that were sent to Russian or German hands for assembly and were then used against their own country in war.

Information was harder to get these days since movement was severely restricted, especially in the Russian-controlled territories, but rumor had it the Americans were still dug in beside the French and British troops. The French were essentially prisoners in their own homes. Attempting to flee the country got you tried as a deserter, and, if you were found guilty, the sentence was oftentimes death, depending on the judge.

There were no underground networks, no rumors swirling that an uprising was in the works. There were a few black markets that popped up every now and then, but without fail, they were infiltrated and disbanded, all suspected vendors, suppliers, and customers hung in the cathedral square without trial. It was an effective deterrent.

Dinner was often a noisy affair, and that night was no exception. There was never enough food to fill their mouths, so conversation took its place.

"Have you heard the one about Lenin and the potato farmer?"

Grumbles spread around the table, but it was no secret that everyone enjoyed Philip's jokes. Although no one more than Philip.

"I have," George replied, slurping on the watery broth and smiling at Marcelle. "The soup is delicious, mon amour."

"So, Lenin goes to visit a potato farmer in the countryside, and the farmer says, 'Comrade Lenin, the potatoes are so abundant that, if we stacked them on top of each other, they would reach all the way to God in heaven.' 'But God does not exist,' replies Lenin. 'Exactly,' says the farmer. 'Neither do the potatoes.'"

Philip's reaction to his own jokes was usually funnier than the jokes themselves, but even Lina, who typically forbid the name "Lenin" to be uttered in their house, cracked a smile.

"Lenin will no longer be in charge soon," Lina said as she cleared the dishes from the table. "You will have to change all your jokes to Stalin now."

"Where do you get your information, Lina?" Philip asked as he pulled Rosalie onto his lap. Lina huffed at him from across the kitchen.

"You have your own bedroom. Is this really necessary?"

Philip and Rosalie had declared themselves husband and wife shortly after the Bolsheviks came to town. The Russians, by comparison to the Germans, kept such elementary records that there was no reason to maintain the charade. The Russians handed out ration cards like a priest might hand out Hail Marys in a confessional. There was no food anyway. What difference did it make to them who had a card?

"Don't be jealous, Lina. There are a handful of men to choose from now." Rosalie was always watchful of Lina. She didn't have to compete for Philip's attention when it came to her physical beauty, but Lina and Philip had a deeper connection that seemed to put her on edge. Marcelle pitied her sister's jealousy. She had no doubt that Philip cared for Rosalie, but theirs was a marriage of convenience. There were no other options. They made a dashing pair, and to an unfamiliar eye, they were a couple enamored with each other, but Marcelle knew about Philip's true love back in America. George had told her all about Dorothy, whose picture Philip kept stashed away from the others. Marcelle wondered if Rosalie had ever seen it.

"Maybe you should put on some of that lipstick I found in the cupboard, Lina," Rosalie continued. "See if you can snag one of those new men in town."

"I have no interest in being a wife," Lina replied. "Trust me, it is quite tedious."

"Poor Lina." Rosalie winked at her from across the table. "You will die a virgin at this rate."

"Who says I am a virgin?"

"Mon Dieu, Lina!" Marcelle covered Gabriel's ears as the room erupted in laughter. Whether Paul understood the meaning of her words or not, he clapped his hands in front of his face and laughed along with the rest of them, delighted to see the Lina he had known from before the Russians.

"Maman, what is a virgin?"

When her son looked up at her, Marcelle could feel the heat rising into her cheeks. She cut her eyes to both Rosalie and Lina, who had joined together in a conspiratorial laughter.

"It is a woman who . . ." She glanced at George, who was rocking the baby beside her, struggling to contain his own laughter. ". . . a woman who . . . well . . . who is not yet married."

"Are you a virgin, Maman?"

Marcelle dropped her face into her hands, unable to hold back her own giggles.

"Poor Marcelle," Philip laughed. "Don't let them do this to you. Come, Rosalie." He guided her to the middle of the room as she protested and tried to resist, knowing what was to come. "Let's take the attention off your sister."

"My favorite part of the night." Lina cheered from the table. "I love watching you dance, Rosalie."

For all her beauty, Rosalie hadn't an ounce of grace. She was clumsy and fantastically uncoordinated, especially next to Philip.

"It is not so easy," she complained. "You try it."

"Come on, Lina," Philip said as Lina jumped up from her chair. "I was going to teach Rosalie the Argentine tango tonight, but I'll tame it down for you, love. How about the foxtrot?"

"I am up for anything, darling."

Despite his grace on the dance floor, Philip had a most

unpleasant singing voice. But since no one else knew any songs to go with the foxtrot, they clapped along to his words and cheered as Lina's feet skipped over the floor, struggling to keep up with Philip's. Lina was quite coordinated, at least compared to Rosalie.

"Excuse me." No one had noticed the dark-haired sister standing at the bottom of the stairs until she raised her voice and knocked on the wall to get their attention. "I am sorry to interrupt you, but my sisters are requesting that you keep the noise down."

Until there was silence, Marcelle hadn't realized how much noise they'd been making with their singing, dancing, and cheering. Gabriel was asleep in her lap and didn't stir when she placed him on the mattress beside Paul, who was still rocking along to the silenced music.

"Come," she said, reaching out for the woman's hand. "We are learning the foxtrot tonight."

The woman glanced up the stairwell to where her sisters were awaiting her return and when she turned back to Marcelle, there was a smirk on her face and a twinkle of mischief sparkling in her eyes.

They danced long into the night, even after les soeurs called down for the dark-haired woman, who was breathless and sweating and full of smiles when she finally retreated to her apartment. It was in these moments that Marcelle understood how her fractured and scarred life was also an amazingly beautiful gift, and how she was wonderfully fortunate to have become a part of this unlikely family.

chapter 32

October 1925

"He should be home by now."

Lina paced by the door, an unfamiliar restlessness working its way through her typically calm demeanor. It was putting them all on edge.

"I'm sure he's fine. He probably met a girl and lost track of time."

Even Philip couldn't make her smile. Paul was missing. He'd only been gone for three hours, but it was not in his nature to wander far from home. Lina often joked he was just like the herding dog her grandfather had on his farm when she was a child. Thirty minutes couldn't pass without Paul peeking his head through the door, checking to make sure everyone was where they should be. She had already searched the entire town for him, knocking on neighbors' doors and combing through the fields.

Something was wrong.

They all felt it, but no one wanted to be the one to give fear a voice, so they sat mostly in silence and let the hours tick by. Even George, who was typically the most pragmatic of the group, was incessantly peering through the curtains out the front window.

The children had spent the afternoon with the sisters upstairs. Gabriel, at six, had finally outgrown his childish antics and, after learning how to be effusive with his charm, was now a favorite with les soeurs. Juliette was never far behind. She watched her brother with the same steady patience she'd inherited from her father. She was a beautiful child, dark and mysterious. There was something so unattainable about her, that, even at two, people just wanted to be near her. She was her father's daughter. Quiet. Contemplative. Perceptive.

The sisters had offered to keep them for the evening. Even they'd understood that something was amiss, that Paul should have been home by now, and that it would be a long and trying night.

"I'm going out to have a look." George pulled the curtain back once more, searching up and down the empty street. "No point all of us sitting around here."

"I will go with you." Marcelle pulled her coat on and tried to follow him out the door, but George was already steering her back inside.

"No, mon amour," he said, kissing her forehead and letting his lips linger for a moment. "It is almost dusk."

The sun would set in less than an hour, and nothing good ever happened in Soissons when the sun went down. The Russian soldiers made sure of that. But as George walked away and Marcelle looked back at Lina agonizing by the window, she knew she had to do something, so she slipped quietly out the door before anyone noticed and headed off in the same direction as George.

The days were getting shorter. Winter was creeping in, running its frigid fingers over the crops in the fields and whispering its icy breath through the leaves in the trees. All around her, the last remaining vestiges of autumn were dying. Marcelle pulled her coat tighter around her body and tucked her chin into the collar as she soldiered on through the cold.

Where was George going?

She'd lost sight of him after rounding the corner at the end of their street and was so preoccupied with trying to find him again that she didn't notice the Russian soldiers standing in the middle of the road until a hand slipped over her mouth and she was being dragged into a back alley.

"I told you to stay home," George whispered, pushing her into the shadows. The light was fading fast as he rushed her through town along silenced streets and between shuttered houses. Marcelle knew where they were headed; it was where she'd assumed George had been going when he'd left home.

The cathedral.

It was locked with chains, and the paint that was splattered over its stones warned the citizens of Soissons to stay away, to reconsider their God. Many had found out too late that it wasn't a request or a recommendation; it was the law, and the consequences for believing in the Almighty were severe, if not fatal.

Max had warned them. He'd told them to get rid of the rosary, but no one had the heart to take it from Paul, who could oftentimes only be placated by running the beads through his fingers. Lina never allowed him to take it from home, but they had searched the entire apartment when Paul had gone missing, and wherever it was, they feared Paul was too.

Où est ton Dieu maintenant?

"Where is your God now?" Marcelle whispered, reading the newest message that had been painted across the doors. She ran her fingers over the beautiful engravings in the wood beneath the paint, remembering the story her father had told her about the cursed doors of the Notre Dame Cathedral in Paris that she had never been to visit. Doors that possessed a beauty and craftsmanship beyond what was possible. Doors that could only have been made by the devil himself. Was he here now? Testing them? Mocking them? Cursing them?

"Where were you going?" When Marcelle turned to face George, she expected another flimsy excuse to go along with all the others he came home with late at night, but for the first time in months, he held her gaze so she could be sure that only the truth would pass his lips.

"I was going to retrieve some of the rubles I've stashed away for our escape," he said. "I thought maybe I could buy Paul's safety. Buy his life back if they haven't already killed him."

"What rubles?" Marcelle asked. "Where did you get rubles?"

"I never got a promotion at work," George replied. "That's not what I've been doing when I come home late at night. I've been selling wine and cigarettes to the Russian guards at the factory. And to the soldiers around town."

George must have been anticipating a different reaction than the one he got. He was braced for the assault of Marcelle's words, but pride was all she felt for her husband in that moment, and disappointment in herself. She'd spent so many years hiding from the monsters, she'd forgotten how to fight them. Where had the fearless woman from Montmirail gone? The one who'd commandeered her own fate?

"Where do you get the wine and cigarettes?" Marcelle asked.

"From the underground. The guards at the factory let me slip out with a handful of bullets or some weapons parts from time to time as long as I keep them supplied with liquor. And then I exchange those parts for more wine and cigarettes from the underground runners."

"Let me help you," Marcelle said, but before George could respond, a scream that would follow Marcelle into sleep pierced the darkening sky around them. It was Lina. Marcelle had never heard Lina scream, but she had no doubt that the shrieks coming from the other side of the cathedral belonged to her. And what lay on the other side of the cathedral was something the people of Soissons avoided with a steely determination.

La potence.

The gallows was never the first place anyone looked, even if it was the first thing that came to mind when a loved one went missing. If night hadn't been looming over them, George would have left Marcelle by the cathedral door. He would have spared her what they both knew they would find behind the church.

Lina stood in the center of the courtyard, and Marcelle could barely resist the urge to steer her gaze up toward Paul's lifeless body above her. His legs hung motionless at eye level, his bare feet clean and well manicured. Lina had trimmed his nails just the previous evening. His brown leather shoes, the ones Marcelle had seen sitting by the front door that morning, had already been taken, along with the woolen socks she had recently darned for him.

Paul had been loved. He had been a bright spot, a single flame shining through a long, dark night, a reminder of why they persisted. Despite the whispers around town, caring for him had never been a chore, especially to Lina. To have been loved by a soul as pure as Paul was a rare gift. To have harmed him, Marcelle imagined, bought you a seat beside the devil for eternity.

Lina's sobs echoed through the courtyard. The words she screamed were mostly unintelligible, but "Bolshevik," "pig," and "hell" were unmistakable. George had to physically pick her up to pry her away from the square, his hand wrapped over her mouth to muffle her words. When they got to the edge of the courtyard, Marcelle couldn't help herself. She turned back and let her eyes drift up the length of Paul's body. She wished she hadn't. It was an image she would spend the rest of her life trying to forget. The bluish tint of his skin, the bulging of his eyes, the unnatural angle of his head. The rosary was twisted around his neck, the crucifix glistening beneath the last fading rays of the sun. George should have let it burn all those years ago. Look what it had done to them.

If Marcelle hadn't been paying attention, she would have missed the flurry of movement from the man on the far side of the courtyard. The limp, the crutches, the shock on his face when he saw Paul's lifeless body hanging in the middle of the square. She was surprised by the dullness in Roland's eyes. There was no fire, no flames. Not even a spark. She hadn't seen him in almost a year, and she rarely thought of him. His name was never spoken in their home; Lina wouldn't allow it.

But now here he was, all alone, hobbling toward them across the courtyard. Marcelle put her hand up to stop him and shook her head. She knew he had nothing to do with Paul's death, and she knew he had kept their secrets safe over the past few years. But she also knew that if Lina saw him in that courtyard, she would do something that would land her either in prison or hanging beside Paul before the night was through.

Roland stopped at Marcelle's signal, and through the last slivers of the fading light, she thought she saw him mouth the words *I'm sorry.* She would often wonder about the verity of that memory. Had he really whispered those words? Had she perhaps misunderstood him? Or had she imagined it because she'd wanted it to be true?

When George went back to the gallows later in the night to retrieve Paul's body, it was already gone. He woke Marcelle upon his return to the apartment to show her the package that had been waiting for him on the front step. The rosary. Marcelle ran her fingers over each bead. How many years had it been since she had prayed the rosary? She offered up a silent prayer for each person in their home, before tossing it into the dirt hole George had dug by the front door. She was torn over her commitment to God. Did she owe Him something? Would He listen to her if she started praying again?

"Wait!" she whispered, before reaching back in and grabbing the crucifix. She held it in the palm of her hand and offered up one final prayer, for Roland, before dropping it back into the hole. Marcelle would never see the rosary again. They would leave Soissons before it could be unearthed, and though her relationship with God would be tested time and again, she would come to believe that the prayer she'd buried for Roland with the rosary beads was like one of the seeds she had planted in her garden when they had first come to Soissons. It would lie dormant for years, but eventually it would find the nourishment it needed and blossom into salvation.

chapter 33

GEORGE

October 1926

"Maman, look! I am a little octobrist." Gabriel beamed up at Marcelle and pointed to a red star that was pinned to his shirt. "Comrade Stalin sent these to all the schoolchildren in France. We are called octobrists because October was the month the Bolsheviks freed the people from the evil tsars. I learned that in school today."

Before he'd even finished speaking, Lina had crossed the room and ripped the pin from his shirt, leaving a hole in the fabric that would need to be mended before school the next day. Gabriel gazed up at his aunt, his mouth gaping and his eyes bulging as if she'd just slapped him across the face. He was seven years old and had recently started school under the new Bolshevik ordinance. Over the past year, since Paul's death, Lina's anger had been incessant, escalating at every new ordinance and law. She was becoming unhinged, and, while George had once believed they wouldn't survive without her, he now worried that Lina would be the root of their downfall.

Stalin had begun a new policy of indoctrinating the youth. It would have been a clever strategy if there were any children in the towns, but war and poverty and famine had skewed the age balance of the population, leaving behind a throng of middle-aged women who had been ground into the dirt beneath the polished boots of the Germans and Russians, and they were immune to propaganda.

"Communist pigs." Lina spat the words out as she crushed

the tin star in her hand. "Do not bring that filth into this house again."

"Lina!" Marcelle wrapped her arm around Gabriel's shoulder and guided him to the bedroom before he could say something to his tante Lina that would get him a real slap across the face.

It was a difficult balance. School was compulsory and Lina's hatred for the Bolsheviks was clashing with the pride Gabriel came home with every day as his confidence and sense of purpose grew. He was a part of a group now; they were children with a common purpose and common goals. What child didn't want that? How could George and Marcelle explain to their seven-year-old that he was being brainwashed? That the young man he was growing into was not the person his parents would have chosen for him to be?

George and Marcelle had managed to squirrel away almost enough money for an attempted escape, and they'd learned from the underground runners that their best chance for success would take them west to the coast and across the English Channel. The world was losing interest in the European War, and American troops were starting their withdrawal process from the front lines. The other Allies would soon follow suit, but it would likely be years before any diplomatic relations would be established within the new territories of France, years before George and his family could seek asylum. The Russians still controlled the northern regions of the country, and while the Germans seemed more inclined to welcome diplomatic relations into their southern territories, possibly even an American embassy at some point, crossing the border from Bolshevik-controlled lands was a monumental task.

Rumors of escape attempts were grim, at best, most ending with no survivors. But they'd recently learned that the local fishermen from the villages up and down the French coast had all been replaced with Russian fishermen who weren't averse to handsome bribes from refugees who could produce

British identification cards. The underground runners hadn't yet heard of any failed attempts, so George and Marcelle had decided that every ruble they'd saved would be put toward that effort.

For ten thousand rubles each, the Russian fishermen would navigate the mined waters between France and England and deliver them to a British humanitarian vessel whose crew would check only for proper identification before allowing them to board. They would then be taken to a holding area for authentication of their identification cards, but as far as the runners knew, no one had ever been sent back to the Bolsheviks once they'd stepped on British soil.

Freedom was finally within their reach, perhaps just months away. According to Marcelle, who had recently had tea with the wife of the forger, their British identification cards would be ready within weeks. She'd left a gift with the woman of four thousand rubles and a list of names:

Georges Fournier, 31
Marcelle Fournier, 29
Gabriel Fournier, 7
Philippe Fournier, 28
Rosalie Fournier, 29
Lina Fournier, 24

Lina's was the only name that wasn't borrowed or made up or attached to a dead man. They'd been advised to travel under one family name. The British preferred it that way. One head of the household meant fewer questions and less confusion. And Juliette would not need an identification card. Children under five could travel under their mother's identity. George had followed every suggestion; he'd taken every precaution to make this trip a success, and he wouldn't let Lina sabotage it no matter how much she detested his feigned tolerance of the Bolsheviks.

"You need to be more careful, Lina." He held his hand

out for the red star, but Lina glared back at him in response. "You're putting us in danger when you do things like this."

"You will just let them take your son? These people who killed Paul and have taken everything from us?" She threw the pin at George's feet. "And your daughter? When it is her turn, will you let them take her, too?"

George picked up the pin and tried to straighten the bent ends of the star. It was cheap and flimsy, and he worried the tips would break if he bent them too far.

"Give it to me." Rosalie reached her hand out for the pin. She was sitting at the table and listening to their conversation, and when George handed her the star, she eased the ends open and flattened it gently onto the wooden table. "Voila," she said. "Good as new."

"Thank you," George mumbled. "Maybe you can help talk some sense into Lina."

Rosalie had no interest in such things, though. Lina's bad side was not a fun side to be on. "I think I'll return this to Gabriel instead," she said, rising from the table and following her sister into the bedroom.

"You're going to get us killed talking like this, Lina. Can't you see that?"

"Can't you see that nothing I do matters?" She spun around and pointed the spoon in George's direction. "Can't you see that fate is stronger than me? I couldn't even protect Paul. I knew the day he would die, and I couldn't even stop it from happening."

"Please stop, Lina." George sank down onto one of the chairs at the table. "There's no way you could have known that Paul would die. You can't really believe that you've come back in time."

Lina snuffed out the fire on the stove and took the seat across from George. Despite the hysterics of her words, her eyes were clear, and her face determined. How could she believe such things?

"I don't need you to believe me to make it true," she said. "When I came back, I did so with the knowledge that I was sent here to save Max from drowning. And I did it because I thought him surviving had something to do with me. But all it did was give him the chance to return to Germany. And Paul is dead. Again. And now Rosalie will be next."

"Stop it, Lina!" George pushed himself back from the table, knocking the chair over as he stood. "That's enough. You can't be saying things like this."

The commotion in the kitchen pulled Marcelle and Rosalie from the bedroom, and as Lina rose from the chair, she glanced from the women in the doorway to the boy between them and then back to George.

"It will be next month on Juliette's birthday," she said, before turning back to the stove and relighting the fire. "You will see."

chapter 34

November 1926

"Joyeux anniversaire!"

It was Juliette's third birthday, and Lina had somehow scrounged up a tablespoon of sugar and a cup of flour to make her a cake.

"Look, Papa," Juliette squealed. "Maman and I have matching teeth."

Juliette had taken a tumble into the side of the stove the previous evening and was proud of her newly missing tooth. Mostly because she thought it made her look like her mother. George had once caught her with a kitchen knife, trying to carve a matching scar into her own cheek. That had been a difficult conversation. He'd spent so much time trying to convince his daughter that her mother's scar was a sign of strength and beauty that Juliette decided she wanted one too. What little girl didn't want to be strong and beautiful like her mother?

Marcelle laughed as she pressed her face up to Juliette's for everyone to see their missing teeth. She was no longer the demure young woman that had made him stutter over his words and stumble over hospital cots. It was her confidence that made her beautiful now. Not the free-spirited and reckless kind of confidence she'd possessed as a twenty-one-year-old, the kind that had gotten her dragged into a German prison and beaten nearly to death. What she possessed now was self-control. Maturity. The knowledge that every move she made reflected upon her family, that her actions had consequences that reached far beyond what was standing right in front of her.

"That's not fair." Philip reached into his mouth and pretended to wiggle a loose tooth. "I have too many teeth in my mouth. Who will help me pull one out?"

"I will do it, Oncle Philippe!" Juliette bounded across the room and jumped into his lap.

"Let me know if you cannot get it, Juliette." Lina laughed from across the room and tapped the rolling pin into the palm of her hand. "I will show you a better way."

Lina was finally starting to let her guard down. She'd been on edge all day, watching Rosalie like a hawk, unwilling to let her step foot outside their house. She was so certain Rosalie would be shot down in the middle of the street in broad daylight—thoughts she'd shared only with George, thankfully—that she hadn't let Rosalie out of her sight all day. It wasn't until the lingering hours of light had all but faded that she'd finally started to breathe again, but that had left her completely unprepared for the Russian soldiers who had somehow found their way to the front door.

"Please, do not stop the celebration on account of us." The soldier who spoke was missing an eye. His face was ravaged with scars and where his eye had once been sat an empty socket of pink, sagging skin. "What are we celebrating today?"

No one answered. An unnatural stillness seized them all, anchoring them in place, and it wasn't until Gabriel stepped forward that the silence splintered around them.

"Good evening, comrades." Marcelle gasped at the sound of her son's voice, and George had to grab her wrist to hold her back. "Welcome to our home. I am proud to announce that I have received my Bolshevik pin from Comrade Stalin last month at school."

The man with the missing eye laughed as he stepped up to Gabriel, but there was nothing jovial in his laughter. It was menacing and ugly, and when he stared down at Gabriel,

George had the sudden urge to strangle him. The soldier by the door didn't enter any further. He was young, with a boyish face that had likely never felt the weight of a razor.

"And tell me, comrade," the man with the missing eye said. "Where is this pin? And why are you not wearing it?"

Gabriel's eyes drifted to Lina, who was still standing at the stove with the rolling pin in her hand, and when the Russian soldier followed his gaze, George prepared himself to pounce. Across the room, as the tension mounted, Philip shifted Juliette's weight to the floor as he too readied himself for the attack. Gabriel was just a boy. They couldn't blame him for what he was about to do. He didn't understand that the choice of his next words could implicate his aunt in anti-communist rhetoric, that by telling the soldiers she would not allow him to wear the pin in their home, he could be putting her life in danger.

"It is in my wardrobe," Gabriel said, turning his attention back to the soldier. "I didn't want it to get ruined before school tomorrow."

"I see," the Russian replied. "But you are supposed to wear it at all times. No?"

Gabriel nodded and dropped his head before the man grabbed his wrist and twisted it to an unnatural angle to get a better look at the watch on his arm. Gabriel didn't startle or wince or cry out in pain. George almost didn't recognize him. When had his son grown into this brave young man who stood unflinching as a Russian soldier berated him and interrogated him?

"Where did you get this?" the man hissed, pulling it up to his good eye and studying it closely. "Is it British?"

It's a Hamilton. They're never wrong.

George could still hear Philip's words from the night in the cellar all those years ago before he and Rosalie had left for the front. He'd given the watch to Gabriel one Christmas with strict instructions to never wear it outside the apartment.

"It is German," Gabriel whispered. "I found it in the cathedral square when the Germans were still here."

All that time, all those years, George had believed he was sheltering his son from this. He thought he'd been allowing Gabriel to be a child, to not worry about the men outside their doors or the food that was missing from their plates. As it turned out, Gabriel had learned those things on his own, and, perhaps, George had just made it more of a challenge.

"You mean you stole it," the man said. "Are you a thief?"

"No, sir," Gabriel replied. "I am no thief."

"No matter. Take it off. This belongs to Russia now."

Gabriel handed it to him obediently, no flashing glances to Philip sitting across the room from him or to George standing behind him. Nobody moved as the soldier secured the watch to his own wrist, and it wasn't until he turned his attention away from Gabriel that George stepped forward and pulled his son to his side.

"And what are we celebrating today?" The man glanced from one face to the next until his gaze settled on Lina. "What are you making, mademoiselle?"

Lina tucked Juliette behind her, so she was wedged against the stove, and stood tall in front of the Russian soldier. "A cake," she said. "Perhaps you would like some, comrade?"

"No." The Russian shook his head and smiled. "But there is something else I might like."

Marcelle was too fast for George. He should have known that his wife would strike, that she would always place herself between danger and the ones she loved, but before he could stop her, she had wedged herself between Lina and the Russian soldier, who stepped forward until they were eye to eye. Two faces carved with stories of brutality and sacrifice and defeat.

"Take me instead," she whispered.

"Nyet," the man replied, as he continued to run his gaze over the line of scar tissue across Marcelle's face. "You have already been taken."

George didn't move, but his eyes darted from the soldier in front of Marcelle to the soldier at the door to Philip at the table. It would be a fair fight.

"You can't have either of them," he said, stepping forward as Philip rose from the chair and the momentum in the room seemed to shift. "It's time for you to go."

The man with the missing eye rocked back on his heels, away from Philip's looming presence, and then laughed.

"Do I look like the kind of man who walks away from a fight?" His attention shifted between George and Philip before he pulled a dagger from the sheath around his waist. "Now, we can do this the easy way," he said, "or we can do this the hard way. It is up to you."

He was not a stupid man. Despite his reckless bravery, he must have known that he didn't stand a chance, because when Philip and George began to close in on him, he did the only thing that could stop them in their tracks. He smiled as he held the edge of the dagger to the pale skin of Gabriel's throat, his empty eye socket stretching and the pink flesh within it glistening.

"The boy or the girl? I prefer the girl," he said, nodding toward Lina. "But I will take either of them."

"Good evening, gentlemen."

Until Rosalie strode into the room, her golden hair flowing down her back and her lips painted a blood red to match the dress that was clinging to her body, George hadn't realized she'd even snuck away. He hadn't realized she'd been edging closer to the destiny Lina had predicted for her.

"What does a lady have to do to get a date around here? It's been ages since I've been out with a man." Rosalie ran her eyes over the Russian soldier who was holding the knife to Gabriel's throat. "I would have thought you were the type of man who preferred women."

Rosalie was stunning, and she knew it. She must have also known that if she was going to save her nephew, she couldn't be refused, and simply offering herself up wasn't good enough. This was a game, a dance through a field of mines where the slightest misstep would leave them all ground to dust.

"Perhaps your partner is the man I am looking for." She winked at the soldier by the door, who shifted nervously from one foot to the other, and then ran her hand through her hair, which she shook out behind her. When she smiled, her teeth sparkled beneath her crimson lips.

The tension in the room swelled. Philip stood by the table struggling to maintain his calm, his hands balling into fists and his jaw tensing beneath his clenched teeth. The tip of the Russian soldier's blade pressed into the soft skin of Gabriel's neck as the boy struggled to quiet the tremors that pulsed through his body. George didn't dare move a muscle as Rosalie stepped toward the door and held her hand out to the soldier who was almost young enough to be her son.

"Shall we?" she said, and as the young soldier tentatively reached his hand out to her, the man with the missing eye finally broke.

"If it is a man you want, then why do you go to the boy?"

She had him. He'd fallen into her trap, and when she turned to face him, she placed her hands on her hips and pulled a sultry smile from her lips before nodding toward Gabriel, who was still trembling beneath the weight of the steel blade.

"Because the man I wanted is more interested in little boys."

Rosalie lured him toward the door, casting out just enough bait to catch his interest. Gabriel stumbled as the man shoved him along, the tip of the knife nicking the skin beneath his jaw until tiny dots of blood popped out like ink blots on paper.

"No, no." Rosalie shook her head and wagged her finger at him. "Leave the boy," she said. "You will have no use for him tonight. I can assure you."

And with that, the man with the missing eye shoved Gabriel toward his family and vanished into the frigid night with Rosalie, who didn't once look back at Philip or Marcelle or the others she'd just saved. She must have known she would falter if she'd had to say good-bye.

Marcelle's sobs broke through the silence like a dam being obliterated by a torrential flood. The children trembled in her arms as Lina pushed them all up the stairs to the sisters, who'd been listening and waiting and praying. They rushed them into the apartment and when the door shut behind them, Philip slammed his fist onto the table.

"I'm going to get her."

"You cannot go after her." Lina stumbled down the stairs after leaving Marcelle and the children with les soeurs. "They will come back for the rest of us if you go. Do not make Rosalie's sacrifice worth nothing."

Lina and Philip went back and forth as George contemplated the various scenarios. The risks, the rewards, the sacrifices. He played out every possible outcome in his thoughts and by the time he was through, Marcelle was standing at the bottom of the stairs, her hair disheveled and her eyes red and swollen.

"Please go get her," she begged. "Please, Philip. Bring her home."

They were running on emotions, reacting to their pain and giving it too much credibility.

"Lina is right," George said, unable to look at Marcelle, who crumpled onto the stairs under the weight of his words. "Rosalie wouldn't want us to go after her. You both know that."

There was no more talk of a rescue as the night wore on. Philip paced by the front door as Marcelle finally gave in to the exhaustion and slept fitfully on the couch beneath the window. The children spent the evening with the sisters upstairs, and Lina, ever secretive, snuck out into the night under a dark and cloud-filled sky. George spent the endless hours by Marcelle's side, trying to soothe her back to sleep from the nightmares that preyed upon her throughout the long night.

"Rosalie!"

He was defenseless against the one that finally stole her from sleep. She shot up from the couch, her screams piercing the air as George tried to quiet her.

"No!"

"It's okay, mon amour," he whispered to her as he ran his hand over the back of her shirt, which was soaked through with sweat, assuring her of things he didn't believe to be true. "She'll be back in the morning."

"No." Marcelle clawed at her chest as if the pain was unbearable, before she frantically jabbed her fingers into her ribs, searching for the beating of her own heart. When her hands finally stilled, she looked up at George with those piercing blue eyes and breathed out the breath she'd been holding. And then she shook her head.

"She is gone."

chapter 35

Marcelle wouldn't speak.

George had brought her coffee and tea and leftover bread all throughout the night and into the morning, but she wouldn't accept any of it. She sat by the window, staring out at the sun rising over the barren streets, and she wouldn't speak. George paced by the door. Lina still hadn't returned from the previous night, and Philip had gone out looking for Rosalie, determined to prove Marcelle wrong and bring her back alive.

"Please talk to me, mon amour." When George knelt down in front of Marcelle, he almost didn't recognize the woman staring back at him. It hardly seemed possible, but overnight the hollows of her eyes had deepened, and the ghostlike pallor of her skin had intensified.

There was no knock at the door before the Russian soldiers poured into their apartment and the man leading the search read the charges against them. Something about conspiring against the communist regime. The incident report indicated that a soldier passing by their apartment the previous night had stopped to address anti-Bolshevik rhetoric coming from their open window, when he and his partner had been threatened by the men in the home and then propositioned by a prostitute also living in the home. The prostitute had stabbed one of the men in the eye and he was now blind.

Marcelle laughed when the commander read that part,

and if Lina hadn't picked that moment to push her own way through the front door, it would have bought her a slap across the face, at the very least.

Instead, he yanked Marcelle from the couch and pushed her out the door before George could comprehend what was happening. He stumbled down the stairs after them.

"Where are you taking her? She has done nothing wrong."

"She is interfering with an investigation." His grip on Marcelle's arm tightened as he dragged her down the middle of the street, barefoot and half-dressed, for all the town to see. "She will be questioned in a more appropriate environment."

"Please." George followed them down the street as nosy neighbors peeked out their windows between half-closed curtains. "Take me instead. She doesn't know anything."

"I suggest you return to your house before we arrest you both."

Lina was standing in the doorway when George turned around. They were the only two left. Their once bustling and overcrowded apartment felt cold and lifeless when George stepped back inside.

Lina locked the front door behind them before shutting the curtains, steering George to the table, and pulling out a package from beneath her dress. She pushed it in front of him.

"I'm sorry, George. I should have come earlier. I didn't think they would be here this early in the morning." She nodded to the package sitting between them. "It is time to go."

George pulled open the paper to reveal four British identification cards.

Georges Fournier, age 31
Marcelle Fournier, age 29
Gabriel Fournier, age 7
Philippe Fournier, age 28

Four names. Four of the six names that Marcelle had delivered to the forger's wife. Juliette didn't have one because she didn't need one. But Rosalie's was missing. And Lina's.

"Where did you get these?" George asked. "And where is yours?"

Lina smiled back at him. It had been so long since he had really seen Lina, really studied her face and recognized all the ways it had changed over the years they'd come to know each other. She was no longer that wiry teenager who'd confronted them in the cellar when they'd first stumbled into Soissons. She had a woman's face now, lined and strong.

"I am not going," she replied. "But thank you, George. I didn't know you had done all of this for us. I had one of my contacts track down the man who forges the identification cards, and we were quite shocked to learn he'd already been provided the list of names I had for him. Or, at least some combination of them."

George nodded before folding the paper back around the cards. "I notice there isn't one for Rosalie," he said, placing his hand over the stack. "Marcelle thinks she's dead. And Philip left hours ago to bring her home."

"We cut her down before dawn," Lina replied. "Buried her in the outskirts of the city in a cemetery we created for the victims of the Bolsheviks. I buried her identification card with her. Someday, when these monsters have left our country, someone will find her, and they will know who she was."

"You were right about Rosalie," George said. "I doubted you, Lina. But you were right."

"Yes," Lina sighed. "Unfortunately, I was right. I would not wish this curse upon anyone, though. To watch the people you love die, knowing there is nothing you can do to stop it; it must be a trick by the devil himself."

As difficult as it was to believe, George knew that what Lina was saying was true, that she had been here before. There was no other explanation that could suffice for all the things she had known would come to pass. "But how did it happen?" he asked. "How did you end up back here?"

"I don't know how it happened," Lina said. "Fate, I suppose. I don't know if fate is a deity, or a cosmic force, or some kind of a witch, but I am certain that she is a woman." Lina shook her head and laughed. "Because she does not forget."

"Forget what?" George asked.

Lina folded her hands into her lap and stared down at them for a moment, trying to find the words to explain a phenomenon that defied reason and logic and every rule of life George had ever known.

"Imagine that you are just going along and living your life," she began, "and one day you die. And you're sent back into your life to a moment that you've regretted in some way. A decision, perhaps, that should have been different. A decision that, no matter how hard you tried to bury it, you were never able to forget. And you think, well great, now I get to do this part over. I can finally forgive myself for what I did all that time ago. And maybe I can change the horrible things that happened afterward, as well. Prevent the deaths. Stop the invasions." Lina took in a deep breath before she pulled her eyes up to meet George's. "But then, over time, you realize it wasn't even about you. It never was. And nothing you did could ever stop death from finding the ones you loved."

"But how do you . . ." George didn't finish his sentence. *How do you do it?* was the question he wanted to ask, but it seemed an unfair question. How does anyone shoulder his burdens? You either do or you don't. You live or you die.

"Would you do it again?" he asked. "Knowing that Max wouldn't save Paul, would you still rescue him at the river?"

"I have spent many hours considering that question," Lina replied. "And I choose to believe that saving Max must have been important, and that fate must have sent me back here for that reason. I have to believe that Max will go on to do something great, something to change history, because otherwise, what is the point of all this? Is it some horrible cosmic joke?" Lina paused for a moment, dropping her eyes to her hands again. "And, if I am being honest," she continued, "I like to think that maybe someday someone will be sent back to change *my* fate. To create a world where someone as beautiful as Paul isn't murdered by these monsters."

When she looked up at him again, George was surprised to see tears in her eyes. He'd never seen Lina cry. He'd never imagined anything could bring her to tears. She wiped them away before they could fall and smiled back at him.

"We have more important matters to worry about now, though," Lina said, but before she could rise from the table, George reached out and placed his hand over hers.

"Lina, wait," he said. "Do we make it out of here? Can you tell me that much?"

Lina paused, the slight flicker of her fingers beneath George's hand a reminder that, despite her strength, she was not immune to the vulnerability that preyed on them all. "Things are a bit different this time," she said. "You were not on the run when we were last here, and while Paul and Rosalie were both killed, they were not hung in the cathedral square like they were this time. So, even though things are different, they are somehow still the same." Lina was silent for so long that George didn't expect her to continue. "But, no," she finally continued. "To answer your question, we do not all survive this, George. That is not how this ends."

"Who is next?"

"You don't want to know." Lina shook her head, trying to slip her hand from George's grasp as he tightened it.

"Please," he begged. "Is it Marcelle? Or one of the children? Please tell me."

"I promise you, George." Lina snatched her hand back and locked her eyes on his before she pulled herself up from the chair. "You do not want to know."

He knew she was right. He knew that knowing would break him, but even so, he would have chosen that over ignorance.

Lina pulled four empty flour sacks from the cupboard in the kitchen before handing two of them to George. "We will have to wait until nightfall to get Marcelle out of prison and to get you all on the road," she said. "I will pack a few things for her and the children. You pack for Philip and yourself. He will not be coming back here. He and the children are in hiding."

"The children? But they're upstairs with les soeurs. How did you . . ."

Lina shook her head and smiled as she turned toward the bedroom. "Just pack."

George was an inefficient packer. He didn't know where they were going or how they would get there, and after throwing some pants and shirts into the flour sacks, he went searching for Lina. He wasn't expecting to find anyone else in their apartment, especially the man who was standing in their kitchen. He never imagined they would meet again.

"I'm so sorry, George."

Roland hadn't changed. He'd been well fed and well cared for under the Bolshevik regime and didn't possess the same gaunt and weary appearance as the rest of them. George couldn't remember the last time he'd seen Roland, and he feared that if Lina walked through the door and saw her cousin standing in their kitchen, they'd have more to worry about than just getting Marcelle out of prison.

"You shouldn't be here." George glanced back toward the bedroom. "Please, Roland. If Lina sees you here . . ." He shook his head and let his words trail off.

"I am here to help you get Marcelle out of prison."

⌁ ⌁ ⌁

If they'd had any other options, Roland would not have been sitting at their kitchen table with them, sipping on watery tea and devising strategies to free Marcelle. As it turned out, he was a wealth of information, and George shuddered to think about what would have happened to Marcelle if he hadn't shown up when he did.

Waiting until nightfall wasn't an option. Prison guards lived a comfortable life from all the bribes they took from drunk and lonely soldiers looking for ten minutes with a prisoner, especially a female prisoner, and those visits started the moment the sun went down. If they didn't break her out before then, Marcelle would be lucky to survive the night.

"How do you get to be the first in line?" Lina asked, but George was already shaking his head. They couldn't risk waiting until nightfall. He couldn't do that to Marcelle. "I know it's not ideal, George. But we must consider everything."

"The bigger the bribe, the closer to the front," Roland replied. "Especially if it is alcohol."

"I don't like this. Even if you got yourself in, there's no way to get her back out without someone noticing." George pushed himself back from the table and paced through the kitchen. "We have to come up with something better. How about rubles? I have plenty of rubles to buy off a guard. Maybe we can go now when no one else is there."

"You cannot buy her freedom," Roland replied. "If she disappears from the prison, the guard who was supposed to be watching her will be killed. He will not take a bribe for her release. He will only allow you time with her."

By the time the sun had peaked in the sky, they'd exhausted every possible scenario and were no closer to a solution. George's thoughts kept bringing him back to the prison in Jaulgonne, the night he and Philip had snuck in to rescue Marcelle. Every dead-end road was leading them back to that moment.

"Can your people get me liquor and cigarettes?" Roland asked.

Lina shrugged in response.

"It depends," she said. "What do you have in mind?"

Your people.

Lina's people. Roland's people. George's people. They all had their own people working under the noses of a communist regime that survived only because of the underground.

"George," Roland said. "I am sorry to ask this of you, but could Lina and I have a moment, please?"

Given their history, George was disinclined to leave Lina alone with him, but when she nodded her consent, he stepped out the front door into the crisp November air. He thought about Marcelle in her thin cotton dress. No jacket. No shoes. Not even a pair of socks to keep her feet warm. She was broken. She would never be the same without Rosalie. They had torn out a piece of her heart and left a gaping wound in her chest that would never heal.

The town was quiet. It was always quiet these days, but there was a different kind of silence forcing its way through the desolate streets on that particular afternoon. An ominous and foreboding presence, like the devil had found his way to Soissons.

George's gaze instinctively dropped to the dirt patch by the stairs, the spot where he and Marcelle had buried the rosary. For two years it had lain beneath the ground. Should he dig it back up? Would Marcelle want that piece of her sister?

Before George could come up with an answer to that question, Lina came out to get him, and the rosary lost its importance. He would travel many miles before he thought about that rosary again, but when it came back into his life, it would carry an entirely new meaning.

〜〜〜

"I don't like this one bit, Lina."

George hadn't fired a gun in eight years, but the weight of the rifle in his hands felt comfortable and familiar. The sun was just starting to set, and he'd been camped out in the field across from the jailhouse for hours, wedged between rows of overgrown and out-of-season crops. It was a small building, perhaps one or two cells at most, and while George could see only one entryway from their location, two guards were visible. Neither had any idea he was being watched.

"You don't have to like it," Lina replied. "You just have to do it."

They had decided on a plan, though it wasn't ideal. Lina was securing liquor bottles to the inside of Roland's oversized coat and stuffing the pockets full of cigarettes. They were counting on it being enough. George had promised them both that, even if Roland wasn't first in line, he would not fire the rifle and he would stick to the plan, but they had to have known he was lying. George had no intention of letting anyone near Marcelle. If anyone but Roland tried to walk through the front door of that building, they would get a bullet to the back of the head.

"Should we go over the plan one more time?" Roland asked. He was nervous. George couldn't blame him. If he was caught, he would be killed.

"I think I've got it," George replied. "Just be the first one in there and we won't have anything to worry about."

"I will do my best, George. I hope you and Marcelle make it out of here, my friend. I wish I had been a better friend to you both. And for that, I am sorry."

"There will be plenty of time for this later, Roland. Just go in there and get Marcelle and we'll call it even."

Roland nodded back at him and smiled before he turned to Lina, who walked him to the edge of the field. She placed an oversized hat onto his head and wrapped a scarf around his face before she handed him a pair of gloves that he pulled over his hands while she held his crutches for him.

It was taking them too long. George was getting restless as Lina fussed over Roland's outfit and they discussed last-minute plans. How many times did they have to go over this? Roland would go in the front door alone and come out the service door in the back with Marcelle. There was only one guard for the back of the prison, and he could typically be found bundled inside his coat, smoking cigarettes, and sipping from his flask.

Roland was confident they could slip right by him, but if not, he'd assured George, as he'd patted the sheath around his waist, there was no one better with a dagger than him. George was there as a last resort. If they didn't make it by the guard, and if Roland couldn't best him with the dagger, George would have to take him down with the rifle, and then the race would be on.

By the time Roland hobbled out of the field toward the jail-house, a crowd was starting to gather, and George's finger was getting restless on the trigger. He wanted Philip by his side. He should have insisted that Lina bring him, but she'd been adamant that he stay with the children because he would've been a liability; he wouldn't have had the patience to see the plan through. The light was fading as Lina hunkered down beside him just in time for Roland's theatrics.

They could hear the other men jeering as he opened his coat for the guard to see what he was offering. Some of the men tried to match him with bottles of what looked like homemade liquor concoctions, but when Roland pulled the cigarettes from his pockets, the deal was done. The guard collected the contraband as Roland took an exaggerated bow, dancing like a jester in front of the crowd of men who were all waiting their turn for a chance at Marcelle. If he thought he could have gotten away with it, George would have shot every last one of them.

When Roland disappeared into the building, George turned his focus to the guard around back. He didn't have a clear view of the back door, but the guard was in his line of sight.

"Why is he taking so long?" How long had he been in there? Neither one of them had a watch.

"Give him some time," Lina replied. "It has only been a few minutes."

The men out front were getting restless. Even without a watch, George knew too much time had passed, and if Roland

and Marcelle hadn't already snuck by the guard, he needed to be ready to take the shot. With his senses heightened and his vision sharpened, he took aim at the back guard. Deep breath in. Long, slow breath out. Steady hands. One finger.

The jolt of the rifle didn't come from the recoil. George never even pulled the trigger. It came from Lina knocking the gun out of his hands.

"Not yet." She grabbed the gun and pointed her finger toward the prison entrance.

Cheers erupted as Roland staggered out the front door, hunched over his crutches and struggling to make it down the stairs and across the road. He was alone. Was he injured? Drunk?

"Where's Marcelle? Give me the gun, Lina."

"Wait!" She pulled a light from her pocket and flashed it twice, but Roland was off course, hobbling toward the field to their east. The men at the jailhouse were jockeying for position as the guard looked over their wares and pointed to one near the back.

George was about to snatch the gun from Lina's hand, but she took off at a sprint, flashing her light on and off until Roland's head suddenly turned in their direction and he changed course.

"That son of a bitch!" George hissed, but Lina was surprisingly fast, darting through the rows and hopping over vines that tangled around George's ankles, tripping him up and slowing him down. "Give me the gun, Lina."

She got to Roland first, knocking him to the ground and ripping his pants off. It wasn't until George was standing over him and saw the leg, the one that should have been missing, unfold from beneath him, that he realized it wasn't Roland. When the hat and the scarf and the oversized coat came off, it was Marcelle staring up at him, her hair shorn from her head and terror flooding through her eyes. George pulled her up and into his arms, but Lina was already pushing them deeper into the field.

"Where is Roland?" George asked, his eyes darting back toward the prison. "Is he coming out the back door?"

"There is no back door," Lina replied, grabbing Marcelle's arm and dragging her barefoot and stumbling through the foliage. "It is time to run."

chapter 36

MARCELLE

Roland was dead.

Marcelle didn't know this with the same certainty she had known her sister was dead, but she believed it, just the same.

She had an arm around each of her children, and George was struggling to soothe her while Lina detailed her escape to Philip. The burdens she carried would soon drag her under. First Rosalie, now Roland. Their souls would forever be tethered to her.

Lina's story had been accurate enough, but Marcelle would never share the details of that night with anyone. How she'd stood naked in front of Roland as he'd dressed her, buttoning up the shirt because she couldn't calm the tremor in her hands. How he'd laid her on the bed and pulled the pants over her folded leg so it would appear to be missing. How he'd sheared her hair off with the dagger, then placed the hat on her head and wrapped the scarf around her face. How a lifetime of memories and familiarity had passed between them in a span of ten minutes. How she'd cried into his chest as he had pulled from her a promise that she would go on, that she would fight for herself and her children, and that she would not allow these sacrifices to be made in vain.

She couldn't imagine a scenario where he'd made it out of that prison cell alive. Had they found him naked? Had he pretended Marcelle had bested him? Had he hopped out of the prison without the crutches she'd taken?

Marcelle's feet were still bleeding. George had washed them off and picked out the thistles and thorns, but they were in bad shape. She'd run barefoot through the fields as Lina had led them to a root cellar hidden in the side of a hill on the outskirts of town. It felt like they'd run for hours through fields of brambles and across rock-filled streams. Marcelle had refused to ask for a break. Even when her lungs burned and her feet bled, she'd kept pace with Lina and George, desperate to get back to her children.

It wasn't until she'd seen Gabriel and Juliette huddled together in the back of the cave that she'd finally broken down and wept. It was just the six of them now, stuck in a dirt hole that had been dug into the side of a hill in the middle of nowhere.

What kind of a life was this? What had she done to her children? Gabriel could have been living a good life with Max and his family in Germany. He could have been eating meals around a table and thriving in school, playing with his friends in the street instead of hiding in a dirt cave, hungry and scared. Why hadn't she let him go, and what wouldn't she give to have that moment back, to change her son's fate?

A stick snapped outside the bunker, a sharp crack, splintering wood beneath a boot.

No one moved. Even when the light from the man's lantern cast his shadow across the wall, no one flinched. He was a Russian soldier, and he watched them in silence, his eyes running over each of their faces until they landed on Lina's. A rifle hung at his side, the strap draped casually over his shoulder. Lina placed a hand over Philip's arm, a warning to stay back, before she stepped up to the man and fell into his arms. He kissed the top of her head and laughed before stepping back to get a better look at her.

"Rosomakha," he said, running his hand over the side of her face. "Are you going to introduce me to your friends?"

Nikolai was the man's name, and he'd come bearing food, water, and flour sacks filled with clothes from their apartment. After Marcelle changed from Roland's clothes into a dress, she joined the others in the field outside the root cellar beneath the stars and listened to the Russian soldier detail the plans for their coming escape. The night sky was still and the air crisp, and the children soon fell into a deep sleep by Marcelle's side.

George had reluctantly forgiven Lina for lying to him about the escape plan at the prison. He must have known why she had done it, that he would never have gone along with it. He was not a man who carried his anger with him, and he knew that, come morning, they would part ways, possibly for good. Marcelle had not allowed herself to think about where this journey might land them, but as she stared up at the vastness of the sky, she couldn't help but let her mind wander. Could they really make it to England? Maybe even to America?

Nikolai's French was flawless. His mother had been from Lille, and he'd spent his summers in northern France as a child. France was in his blood. His father had been a high-ranking officer in the Russian army until the Romanovs had abdicated and Lenin had taken over. His father would have been shattered if he'd lived long enough to see his son in a Bolshevik uniform. But what else could Nikolai do? His father's Russia was gone.

Nikolai was no one important in the Bolshevik army, but in many ways that worked to his advantage. No one watched him; no one expected anything from him. Over time, he'd worked his way into the position of a driver, hauling produce and metalworks to the bigger cities where farmland and factories were scarce. The guards at the checkpoints knew him and waved him through without question, especially when he came bearing gifts of cigarettes and homemade wine and seedy magazines.

"We will leave at dawn," Nikolai explained. "You must remain under the tarps with the vegetable crates, but I do not expect any problems. I can get you as far as Abbeville, but beyond that we would be stopped and searched."

They all nodded in agreement. The events of the past few days had taken their toll, and no one was much for talking. When Lina's head lolled against his chest, Nikolai pulled her in closer. "I suggest you all get some sleep," he said. "The next few days will be long."

George carried the children into the shelter of the cave before he came back out and whispered a goodnight into Marcelle's ear. He didn't ask her if he should stay or when she would come to bed. He didn't have to ask her those things. He knew Marcelle like the stars knew the moon, and he knew she needed this time to say good-bye to Lina.

Lina looked like a child beside Nikolai—petite, delicate, and vulnerable—not at all like the woman Marcelle had come to know over the past eight years. How long had it been since she had seen this side of Lina, the one who'd found comfort in her mother's arms at the news of her father's death?

"What was that word?" Marcelle asked, looking up at Nikolai, whose eyes were an even deeper brown than George's. "When you first entered the cave, you called Lina something. Rose . . . Rosa something."

"Rosomakha?"

"Yes. That was it. What does that mean?"

"Rosomakha is wolverine. It is a small animal in Russia. Unassuming. Everyone says that the bear is the fiercest animal in Siberia, but the natives, they know the truth. The wolverine rules the taiga."

Marcelle watched Lina sleep. Small and unassuming. Lina was one of the fiercest people she had ever known. She would outlast them all. There was so much Marcelle wanted to tell her, so much she wanted Lina to know. She had been everything to Marcelle: a loyal and true friend, a protector, a sister. How could she walk away from this life without her?

"She knows." Nikolai watched her through the dim light

of the lantern. He must have said his own share of good-byes over the years, and Marcelle was thankful that he was a man of few words. She had no interest in words tonight. Words were useless in times like these; in most times, she supposed. They would leave the next morning, before the sun would even have a chance to rise. There would be no long and drawn-out good-byes. Each woman would offer a kiss on the cheek to the other with a promise they would meet again, a promise this would not be their final good-bye.

chapter 37

They made the four-hour trip to Abbeville hidden beneath a tarp and wedged between crates of vegetables. The checkpoints had been never-ending, the stop and go of the truck rattling their bones as their bodies had banged against the hard wooden floor. But Nikolai had been a master negotiator, managing to avoid inspections at every stop by trading wine and cigarettes to the guards for safe passage.

Gabriel had been an excellent traveler, he and Philip wedged into the front of the truck bed together and whispering jokes between checkpoints. Philip had been folded around the crates like an accordion, but had never once complained, even as he'd carried Juliette on the five-kilometer trek that took them from the truck to the one-room cabin on the banks of the canal. Their hike had been fraught with obstacles—hidden tree roots, deep embankments, rocky streams—but they'd somehow managed to step into the cabin just as the sun was disappearing beneath the trees.

By the time Marcelle got the children settled, George and Nikolai were deep in conversation about the coming days. George would travel alone for the first trip to deliver half the wine and cigarettes, half the rubles, and their identification cards to a man Nikolai had found living about ten kilometers up the canal toward the English Channel in another one-room cabin. He was a Frenchman, and an untrusting one at that, with strict rules: He only worked for cigarettes and wine, he only dealt with Frenchmen, and he only allowed one person in his cabin at a time. George seemed pleased with the rules. He had an appreciation for men who were methodical and precise, especially since he was one of them.

Three days later they would all return together with the rest of the goods and the rest of the rubles, in hopes that the Frenchman in the cabin had been able to secure transport for them with one of the Russian fishermen.

"Why does he want the identification cards now?" George asked, nervous to part with them after having gone to such lengths to secure them.

"The fishermen will not take anyone without proof of identification. No matter how much they pay. And they want that proof before they agree to a trip. It is too risky for them once they get into British-controlled waters. A boat full of people claiming to be British with no identification makes people suspicious. Do not worry, George. He has been vetted."

Aside from the clothes on their backs and their bags full of supplies, Nikolai left them with a few days' worth of food and water and his word that he would take care of Lina. Marcelle watched him disappear into the forest beneath the darkening sky and wondered if they would ever meet again.

She was restless, busying herself with an old straw broom she'd found outside the door as Juliette watched her from the corner atop a bed full of clothes. Something didn't feel right. She knew the man George was going to visit in the morning had been vetted, but something still felt off, like the night she had delivered the book to the man with the black beret beneath the cherry tree in Montmirail. Her gut was trying to tell her something.

"It will be fine, mon amour." George was watching her. He had packed his bag for the last time and was tucking his identification cards into his pockets. French on the right, British on the left. He never went anywhere without his identification card, not even to bed. Marcelle's scarf fell from her head as she wiped her brow with her forearm. The last time a man had shorn her hair with a dagger, she had been too self-conscious and insecure to let anyone see it. It wasn't until it had grown out enough for a trim that she'd even left her room without a scarf. She was a different woman now, though. The vulnerability she carried was no longer tied to her beauty; it lay in her family.

"I will go with you, Papa." Gabriel was an attentive boy, becoming more like his father every day. At seven, he seemed more like a man than a child, and Marcelle often wondered if it was too late to bring childhood back to him. Was he too far gone from the boy who'd once played with toy airplanes and stolen sugar from the pantry? Would he ever really know what it meant to be seven?

"You would be a fine partner, son." George placed his hands on Gabriel's shoulders and leaned in close before whispering to him in a conspiratorial voice. "But I will need a man here to help Oncle Philippe take care of your maman and Juliette. Do you think you can do that for me?"

"Oui, Papa." When Gabriel glanced back at Marcelle, she had to hide the smile from her face and pretend she was not eavesdropping on their conversation. "I will take care of them."

Night came quickly.

After a light dinner of bread and cheese, Juliette fell asleep in her father's arms. The days had been long for all of them, but especially for Juliette. When George laid her tiny body beside Marcelle and Gabriel, she didn't budge. Her breaths deepened until she was lost to the world, and soon after, her brother followed her into sleep.

Marcelle fixed a separate bed for her and George, but she couldn't find comfort on the wooden floorboards; she couldn't trick herself into sleep. When she finally gave up, she stared into the blackness around her and listened to a conversation that was as stale as the bread they had just eaten for dinner.

"Do you ever think about that night?" Philip was always the

one to start it, the one who couldn't figure out how to bury the memories of a battle he was certain they should have won. "It's just . . . well . . . you never bring it up," he said, "but . . . I guess I always wonder if you think about it."

"I try not to," George replied, and Marcelle knew that was the truth. George had been dreaming about that night repeatedly over the past few weeks, waking in such a frenzied and terrified state that Marcelle could barely soothe him.

"What do you think might have happened if we'd been able to take that hill back?" Philip asked.

"I don't know," George sighed between them. "Maybe you're right. Maybe I made the wrong decision."

"That's not what I meant, George. I know you saved my life out there. And you know I would have done the same thing for you if the situations were reversed. Even if you didn't want me to." When Philip hesitated, Marcelle turned her head slightly so she could hear them better. This was a new twist on an old conversation. George had never once conceded that his judgment might have been in error, and Philip had never once acknowledged that what George had done was out of love. "I don't know what's wrong with me," Philip said. "I just feel like I'm always going back to that moment. Like it was supposed to have ended differently somehow."

George didn't respond, and as the silence settled around them, Marcelle thought about her own memories that wouldn't stay buried, the secrets she had carried with her over the years. "I hope you know that you don't have to worry about Marcelle and the kids if . . . well . . . you know." Philip hesitated before he continued. "If something happens and we have to run, I want you to know that I'll take care of them. That I would defend them with my life."

"I know you would," George said. "And there's no one I would trust with my family more than you. If I'm not back by nightfall, get them out of here. Take the money and the rest of the cigarettes and wine and disappear."

Marcelle pressed her face into the back of her arm and sobbed silently. She couldn't lose George. When the conversation finally ended, and he slid into the space beside her, she pressed her body up to his with a need so deep she didn't even care that her children were asleep in the corner or that Philip was settling in across the room. Her back arched against the wooden floor as George's weight pressed down on her, their bodies tensing together.

He kissed the tears from her cheeks, running his lips across her face until they lingered just over her mouth. She closed her eyes and breathed in the warmth of his exhaled breaths, filling herself with him, needing his strength inside of her.

"Come back to me," she whispered. "Please come back."

"I am right here, Marcelle." His words mixed with hers in the air between them as he ran his finger along the delicate ridge of the scar on her cheek before sliding it down her neck. "I am always right here," he whispered, placing the palm of his hand over her heart. "And I promise, I will always come back to you, mon amour."

chapter 38

GEORGE

They would come for him.

Even through the mist of the morning fog hanging over the water, they would see him digging in the mud by the banks of the canal. George was sure of it. He couldn't calm his breaths. They were too loud, and the Russian soldiers who were inside the Frenchman's cabin would hear him, and then they would come for him.

The blast of a rifle pierced the air, forcing George to his knees, before sending a flurry of birds from their roosts as they chased its echo over the water. They had killed the finder, the man whose cabin they were now ransacking, and they would come for George next.

He ducked his body even further beneath the line of bushes sheltering him along the shore and tried to smooth the mud at his feet. His hands were clumsy, numb from the cold, and he feared the hole he'd dug for the sack with the wine and rubles and identification cards wasn't deep enough. The water was frigid as he rinsed himself off before putting some distance between him and the hole. If he was caught, the Russians had to believe he was traveling alone.

The light was starting to filter in through the trees overhead, starting to burn off the fog that had blanketed him beneath it. George flattened his body against the ground and slithered between coppices of trees. He had to stay ahead of the soldiers; he had to get to his family first.

From his position, he could see the soldiers' boots as they stepped from the cabin onto the grass below. They had already broken into the wine and cigarettes, their voices carrying with the wind, growing with each uncorked bottle. George had no choice but to wait them out. There was no cover beneath the rising sun. He counted the pairs of boots.

. . . five . . . six . . . seven

There were seven of them. Or was it six? He counted again.

. . . four . . . five . . . six

When he heard the stick snap behind him, the image of Philip's smiling face at the prison in Jaulgonne popped into his mind. Would his friend be there when he looked back? Would they storm up the hill together and kill the Russian soldiers? Would they find their way to freedom?

——— ⌣ ———

"Skazhi eto po-angliyski." *Say it in English.*

"I don't speak English," George replied in Russian. "Only French, German, and Russian."

"Say it in English!" The smell of onions and sauerkraut filled the air between them as the man leaned in closer to George's face. He smelled like a German, but he spoke Russian, and the glistening medals pinned to his coat were Bolshevik. The two identification cards George had been carrying in his pockets were sitting on the table between them. He could barely see them through the swelling of his beaten eyes, but he knew they were there. He should have buried them in the mud with the others. They thought he was a British spy. If they only knew the truth.

"I don't speak English," George muttered again, his tongue running over the jagged edge of a cracked front tooth that had been broken the day he'd been captured outside the finder's cabin. He was going on his third day, and he was arguing in vain. He'd be beaten either way, and English was bound to slip out. Marcelle and Philip would have figured out by now that he wasn't coming back, that they would have to find a different route.

"Anglisyskiye svin'i." *English pigs.*

George didn't flinch when the spit landed on the side of his face or when the table between them was toppled. He sat quietly, waiting for the next barrage of fists and fury that never came. The message that interrupted round three of interrogations must have come from the top, because when it was delivered, the commander left the room.

It wasn't long before he returned, snapping at the guards in the corners to right the table and settling himself across from George. When he smiled, his yellowed teeth glistened under the glow of the lamplight, highlighting the rot that was spreading along his gum lines. Juliette would have cried if she'd ever come face-to-face with him. She would have thought the man sitting across from her papa was the wolf from the fairy tales Marcelle recited to her at night. George was beginning to wonder the same thing. He was a mountain of a man, propped atop a throne-like chair that looked like it had once belonged to a Russian tsar.

"Cigarette?"

The man pulled out a sterling silver case, intricately engraved with throngs of ivy and flower petals. When he popped it open, George caught the woody scent of real tobacco and marveled at the row of perfectly rolled cigarettes that were lined up as straight as a formation of soldiers. As much as he yearned for the taste of one, he kept his hands in his lap.

"No, thank you," George replied, troubled by the sudden shift of energy in the room.

"Suit yourself," he mumbled around the cigarette that rested between his lips before pulling out a sterling silver lighter to match the cigarette case he must have pilfered from a wealthy French family along the way. When the scent of burning tobacco reached him from across the table, George could feel his resolve waning. The air was thick with smoke before the commander coughed into his fist and cleared his throat.

"Your wife is a beautiful woman," he said, and while the words hung between them, floating just beyond George's reach, there was nothing he could do to prepare himself for the moment they would hit. There was no amount of armor that could have defended him, and no barrage of fists that could have come close to the blow of the commander's words. He stubbed the end of his half-finished cigarette into the bottom of his boot before he flicked it into the corner and leaned forward across the table.

They didn't make it. Philip and Marcelle and the children had been captured.

"Please," George begged.

"Do you know the penalty for being a British spy?"

George didn't respond. He knew the penalty. He knew that if he was convicted of being a British spy, the penalty for all of them would be the same. Death.

"Please. She is innocent. I am French. The British card is fake. I can show you how I made it."

The commander rose from his throne, the clicking of his heels beating like a metronome onto the concrete floor.

"Marcelle," he said. "It certainly sounds French."

As he watched the commander pace back and forth before the table, his arms clasped behind his back like a revered professor, George couldn't quiet his mind. He should have found a way back to them, a way to warn them. What could he have done differently?

"And your son," the commander continued. "Gabriel. Very French indeed."

He flicked his hands toward the guards, who scurried from the room like the rats who'd once scattered through the hayloft in George's old barn in Alabama, and then he sat back down.

"You have two options," he said, waiting for the door to

shut behind the last guard before continuing. "If you are indeed a British citizen, as your identification card indicates, then you and your family will be sentenced as enemies of the state, which, I am afraid, carries the penalty of death. There is another way, however. I am looking for credible information about a certain network of French and British citizens that has been a thorn in my side for some time, and I am confident you possess this information. I need to know who made this identification card for you." He held up the card in front of George's face. "I need names, dates, locations. All of it. If you can provide this to me, I will destroy the card, and you and your family will be sentenced as deserters."

"And what would that look like?" George asked. "What would the sentence for a deserter's family look like?"

"For attempting to abandon your country and its people, you and your wife will be rehabilitated at a work camp," the commander replied. "Your son will spend ten years of his life in a juvenile camp to help pay for the crimes of his family. But he could have a bright future as a Bolshevik when his debt is fully paid."

George's mind was spinning as he tried to process the commander's words. You. Your wife. Your son. What about Juliette? And Philip?

"What about . . ." George stopped himself before he let the words spill out between them. Something was off. A nagging voice was whispering through his thoughts that he was missing something. Something vital.

"The man traveling with you?" he replied, and when George nodded his head, the commander smiled. "Philippe Fournier? Your brother, I assume? He will of course join you and your wife at the work camp."

Philippe Fournier.

George knew only one Philippe Fournier. He'd created him before they'd left Soissons and he'd buried him in the mud on the banks of the canal. They'd found the sack. The commander

hadn't mentioned Juliette because there was no British identification card for her. He had four cards in his possession, but
not George's family.

George leaned back into the chair. If he was wrong, the consequences would be dire. But if he was right, then his family
was somewhere out there working their way toward freedom,
and the real issue became George's life versus the network of
people who'd created the fake papers for him. Maybe even
Lina.

"My wife, Marcelle," George said, sighing into the space
between them. "I worry about her. I don't know that she is
strong enough to survive a camp."

The commander nodded back at him. "Perhaps other ar-
rangements can be made for her," he replied. "Like most Frenchwomen, she has a softness to her. A weakness. Not a good trait
during these difficult times, would you say? You should have
gone with a Russian woman. Maybe even a German."

George nodded and laughed along with the commander.
"Yes," he replied, picturing Marcelle's chopped hair and
scarred face, the missing tooth that no longer troubled her.
No one who laid eyes on Marcelle would ever describe her as
weak. "Always so worried about beauty." George smoothed
his hands across his cheeks. "The skin, the hair, the teeth. So
exhausting keeping up with it all."

The commander laughed as he offered George another cigarette. "Well, she certainly knows how to keep herself beautiful. I think we can work something out for your wife. Let her
hang on to that beauty. We want you to have something to
look forward to when you are released from the camps." He
nudged the cigarette case closer to George. "A cigarette?"

"Yes." George reached over and pulled one out. He ran it
under his nose and breathed in the scent of it. "I think I will,"
he said. "Thank you."

"So, Monsieur Fournier. Have you decided then?" The

commander leaned across the table and lit the end of George's cigarette. "Are you a deserter or a spy?"

George was tired. How many times had he escaped death? He was tired of running from it, tired of hiding. His family was safe, and he would never offer up information that might put Lina at risk. He was out of options. This was it. This was the end. He took one last puff from the cigarette and inhaled the smoke deep into his lungs before he watched it drift out into the air, into a freedom he wanted so desperately to taste, and then he looked at the Russian commander, and he smiled.

"I am a spy."

chapter 39

The blast rang through his ears.

But the bullet, suspended in the air between him and the man who'd fired it, wasn't the last thing George saw. It was the man's eyes. In that moment of hesitancy, that brief instant of anticipation, their gazes locked, and George could see all the fear and sorrow and regret in the eyes of the man who'd been ordered to send death his way.

He would never forget those eyes.

When his world disappeared, and the thrumming of his heart beneath his chest stilled, he could hear the man's words as if they were being spoken inside his mind.

"This is not who I am. This is not the man I was meant to be."

"Who were you meant to be?" George asked, but the man was already gone and when the light came back, it was the sun rising over the endless pastures of his home in Alabama. A woman was walking toward him, and he knew, without having to see her face, it was his mother.

"You're here, George." Her words carried across the field in the soft southern drawl that always reminded him of home. She was beautiful and young and the exact image of the woman he'd seen only in his dreams for the past twenty-seven years.

"I missed you so much, Mama."

When she held him, he was six years old again, certain that his mother's arms would protect him from all the horrors of the world.

"My boy," she whispered into his hair. "I'm so proud of you. I wish you could stay."

George reached for his mother even as she slipped through his fingers and vanished into the air like a fine mist. His legs wouldn't move. He lay on the ground, staring up at the blazing sun and trying to force out the words that droned through his mind. Russian words. *Is he dead? Why are his eyes open?* Russian soldiers. They stared down at him as the gravel beneath his body bit into his skin.

"You just gonna lay there and mope? Or are you gonna get up and play?"

His brother was staring down at him, and when George looked up from the ground, he was eight years old, and had just twisted his ankle trying to catch a pass. He remembered the day well.

"Come on, boy. When was the last time you threw a football?"

His brother tossed him the ball when he got up. It felt strangely familiar in his hands, and when he threw back a perfect spiral, he laughed out loud. "I've still got it."

"You're all right," his brother laughed. "I'm sorry about everything you went through, little brother. But you know what you have to do, right?"

George caught the football again, feeling for the laces with his fingers and running the question through his mind. You know what you have to do, right? He threw it back to his brother without answering.

"Nice throw, Papa. When are you going to teach me how to do that?"

Gabriel stood before him, his cheeks rosy and full, a typical seven-year-old boy who hadn't grown up starving and tormented.

The house in the background, the one George had always hoped to bring his family back to one day, was the same one he'd grown up in.

"I'll teach you now," George replied, but as he walked toward his son, Calypso whinnied behind him.

———～～———

The horse snorted, pawing at the dust on the ground. The poor animal was too starved and wasted to fill out the harness that secured him to the cart. More Russian words. *Load him up. Give me a hand.* More Russian soldiers. His body felt light, drifting through the air along with the aroma of the homemade wine George had sold for their freedom. It was the scent of Russian soldiers. The horse whinnied again as the gate to the prison opened and his body was carted away.

———～～———

"I like when she talks to me," Juliette said, reaching her hand out toward Calypso.

"You better be careful with this one," George said, walking up beside his daughter. "She's been known to try to take off a finger or two."

"It's okay, Papa. She likes me." Just to prove him wrong, the black mare pushed her nose into Juliette's hand and nickered. "Will you teach me to ride her?"

When George smiled down at his daughter, she was a teenager, looking up at him with those brown eyes that always melted him. This was where Juliette belonged, taming her own wild mare.

"I would love to do that," he said.

"Oncle Philippe wants to talk to you first." She nodded toward the gate behind him, where Philip was sitting with his back toward them and gazing out over the pasture.

"This is some place," he said. "I sure am glad you brought me here."

"I'm glad you're here too," George said. "I always hoped we'd make it back here someday."

"I'm sorry you don't get to stay."

"What do you mean?"

When Philip hopped off the fence and turned around, he was the twenty-year-old kid George had met in Châteauvillain all those years ago. The boy whose hands had never been stained with blood and whose idealism hadn't been crushed by prison camps and starvation and executions. He'd forgotten Philip had ever been this young.

"I could have stopped them, George. If you had just let me go, we could have taken the hill, and everything would have been different."

"I thought I already apologized for this."

"It's not an apology I'm looking for, my friend. I just need you to know how pivotal that moment was. I need you to really understand that before you go back."

The darkness surrounded him. It pressed on his skin and through his body and into his mind until he couldn't move for fear it would suffocate him. It wasn't the vast darkness of the midnight sky that had found him. It was the kind of darkness that came when the walls closed in. When the box was shut. When the coffin was sealed. Something rustled beside him, scratching at the surface of his thoughts and breathing out words in a language he hadn't spoken in years. English.

The laughter pulled him from the void. It was light and carefree, and he hadn't heard it in years. Marcelle was swinging on the old tire swing his father had hung for him when he was just a boy, her head back, her face to the sun, her hair flowing beneath her. She jumped up when she noticed George watching her.

"*I bet you can't catch me,*" she teased, and darted off through the grass with her bare feet.

"*You made it too easy,*" George laughed as they lay beneath the giant oak and stared up at the sky.

"*You have to go back, George. There's a special purpose for you.*"

"*What special purpose?*"

"*You know what you have to do.*" Marcelle leaned over him and smiled. No missing teeth. No scars. No pain.

George shook his head.

"*I think I'll just stay here forever,*" he said. The blue of Marcelle's eyes was a perfect match to the endless sky above her, and as she leaned in closer to him, her hair brushed across his face. She placed her finger on his forehead, over the spot where the bullet had entered his skin.

"*Open your eyes,*" she whispered as he let them drift shut and took in the chorus all around him. The birds. The wind. The sound of Marcelle's voice. "*Open your eyes, my love. Open your eyes . . .*"

part III

chapter 40

GEORGE

The air that filled George's lungs when they finally kicked back into action tasted thick with sweat. It was stale and stagnant, and the light that trickled in from his periphery was muted and gray. The abrasive contrast between the two worlds felt like sandpaper over his skin.

"You okay, buddy?"

English. Someone was speaking English. American English.

"I think he was having a nightmare."

There were too many voices. Too many bodies in the room. Too many men stacked together and fighting for the same air that was too thick to sustain them all. He had to get out. There had to be an exit. As he scrambled to get away, his hands and knees dug into the ribs and limbs of all the bodies that were packed in around him. They were yelling at him by the time he reached the door, but when he yanked at the handle, it wouldn't budge.

"Ouvrez la porte!" George begged as he clawed at the door. "S'il vous plait!"

The room descended into silence as one of the men stepped over the others and unclasped the wooden bolt holding it in place. George fell to the ground as a chilled gust of fresh air flowed over him and the wind swirled into the room. The man who'd opened the door kneeled beside him and pushed it shut.

"You okay? Sounded like you were having one hell of a nightmare in there."

"Philip!" George reached out and grabbed his hand. "Please, for the love of God, tell me you got Marcelle and the kids out of France. Please!"

Philip pulled his hand back and coughed uncomfortably into his fist. "Sorry, buddy," he said. "I'm not sure I know what you're talking about."

George would have stood if he thought his legs could hold him, but his thoughts were spinning through his head in such a frenzy they were making him dizzy. He reached for his forehead, for the spot between his eyes where the bullet had been barreling down on him. "Ils m'ont tiré dessus."

Philip watched him through the pallor of the moon that sat high above them, casting a flimsy light through the film of clouds around it.

"Is that French you're speaking?" Philip asked.

"They shot me." George rubbed at the spot where the bullet had entered his flesh. "They killed me, Philip. Did they kill you, too? Is that why we're here together? Where are Marcelle and the children?"

Philip eased himself to the ground beside George. "Listen, Mountcastle," he said, clearing his throat before he continued. "I think you're a decent guy, but not everyone is cut out for the stress of war. I don't want to do anything to get you into trouble, but if you keep talking like this in front of the other guys, someone's going to say something to the higher-ups and you're going to be sent packing. You sound like you're cracking up."

It was the name Mountcastle that threw him. Whatever words Philip said about the state of George's mental health meant nothing compared to the word Mountcastle. He hadn't been called that name in almost a decade, even by Philip. He felt like an impostor just hearing it.

"You don't remember any of it, do you?"

Philip didn't respond. He was close enough now that George could see his face clearly by the light of the moon. It was the face of the twenty-year-old man who'd visited him on his farm in Alabama before he'd come back.

The details were still sketchy in George's mind, but he'd been shot at the Russian prison, he'd gone home to Alabama, and then he'd woken up in . . . where?

The American men piled together in the farmhouse, Philip at twenty years old. George knew where he was. He turned and looked back toward the stables that weren't visible through the darkness.

"This is Châteauvillain, isn't it?" he whispered, turning back toward Philip. "And it's 1918."

George ran his fingers over the smooth skin on his forehead. He was dead. He knew this with the same certainty that the Philip he'd left in the cabin in Abbeville would have sacrificed himself to get Marcelle and the kids out of France. But where was that man now? Where were his wife and children?

Philip stood up beside him and stretched his arms high above his head before he glanced at the watch on his arm. It was Gabriel's watch. The one his oncle Philippe had given to him. The one that had stopped when they had taken that tumble down the hill. The one the Russian man with the missing eye had taken from his son.

"Maybe it wouldn't be a bad idea if you requested some time off," Philip said. "Get your head straightened out before we go into combat. I'll go with you tomorrow to talk to Colonel Mac. What do you think?"

"Sure," George replied. What else could he say? How could he explain to his friend that the war they were fighting would eventually lead them to a small town to the north where they would spend years with people he'd never met, fighting against an army he'd never seen, and risking their lives for a world he'd never known. Or maybe Philip was right. Maybe he'd lost his mind.

George spent the remainder of the night lying beneath the

stars, unable to sleep or calm his thoughts, still not certain that what he was experiencing was even real. It felt real, the crisp air biting at his lungs when he inhaled too deeply and the dew of the grass cooling his skin when he ran his fingers over the ground. Whatever lingering doubts George held about the veracity of Lina's words vanished overnight.

Morning came like the budding of Marcelle's roses, silent and unseen, its presence sudden and magnificent. George had never noticed the sunrise over the Aujon River in Châteauvillain. At twenty-three, he hadn't understood beauty.

The men were starting to awaken. They passed by George on their way to the latrine, and, while a few mumbled greetings to him, they'd obviously been warned to keep their distance. George didn't bother freshening up. He pulled on his trench boots and slid into his overcoat before heading to the hill that led to the horse stables.

The corrals hadn't changed. They looked like they'd been frozen in time for the past eight years, and when the black mare spotted him, she snorted and pawed at the ground. George could only see her wasted corpse lying beside the tracks on the road to Montmirail. Did she remember that, too? Did anyone here remember what they'd been through?

I wish you could stay.

I'm sorry about everything you went through, little brother. But you know what you have to do, right?

I could have stopped them, George. If you had just let me go, we could have taken the hill and everything would have been different.

You have to go back, George. There's a special purpose for you.

His mother. His brother. Philip. Marcelle.

Lina hadn't been there, in that in-between world, but perhaps she had told him everything he needed to hear at their kitchen table in Soissons the night before they'd fled. Perhaps she had known all along that George would return. And Philip, had he known? All those conversations they'd had about that battle. His insistence that he was supposed to have been there, that he was meant to defend that hill. Had they really been just speculation? Or had he known?

As he looked out over the herd of starved and weary horses, George wondered if this was Philip's moment to be the hero, Philip's chance to end all the suffering that had happened at the hands of the Germans and the Bolsheviks.

The black mare whinnied as she chased the other horses from the feeding trough. It was empty. Whatever hay had been tossed down for them was long gone, and whatever they found today would make no difference. Most of these horses wouldn't even make it to the front, and those that did would end up burning in the stables that would be bombed during the battle. That was the way it had happened, but as George saw the whip coming down over the black mare's back, he could almost hear Colonel Mac's words as they danced through his mind from that same memory.

I'm afraid we're about to find out just how useful a healthy herd of horses would have been.

Hadn't the nurse at the chateau on the water's edge once offered him the supplies from their stables? What if George could change the playing field? What if he could prepare the horses and the men for the battle he knew was coming and change the outcome of the war? Philip didn't have to die. He could return to his family in Pennsylvania. George and Marcelle could raise their children in freedom, maybe even settle in America, and France could finally crawl out from under the years of oppression that had stolen her spirit and broken her back.

George raced down the hill, excitement and anticipation drumming through his body like a current. He would need some help to get this done. He stopped only long enough at the farmhouse to see that no one was there, and then continued to the training grounds. The men were hunkered down in the trenches, Philip's head poking up above the others. George could tell by the way it was bobbing that he was laughing about something. The other men were so focused on what was going on down the trench line, they didn't notice when George slipped in beside them.

". . . the German doctor returns and says, 'Ve haf more bad news. Now ve haf to amputate your leg.' The Englishman is distraught and says . . ."

George had heard this joke before. He remembered the day Philip had told it, the day they'd been hunkered down in the trenches, waiting their turn during grenade practice. When he'd finished the joke . . .

"Stop!" George pulled himself to his feet, slipping down the muddy embankment of the trench wall as he stepped over his fellow soldiers and tried to gain a foothold. "The grenade," he said, struggling to pull himself over the edge of the wall just as a pair of hands wrapped around his ankles. "It's going to explode inside the dugout. We have to warn them."

"Get down, Mountcastle." Philip yanked him back into the trench just as the deafening blast from the hand grenade and the force of the explosion threw them both against the mud wall. George was up before the first shower of dirt could fall over them, clambering out of the ground and sprinting toward the chaos. He wouldn't feel the pain in his hands from clawing at the earth until later in the day, after the shock had worn off, and it wasn't until some of the other men joined in that he realized he'd already dug out one of the soldiers.

He left the man with the medics who descended on him like vultures to a carcass, and, when he turned back around, another soldier was being pulled from the wreckage. It was the man who'd been holding the grenade. Half of his head was missing, along with three of his limbs. George stumbled backward as he watched one of the medics toss a sheet over the man and then move on to the next casualty. By the time it was over, three men were dead, the same three who'd been dead eight years earlier, and George had been too late.

"Mountcastle." Philip was standing beside him when he

snapped out of his daze, no streaks of dirt across his face, no blood on his hands. George held his own hands up with the sudden realization that even though everything was different, it was somehow all still the same. The morning was still ending with the same three dead men under the same white sheets. The only thing that had changed was the man with the blood on his hands.

"You cannot just walk in here and take whatever you like."

Anna watched as the men hauled fencing material from the chateau's barn to the pastures by the horse corrals. The British nurse George had first seen storming down to the river to scold the American men galivanting in the water eight years earlier wasn't aware that another version of herself had offered him free access to everything in that barn. A lock of hair fell from her cap, a brown curl bouncing in time with her words.

"This is private property. You Americans think the world belongs to you."

"I apologize, ma'am." George tipped his hat to her. "I should have come to you first. We're just trying to get the horses into working shape before they're sent to the front, and I heard these supplies weren't being used."

She faltered for a moment at his reasonableness, adjusting the cap on her head and clearing her throat. The little girl with the flaming curls, the one who had kept him company with the horses all those years ago, bounded through the door, and when she looked up at George with those deep and knowing eyes, he could almost hear her giggling as the black mare chased him through the corral.

"Bonjour, Louise," he said, reaching up and touching his hat in greeting. "Comment vas-tu?"

The little girl didn't respond. She watched him with the same suspicious eyes that had tracked his movements the last time he was there and slid her hand into the nurse's.

"You speak French?" Anna asked.

"Oui," George replied, smiling back at her as a familiar blush crept into her cheeks. She fiddled with the curl that wouldn't stay put behind her ear, twirling it around her finger.

"How lovely," she exclaimed. "I think you're the first American soldier I've met who speaks French. Not that I spend my time consorting with American soldiers, or any soldiers for that matter. I am far too busy at the hospital for that sort of thing. Of course, even if I weren't busy, that is absolutely not something I would be doing."

George nodded along and tried not to laugh as she fell deeper into the hole she was trying to dig herself out of.

"Of course not," he agreed, when she finally stopped talking. "I'm sure England only sends its finest nurses to represent its people. And we certainly appreciate the work you do for the soldiers."

"Yes, well, thank you," she said, before fixing her cap one more time and gesturing to the supplies around the barn. "And, please, take what you need. It is simply gathering dust in here. No need for it to go to waste if it can help our men at the front."

"Thank you, ma'am."

She nodded in response and took a few steps toward the door before spinning around as if she'd forgotten something.

"Oh, and Private. Take care of yourself out there. I hear the Americans will be leaving for the front soon."

"Yes, ma'am," George replied, smiling and tipping his hat to her one last time. "I certainly will."

Philip was watching him when he turned around. He was no longer suggesting a visit to the colonel or a leave of absence to get George's mind straightened out, but he knew that something wasn't right. This wasn't the sort of problem Philip was used to solving, and George was impressed with the discipline he'd shown in handling it with such patience and finesse. At some point, he would sit down with him and tell him the truth, but that was a conversation for another day.

"Who's responsible for this?"

The voice that put a sudden halt to their work belonged to a man who was used to commanding an immediate audience. Colonel McAlexander walked the path that had been cleared for him, approaching George with the same scowl he'd worn during the last war they'd fought together. George remembered him well. His bark, his swagger, his bravado. His personality was everything that George's wasn't.

"I like to see this kind of initiative, son." The colonel laid the same heavy hand on George's shoulder that he'd used to pull him from the path the mare had been plodding over during their trek to Montmirail. "Not too many men understand the worth of a good horse."

"Yes, sir," George replied.

"You let me know if there's anything else you need." When George followed his gaze to the other men around him, he could see so clearly the scene in the Surmelin Valley from the night the colonel had slammed his fist over the map on the makeshift table in his bunker the moment he'd learned the French had abandoned Hill 231. He could hear the words the colonel had said when he'd sent the men back to the front, back to the guns, back to a certain death. And he wondered, how could you ask a man to die for you, when you didn't even know him?

"Actually, sir," George said, turning to look the colonel in the eye. "There is one more thing."

chapter 41

It took the whole day and half of their company to erect the fences and construct an irrigation system that fed into the pastures, but they'd done it. The fences covered more ground than George had imagined possible, and as he watched the horses grazing along the hill beneath the setting sun, his thoughts were with Marcelle and his children. He'd been diligent in his refusal to acknowledge the question that had been knocking at his mind.

What would happen when he warned Marcelle away from the man in the black beret? In all their years together, she had spoken of him just once. The man who'd stood beneath the cherry tree and led her straight into German hands. The man who'd delivered her to the general at the prison in Jaulgonne. Without that man, without the general, Gabriel wouldn't exist.

A splash of color, stark against the sun-dried fields, caught George's attention. When he squinted toward the setting sun, he saw Louise standing in the swaying grass, watching him like she'd done so many times before. He held his hand up in greeting.

"Bonjour, Louise."

She moved like a cat through the tall grass, her footsteps delicate and precise, her gaze on George's face unfaltering. "You didn't speak French yesterday," she said, stopping in front of him.

"No," George replied. "I didn't. But yesterday was a long time ago."

Louise's dark eyes were filled with the same intensity he

remembered from the last time he'd been there. She reminded him of his daughter with her unobtrusive and contemplative presence. Louise sat down in the grass by the fence and folded her legs beneath her. She looked even smaller against the backdrop of the horses in the distance, petite and unassuming. George pushed some of the overgrown weeds aside and flattened the grass before he eased himself onto the ground.

"Will you be leaving soon, monsieur?" she asked as George settled beside her. He nodded, unable to pull his eyes from the blade of grass in her hands as she peeled it down the center.

"Yes," he said. "I will be heading to the front soon."

"What will happen to us here in Châteauvillain? Will the Germans bomb us?"

George's instinct was to say no, to assure the little girl beside him that she would be safe and protected, that her maman and papa would not allow anything bad to happen to her. But Louise didn't have a mother or a father to protect her. She had no Tante Lina or Tante Rosalie, no Oncle Philip. She was an orphan with only a British nurse to love and protect her. But that British nurse would soon move on, and then what would happen to Louise? What *did* happen to her all those years ago?

"They will try," George said as he scooted himself closer to Louise and draped his arm over her shoulder. "The Germans will try to take Châteauvillain, but I will do everything to stop them. And then I will come back to make sure you are safe."

"Do you promise?" Louise wiped at her eyes, doing her best to hide the tears that were beginning to surface.

"I promise," George replied, pretending not to notice, and pulling her in tighter. "When this war is over, I promise I will come back to find you."

⁓ ⁓ ⁓

"Au revoir, Louise."

She couldn't hear his whispered words over the train engine, but George held his hand up and watched the barefoot little girl on the platform until he could no longer distinguish her tiny body from the background of Châteauvillain, and then he took his spot beside Colonel McAlexander.

The train rolled out just on time, and the colonel, true to the promise he'd made George in the chateau's barn, skipped the Cadillacs and joined his men for the trip to Montmirail.

"You sound like a Frenchman," the colonel said as George settled down beside him. "You have family in these parts?"

"Yes, sir," George replied. It wasn't exactly a lie.

"That's good to know. I might need your help with translating out there."

"Yes, sir."

"What about you?" The colonel turned to Ricci, who was settled in beside him. George had rarely thought about Ricci since he'd last seen him running panicked through the battlefield without his gas mask. It had been a valuable lesson, and one George had tried to pass on to the other men in his unit. He was endlessly encouraging them to fight through the panic of the gas masks during training, insisting their survival would depend on it. "What's your story, son?"

"I came to America from Italy," Ricci said.

"Italy." The colonel nodded. "I've known some fine Italian soldiers. And how long have you been in America?"

As the conversation continued, the men in the train car began to relax. There was an unexpected easiness to the back-and-forth between the colonel and his men. They all wanted the spotlight; they all wanted the chance to talk about their homes and their girlfriends and their futures.

Milo, as usual, was not a part of the conversation. He was leaned up against the side wall, puffing away at a cigarette, and listening quietly. George couldn't blink away the image of the Howitzer on the side of the hill, Milo's body draped over it, and his fingers—what was left of them—scraping the ground.

Philip watched him from across the train car, and when George nodded to him, he didn't nod back. In all the years

George had known him, he'd never seen Philip so out of sorts. He'd seen him juggle anger and sorrow and even fear, but he'd never seen this man who was cloaked in uncertainty and doubt. They were not traits he wore well.

"Me and my cousin," Ricci was saying when George tuned back in, "we went on a big ship from Italy to New York together. We were so sick." He grabbed his stomach and moaned, pretending to vomit over the edge of a ship. "And then we joined the army and came here in another big ship."

Ricci's laughter was contagious, and the men were enjoying the camaraderie with their colonel until the train came to a sudden and jarring stop. George had forgotten about the mechanical issues with the Cadillacs, and the black mare, and the man whose arm had been ripped off by the passing train.

His eyes danced over the horizon, scanning from left to right. Who would come first? The black mare stumbling on her way to the front or the train full of German prisoners on their way out?

When the train cars started overheating from the summer sun, just like George knew they would, he followed the other men through the meadow and toward the shade of the tree-lined ravine. The grave markers dotting the field were overgrown with weeds and encased with vines, but they were no longer just wooden crosses and stone monuments to him now. Each one was an individual man who, like George, had understood the real terror of the battlefield. George knelt down before one of the markers and pulled away the weeds before he ran his hand over the French inscription.

For glory of his country.

How many men would die for this country? How many women? What cost was worth their freedom? No one who'd ever gone without freedom could truly answer that question. George turned his gaze to the north, toward the front, toward Marcelle. She was like a flame in the distance, drawing him in, luring him to her. But fire burned, and he was fearful of what would happen when he got too close. He'd avoided the question that was looming over him with an undeterred resolve.

Should he warn Marcelle about the rendezvous with the man in the black beret?

It was an agonizing question, the answer so obvious that it didn't even warrant asking, but here it was, floating through his thoughts and taunting him with *what if.* What would Marcelle tell him to do? He knew the Marcelle he'd left behind would walk into that prison without hesitation to get her son back, but this was George's burden, and regardless of the choice he made, the consequences would be bound to him forever. Could he send his wife to be tortured and raped so their son could be born?

The black smoke swelled into the sky over the horizon as the train carrying the German prisoners rounded the bend. There was no sign of the mare, but the men from George's unit were already lining up along the tracks, and though the train was still at least a kilometer away, their insults were already sailing through the air.

There were too many men. As he scanned over their faces, George worried he wouldn't be able to pick out the one who'd gotten himself killed the last time they were here. But it wasn't the man's face he needed to remember. There was only one soldier foolish enough to dance on the tracks as the train rolled closer, his brazenness intensifying as the prisoners neared.

George couldn't stop him. He couldn't distract him or reason with him or convince him that what he was doing was going to get him killed, so he did the only thing he could think of to prevent a man from jumping to his death. He tackled him. He held him to the ground as the train rolled by, and perhaps, if he'd been a bit stronger or even heavier, he would have been able to keep the man from escaping his grip and fulfilling his destiny.

The soldier never made it onto the side of the train car. By the time he'd freed himself from George's grip, the train was picking up speed and the jump that was supposed to land him onto the thin ledge of the nearest door sent him instead into the void between two cattle cars. He simply disappeared.

It wasn't until the train passed that they found him again. There was no need to summon the medics. This time, he wouldn't make it to the tent hospital in Montmirail, and as George ran through all the things he could have done differently, he felt more and more certain that Lina had been right; nothing would have changed the outcome of that moment, because fate hadn't sent George back for that man.

The last leg of the trip was a somber affair. Colonel Mac continued to chat with the men, but the mood was more subdued, and as they neared the front, and the shelling in the distance intensified, the intervals of silence lengthened.

There was no black mare on this trip, no corpse on the side of the path. Draft horses trudged along at a steady pace hauling supplies in one direction while families heading the opposite direction balanced equal amounts of fear and exhaustion in addition to their meager possessions.

Could one man change this? Even with the knowledge he possessed, how could he change this monstrosity that had already been set in motion?

When the train came to a stop, they were not in Montmirail. Colonel McAlexander hopped from their compartment after mentioning something about hiking the rest of the way in, and by the time George had gathered his senses, the rest of the men were following him out.

"Something wrong?"

Philip stood beside him wearing the same watchful and guarded expression that was fast becoming his trademark. The garrulous man who'd led their company eight years earlier had been replaced by someone George barely recognized.

"This isn't where we were supposed to stop," George replied.

"And where, exactly, were we supposed to stop?"

"Montmirail."

Philip nodded as they watched each other in the doorway of the train car, bodies flowing around them like river water flowing around rocks in a stream. His eyes hadn't changed. They looked just like the ones that had watched Rosalie dance off into the night to her death. Was there some part of him that knew?

"What's in Montmirail?" he asked.

When George hesitated to answer, Philip shook his head and waved the question away.

"Never mind. Go ahead, Mountcastle. I'll cover for you if anyone comes looking. I'll tell them you're off in the woods somewhere. A sour stomach."

George used that same excuse to slip off from his company when they came to the crossroads that would lead them to the fight. He sat in the bushes and watched through the breaks in foliage as his entire unit continued their march to the north, the summer sun beating down and fatiguing them. When the final boots were kicking up dust in the distance, he stepped from the bushes and onto the road to the west, the road to Marcelle.

It wouldn't matter how many times George stepped into the chaos of the platform hospital in Montmirail; it would always be mayhem. Doctors and nurses, covered in blood and barking orders, dashed from tent to tent. War-weary soldiers, staggering around the grounds, searched for missing friends and lost units. Wounded and dying men, laid out across lawns and steps, cried for their mothers.

George searched each tent and platform and lawn. He traced and retraced his steps, questioning nurses and doctors alike, begging information from servicemen and clergymen and orderlies. It made no difference.

Marcelle was nowhere to be found.

It was the rosary he found first, the beads sparkling beneath the bright July sun. The crucifix had recently been shined, and as George pictured it buried beneath the dirt by their front door in Soissons, burned and battered and broken just like the rest of them had been, he couldn't contain the grief that washed over him.

Rosalie didn't recognize him. She stared back at him as he struggled to conceal the tears that were stinging his eyes, tears he'd never had the chance to shed for her. He wanted to thank her, to reach out and embrace her and tell her what her sacrifice had meant to him, to all of them. He wanted her to know that she'd been mourned and loved, and that they had planned to take her with them, that she'd been buried with the papers that would have bought her freedom. But, instead, he could only stare back at her and force himself not to weep.

"Can I help you?" she asked, placing an identification tag from one of the dead soldiers at her feet into the bag in her hand.

"That's a beautiful necklace." George nodded to the rosary around her neck. "It must be very important to you."

Rosalie's fingers worked over the crucifix as she considered the question.

"It was my sister's," she finally said, smiling as she looked down at it. "I cannot seem to get her into a church these days. Every night I try. I thought maybe wearing her rosary would remind her of what she has given up."

"It's Marcelle's?" George remembered the night they'd buried it, the night Paul had been hung and Marcelle had reached into the hole for one last prayer. Rosalie's eyes shot up at the mention of her sister's name.

"You know Marcelle?"

"Yes . . . well . . . it's complicated." As George stumbled through a messy response about their paths having crossed at one point, and Marcelle being someone very important to him, Rosalie simply smiled back at him.

"You seem like a nice man," she said, pulling the rosary from around her neck and handing it to him. "And you seem to be quite taken with my sister. Perhaps if she sees you with her rosary, she will consider giving God another chance."

George stared down at the necklace in his hand as Rosalie went back to work, the whispered words of her Hail Marys interrupted only by the clinking of the dead soldiers' identification tags landing in the bag. He slipped the necklace over his head before he turned back toward the rail station and came face-to-face with a woman he hadn't seen in eight years.

The blue of her eyes that he still couldn't get quite right, the slope of her nose, the smoothness of her skin. She looked like a child. How could this have been the same woman he'd left in another life?

Her smile was tight-lipped as she passed him on the way to her sister, and it wasn't until George said hello that she gave him any notice.

"Je ne parle pas anglais," she said, with barely a glance back in his direction, but when George laughed in response, her steps slowed, and she steadied her gaze on his face.

"Now I know that's not true, mademoiselle," he replied in French. "I happen to know that your English is quite good."

Marcelle stepped cautiously forward before her eyes caught the rosary around his neck. She glanced in the direction of her sister, who was too busy with her work and her prayers to notice them, and then back to the necklace.

"Why are you wearing my sister's rosary?"

"Marcelle." George ran his fingers over the beads and smiled down at her. "I never knew this was yours."

"Why would you?" she asked. "Have we met?"

He nodded back at her. He couldn't remember her face without the scar, or her smile without the missing tooth. He couldn't remember his life without her and Gabriel and Juliette, and the decision he'd been putting off since returning from that world was looming over him now, the urgency of it weighing down on him with the force of one of those German tanks that had barreled toward them across the Surmelin Valley.

Though he hadn't been able to acknowledge it, even to himself, there had been some part of him that had hoped, perhaps even *believed*, Marcelle would remember him. That when she saw him, the memories of who they had once been, or who they would one day become, would come flooding back to her like a deluge through a broken dam.

But that wasn't how it happened.

The Marcelle standing before him didn't know what they had endured together. She could no more give him advice on what to do about their son than she could tell him their son's name.

"Well," she said, turning toward her sister. "I should really be getting back to work."

"Marcelle, wait."

When she faced him again, George could almost feel the beating of her heart against his chest as they had lain together during that final night in the old, abandoned cabin. The silence between them grew heavy as time ticked away, unwilling to pause or even slow down for this beautiful and arduous moment.

"Josephine LeBlanc will be captured by the Germans tonight if she goes to deliver the message to the man in the black beret."

"What did you say?" Marcelle's voice was just a whisper as she took a quick look back at her sister and stepped closer to George.

"Charles will ask you to deliver a message tonight to a man in a black beret," George continued. "And even though you will know something is not quite right when you see him, you will step up to him. And then it will too late."

"Who are you?" Marcelle asked. "Who sent you here?"

"I can't explain it to you. There's no time right now. But I'll come back, Marcelle. I promise. After the battle, I'll find you and explain it all to you."

"Did Charles send you here?"

"No, Marcelle. I can't explain it right now, but I wouldn't have come here if it wasn't important. Bad things will happen if you get captured tonight. Please trust me."

"Marcelle?" Rosalie stepped up beside them, her hand reflexively reaching for the crucifix around her neck before remembering she'd given it away. "Are you going to introduce me to your friend?"

Marcelle looked from her sister to George to the rosary around George's neck.

"You don't know him?" she asked. "But why would you give him . . ."

Her question drifted away with the wind as she tried to decide what to do with the information she'd just received. Caution hadn't yet been beaten into her. This Marcelle was not the same methodical and deliberate woman who'd navigated Soissons with her starving children. She didn't know about the hungry men who came knocking at the door, about the cruelty of war that extended far beyond the bombs on the battlefield.

"Marcelle was just telling me that she would like to join you at church tonight," George said, smiling at Rosalie and running his fingers along the beads of the rosary around his neck. "Isn't that right, Marcelle?"

When he turned back to her, she was glaring up at him, and George finally saw the woman he'd been looking for. The tilt of her head, the slight lift of her chin, the narrowing of her eyes. It wasn't the woman he'd come to know over the past eight years, but it was the woman he needed her to be in that moment.

"I suppose," she said, a smirk on her face and a familiar glint in her eyes. "Since I have no other plans for the evening."

chapter 42

MARCELLE

Montmirail, France
July 1918

"You are no witch."

Until that moment, Marcelle hadn't been paying much attention to the prisoner sitting across the table from her. Charles had replaced the man's uniform with prison pajamas before sticking him in the interrogation room, but Marcelle knew from his stiff back and broad shoulders that he was most certainly a high-ranking German officer. She didn't need a uniform to tell her that. She'd been questioning him for almost thirty minutes, but she was too distracted to get anything of value; she couldn't tear her thoughts away from the man in the black beret who'd been waiting for her beneath the cherry tree.

The American soldier had been right.

She and Charles had watched "Oncle Henri" from the shadows, and when Marcelle hadn't greeted him with a peck on the cheek and a gifted book, he'd been carted off into the night by two German-speaking operatives who'd been waiting in their own shadows.

Marcelle took a cigarette from the case on the table and leaned back into her chair before lighting it and drawing the smoke deep into her lungs. The room was windowless and barren, aside from two wooden chairs and a table, and the air was thick and stagnant.

"You are right," she said, blowing out the smoke between them until it hung in a stubborn cloud above their heads. "I am not a witch. But I wish I were." She tapped the ash from the end of her cigarette onto the floor. "It would make my job so much easier."

When the man laughed, Marcelle smiled back at him.

"As it stands, I am just a woman who has been sent in here to convince you to talk." The prisoner's eyes didn't leave hers when she pushed the cigarettes and matches to his side of the table. "So," she said, "let's talk."

"What is on your mind, mademoiselle?" the man asked, switching from German to French. He fiddled with the case of cigarettes but didn't take one.

Marcelle shrugged.

What was on her mind? Too many things to keep straight. The man in the black beret had shaken her. In all her days with British intelligence, she had never once felt so exposed. What would have happened if she'd been captured? Would she have been tortured? Killed? Would she have cracked under the pressure?

"War, I suppose," Marcelle finally replied. "What is on anyone's mind these days?"

The man nodded. "War," he said. "But there must be more to talk about besides war. How about hobbies? Or family? Or the weather? It is a particularly hot summer, don't you think?"

"As much as I would love to chat about the weather and such, my job is to get information from you about battle plans, troop locations, things like that."

"Ah, yes," he agreed. "Back to work. And you think you can get this from me?"

"I am quite good at it," Marcelle replied, dropping her cigarette onto the floor and crushing it beneath her shoe. "Or so I have been told."

"Yes," he laughed, pushing the cigarettes back across the table without taking one. "I have heard that about you. And I must admit, when I was captured, I was hoping I might get to meet *la sorcière de la rivière*. Everyone wants to know about the witch of the river."

He was right. Men were endlessly curious about her, always looking for something to take back with them, wanting to claim some piece of her. Too much of Marcelle's time was spent with men these days, and she was tiring of them, tiring of their need to possess her. Why did men always feel the need to conquer? The need to know, to take, to own?

"What do you want to know about me?" Marcelle asked. She had danced this evasive dance with men so often, it was starting to wear on her. "Am I married? Widowed? Do I have children?"

"I already know those things, mademoiselle. There is no husband. Yet. And certainly no children."

"Interesting," Marcelle responded, scraping her teeth over her bottom lip. He was fishing; he had to be. She never shared anything about herself with anyone, especially German prisoners, so there was no way he could know those things for certain. "And how can you be so sure, monsieur?"

"You are too reckless to be a mother," the man replied. "You do not understand vulnerability. That is why men call you a witch."

"What do you know about vulnerability?" Marcelle huffed. "You sit behind your tanks and guns and attack innocent people, and then you call me reckless because I do not back down from you? You think I am a witch because I am not vulnerable? Not weak?"

"You mistake vulnerability for weakness, mademoiselle. They are not the same thing."

"I did not realize I would be getting a lesson on vulnerability today," Marcelle retorted. "Please, continue."

"It is not a lesson," the man said. "Vulnerability cannot be taught. It is when you value another person's life over your own. When your usefulness is limited by the susceptibility of other people. That is vulnerability."

Marcelle was suddenly seventeen again, standing in an abandoned alley of Soissons and stepping in front of her sister with no fear of the bullet she knew was coming her way. Rosalie made her vulnerable. Pierre too. The man in the black beret had already made her see that. They were the two people Marcelle feared would reap the consequences of what she had become. *La sorcière de la rivière*. She had finally gone to mass with Rosalie not long after she'd watched the man beneath the cherry tree being carted away by the Germans, and she had already decided this would be her final interrogation. She and Rosalie would soon return to Paris.

"Perhaps you do understand vulnerability," the man said, studying Marcelle's face. "Perhaps you want this war to end just as much as I do."

"Then tell me what we need to know to put an end to it, and we will make it happen." When he didn't answer, Marcelle shifted forward in her chair. "When is the next assault scheduled? And where will it be?" She leaned into the space between them, pressing closer with each question. "Where are the locations of your heavy artillery? When are your reinforcements due? Tell us what we need to do to win this war, and we will offer you protection. A new life."

Marcelle embraced the silence that descended upon them. She had navigated this final dance well. The man wanted to talk; he just needed a moment to realize it.

"There is an assault being planned," he finally said. "I do not know the details, but it will happen soon. General Ludendorff will not be releasing the battle plans until the attack is imminent, for fear they will be leaked into enemy hands."

"Can you get them?" Marcelle asked. "If we make it worth your effort, can you get the battle plans if we send you back? The exact time and location?"

"I cannot go back there," the man replied. "Even if I could get my hands on the plans, they would know what I had done if I suddenly disappeared with them."

"But you would be gone by then. You would be safely back in our custody by the time anyone figured it out, and . . ." Marcelle stopped, her words fading between them and her thoughts carrying her back to their conversation about repercussions and vulnerability. "Who is it that makes you vulnerable, monsieur," she asked, and when he refused to answer her question or even make eye contact with her, Marcelle understood all too well what was at stake for him. "We can send operatives in to get your family out of Germany," she continued. "But whether for persuasion or protection will depend on you."

"This has nothing to do with them," the man replied, straightening his back in the chair and scowling at Marcelle. She imagined he would have been quite intimidating had he been wearing his uniform, but in his prison pajamas, he was just a man like any other, desperate to save his family. "And you are not the sort of person to sacrifice innocent women and children for battle plans," he continued.

"Perhaps you are confusing me with the person I was five years ago," Marcelle replied. "If so, then you are correct. That woman would not have understood your lesson in vulnerability. And she would not have had the callousness or the audacity to threaten your family for the sake of her country. But war has changed us all, has it not?" As they watched each other through the silence, Marcelle wondered where that girl had gone, and if, in some other world, in some other circumstance, her sense of decency would have survived. "Tell me, monsieur," she said. "Would you sacrifice me for the safety of your family?"

The man didn't respond; there was no need. The answer, of course, was yes.

"I want my family here first," he finally said. "And a guarantee from your bosses that they will be relocated to British soil as citizens after the war. I want to see them holding their British passports before I go in and get the battle plans."

Vulnerability.

This was vulnerability. A man willing to face beatings and torture and death to save his family, a man willing to surrender his country for love.

"This is not a promise I can make," Marcelle said, rising

from her chair and pausing before heading to the door. "But I will plead your case to the men in charge."

Marcelle was not a part of the team that sent for the German soldier's family or made the decision to offer them asylum. It happened behind closed doors between men whose importance far outweighed hers. She only learned of their decision when she saw the man's wife and their two sons being escorted from his prison cell the day he was to be sent back to the Germans, the day he requested to see Marcelle one last time.

"I wanted to say good-bye," the man said as Marcelle stepped back into the room. She was startled by his height and couldn't pull her eyes from the medals adorning his coat. He was a well-decorated officer, more so than any soldier Marcelle had ever seen, French or German alike, and Charles had been right to put him in pajamas before sending her in for the interrogation.

"So, you are going back, I see." Marcelle nodded to his uniform. "And you will return with the battle plans?"

"I will do my best," he replied. "It is not so easy to get across enemy lines without being shot by one side or the other, but we have worked out a crossing at the river once I have secured the information, and for the sake of my family, I will not miss the rendezvous. I will do everything in my power to make it back with the plans in hand."

"Good luck, monsieur," Marcelle said. "I hope to see you again one day."

"And I, you," the man replied. "And I wanted to thank you for getting my family here safely."

"I am not the one who brought your family here," Marcelle said. "I am not the one you should be thanking."

"I beg to differ, mademoiselle," he replied, smiling back at her. "I know that you would not have sacrificed my family, and I don't just say this because I have seen that they are safe. You are a remarkable woman, and while you will never be awarded a medal for your service, and your name will not be mentioned in the history books, what you have done for your country is nothing less than valiant. If we can pull this off," he said, adjusting the cuffs on his shirtsleeves and preparing to be sent back into battle, "you will have played a bigger role in bringing peace to Europe than anyone will ever know."

chapter 43

MARCELLE

Soissons, France
May 1991

"Do you have a cigarette?"

Marcelle's hands trembled as she pulled herself up in the bed. Night had long since settled around them, the creatures of the day having been silenced and tucked away for hours.

"A cigarette?" Juliette set the diary onto the bed between them. "I have never known you to smoke, Maman."

Marcelle couldn't quiet the humming in her chest as it pulsed through her veins and seeped into her muscles. How many years had it been since she'd felt the numbing calm of nicotine and tasted the bitter tang of tobacco? She'd quit shortly after the war, and though she'd had cravings on occasion over the years, she'd never had one as potent as this.

"Are you unwell?" Juliette asked, placing the back of her hand over Marcelle's forehead. "You seem a bit pale."

"I am fine." Marcelle waved her daughter's concerns away and leaned back into the pillows. The night was wearing on her, but she was certain sleep wouldn't come until her daughter finished the story in the diary. "Let's just get to the end, shall we?"

"Maman?" When Marcelle looked up at her daughter, she could almost see the little girl she and Pierre had taken to the river for picnics when they were young and fearless, when their futures were laid out for miles before them. How many years ago had that been? "Was that part true?" Juliette asked. "Did you really interrogate that German officer?"

Even as a child, Juliette had been uncommonly perceptive, always attuned to the emotions and nuances of the people around her. Marcelle should have known that her daughter would pick up on that.

"Yes," she replied. "It was true." But even as Marcelle said the words, she wasn't quite certain she could trust them. Her memory was becoming more unreliable by the hour, and she could no longer parse out fact from fiction in these two conflicting versions of her life.

"But Maman," Juliette said, "how could George have known about the German officer if he wasn't even there with you?"

Marcelle smiled, recalling a conversation she'd carried with her for decades, a conversation that was as beautiful as it was enigmatic. "I have a feeling you're about to find out," she said, nodding toward the diary.

"You know what's going to happen?" Juliette held the journal up between them. "You think this is true? What he has written in here?"

"I don't know for sure," Marcelle replied. "Most of that diary is not the life I remember, but there are parts in there that are . . . well . . . they're real. They are true. It is almost as if he has gotten back on track with real life. These are the memories I have carried with me all this time. The man beneath the cherry tree that he warned me away from. The German officer I interrogated at the prison. This is the life I have lived."

"Do you think maybe this story in here," Juliette said, tapping on the diary she was still holding up between them. "Do you think this is the life George lived?"

Marcelle smiled back at her daughter and shrugged. "I'm beginning to wonder."

chapter 44

GEORGE

Château-Thierry, France
July 1918

"Incoming!"

George ducked into the trench and held his helmet in place until the earth stopped trembling and the dirt stopped raining down on top of them. He was back in the trenches, digging and dodging the mortars that were falling like the slow and steady beat of the giant raindrops that used to come before a heavy downpour in an Alabama spring sky.

"Where you been, Mountcastle?"

Ace was digging beside him. George's familiarity with Colonel McAlexander had made him a bit of a celebrity to the other men, so when he'd gone missing during their march to the front, rumors had abounded.

"I told you," George said, tossing a heap of dirt over the side. "I got lost."

No one wanted to hear that version of the story; they wanted something better, maybe something about beautiful and lonely Frenchwomen who provided services to the American servicemen who'd come to save them. But George couldn't offer them that. The beautiful Frenchwoman he'd gone to see was off-limits. Who knew what they would do to her in their dreams?

George paused for a swallow of water from his canteen. The air was cooler without the weight of the sun, but the nights were longer than he remembered, even if the work wasn't quite as exhausting. He didn't complain about digging this time. His muscles were well fed and his endurance boundless, the constant aches that had plagued him in Soissons conspicuously absent in this younger, more well-nourished body. George dug through the blisters, encouraging the men beside him to do the same.

The river was just a vast expanse of blackness when George gazed out at it beneath the night sky, trying to imagine the German soldiers on the other side digging their own trenches and preparing to face their own demons. Did they know what was coming? Were the foot soldiers up front aware they would soon be launched into battle?

Colonel Mac had been right all along. The elastic defense had been useless, and allowing the German troops to land on the south shore had been a grievous mistake. They had targeted the valley floor from the onset of the battle, needing a flat and open area to get their heavy artillery and tanks into position. There had been no driving them back once they'd crossed the river, and no stopping them as they'd barged right through to Paris.

George clambered out of his hole at dusk the following day. He caught up to Colonel Mac, who was walking the perimeter of their territory, like he did every evening, and got in line behind the field officers. More trenches. More guns. More artillery. They were the same orders he'd barked eight years earlier, to the same men, about the same battle.

"Sir." George tagged along behind them, trying to get a word in to the colonel who was surrounded by his officers. "Excuse me, sir." He buzzed like a gnat around the periphery of the group. "Colonel McAlexander!"

The officer beside him jumped.

"Private, you will return to your company at once," he snapped. "There is a chain of command. And you will follow it."

"What is it, Private?" Colonel Mac asked, holding his hand up to silence the man beside him.

"You were right, sir," George said. "The elastic defense won't hold."

The silence that followed was enough to make the other men squirm, but George didn't falter under Colonel McAlexander's gaze. He waited patiently as the colonel tried to piece together his words. He was a contemplative man, a natural leader who wouldn't let rank or pride get in the way of success.

"And what makes you think the elastic defense won't hold, Private?" he asked.

George nodded toward the hill to their east, Hill 231, the one the French had abandoned when the Germans launched their assault.

"You were right about the French. They will flee the moment the Germans land on the south bank, leaving our entire right flank open. Once the troops and the tanks have crossed the river, the Boche will swarm in from the east with their Howitzers and Sturmtruppen and take out the artillery and heavy weaponry from our back lines. It will be a massacre. There won't even be a chance to retreat."

"Private, that is enough—"

"Wait." Colonel Mac cut off the major beside him and stepped closer to George. "What makes you think this will happen, Private?"

"The French are tired, sir. Their men have spent years in these trenches. They have no will to keep going, and they have no confidence in a German defeat, regardless of who is by their side. They haven't even dug in yet. You can see for yourself."

"And what do you suggest we do?"

"I don't know anything about military tactics, sir. But I know people. And I know that you've already decided you want control of that hill." The men followed George's finger as he pointed toward the sloped fields and forests to their east. "But you're not going to get the commanding officers to agree to it by marching in there and barking demands. It's going to take finesse."

"Finesse." Colonel Mac laughed at George's choice of words, while the officers around him shifted nervously at the bluntness of their conversation. "And I suppose you're going to tell me how to do this?"

"No, sir," George replied. "But I suggest you use everything in your power, because we don't stand a chance without it."

Colonel Mac looked out over the valley toward Hill 231, but the sun had already set and there was nothing to see but the intermittent glow of incendiaries screeching through the air.

"Is there anything else, Private?"

"Yes, sir," George replied. "I know when the Germans will strike."

~ ~ ~

"Did you hear the one about the tank that ran over a box of Cracker Jacks?"

Philip was slowly transforming back into the man George had known him to be. His jokes were stale, his energy was boundless, and his ego was brimming with confidence.

"Killed two kernels. God rest their souls," George mumbled under his breath, but they were all packed so tightly together in the trench that the other men couldn't help but hear him.

"I thought these were originals, Foster," one of the men yelled out. "Mountcastle's already heard them all."

The sun was still high in the afternoon sky, and the men were still hunkered down in hiding from the German planes overhead. They'd covered their position with hay and brush and anything else to blend into the surrounding foliage, but it was an unsettling phenomenon to look up and see the underbelly of a German Albatross. George couldn't sleep as he imagined the upgraded planes the Germans had been working on.

His unit had been at the front for over two weeks, but he hadn't seen Colonel McAlexander again, not since he'd given him news of the attack. None of the officers had believed him about the date and time, not even the colonel. They'd all agreed that Bastille Day would be too obvious and that the Germans would know the Allies were expecting it. History had already proven that to be untrue, but George's contributions to the defensive battle plans were not as well received as he had hoped they would be.

"Hey, Mountcastle." Philip was holding up a pack of cigarettes and nodding toward one of the dugouts further down the trench line. "Smoke?"

George scrambled to his feet and followed him down the line, settling in beside him with his back against the parapet. They'd reinforced the front wall of the trench with both wood and sandbags and had added an extra roll of razor wire along the ground between them and the Germans. The countdown was on. In less than a week, the German Army would be rolling over them if they weren't prepared.

With the first draw of smoke into his lungs, the humming in George's chest instantly settled. He closed his eyes and let his head fall back against the wall, exhaling between parted lips and vowing to never take real tobacco for granted again. Philip was watching him when he opened his eyes.

"Who are you?" he asked, blowing out his own cloud of smoke. "You're not the same guy who got off the transport ship with me a few months ago. That guy didn't know anything about war. And he didn't cozy up to high-ranking colonels. And he sure as hell didn't speak French."

"You're right," George agreed, before taking another draw from his cigarette. "I am a completely different man. And I don't know how I'm going to explain this to you without you thinking I've cracked up, but I'll try."

He didn't know where to begin. How could he convince Philip that he'd already seen his future? That they were more brothers than friends? That they'd suffered under the occupation of Germans and Russians alike?

"Dorothy." George pointed to the pocket on Philip's coat. "In your pocket you have a photo of a girl named Dorothy. You told some of the guys that she was your sister when they found it, because you were worried they wouldn't think she was pretty enough. But she's not your sister."

"What do you know about Dorothy?" Philip's hand instinctively went to the pocket over his chest before he pulled out the photo of her. "You been snooping through my stuff?"

"Everyone thinks you'll marry the beauty queen, but Dorothy's the one you love. She's smarter than the others." Philip's eyes grew wide as George recited the words he'd said in confidence to him on the cellar floor in Soissons all those years ago. "And your watch," he continued. "It's a Hamilton. Your grandfather gave it to you when you enlisted. Your little brother was so jealous you were scared he'd try to enlist just to get one for himself."

The shake of Philip's head was so subtle, George couldn't be sure he'd actually seen it. He thought about continuing, about mentioning the tiny town of Meadville, Pennsylvania, and the Meadville Market House where Philip had spent his entire life before joining the army. But he didn't need to go on.

"How do you know all this?"

"I've been here before," George replied. "We both have. We fought through this battle and lost and spent the next eight years just trying to survive. You fell in love again. Her name was Rosalie. And maybe you didn't love her the same way you love Dorothy, but she was someone special to you."

"Rosalie."

When Philip whispered her name, George could almost see them dancing and laughing in their tiny apartment, surrounded by their family. That same familiar call was taking him back there. The closer he came to losing it, the stronger he felt the pull. Despite all the horrors of that world, there were moments when he found himself yearning for the life he'd left behind, yearning for Philip's bad jokes, and Marcelle's spring garden, and Paul's contagious laughter.

"How is it possible?" Philip was still shaking his head, still unable to grasp what George was saying to him. "How could you live a life and then come back?"

"I was killed. I don't really understand it myself, but when I died, I went through a sort of in-between world. You were there. And others. And you were all trying to convince me that I was being sent back for a specific reason."

"What reason?"

How many times had they talked about that night? How many times had Philip insisted that he was supposed to stay with the Howitzer and take back that hill? George could still feel the dirt and rocks and twigs digging into his side as they'd tumbled down the hill.

"We were trying to take back that hill over there." He jabbed the air with his thumb, pointing it toward Hill 231. "The one the French are defending. The Germans had taken control of it early in the fight and had moved some artillery guns into position. We'd taken one of their Howitzers, and you wanted me to get reinforcements to help turn it around. You said you'd hold them off until I returned." When he stopped talking, Philip scooted in closer to him, eager to hear the rest of the story. "They would have killed you," George said. "The Germans kept swarming over the top of the hill, and you didn't have enough ammunition to hold them off."

"So what happened?"

"You wouldn't listen to me. I ended up having to knock you down the hill. And then we surrendered."

George had spent years trying to forget that moment, but he could tell from the faraway look on Philip's face that he was desperate to picture it in his mind, amazed that some other version of himself was already a battle-tested soldier.

"And that's why you were sent back here?" Philip asked. "I still don't understand."

"You were always convinced that you were supposed to be on that hill defending that gun. And when I came back, it was clear that I was meant to let you stay. To get reinforcements and take back the hill. But it's different now. I'm working hard to put us in a better position to defend the hill and the valley floor."

"I'll do it."

Philip couldn't hear him. He was no longer listening to George's words about the information he'd passed on to Colonel McAlexander, or his hopes that the colonel was already implementing some new strategies to put them in a stronger position before the Germans made their assault. Philip had never known the horrors of the battlefield; he didn't understand what he was saying. He just wanted to be the hero again.

"You're not listening," George said. "It won't come to that this time. We can win this battle without having to relive that moment."

Philip scooted back against the wall just as another German Albatross soared over their heads. They both tilted their faces up to watch it pass, as George tried to block out the image of that Howitzer on the hill. That chapter was done. The new one they were writing would end with an Allied victory and take them both home.

"I hear what you're saying," Philip said, and when George looked over at him, he could almost see the hardened lines and the furrowed brow of the man who'd promised to defend Marcelle and the children with his life the night before George had been captured by the Russians. "But I just want you to know that if it comes down to it, if it's the only way we can beat the Germans, I'll do it."

George was doing his best to ignore the banter between Philip and Ace as they paddled across the river on their last reconnaissance mission, their last attempt to snag a German soldier. Ten boats had been sent out that night—French, British, and American—with very specific orders to be on the lookout for a German officer on the other side of the river and to bring him in alive. George was so busy devising strategies to get Colonel Mac to heed his warnings about the coming battle that he didn't notice the man standing on the shore. It wasn't until Philip was pointing him out and Ace was paddling closer that George even saw him.

"Is that a Boche?" Philip said.

It was him.

It was the man George had seen standing beside the river eight years earlier, the man who'd disappeared into the mist like a phantom. Only this time, he was real.

Ace had just gotten them up to the bank when Philip crashed onto the shore with his rifle at the ready. But there was no struggle, and though he carried no weapon and held only a letter in his hand, Philip kept his rifle aimed at the man's back even after he'd stepped quietly into the boat and Ace had rowed feverishly to distance them from the shore.

He was an officer, and a high-ranking one at that, his medals glistening even beneath the moonless sky. He held the letter out for them to see. "Ich habe die Pläne hier," he said. "Sie müssen mich zu Ihrem General bringen."

I have the plans here. You have to take me to your general.

"What did you say?" George whispered the words back in German, the steady rocking of the boat making him dizzy and unbalanced.

"You have to take me to your general," the man said, threads of panic winding through his words as he pushed the paper into George's hands. "I have them here. The plans. Please, the witch of the river sent me. You must get these battle plans back to her."

"The witch of the river?" George's stomach lurched and his hands shook as he took the letter from the man and glanced back to the shore where he'd been standing. "Where is she?" he asked. "The witch of the river? Has she been captured?"

"No," the man said, shaking his head and urging Ace to

keep paddling. "Please! We must keep going! She is fine. She is with the British intelligence—"

When the shot rang out from the shore and the German collapsed into George's lap, Ace was the one to spring into action. "Get down!" he yelled, grunting with the effort of each stroke until the boat finally crashed into the south shore.

"What just happened?" Philip pulled the dead man off George before they jumped out of the boat and scurried up the bank to safety. "Who was that man?"

"Are you a fritz, Mountcastle?" Ace threw the paddles into the rowboat and stormed up the bank, poking his finger into George's chest and then back toward the river. "Who the hell is that dead man in the boat? What did he give you? Hand it over."

George's fingers were clenched so tightly around the paper that Ace would have needed pliers to remove them, and it wasn't until Philip stepped between them that the tension finally broke.

The witch of the river.

"Marcelle," George whispered, tucking the letter deep into his pocket. "We need to get this letter to Colonel Mac."

chapter 45

It was a night with a darkness you could feel.

The French were in the midst of their Bastille Day celebrations, and the hour was drawing near. There had been no news yet from the top about the attack, and George was worried the battle plans he'd given to their major hadn't found the right hands.

He couldn't stop seeing the man from the river, and the ethereal version of him that had been standing on that same riverbank eight years earlier. *The witch of the river sent me.* Maybe this had been fate's plan all along. Maybe saving Marcelle from the prison in Jaulgonne had been the real reason George had been sent back and Philip's sacrifice wasn't even a part of the plot.

As the hour drew near George did what he could to prepare the men around him for what he knew was coming, but Philip was the only one listening. He'd cracked his last joke two hours earlier and was checking his watch incessantly as the minutes ticked by.

Three hours.

The valley floor was ready for the attack, even if the men weren't. Artillery guns surrounded the perimeter, a new system of trenches had been dug to defend their right flank from an ambush from the east, and Colonel Mac had been given permission to appropriate a good section of Hill 231. Individual slit trenches had been dug into the side of the hill furthest from the river to protect the men against German artillery fire being lobbed their way, and the company being tasked with defending that hill was already in position. There would be no elastic defense this time.

There was an unnerving and familiar feel to the night as George listened to the words of the French songs, the ones he hadn't understood the last time he'd been there, drifting over the valley.

To arms, citizens . . .
Train your battalions . . .
Let's go, children of the Fatherland . . .
The day of glory has come . . .

"How much longer?" Philip was getting restless beside him, burning through cigarettes and checking his watch with a dogged consistency.

"Two hours."

The words had barely left George's mouth when Colonel McAlexander came galloping in on horseback, sitting tall under the open sky. He dared the enemy to come for him, and when the field officers begged him to take cover, he stubbornly rebuked them, insisting that when God was ready to take him, he would be ready to go.

"The Germans will attack tonight." As his words echoed through the valley, the constant angst that lived beneath George's skin squeezed around his chest in anticipation of the battle. Marcelle's message had gotten through. They were preparing for the attack that George had already known was coming.

"At ten minutes after midnight, the Boche will send over mortar shells and bombs filled with smoke and poisonous gases." The colonel struggled to steady the horse that fretted beneath him, waiting for its chance to bolt. "They think they will shake us before they make their assault across the river.

They think we are unprepared. They think the Americans will quake with fear, fall back, surrender. And while it is true that we have not been tested in battle, tonight we will show them who we are."

He spun his horse in a tight circle as the men around him hollered and cheered. Philip raised his rifle into the air and yelled along with the other soldiers, ready for the fight to begin. George could still hear the words he'd said to him on the cellar floor in Soissons:

I'm a fighter, Mountcastle. That's what I do. Stick me on a battlefield and put a gun in my hand and I'm your man. But you. You're a survivor.

"This Surmelin Valley is the gateway to Paris," Colonel McAlexander continued as he pointed his cavalry sword toward the valley floor. "And you men have been tasked to defend it with your lives. We will not fail. We will not fall back. We will not allow the enemy to cross that river. We will be the rock of this valley. Tonight, we make history. And tomorrow they will sing praises about the men of Colonel McAlexander's Thirty-Eighth Infantry."

Cheers followed the colonel as he galloped down the trench line to deliver the same speech to the next company of men, and as the field commanders gathered their troops for last-minute preparations, for the first time in weeks George felt unprepared for what was to come. He was heading into uncharted territory.

The Allied attack would begin at midnight. The French and their allies would launch a barrage of bombs and gas and incendiaries over the Marne River ten minutes before the scheduled German assault in hopes of sending their troops into disarray, and when the Germans came, there would be no falling back. No elastic defense. The gunners were in place. Machine gun pits had been fortified, artillery guns had been mounted, and the frontline trenches had been packed with riflemen whose orders were to kill anything that moved in front of them.

As midnight approached and the French stopped singing,

the silence that descended upon them was oppressive, the anticipation agonizing. The weight of the fear that latched onto George in expectation of the battle was almost as heavy as the fear that had carried him *through* the battle eight years earlier.

Philip checked his watch one last time.

"Five minutes."

Marcelle's face was all George could see as he pulled his gas mask over his head and double-checked the bayonet at the end of his rifle. Her smile when he'd first flirted with her at the train station in Montmirail. Her tears when he'd asked her to marry him on the floor of their apartment. Her frown when he'd laughed about women spies at Max's house.

They were beautiful memories, but they were sprinkled over a life that was fraught with pain and sorrow and loss. A life that would have a new course if George and the men around him could stop the Germans.

When midnight struck, and the bombing started, the explosions that rocked the ground were so close that George couldn't be sure they'd landed on the right side of the river. Less than seventy-five yards away, incendiaries lit up the sky to reveal nests of panicked German soldiers diving for cover and fumbling with gas masks, pulling camouflage covers from the Howitzers that were lined up along the north bank. They were flustered and disorganized and couldn't get them loaded before the gunners from the Thirty-Eighth were able to take several of them out.

It wasn't until the shells were streaking through the air overhead and pounding into the ground around them that George knew the fight was really on. It didn't matter how many times he'd relived this moment in his dreams, when the incendiaries lit up the scene around him, revealing the chaos of the night, George couldn't stop the skeletal fingers from reaching into his chest and squeezing the breath from his lungs.

Philip was already at the parapet, his rifle propped between the sandbags and aimed across the river, his finger steady on the trigger. The men beside him followed his lead, and by the time George got into position, thousands of guns were aimed at the German front, awaiting the monster that would soon come to life.

The Sturmtruppen were the first to cross the river, and when the men of the Thirty-Eighth began their stand in earnest, it was the deafening roar of rifles, artillery guns, and exploding hand grenades that stunned George's senses.

He'd spent his last battle on the run; dodging, evading, and retreating, surviving by observation and deliberation. This was something new. As every nerve in his body screamed for him to run, George remained. He carted ammunition to machine gun nests, he covered the gunners while they reloaded, he dragged wounded soldiers to the medics. He let his body be ruled by instinct and reaction rather than thought and reason.

"Do they ever stop coming, Mountcastle? How long does this last?"

Philip was still by his side. He'd been tossing hand grenades over the razor wire for the past hour in regular increments, doing his best to keep the Boche who had already crossed the river from slipping into their trenches. Ricci had gone to fetch him another box, as George tried not to listen to his questions. He tried to forget what he knew about the last battle, where Ricci had run off to his death beneath a blackened sky and Milo had been torn apart piece by piece throughout the night.

"Everything's different this—"

"Grenade!"

Before George could get his words out, an explosion rocked the trench walls, breaking through the wooden reinforcements and sending dirt and debris over their heads. When the smoke drifted into the sky and the dirt settled at their feet, Ricci's body, or what was left of it, was crumpled over the decimated sandbags along the far side of the trench wall. His gas mask had been ripped off and the whites of his eyes shined through the darkness. George couldn't pull his gaze away. Philip was still by his side, shouting something into his ears, but it wasn't until the medics dragged Ricci's body away that the words hit him.

"Captain Reid needs us on the hill."

Bullets continued to whiz by their heads, explosions pounding into the ground around them, as George tried to make sense of Philip's words. A runner had been dispatched from the commander in charge of the troops on Hill 231, the hill on their right flank, the one the French had already abandoned. They couldn't hold the Germans back. They needed reinforcements.

George was on the run again, crossing wheat fields and dodging mortar shells along the way. He pulled his gas mask off before splashing across the stream that had carried them up this same hill under the same sky eight years earlier. Halfway up the hill they came upon the slit trenches that had been dug into the side of the hill for extra cover. Judging from the number of dead bodies surrounding them, they were not effective.

What was left of the company of men who'd been manning the machine guns mounted in front of them was taking shelter from a German plane that was skimming so close to the ground, George feared it might crash into them.

"Get down!"

He dove into one of the trenches just as a spray of bullets washed over the ground around them. The thirty other men who had arrived with him from their company were spreading out along the hill, being plugged into the lines where they were needed.

The Germans had already crossed the river in front of them. They'd taken the position on top of Hill 231 and were rolling their artillery guns into place as George and the men around him tried to pick them off one by one. There were too many of them, and the machine gunners who were trying to hold them off were running out of rounds. The runner who'd been sent to retrieve more ammunition had been gone for at least an hour, and they had to assume he was dead. But the next runner they sent out didn't make it more than a few feet from the trench before a German machine gunner felled him. Their right flank was overrun too, and it was no longer a question of if, but when, they would be completely surrounded and cut off from their own troops.

The trenches felt like tombs. There couldn't have been more than fifty of them left on the hill, men from all different companies and all walks of life. By the time the next plane floated overhead, grenades and mortars were being lobbed at them from every direction. They were surrounded. The trenches were no safer than the fields around them, and the men were diving from one slit trench to another, piling on top of each other, desperate to find cover. But there was nowhere to hide.

The communication lines were all down. The carrier pigeons were all dead. The runners were all trapped. Support wasn't coming. No one out there knew they were out of ammunition and down to their last men.

Captain Reid was shouting over the din of the explosions that were engulfing them, but he was talking mostly to dead men. The bodies were mounting even as he made his way across the line, but the few men who could still hear him listened carefully to his words.

"We must take back this hill!" he yelled, and as George followed his gaze to the men who were hunkered down beside him, for the first time since the fighting had begun, he wondered what he'd done wrong. What could he have done differently? What would have changed the outcome of this battle? "If we don't take back this hill," the captain continued, pausing only to take cover from an artillery shell that pounded into the ground less than twenty feet away, "then all those men down there in the valley will be decimated. Let us make no mistake about it. This battle ends here, on this hill, one way or another."

Philip and Milo were the first two men to volunteer for

the mission Captain Reid was detailing. The German gunners on their right flank would be their first targets. A small party would sneak through the wheat fields between enemy lines and take out the artillery gun that had been set up to their east. Once that section was cleared, another party would work its way around to the south and take out the guns behind them, continuing on until they were ready to face the biggest threat, at the top of the hill to the north.

George was attached to the first party, slithering on his stomach through the wheat fields behind Philip and Milo just as he'd done eight years earlier. The sun was starting to rise above them, but the Germans were unsuspecting when they made their move, only managing to get off a few rounds from their machine guns before they went down.

"Bingo!" Philip scampered up the hill to the artillery gun before turning it toward the front, as Milo hopped around behind him clutching his arm.

"Shit!" he yelled, squeezing his arm to his side. "Son of a bitch got me."

Three of his fingers had been shot off his left hand, and as one of the men pulled a wrap from his first-aid kit to stop the bleeding, George couldn't tear his eyes away. The drumming of the artillery gun and the thudding of the bombs shaking the ground around him began to fade from his senses as his world stilled in this one moment. Was this where he was meant to be? Was this how it ended?

The hoofbeats were the first thing George heard as the scene came crashing back to life. Over the thunder of battle came the steady and familiar beat of a galloping horse. He spun around just in time to see the horse rear as the rider on its back was shot off by a spray of machine gun bullets. George grabbed the horse's bridle, but it was panicking and throwing its head and he was worried they were both about to be gunned down.

Milo was on the ground, tugging at the rifle that was strapped to the dead man beside him, while Philip was turning the artillery gun toward the Germans who'd snuck up on them. They were barely visible through the mist, but George could see them going down as Philip returned fire.

"Whoa," George whispered as the horse reared again, fighting to break free from his grasp. "Easy."

It wasn't until he placed his hand over the horse's nose that George recognized her. The black mare from Châteauvillain. Against all the odds, they'd somehow found each other, somehow been brought back together for this one moment.

"We need reinforcements!" Philip had abandoned the artillery gun that was out of ammunition and was screaming over the rat-tat-tat of the machine gun he'd picked up as he fired into the line of approaching German soldiers. He paused only briefly as he turned to face George, nodding toward the horse. "Go, Mountcastle. I've got this."

George looked down at Milo, who was doing his best with the rifle, and then back at Philip, who was pulling another spent cartridge from his machine gun. This couldn't be the end. He'd done everything to prevent this moment, but, somehow, it had still found him.

"No!" George yelled, grabbing Philip's arm and struggling to pull him from his post. "Let's go! We'll fall back to the other troops and make another push when we have reinforcements."

"I'm not letting go of this position." Philip shoved George's hand away and loaded the last clip into the machine gun. "You know this is the way it has to be."

There was no stopping Philip this time, no tackling him or forcing him down the hill, no surrendering to the enemy. As he mounted the horse who'd come to save him, George suddenly realized this was the path he'd already set in motion, and, in some hidden recess of his mind, he must have known that this was always the way it was going to end.

He settled into the saddle as the mare danced beneath him, anxious to escape the terror surrounding them. They'd made it just halfway down the hill before he pulled her back to steal one last glance at his friend. From afar, he could see the line of approaching Germans. Milo had managed to take out a small group on their right, but the few who'd snuck by were almost upon Philip by the time George got the horse steadied beneath him. He pulled the rifle from his shoulder and took aim.

"Easy, girl," he whispered, his vision sharpening as he focused in on his target. Deep breath in. Long, slow breath out. Steady hands. One finger. Squeeze. The man went down. And the next. And the next.

Philip watched the men fall beside him before turning back to George and waving him away. *Go.* The word hung between them as George swung the rifle back over his shoulder and the horse began to fuss beneath him. They watched each other for only a moment, Philip beside the artillery gun and George atop the mare, a second or two at most, but it was a moment that would live in George's memory forever. Through the low fog that hung just above the wheat fields, and amidst the blasts that crashed all around them, the two friends said good-bye as fate finally pulled them in two opposite directions.

The black mare didn't hesitate. She galloped between exploding artillery shells and over felled trees, the drumbeat of her hooves a constant through the shrieking mortars and thundering cannons. Her nostrils flared, and her body heaved, and by the time George reined her in, her coat was slick with sweat. He leapt from her back and dove into the dugout, where Colonel McAlexander listened to his report and jumped into action. It was Major Rowe's company that would join him. They had both men and ammunition to spare, and as George led them back through the fields toward Hill 231, he felt a sudden peace come over him, as if these were the footsteps he'd been meant to walk all along.

By the time they made it back, Captain Reid and his troops had already taken out the gunners to their rear, and with the added reinforcements, they were ready to make a push to the crest of Hill 231, ready to drive the Germans back across the Marne.

It would be another dawn before George would find his way back to Philip, another sleepless night as the men of Colonel McAlexander's Thirty-Eighth Infantry held their line, refusing to back down. When the artillery guns were destroyed, they fought with their hands; when the ammunition ran out, they charged with their bayonets; and when fleeing troops urged them to retreat, they regrouped and rose again. It wasn't until the sun peeked over the horizon on the third day of fighting that the German Army finally retreated, and George stumbled back to the side of Hill 231.

Back to Philip.

He and Milo were propped up against each other, each with a German pistol in his hand. Except for the bullet holes riddling their bodies, they looked like they were sleeping. The artillery gun they'd defended was at their backs and there were at least a dozen dead German soldiers scattered around them, all reaching for the gun. A scene frozen in time.

George sat down beside them and gazed out over the Surmelin Valley. It was a scene so horrendous it would rarely be spoken of by the French and Germans alike, and though George would spend years trying to forget it, he would carry it with him to his grave. He would never speak about the Battle of the Marne again. He would never share the details with anyone.

"How am I going to leave you out here?" he said, his words drifting over the stillness of the battlefield. The tears were spilling down his cheeks before George even realized he was crying. How many years had it been since he'd wept? How many lifetimes ago? Philip was just one of the dead now, just one of the hundreds of thousands of men who wouldn't be returning home. But, to George, he was so much more than that. He was a friend, and a confidant, and a brother. How would anyone know how bravely he'd fought and how pivotal his sacrifice had been?

"I'll go visit your parents at the Meadville Market House and tell them . . . and Dorothy . . . I'll make sure she knows how much you . . ." The words just wouldn't come. "I'm sorry," he sobbed.

I'm sorry.

They were the only words that made any sense. George would spend his life going back to that moment, always regretful, always wondering what he could have done differently. When the sun finally peaked in the noon sky, and he knew it was time to go, he mopped up his tears and rifled through Philip's pockets, pulling out the photograph of Dorothy. He smiled as he ran his finger over the mischievous grin of the woman who'd always had Philip's heart, before tucking it back into his friend's pocket. Philip's army tag clinked against his own when George slipped it over his head and the Hamilton watch with the unbroken face ticked heartily as he secured it to his wrist. He fixed the collar of Philip's jacket, folding it back into place, before he finally pulled himself from the ground and thanked his friend one last time for the tragic and beautiful life they had shared together. For every stale joke, every late-night conversation, every heartbreaking sacrifice. He offered one last salute to both Philip and Milo, before he turned around and walked away from the best friend he would ever know, taking his best memories with him.

"What month do all soldiers hate?" he said, his voice fading into the valley as he stepped over the wreckage of the battlefield on his way out. "March . . . Have you heard the one about Lenin and the potato farmer . . . So, Lenin goes to visit a potato farmer in the countryside, and the farmer says . . ."

chapter 46

"Marcelle?"

The red dress flared around her legs when she spun to face him, and George was almost knocked back by her beauty. He'd never seen the woman standing before him. He'd never believed the youthful and carefree girl who'd walked the streets of Soissons before the Germans had come had really existed. But here she was, right in front of him. Her smile was radiant, and the dull sheen that had once obscured her eyes was now replaced with a spark that set her alight.

The Germans had surrendered. Months had passed since the battle along the Marne River, and George and the rest of the men from his unit had marched across France, carving away at the German forces battle by battle and setting the country free. But freedom had taken its toll. It hadn't been as simple as Marcelle getting the battle plans from the German officer or Philip's sacrifice on the battlefield. They had both been crucial pieces of the puzzle, necessary for victory, but there had been thousands of other pieces, thousands of decisions and sacrifices that had led them to this moment.

The nightmares were endless, and in order to escape them, every spare second of George's time had been spent imagining this moment, every dream bringing him back to this woman.

"You look stunning," he said, astounded by the softness of her features and the quietness of her eyes. Gone were the darting glances and the furtive stares. When she placed her hand on his arm, George was suddenly infused with the memory of their bodies pressed up against each other, the feeling of her heart beating against his as they'd said good-bye.

"You!" she exclaimed, squeezing his arm. "You were right. You saved my life. Wait here a moment. There is someone I want you to meet."

Festivities were underway across the country, and Montmirail was no different. When George had found her, Marcelle had been in the thick of a celebration, laughing and chatting with nurses and orderlies and patients alike. As George watched her disappear into that same crowd, he felt a strange yearning for the woman he'd left in the cabin by the canal, the broken one with the shifting eyes and the tortured soul, the one he'd promised to save. But that Marcelle was gone, and the one that reemerged from the crowd held her shoulders back and her head high, dragging a man with a shock of red hair behind her that George recognized instantly.

"Charles, this is the man I was telling you about," she said, gesturing to George. "The one who warned me about the man beneath the cherry tree."

"Outstanding." When Charles reached out to shake his hand, George couldn't blink away the image of him tied to the pole at the prison in Jaulgonne. It would forever be burned into his memory. Just another one of Marcelle's ghosts. "How did you know?"

"Dumb luck," George muttered, waving away the praise. "I stumbled across the information on my way to the front. It's not important now."

As Charles went on about lucky breaks and extraordinary coincidences, his words began to fade from George's mind, and all the sounds around him ceased to exist. The singing nurses, the blaring radio, the celebrating men. Gone. All of it gone as the face of his son appeared from the crowd on a man George had seen just once in all his years. The other man from the prison in Jaulgonne. The one with the missing arm who'd died beside Charles.

Gabriel's father.

When he walked up and pulled Marcelle to his side, George couldn't shake the image of her body crumpling to the ground the moment he'd been shot, and with each passing moment, he felt her being torn from his reach. Every hurdle, every sacrifice, every heartbreak. All the hazards that had littered their life were nothing more than memories now. But even with the pain of this realization, there was the dichotomous joy of knowing that Gabriel was here, that he had come back to them.

"You're already . . ." George breathed out the words, unable to finish them, but when he gestured to Marcelle's belly, to the baby who'd already been growing inside of her when she'd been captured by the Germans and taken to the general in Jaulgonne, Marcelle knew what he meant to say.

"Could you give us a minute, please?" She turned to the men beside her, smoothing out the front of her dress where a slight bloom was just starting to show beneath the black belt that was cinched around her waist. "I'll be back in just a moment." Marcelle placed her hand over her belly, waiting until the men were just out of earshot. "How could you possibly know that?" she asked. "Pierre is the only one who knows, and he—"

"Pierre?" George looked back toward the festivities for the men who had already been swallowed up by the crowd. "But I thought Pierre died at the front."

"What are you talking about?" Marcelle took a cautionary step back as George tried to work through the magnitude of this news. "Who are you?" she asked.

"You wouldn't believe me if I told you," George replied, still struggling to comprehend what he'd just stumbled into. So many secrets. He thought he'd known about all the burdens weighing down on Marcelle, but this was the one she'd kept to herself. Had she known whose baby she'd been carrying?

When had she figured it out? Was it the moment Gabriel had first been placed in her arms? Was it when he'd said "Maman" for the first time?

George didn't fault her for her silence. Whatever secrets she'd held from him in Soissons were not out of malice. She had done it to spare him. She had done it to spare Lina and Roland, too. Marcelle had understood too well what it would have done to them to know that Pierre had come back but had chosen a life without them. George nodded toward the walking path that led to the river. "Will you walk with me?" he asked.

Marcelle kept her distance as she followed him along an ambling path that wound beneath a canopy of cherry trees. A cotton-filled sky hung overhead, the clouds careful not to veil the sun that shined down upon them. George felt nothing but sadness as he took in all the beauty around them, regret that he and Marcelle had never been able to walk along a river or take their children to a park or share a family picnic. Their world had been nothing but survival.

He stopped when they got to the bridge, stepping up onto the wooden planks and offering Marcelle a hand. She accepted it just as a breeze caught a tuft of her hair. She pushed it out of her face and smoothed down the bottom of her dress that billowed up with the wind. It was a beautiful dress, but when he looked at it, George could only see Rosalie the night she'd given her life for them in her own red dress, with her golden locks and scarlet lips.

He shook the memory away and leaned over the railing to watch the water flow beneath them. It meandered carelessly around rocks and branches, shouldering each blow that fate sent its way.

"I got your message," George said, turning back to Marcelle. "I thought you might like to know."

"What message?"

"The German officer you interrogated. He handed me the

battle plans you sent him back to retrieve. They were very useful. Thank you."

When Marcelle's face lit up, George could almost see the woman who'd laughed behind the glow of the candlelight during their first Christmas celebration together. He missed that woman. He missed her smile. "He made it," Marcelle exclaimed. "And how fortuitous that you were the one to receive it."

"Yes," George replied. "Fortuitous."

Fate was a skilled impostor, passing herself off as luck and chance and prayers fulfilled. Lina had been right; fate was most certainly a woman. She was too shrewd to be anything else.

George turned back to the water beneath the bridge. He didn't tell Marcelle about the moment the German messenger had been shot, or that the man had died in his lap. It seemed unnecessarily cruel, and it wasn't what he'd come to discuss.

"Will you marry him?"

Marcelle didn't respond right away. She stepped up beside George and cautiously peered over the railing of the bridge, as if the drop frightened her. Was she scared of heights? Or water? He'd never known these things about his wife. He'd never had the chance to learn them. "Yes," she finally replied, stepping back from the edge. "I will marry him."

"Do you love him?" George followed her over the bridge, as they made their way to the other side. Marcelle didn't answer him, but there was no need. Of course she loved Pierre. George had known about Marcelle's love for Pierre since the moment he'd stepped into the man's life all those years ago, taking what he'd been forced to leave behind, and as he thought about the choices he'd made over the past few months, he wondered what he would have done had he known about these consequences. Would he have let Marcelle get captured by the Germans? Would he have let Pierre die so he could have his family back? When they got to the far side of the bridge, and George turned to face Marcelle, he was suddenly thankful that he hadn't known, thankful that he hadn't been forced to make that decision. He wanted everything this man would now take back from him: his wife, his son, his family.

"What about the baby?" George asked, remembering the March rains that had welcomed Gabriel into their life. "When will the baby come?"

"Early spring." Marcelle rested her hand gently over her waist.

"And do you have a name picked out yet?"

"I have a couple in mind. If it is a girl I thought I might name her after my sister. But if it is a boy . . . well . . . I guess I would need to talk to Pierre about that."

"I think Gabriel is a fine name." As the words left George's mouth, Marcelle gasped, reaching her hand out for his arm.

"That is my father's name," she said. "How could you know that was the name I had chosen?"

George didn't dare move a muscle. He wanted nothing more than to feel the warmth of Marcelle's skin upon his, to hold her in his arms as he told her all about their son. How she would fall in love with him the moment she held him. How he would be the smartest baby ever born. How he would be so brave that sometimes she would forget he was just a child. And how, one day, she would look around and wonder what happened to the little boy who had flown toy airplanes around the house and thrown temper tantrums on the floor.

And Juliette. He knew with a certainty that he couldn't explain that Juliette would return to her maman. He wanted so desperately to share that with Marcelle. To tell her how the wisest and purest and most beautiful soul she would ever know would someday be her daughter. How, just like her mother, she would be both fearless and kind, the very embodiment of strength and virtue and grace. But Marcelle would learn these things on her own. She would live these moments and discover each of them in her own time.

"I know you, don't I?" When Marcelle looked up at him, George could almost see his wife standing before him with her chopped hair and broken smile, daring him to lie. Daring him to make up a story that she would pick apart piece by piece. "I feel like we've been here before," she said. "Like we've already had this conversation."

George smiled back at her. He wouldn't lie to Marcelle; he didn't know how. He'd tried, on occasion, but she'd been able to read him as effortlessly as she'd read those fairy tales from the book Max had given to her on Gabriel's first birthday. When the tears swelled in her eyes, pooling in her lashes, he knew that she finally understood the significance between them, even if she couldn't voice it.

"If you had come before Pierre . . ." she whispered, as the tears finally spilled onto her cheeks, and she stepped into his embrace.

George had never come before Pierre, that wasn't the way fate had written his story, and as he considered stepping back into that man's life and taking back everything he'd lost—Pierre's name, Pierre's wife, Pierre's son—he could suddenly see this new version of Marcelle's life playing out before him. The real Pierre standing by her side when Gabriel came kicking and screaming into the world. Her parents celebrating weddings and birthdays and Christmases with their daughters. Rosalie and Marcelle growing old together in Soissons, watching their children and grandchildren play by the river.

"You should go," he said, pulling from their embrace but still clutching Marcelle's hands, not yet ready for the end to come. Her tears were slowing, but her grip didn't loosen, and she made no move to leave. He would never stop loving Marcelle. He would never forget about the sacrifices she had made for the people she had loved, about the family they had created together, and about the brokenness of her life that had been pieced back together to make something beautiful. She was no longer that broken woman, though, no longer destined to travel down the broken road that had once led her to George. He had to let her go.

"You should go."

Marcelle simply nodded before wiping the remnants of her tears away, and when George leaned in and pressed his lips to the side of her unscarred cheek, she closed her eyes and welcomed his kiss, clinging to him until he pulled his hands away and stepped from their embrace. For the rest of his life, he would wonder how he had done it. How, in that tragic moment, he'd had the strength to let her go.

"Good-bye, mon amour," he whispered as he watched her walk over the path beneath the cherry trees. She looked back just once, this woman with her flawless skin and perfect smile. She was beautiful, breathtaking really, but not nearly as beautiful as the woman he'd left behind.

epilogue
MARCELLE

Soissons, France
May 1991

"Maman?"

When Marcelle opened her eyes, she was surprised by the soft light filtering in through the sheers on the windows. Juliette sat beside her on the bed, still rummaging through the box that had been sent from America. The bags beneath her eyes told the story of a long and sleepless night.

"Have you been up all night?" Marcelle asked, though she knew the answer. She struggled to pull herself upright as Juliette ignored the question and propped some pillows behind Marcelle's back.

"I can't stop thinking about the story," Juliette said. "Do you think it was real? Do you think this man, George, lived a different version of a life with us?"

Marcelle's heart said yes, even if her mind told her no. She could see so clearly the life they'd once lived together, the laughter and joy that had been balanced with equal amounts of sorrow and heartbreak. She could hold each memory as if she owned them all.

"Yes," she finally said, nodding toward the journal on the bed. "I believe we were once a part of that life."

"I do, too," Juliette replied. "Although it is strange to imagine another man as my father. This man, George, the way he described me. Was he right?"

Marcelle nodded and let her memories take her back to the moment Juliette had first been placed in her arms. The depth and wisdom of her eyes; the quietness of her soul. "He was right," Marcelle said. "About you and Gabriel and Lina. All of us, really. Even Rosalie, I think."

The Rosalie from George's diary had not been the same devoted wife and mother and servant of God that Marcelle had known in this life. She hadn't been the woman who'd attended mass daily until the week before her death or the woman who'd recited Hail Marys with an unrivaled obedience. But she'd been an equally devoted servant to her makeshift family. And it wasn't a stretch to see that the Rosalie who'd gotten American soldiers through German checkpoints, the one who'd given her life for her family when the Bolsheviks had come, was the same woman Marcelle had known and loved until she'd been buried in the cemetery behind the cathedral square four years earlier.

They had shared a wonderful life, raising their families together in Soissons as their relationship had evolved and strengthened over time into a bond that could endure any storm. There had been secrets, of course, as in all relationships. Marcelle had never told her sister about her work as a spy. It was a history she and Pierre had kept to themselves, both to preserve the sacredness of those moments together and to spare the families they'd lied to for all those years. Pierre's mother would have been crushed to learn that her son had returned from battle but had chosen not to return to her. Their reunion had been a beautiful one, and the joining of the two families who had fought and grieved and survived through the long years together with the marriage of Pierre and Marcelle had been the ultimate celebration of devotion, perseverance, and love.

"Your father and I never told anyone about our work with British intelligence," Marcelle said. "I don't think our parents would have approved. Or Rosalie."

"Did you know the German prisoner died?" Juliette asked. "The one who was sent back to get the battle plans?"

Marcelle shook her head. She was saddened by that news. George had been right to keep it from her.

"He was right," Juliette continued. "You should have gotten a medal for that, Maman. You helped win the war."

"I have no interest in medals," Marcelle replied. "No wish to celebrate anything about that war."

"Even so," Juliette muttered, before pulling a newspaper clipping from the trunk. "Look," she said, holding up the paper for Marcelle to see. "Max Neumann. I feel like we know him now." Marcelle watched as her daughter scanned over the article. "Tante Lina would have been happy to hear this," Juliette continued. "It turns out there was a very good reason to save this man."

Juliette read aloud from the article that detailed the bravery of a German officer who had risked his life saving Jewish families during World War II. A man who had brought Jewish children into his home to raise as his own. A man whose wife had carried on his work even after the Germans had sentenced him to death.

"Lina would have been very proud to have known that man," Marcelle agreed, thinking about the fiery woman who'd been taken from them far too soon. Despite her life having been cut short, Lina had lived it fully. She'd been a loving and devoted sister to Marcelle from the moment she and Pierre had been married, and, like the girl in George's diary, a fierce defender of France, especially during the second war with the Germans. The one that stole her life. From rumors after the war, Marcelle and Pierre had learned that both Lina and Roland had saved countless lives, sneaking Jewish citizens and political activists out through a network across France before being captured and taken to a camp in Germany. The two had found a common enemy in the Nazis. Neither had returned after the war, and, though they had tried, Marcelle and Pierre had never found any record of them.

Half the contents of the box were spread across the bed between them, but Juliette continued to pull out papers and photographs, scanning quickly over the ones that held no interest and tossing them to the side. She finally stopped when she got to the rosary, and when Marcelle looked at it, she could still see it hanging around George's neck the day she'd first met him in Montmirail. She remembered how amazed he'd been that it had once belonged to her and how grateful he'd been that Rosalie had gifted it to him.

Marcelle pulled it over her head. She'd thought about that rosary from time to time, though she'd never come close to understanding its significance to George. It must have brought him great comfort throughout his life, and great sadness too. Had he thought about Rosalie and her divorce from God when he'd looked at it? Or had he thought about Paul and wondered what had become of him?

Marcelle had been heartbroken to learn of Monsieur Bauer's death upon her return to Soissons after the war. Her beloved German teacher and his wife had both been killed, and Paul had been sent to live with Monsieur Bauer's sister in Lille. Marcelle had seen him from time to time in Soissons, visiting his parents' graves with his aunt. She couldn't remember the last time he had visited, but she did remember that his hair had been graying and that he had been balding at the top.

"It is still ticking." When Marcelle looked up at her daughter, she was holding a watch up to her ear and smiling. "After all this time," Juliette said, peering through her glasses at the unbroken face. "It's a Hamilton. Do you suppose it was Philip's?"

Marcelle held it up to her own ear when her daughter handed it to her, though she needn't have. It was loud and vibrant, and as she ran her fingers over the glass on the front, imagining all the horrors that watch had seen, she felt a sudden sense of pride. Fate had manipulated their lives to set the timeline right, but fate would have been powerless without the labor and sacrifices of people like George, and Philip, and Lina, without Max and the German prisoner who'd given his life to end the war, without Rosalie, who'd given her life to save her family. Fate needed them.

Marcelle was beginning to tire, but the next photograph Juliette pulled from the box caught her attention immediately. Like the others, it was old and faded, but when her daughter turned it over and read from the back, Marcelle was instantly awakened.

"It says Anna, Louise, and George. Châteauvillain, France. November 1918." Juliette's eyes shot up in surprise. "Louise," she said. "He went back for the little girl from the horse corrals just like he said he would. And the British nurse Anna is with them. What a great photograph. They are standing in front of a train, and George is laughing at something Anna is saying. Louise looks very happy between them." Juliette smiled as she studied the photograph more closely. "Louise has bright red curly hair. She is very cute. Anna has curly hair, as well, but it is brown. And she is wearing her Red Cross uniform. They seem quite happy."

November 1918. That was the month George had come to visit her in Montmirail after the war. She remembered that day well. It was one of the few moments from her life that had been locked into her mind, safeguarded from the thief that had stolen so many of the others. It was the last time they had ever spoken. The day they'd said good-bye. She glanced at the diary beside her on the bed. Were those the memories he'd been carrying with him when he'd said good-bye to her on that bridge? Was that the reason she'd felt she'd known him forever? Had it broken him to let her go?

"Look at this one, Maman." Juliette held another photograph up for Marcelle to see. It was larger than the others, large enough that Marcelle could make out some of the details: the house in the back, the tree out front, and the people on the porch. She took it from her daughter and studied it. There were at least fifty people in the photo, generations of families. Some were old like Marcelle and some just infants. A few of the children had flaming red curls. She turned it over to see if there was a description on the back, but the words blurred together.

"Could you read this to me?" she asked, before handing the photo back to Juliette.

"It says George and Anna Mountcastle. Pine Creek, Alabama. Six children, fourteen grandchildren, and thirty-three great-grandchildren. It looks like they had quite a life together."

Marcelle smiled as she picked up the diary from beside her on the bed and leaned back into the pillows. She clutched it to her chest as her eyes drifted shut, certain she could almost hear the wind blowing through the tree branches above the porch from the photo she'd just seen. She was tired. Time kept skipping forward with each flutter of her eyelids, a new scene greeting her each time she opened them. Juliette on the bed beside her. Juliette on her way out the door. Juliette gone with the box from America.

The room was silent, but for the ticking of Philip's watch beside her, and as Marcelle felt herself sinking back into sleep, she clutched the diary more tightly to her chest, worried the story might disappear from her memory if she let it go. The winds picked up again, the trees from her dream rustling overhead as the constant and steady beat of time marched her forward, pushing her into a world that had always been buried somewhere inside of her. The voice that called to her was instantly familiar. It belonged to a man she had once loved in another life, a man she was certain she would love through eternity, and when she listened closely, she could almost hear the words he'd whispered to her on the floor of a cabin beside the banks of a canal when they'd last said good-bye.

I will always come back to you, mon amour.

author's note

While I don't think it is necessary to point out that *Midnight on the Marne* is a work of fiction, threaded throughout the story are depictions of real people, places, and events that played crucial roles in World War I.

The most significant of these, in my opinion, is the role of Colonel McAlexander's Thirty-Eighth Infantry Regiment of the U.S. Army's Third Infantry Division.

Despite orders from the division commander to employ an elastic defense, as described in part one of *Midnight on the Marne,* in real life, Colonel McAlexander insisted that his regiment make a stand on the banks of the Marne River with a rigid defense intended to disrupt the cohesiveness and force of the German troops when they made their move.

And the men of the Thirty-Eighth did just that.

Despite their lack of experience and training, and against seemingly insurmountable odds, they held the stretch of land on the south bank of the river and were not only credited with disrupting the final German offensive assault of the war, but were given a nickname that has endured for over one hundred years: the Rock of the Marne.

Obviously, neither Colonel McAlexander nor the men of the Thirty-Eighth had the foresight of a failed elastic defense as was detailed in *Midnight on the Marne,* but with cunning instincts, innovative leadership, and unrivaled bravery they succeeded in writing what General John Pershing, the commander of the entire American Expeditionary Forces at the time, called "one of the most brilliant pages in the annals of military history."

If you have any interest in learning more about this amazing feat and the specific men who played a role in the Second Battle of the Marne, Stephen L. Harris's book *Rock of the Marne: The American Soldiers Who Turned the Tide Against the Kaiser in World War I* is a magnificent resource and was one of the most valuable tools during my extensive research of WWI.

As always, with works of fiction, many liberties were taken with historical modifications to fit the narrative, so any misrepresentations of timelines or tactics or battle plans are entirely my doing and should not be attributed to any historians or researchers I may have mentioned in my author's note or acknowledgments.

acknowledgments

I have the excellent fortune of being surrounded by an amazing team of people whose hard work and dedication have turned my words into novels, and while they all deserve more than the brief mention they're about to receive, I have already stretched this book far beyond its allotted word count, so I will be succinct . . . said the author.

To my agent, Stephanie Rostan, who has been with me since day one of my writing journey, *thank you* is never enough. Your support and advice and expertise have always been—and will always be—invaluable to me. Thank you also to Courtney Paganelli and the rest of the crew at LGR. I'm so honored to be a part of your team.

To my editor at Forge, Kristin Sevick, I can't even begin to express what it meant to work with you on this book. I enjoyed every email and phone call and brainstorming session, and I am so appreciative that through it all, you always kept my vision in mind. Laura Etzkorn, my publicist at Forge, thank you for your behind the scenes work and the many hours you've spent walking me through computer glitches. Who knew that would be part of the job? To Troix Jackson and the entire Forge team, you all deserve a huge nod of appreciation. Devi Pillai, Lucille Rettino, Linda Quinton, Eileen Lawrence. Thank you to Katy Robitzski, Amber Cortes, and Dakota Cohen of the Macmillan audio team. To Christina MacDonald, who painstakingly corrected my inappropriate use of italics and capitalization, I'm sorry, and I thank you.

For everyone wondering who is responsible for the gorgeous

cover of *Midnight on the Marne*, credit goes to The Book Designers at bookdesigners.com with the assistance of Katie Klimowicz, who served as art director.

To my team of translators, thank you for slugging through the various drafts with me and not taking offense when I butchered your respective languages: Anne-Laurence Bertrand for French, Christina Cesulka for German, Yekaterina Karpitskaya for Russian, and Erica Cremonini for Italian.

To my older brothers, Sam and JJ Festoso, thank you for instilling in me an appreciation of history and war as a child by wearing out the VHS tapes of *The Longest Day, Von Ryan's Express,* and many others, as well as casting me as a combat-trained and battle-tested Polish war baby in your classic home-movie *Polish War Babies.* To my older sister, Ellen Duffy, who was too big to play the part of a Polish war baby, I'm sorry you missed out. And to my oldest brother, Philip Festoso, who would never have tolerated such foolishness, I can probably get you a copy of that tape.

To my parents, Philip and Annelise Festoso, to whom this book is dedicated, thank you for teaching me the importance of family and for demonstrating every single day what it means to endure. Your examples, the lives you have lived, have taught me how to persevere even through impossible odds and how to achieve goals that I would have otherwise thought unattainable. God only knows what you have both endured.

To my daughters. My earth. My wind. My fire. Never let this world dampen your spirits. As I wrote the characters in this book, especially the teenage versions of Marcelle and Rosalie and Lina, I couldn't help but think of you three: Mari, with your boundless acceptance and love; Vidy, with your unfaltering determination and resolve; Jiya, with your infinite compassion and zest for life. Thank you for understanding each missed meal and skipped weekend outing when I had to "type, type, type" and for always supporting me in my dreams. Whatever this world throws at you, stick together and allow your strengths to complement each other. You'll no doubt come out stronger versions on the other side.

To my husband, Sati Adlakha, what would I do without you? This book would never have found its way out into the world this year if you hadn't been standing by my side and patiently wrangling in all my anxieties about time constraints and work and kids and life. Thank you for never doubting me and refusing to let me quit even when I insisted that the timing just wasn't right and that my goals were too lofty. Thank you for loving me more than I sometimes deserve and for always being willing to step up when most of the world is stepping back. The smartest decision I ever made was marrying you in a hot air balloon over the Arizona desert twenty years ago.

And last, but certainly not least, a shout-out to a couple of furry four-legged friends. I'm not sure how many horses have ever made it into the acknowledgments section of a novel, but I can't leave our Izzy out. Thank you, Izzy, for teaching me how to love obstinate and ornery mares. You were absolutely the inspiration for the fearless black mare who saved the day on the battlefield. And Hanzi, my pup, thank you for your constant companionship and for sticking it out with me through the long days and nights even when the treats weren't flowing and you would rather have been snuggled up in your dog bed. You're my good boy.